Suzanne Arruda, a zoo keeper turned science teacher and writer, is the author of several biographies for young adults. An avid hiker and gardener, Suzanne lives in Kansas with her husband, and her cat, Wooly Bear.

Visit the author's website at:
www.suzannearruda.com

STALKING IVORY

On a photography assignment in the northern territory of Mount Marsabit, Jade hopes to film the area's colossal elephants. Instead, she discovers the mutilated remains of four elephants and a man. Although the authorities suspect Abyssinian poachers in search of ivory and slaves, Jade has her own suspicions. When the Kikuyu boy accompanying her is captured by slave traders, Jade must join forces with the handsome Sam Featherstone to rescue her guide, protect the animals, and expose one shocking conspiracy.

Books by Suzanne Arruda
Published by The House of Ulverscroft:

MARK OF THE LION

SUZANNE ARRUDA

STALKING
IVORY

Complete and Unabridged

CHARNWOOD
Leicester

First published in Great Britain in 2010 by
Piatkus
An imprint of Little, Brown Book Group, London

First Charnwood Edition
published 2011
by arrangement with
Little, Brown Book Group
An Hachette UK Company, London

British Library CIP Data

Arruda, Suzanne Middendorf, *1954 –*
    Stalking ivory.
    1. Del Cameron, Jade (Fictitious character)- -Fiction.
    2. Americans- -Kenya- -Fiction. 3. Women private
    investigators- -Fiction. 4. Poaching- -Kenya- -Fiction.
    5. Slave traders- -Kenya- -Fiction. 6. Wildlife
    photographers- -Fiction. 7. Detective and mystery
    stories. 8. Large type books.
    I. Title
    813.6–dc22

    ISBN 978–1–4448–0864–3

Published by
F. A. Thorpe (Publishing)
Anstey, Leicestershire

Set by Words & Graphics Ltd.
Anstey, Leicestershire
Printed and bound in Great Britain by
T. J. International Ltd., Padstow, Cornwall

This book is printed on acid-free paper

This book is dedicated with all my love to
Joe, the love of my life.

Acknowledgments

My thanks to the Joplin Writers Guild for help with chapter 21; the Pittsburg State University Axe Library Interlibrary Loan staff for all the books; National Wild Turkey Federation's Women in the Outdoors program for continuing opportunities to experience aspects of Jade's adventuresome life; Dr John Daley for information on rifles and sidearms; Dr Stephen L. Timme for valiant attempts to help me track down the as yet elusive *Premna maxima*; my NAL publicists, Tina Anderson and Catherine Milne; my agent, Susan Gleason; and my editor, Ellen Edwards, for their continued belief in the series; all my family — Cynthia, Dave, Nancy, The Dad, James, and Michael — for helping me shamelessly promote the book; and my father (The Dad) for teaching me never to feed an elephant bean burritos around open flames. I especially wish to thank Joe, the greatest husband a writer could ever want, for all his help and support.

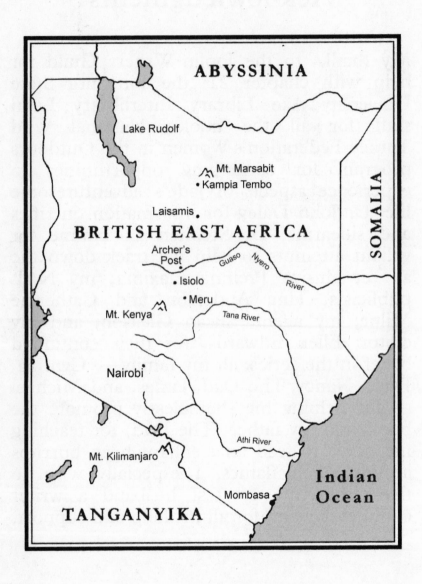

1

AFRICA, *January 1920*

*Many people who consider themselves
experts on Africa have no more experience
than what they read in an Edgar Rice
Burroughs book. The genuine article is
much more intriguing.*
— The Traveler

The last elephant cow smacked her baby on the
rump with her trunk, and the calf squealed and
trotted after the rest of the herd.

'I'm betting if it hadn't been for that lovesick
bull elk, I wouldn't be stuck up in this tree with
you, Bev, hiding from elephants.'

Jade del Cameron watched her friend's wide-
eyed reaction with a great deal of amusement.
The herd had passed beneath them, brushing
their bulky sides against the stinkwood tree's
trunk. Jade's former ambulance corps comrade
Beverly Dunbury had clutched an overhead limb
for dear life, her blue eyes bugging out of her
head. Once the pachyderms melted back into the
forest, Bev relaxed her grip on the branch and
sank onto the blind's planking. The scent of
bitter almond hung heavy in the air from the
bruised leaves. Jade shifted in the tree blind and
resumed setting up her equipment for a night
shot.

'You will simply have to explain that to me,' Beverly whispered as she fanned herself.

'Of course. Several years ago there was this *big* bull elk hanging around my family's ranch in New Mexico. Eight points at least. That's the size of his rack, his antlers.' She paused to see if Beverly understood and decided she didn't. 'It shows he wasn't a calf and not a real old-timer, either. Anyway, it seems he fell head over hooves in love, so to speak, with one of our horses, and — ' Jade cut her narrative short as a loud trumpeting ripped through the forest. 'Whoa, now. Speaking of bulls, that sounds like our big old fellow. Gads, but I want to get a good photograph of him. He's so ancient that his tusks nearly cross each other. Probably would if he hadn't broken one of them.'

'Too far away to hunt up tonight,' added Beverly's husband, Avery, from the other side of the tree blind. He patted the book in his hand, which he'd been reading. 'If Africa were anything like this chap's tales, we'd run across a snarling lion every ten yards and rampaging elephants once a day. I say, his jungle is positively oozing the brutes. You can't take ten steps without kicking one.' He closed the book with an audible snap and sighed. 'I haven't seen a single lion since we entered the Northern Territory.' He glanced over at Jade and recalled her Swahili name of Simba Jike, 'lioness.' 'Well, only one.'

'Is that one of those new Tarzan books I bought for you?' asked Beverly. She glanced at the title, *Tarzan and the Jewels of Opar*. 'Edgar Rice Burroughs may not have the animals quite

2

right, but he does know how to describe a handsome, brave British lord.' Beverly saw her husband's scowl and added, 'It's as if he meant you, darling.'

'He's American,' Jade said as she twisted a slender wire onto a battery's positive terminal.

'No, Tarzan is Lord Greystoke. He's British.'

'Not Tarzan, Burroughs. He's an American.' Jade picked up the coil of wire and looked up in time to see Beverly reach for the first wire. She slapped Bev's hand away. 'Don't touch that.'

'Is this contraption really going to take pictures?' Avery inquired. He put down his book and scooted over the narrow planking to inspect the work in progress.

'It did in Nairobi, but we'll get our field test tonight,' Jade said. 'In theory it should. At least I've rigged it correctly up here.' She patted the Graflex gently.

'When did you test it in Nairobi?' asked Beverly. 'Did you set something up by the pond at our house?'

Jade chuckled, her voice warm and mellow. 'Now what would I photograph at your house, Bev? I'd have done better at Neville and Madeline Thompson's coffee farm. At least that looks African. You've turned yours into a proper English estate with all those rosebushes.'

'You might have taken a picture of whatever ate all her peacocks,' suggested Avery. 'Lion, I suspect.'

'Well, unless you wanted to offer him another peacock as bait, I doubt I'd have seen him. No, I rigged up a test line outside of the Muthaiga

3

Club. Put it near some of the cars during the party Lord Colridge threw for his son Edmunde's homecoming.' What an evening that had been, most notable for the conversation she'd had with Blaney Percival, the Protectorate's chief game warden. It had all seemed so incongruous: her dressed in her best apricot-colored gown, Mr Percival in evening kit, surrounded by half of Nairobi society, discussing elephants and dangerous poachers as casually as the others talked of dinner parties and flirtations.

'I wouldn't recommend this sort of trip to a woman, but I believe you could tackle it, Miss del Cameron,' Blaney Percival had said over the blare of the gramophone.

Jade's skin tingled as he spoke those words. 'Would I find many elephants?' she asked. 'More than at Mount Kenya?'

'Undoubtably, and I'll even send word to Isiolo to let the patrol up there know you're coming. In return, though, I want you to do me a favor . . . '

'Jade! Pay attention. I'm trying to talk to you.' Back in the present, Beverly put her hands on her hips and scolded Jade. 'You're a sneaky little devil! I'd wondered where you'd gone off to during the dancing and why you looked so smug when you came back. All this time I'd hoped you were off having a romantic tête-à-tête with someone.'

Jade snorted and adjusted the camera's lens again.

'So *that's* what made that bang and glaring white light,' said Avery. 'As I recall, our Jade told

4

everyone it was just someone taking potshots at the electric lights again.'

'I remember Mrs Seton shrieking like a peacock,' said Jade. 'Did you see the expression on Colridge's face?' She hooted and slapped her right thigh. 'What am I thinking? Of course you didn't. It was shoved in Mrs Seton's bosom when she clutched him like he was the last life raft on the *Titanic*.'

Beverly folded her arms across her chest and tapped her foot. Only a few lip twitches betrayed her amusement at Jade's story. 'Well, are you going to keep us in suspense, or are you going to tell us what set off the flash?'

'It must have been an animal, correct?' asked Avery. 'Everyone else was dancing or in the bar.'

'Wrong.' Jade wiped her eyes with the back of her hand and picked up a roll of slender wire. 'I caught a lovely picture of Dorrie Woodard and Mr Seton. I think Dorrie was trying to get into Seton's car and he was trying to get in, er, other places.' She shouldered the roll of wire. 'All that remains now is to anchor the trip wire across the trail. Cover me, Avery.'

Avery hefted his Mannlicher rifle and scouted the surrounding brush for any hidden danger. 'All clear.'

Jade shinnied down the stinkwood tree. The daughter of a New Mexican rancher, she always felt more at home in the wilderness than with crowds of people, and her current position as a writer and photographer for *The Traveler* suited her temperament well. Her first assignment, after her stint as a frontline ambulance driver with the

Hackett-Lowther unit in the Great War, took her on safari in Tsavo near Mount Kilimanjaro and gave her a taste for Africa and its wild expanses. Unfortunately, as she was also searching for a murderer at the same time, it also exposed her to the seamier side of Nairobi's population.

That was why, when Jade had accepted another assignment in Africa from her editor, she had specifically requested to photograph wildlife in an area relatively uninhabited by people. She would have been the first to admit that what she really wanted was to be as far away from humanity as possible and this seemed the easiest way to do it. She'd had enough of people to last a lifetime. Of course Beverly, and Beverly's husband, Lord Avery Dunbury, didn't count. They were friends. They now owned some land and a beautiful stone house a few miles outside of Nairobi, and since they planned to make British East Africa their home, Jade had let them tag along.

As she eyed the thick woods surrounding the game trail, she knew she'd gotten as close to her wish for isolation as possible. Mount Marsabit was as remote an area in the Protectorate's northern frontier as she could have wanted. The heavily forested volcanic craters were an oasis of wildlife in the middle of desolation. To the southwest lay the Kaisoot Desert; to the east the Chalbi; and to the north, the even more inhospitable black lava wastes of the Dida Galgalla Desert. Somalia sat two hundred miles east and Nairobi, with all its pretension, was at least a blessed 250 miles away as the crow, or in

6

this case the cape rook, flew.

Unfortunately, other people sometimes stalked these forests, and Jade's conscience reminded her that she hadn't come just for the solitude. A distant echo of rifle reports emphasized both points. Blaney Percival had told her about this hidden spot when she asked for a good location to photograph elephants. In return, she promised to relay information on the current poaching. So far she hadn't seen any evidence, but she didn't kid herself. Where there were this many elephants, there would be poachers.

Jade chose an African olive tree across the game trail and tied the wire around its trunk. Then she ran the thin strand a few inches above the ground to her stinkwood tree blind, passed it under a spool that she'd staked into the ground, and tossed the rest of the coil up to Beverly.

'Does this end go to that little switch?' Beverly asked.

Jade scrambled back up the tree using a rope ladder and reached a hand up for Avery's assistance. 'That's correct,' she answered as she swung a leg over a floorboard.

Avery lowered his rifle and studied the setup. 'I see. Rather ingenious actually. I wondered how you planned to take a photograph in the dark without being here.'

'Hopefully this switch at the battery will set off the magnesium flash powder in that pan at the same time as the shutter is released,' Jade explained. She gingerly slipped a nooselike piece of wire over the shutter release.

'But won't the elephant, or whatever strolls by,

just pull the whole contraption out of the tree?' asked Beverly.

'I've anchored the camera down with clamps. The trip wire is close enough to the ground to be stepped on, but if an animal did snag a foot on it, the wire is so thin, it should snap as soon as it pulls any farther than I've allowed.' Jade stepped back and examined her work. 'At least under the weight of an elephant,' she added. 'I'm counting on smaller animals missing it entirely. Just keep your fingers crossed and pray I've set the focal plane correctly.' Jade fussed with a rubberized hood that covered most of the camera. 'I'm more concerned with moisture on my lens than anything.'

'The long rains aren't due for another month at least,' Avery reminded her.

'That doesn't stop the fog every morning,' Jade replied as she gave a final tug to the hood.

'Oh, hang the fog!' declared Beverly. 'What happened with the lovesick elk? You didn't finish your story.'

'Oh, him? Where'd I leave off?' She paused in thought. 'Right, the horse. So this big old bull elk, he really had a passion for one of the old cow ponies.' She laughed. 'No question of taste, I guess. Anyway, he hung around that paddock for several days till one day he just went berserker and kicked in a section of the fence. Trotted in there as proud as you please, rack held high. Strutted around like some . . . ' She paused to mull over an appropriate description.

'Like a rooster in a henhouse?' suggested Avery.

'More like a duded-up dandy with fifty dollars loose in a floozy house.'

Beverly blinked, her mouth hanging open. 'I *don't* want to know how you know that.'

'Of course that cow pony wanted nothing to do with him.'

'I presume the mare was in heat?' asked Avery, trying to get Jade back onto the story.

'No. That's the funniest part of all — the horse was a gelding.' Jade bent over to gather up her knapsack. 'So the pony,' she began, but she never got any further. At the instant she leaned down, something whizzed a few feet above her head, the sound punctuated by the crack of a distant rifle.

'Thunder and blazes!' exclaimed Jade.

She dropped the pack, snatched up her Winchester, and bolted for the rope ladder as more reports exploded in the distance.

'Jade!' yelled Beverly as she grabbed her friend's sleeve. 'Where do you think you're going?'

'Let go, Bev,' Jade said, her voice low and husky with anger.

'No! Avery, help me hold Jade.'

Avery grabbed for Jade's right arm, pulling his head back to avoid being clobbered by a rifle butt when she tried to swing free of his grip.

'Blast it, you two,' Jade snapped. 'Let me go. Someone's shooting at us.'

'We're not letting go,' retorted Beverly, 'until you settle down and act like a rational human instead of a wound crazed buffalo.'

When Jade didn't immediately agree, Avery

9

added, 'I have rope if I need it, Jade. Be reasonable. Much as you may enjoy it, you cannot go off into the forest and pummel someone.'

Jade exhaled with a tremendous sigh, her shoulders sagging as she admitted defeat. 'All right. I promise. But,' she added as her friends released her, 'they better hope I don't find them.'

Beverly behaved more stoically. 'Settle yourself, Simba Jike. We don't have a game permit for shooting nearsighted hunters.'

'You don't need a permit to shoot hyena, jackal, or jackass,' countered Jade. 'If I hadn't bent over at just that moment, that bullet might have gone through me rather than the tree. Worse yet, it nearly hit my newest Graflex. People heal up, but a shot like that would be fatal to a camera.'

'As long as you have your priorities all squared away, love,' cooed Beverly. 'I'm famished,' she added to change the subject. 'Are you about ready to head back to camp?'

Jade shook her head in disbelief. 'Your appetite is amazing. How can you think about food when we're being shot at?' Back when the pair had transported French wounded from the front lines, Bev had reacted to the stress of shellfire by focusing on something distant and pleasant rather than the falling artillery. After trying unsuccessfully to think about pretty scenery or parties, she had focused on favorite foods. Apparently, thought Jade, she still did.

'Oh, I'm sure it was an accident and they're probably gone by now, anyway,' Bev said. 'I want to eat.'

'I haven't rechecked all my connections. All that shaking from you two might have jarred something out of alignment. Give me another fifteen minutes.' The Dunburys waited patiently while Jade reexamined every wire. *Blasted poachers!* She shrugged off her annoyance and concentrated on readjusting the camera's focus. Finally she couldn't find anything else to adjust and agreed to leave. The trio climbed down Jade's rope ladder one at a time, Avery first, followed by Beverly and Jade.

Beverly's stomach growled and she patted it as though it were an entity that needed to be appeased. 'It will take us at least an hour to walk back. I wish there was some way to get there more quickly.'

Jade opened her day pack and took out a handful of figs. 'Chew on these, Bev. They should tide you over.'

Avery reached behind and patted the book lying in his pack. 'That Tarzan chap covered ground quickly by swinging from tree to tree.' He looked up at the forest surrounding him. 'Right. Well, he certainly did not live around here. I don't see any vines up there that would support a grown man's weight.'

'He must have 'hung around' some other part of Africa,' Jade said. 'That was a joke, by the way.' She scanned the trees for her blaze, a shallow V carved into the bark, which marked the route back to camp along the myriad game trails.

'I'm not sure how anyone managed safaris before trucks,' Avery said. 'But then I don't suppose they attempted to haul around an entire photo lab with them like you, Jade.'

Beverly's stomach growled again, this time loudly enough that Jade turned to stare at her. 'Better stop that, Bev. I thought some wild beast was stalking us.'

'I told you I was famished and I meant it. I want to devour an entire roasted bustard. We shot five of the ugly birds this morning. I should be allowed a whole one for myself.'

'Hear, hear,' echoed her devoted husband. 'And since we had the foresight to send back most of the men to Isiolo once they unloaded the supplies, we don't have nearly the number of mouths to provide for now.'

'True,' Jade added. 'At least we're not eating those horrid Grant's gazelles. Blasted things are too wormy. You have to char the meat to make it edible. But if you eat an entire bustard, Bev, we'll need those men to come back and carry you home.' She looked her friend over. 'Your appetite is amazing.'

Beverly stuck out her tongue. 'Be careful what you say, missy, or I'll tell Madeline and she'll put it all down in a second book about you.'

'That's blackmail, Bev. Madeline's in enough hot water already for making up some silly, over-romanticized tripe about me.' Jade had become friends with coffee farmers Madeline and Neville Thompson last year, and Madeline had been with them in Tsavo. If Jade had known the woman would tell the entire world her darkest fears in a novel that was about to be published, she'd have left her at the station in Nairobi.

Beverly laughed, her voice rippling like

12

dancing water. 'As I recall, Jade, getting her to write a book was your idea.'

'But *not*,' said Jade, 'about me. *That* was *your* doing. And I never said 'Eat my bullets!' to anyone. I should have burned the blasted manuscript when she first showed it to me.'

'Well, I thought it was romantic,' said Beverly. 'She gave me the carbon paper copy, you know.'

'Now, ladies, I really think that sort of thing needs to stop,' suggested Avery when he saw Jade's eyes flash in a cold green fire. 'You didn't finish telling us about that elk, Jade,' he reminded her. 'You left off when the beast kicked in the fence.'

'Right. So this bull elk kicked in the fence and got in with one of our horses, only the horse didn't want anything to do with this hooved lothario. Just as the elk started making his amorous advances, that horse bolted clean through the break in the fence and ran off.'

She paused again to read the trail blazes and chose a narrower path off the larger elephant trail. 'He didn't appear to want to come home, either, so we sent our border collie, Scout, to herd him. Now, the dog chased the horse back, but not before Scout visited the neighbor's — ' Jade stopped abruptly and cocked her head to one side, listening. A faint wheeze reached her ears, as though something large labored to breathe.

'It's over there,' she said, and pointed off in the direction of the original elephant trail. The three of them ran back up the narrower path, then walked cautiously along the larger trail, eyes and ears alert to danger. The labored breath grew louder and more irregular, and the metallic smell of blood permeated the air. As they approached, the wheezing stopped with a shuddering sigh. Jade and her companions stepped into a small clearing.

'Oh, hell!' Jade swore.

Four giant gray corpses littered the ground. The tusks of each one of the slaughtered elephants had been sawed off. Their thick hides bristled with arrows, and opportunistic flies buzzed around, laying eggs in open wounds, a lot of wounds. A broken arrow shaft protruded from one female's gut and a ragged hole yawned where her left eye used to be.

'Merciful heavens,' muttered Beverly. She immediately turned her head to retch.

'None of the arrows are in a fatal spot,' observed Avery. 'It looks like they must have used poison on the arrows to incapacitate them. Then they shot them up close with a rifle to finish them off.' He looked at Jade for confirmation and shuddered.

Jade's exotic, olive-colored face had frozen into a stony mask. Avery followed her gaze and tensed. Beverly turned back, wiping her mouth with a kerchief. She saw Jade's face at the same time and started to go to her friend. Avery put out an arm to restrain her and shook his head. When Jade looked like that, it was the better part of valor to stay out of her way.

In between Jade and the Dunburys lay one of the elephant cows, blood dribbling from her side and open mouth.

Rough stumps appeared where her tusks had been. The sight was horrid enough, but Jade's gaze was fixed on what lay behind her.

'It's worse!' she whispered. 'They killed her baby, too.'

Beverly broke past her husband and ran around to her friend.

'This is the same baby and mother we saw trailing the group today,' Jade said. She bent and inspected the infant's mouth. Her voice broke in a low, husky tone. 'The bastards actually killed the calf for its baby ivory.'

'They didn't just kill elephants,' said Avery. 'There's a man over here.' He pointed towards a collapsed body dressed in a bloody blue uniform shirt and shorts lying in a clump of olive trees. 'Looks like an askari, a soldier in the King's African Rifles, judging by the uniform. Probably caught the poachers in the act.'

Jade stepped around the elephants and squatted down near the body. He was on his knees, his upper torso bent over until his face touched the ground like a Muhammadan in prayer. His red fez lay beside him, and a small red hole marked the back of his head. Two arrow shafts protruded from underneath him. 'Help me lay him out, Avery.'

Gently they turned the man over and straightened his legs. The arrows had penetrated the man's gut, but were probably not the immediate cause of death. Jade heard Beverly gasp. 'Maybe you should wait by the trail, Bev,' Jade said gently.

'No. I'll be all right. I want to help.' Beverly

15

stepped closer and shuddered when she saw the extent of his wounds. 'He faced his attackers to begin with,' she said, her voice quavering.

Jade knew that her friend, who'd seen worse during their ambulance-driving days of the war, was trying to maintain a grip on reason by voicing her thoughts aloud. Jade pointed to two indentations on the ground. 'Looks like he fell to his knees here after being shot in the gut with arrows. Someone must have come up from behind and shot him in the head, execution-style.'

'Judging by how much of his face is missing, he was shot at close range with a pistol,' added Avery.

'Savages,' said Beverly softly. Avery placed his own pocket handkerchief over the African's face and went to comfort his wife.

Jade's gaze swept the ground, looking for telltale signs left by the killers, but the earth was too trampled for her to make out any footprints. Something metallic glinted through the under-brush and she retrieved a spent cartridge from an elephant gun. She slipped it into her pants pocket.

Suddenly one cow's huge frame shuddered as she struggled to take in a final breath. Her lungs wheezed as air leaked from them.

'And those bastards didn't even finish the job,' Jade said. She rose and stood rigid, feet apart, her face once again a stony mask. The cow's labored breath rattled, and more blood dribbled from her open mouth. 'Hand me your Mannlicher, Avery. I doubt my Winchester could penetrate her skull.'

Avery shook his head. 'I'll finish the job, Jade.' He gently released his wife and stepped back to Jade and the dying cow. Taking careful aim, he shouldered his weapon and fired a round into the elephant's brain. The wheezing stopped.

Jade's rage remained. She took a silent oath to find the bastards who'd done this and make them pay.

2

MOUNT MARSABIT

*The Northern Territory of British East
Africa is a valuable wildlife refuge in a land
fast running out of wildness. Farther south,
colonists and native Africans both are
exchanging game trails for paved streets,
wild animals for domestic cattle, and the
acacia tree for rose gardens.*
— The Traveler

'We can't just leave him here,' said Beverly.

'We'll have to for a short time, darling,' replied
Avery. 'We have neither a shovel to bury him nor
anything to carry him back on.' He placed his
hands gently on his wife's shoulders and held
her. 'If you and Jade go back to camp, Jade can
return with a few of the men and a blanket. I'll
stay and guard the body.'

'Jade?' Beverly called to her friend. 'Is that all
right with you?'

Jade held up her hand for silence and cocked
her head to listen. 'Someone's coming.'

'Someone or something?' whispered Avery.

'A human, not an animal.' She listened a
moment longer and amended her statement with
two upraised fingers to indicate two humans.

Avery pulled back the bolt on his Mannlicher.
'If it's the poachers,' he whispered, 'they're going

18

to find a welcoming committee.'

They formed a defensive triangle in case someone else was sneaking up from behind, crouched and waited, rifles ready. The sound of bipeds walking along the trail grew louder. Jade assumed whoever it was would not know they were there, and decided to alert them before that someone became startled and fired in panic.

'Halt and identify yourself before we shoot,' she called.

The footsteps immediately stopped. After a moment's hesitation, a decidedly male British voice replied, 'Captain Barnaby Smythe of the King's African Rifle patrol.'

Jade relaxed her grip on her Winchester and held it across her chest as she rose. Soon Smythe appeared, followed by one native askari. Jade took in the features of both. The captain stood about five feet, ten inches, with broad shoulders and narrow hips. His field hat, a solar topee clamped tightly on his head, hid his hair, but his thin brown mustache indicated the color. The native soldier traveling with him remained a few feet behind his superior officer, black skin melting into the forest's gloom. Only the red fez atop his head stood out.

Avery took the initiative and held out his hand. 'Lord Avery Dunbury at your service, Captain.' He shook the other man's hand. 'This is my wife, Lady Dunbury, and our friend Miss Jade del Cameron.'

'Surprised to see anyone on this trail,' Smythe said. 'Where are your gun bearers?'

19

'We're our own bearers today, Captain,' Jade answered.

Smythe's eyebrows arched in surprise. 'An American. Well, I should warn you all that you are in dangerous territory.'

'We're aware of the elephants, Captain,' Jade said.

'I'm not referring to the elephants, Miss — er, what was your name again?'

'Del Cameron.'

'Ah yes. I've heard of you. Some hyena trouble down in Tsavo, as I recall. Well, you're in frontier territory and a bit too close to Abyssinia for your own good.'

'We're nearly a hundred miles away,' Beverly said.

'And that's a hundred twenty miles too close. Don't think for a moment that being in the Protectorate is any protection here. We're far too short staffed to patrol the entire border, and raiders have been making forays both here and to the west more frequently. I just sent part of my patrol back to Isiolo with several captives. The whole bloody thing's gone wild since Emperor Menelik died several years ago.' He looked past them at the slaughtered elephants, as though he had just now noticed the carcasses. 'I heard a shot recently. Is this your doing? Where are your permits?'

'We didn't shoot them,' replied Jade. 'We're photographing elephants, not killing them. We stumbled on this.' She pointed to the cow that Avery had shot as a mercy killing. 'This cow was left to bleed to death. What you heard was Lord

Dunbury putting her down.' Jade handed Smythe the spent cartridge she'd pocketed. 'I found this. As you can see, it doesn't match anything we're carrying.'

Smythe nodded and surveyed the carnage. 'Poachers.'

'Murderers, too,' added Jade. 'You should see this.' She led the way to the dead man and watched while Smythe examined the body. 'One of yours?' she asked.

Smythe nodded. 'Too much of his face is missing to be sure, but judging by the build and height, I think I know who it is. New recruit, very gung ho sort of lad.' He looked up at Avery and directed his questions to him. 'You say you found him like this? Did you see anyone else?'

'We found him kneeling on the ground, shot in the back of the head.' He pointed to the knee marks next to the body. 'There was no one else around.'

'So you moved the body.' Smythe's tone was accusatory.

'It seemed disrespectful to the man to leave him in that demeaning, groveling position,' replied Beverly.

'It looks like an execution,' said Jade, bringing the conversation back to the crime.

Smythe nodded. 'Probably caught the poachers in the act.'

'So these Abyssinian raiders you spoke of are poaching ivory?' Avery asked.

'Mostly, at least around here. But slave raiding has increased as well.'

21

'And why would that be?' Jade asked, her voice snappish. Smythe had all but dismissed her, which irritated her to no end.

'Their entire system is feudal, Miss del Cameron. The emperor hands over the government of the various regions to his appointees and demands tribute from them all. But once the old emperor dies, all the governors know they'll be replaced. So they take everything they can get and head out. That means the new regional lord has to raid and pillage to get enough goods for tribute or until he can manage to capture enough slaves to plant his fields. Others sell the slaves to North Africa, where they fetch a good price. Sometimes it takes years for them to accumulate their own wealth.'

'And you're suggesting that we're in danger of being taken for slaves?' asked Jade.

'No!' he retorted. 'I'm suggesting you might get in their way and be shot.'

Jade and the Dunburys exchanged glances. 'That might explain that stray bullet today,' Beverly suggested.

'Someone shot at you today?' Smythe asked.

'If they did, they had bad aim,' Jade replied. 'More than likely it was a shot gone wild. Perhaps your man startled them in the act.'

'Well, chances are it was a warning shot,' Smythe concluded. 'You should take the hint and move on farther south.'

'I'm not moving anywhere unless the elephants move, and as I understand it, they won't leave until the big rains begin,' replied Jade. 'I came here to photograph them and I hit the mother lode. But we'll keep watch for more than wild animals now.'

'I should hope that this would prove to you just how dangerous it is for you to remain here, miss,' said Smythe.

Jade considered the officer for a moment before she added, 'Isn't it dangerous for *you* to be out here with only one man backing you up?' She nodded to the lone askari standing in the shadows.

Smythe scowled, planted his feet farther apart, and thrust out his chin. 'See here, young woman. I cannot guarantee your protection if you remain. We have a lot of territory to patrol and I'm stretched far too thinly as it is. It takes weeks, months as it were, to canvass it. I left a small contingency under Lieutenant Fitzpatrick near Isiolo, but most of my company is patrolling the Somalian border. As their captain, I need to join them, so my small reconnaissance here must end as soon as I bury this chap.' He looked beyond her to Avery. 'Lord Dunbury, I leave it to you to take charge of this matter and get these women out of here. Now if you'll excuse me, I'll find the rest of my men and take care of the body.'

Avery bowed slightly in a manner that could mean anything from acquiescence to merely acknowledging his suggestion.

Jade watched Smythe march down the game trail, his lone askari tailing him. 'Most curious, he didn't really answer my question.'

'Probably felt it was impertinent,' said Avery. 'After all, he is an officer in the African Rifles. I

23

suspect he's immune from attack. A uniform does frighten many of the locals.'

'It didn't help this poor man,' Jade said as she nodded to the slain soldier. 'Are they really spread that thinly?'

'The Rifles went through a reorganization after the war,' said Avery. 'I believe there really is only one regiment for the entire northern frontier, but I honestly don't know how many companies it has. Most of these askaris saw hard service during the war. Officers, too. I'm sure it took a terrible toll on their numbers.'

As they resumed their trek back to camp in silence, Jade wondered if Avery would insist on removing Beverly from danger. They also knew that Blaney Percival wanted a report on poaching, but the danger hadn't seemed real to them before. Plus, she had an article for *The Traveler* to research, and only a month to do it before the rains set in. In any event, Jade didn't plan to move on, but considering they each had a share in the supplies, she couldn't very well stay on without the Dunburys or insist that they leave much of the stores behind for her. Then again, Beverly had never run from danger during the war.

Jade smiled to herself as she recalled some of their escapades during their ambulance-driving stint with the Hackett-Lowther unit. As one of the few women's units allowed near the front lines, they'd had many close calls driving the wounded during air raids and shellings. No, Beverly hadn't run from the Germans' 'Big Bertha.' She wouldn't run from a few armed raiders.

Jade led the way through the ancient forest along antiquated trails formed by untold generations of elephants. Mount Marsabit was actually a chain of volcanic craters, and their camp lay on the western side of one crater, Gof Sokorte Guda, which housed a beautiful lake. During the dry seasons, the elephants and other wildlife clustered around the large lake and the smaller ones that circled it like ladies-in-waiting surrounding the queen. The entire mountain chain existed as a green jewel amid the blazing deserts.

Jade took her eyes from the trail for a moment and spared a glance for the massive trees around them as they walked. Some of them sported buttresses; others, like the rarer figs, were stranglers that took hold of a smaller tree and gradually covered it, leaving a hollow core under a latticework of growth. Silver-green moss draped all the trees, and blue butterflies adorned them like living ornaments. *Sweet Saint Peter's little fishes, but it's beautiful!*

The forest maintained a cathedral-like silence during much of the day, while the elephants lounged in the pools or enjoyed dust baths elsewhere. At night, though, Jade knew it would come alive with the tremendous cracking of branches when the elephants fed. *All but four cows and one baby,* she thought, *and one poor soldier who won't sit down to evening mess with his comrades.* She gritted her teeth, finding it hard to accept so much death and mutilation in this stunning landscape.

Less than a quarter mile from their base camp,

25

Jade stopped and held up a hand to signal an immediate halt. Then she put one finger to her lips for absolute silence. After turning her head to the side and listening, she pointed to the trail ahead. She mouthed the word 'animal' and held out her hand, waist high, to indicate its general size.

Avery glanced at his wife and pointed to her stomach. Beverly shook her head to say that whatever Jade heard, it wasn't another stomach growl. Avery shrugged. Neither of them had heard anything, but both trusted Jade's instincts. They knew leopards were nocturnal and lions rare in this isolated sanctuary, but they raised their rifles in preparation for anything. Jade continued to stare into the brush ahead and listen.

Light filtering though the treetops teased them with patches of visibility like a game of peekaboo. Jade knew that any predator's vision in low light would be better than hers. She watched instead for small movements indicating an ear twitch or the quivering of hindquarters, and listened for the slightest brushing of foliage.

Gradually she filtered out the surrounding noises of their breathing and her heartbeat and concentrated on a very subtle sliding noise, as if something small was being dragged along the forest floor. A soft chirp followed.

The faintest trace of a smile twitched Jade's lips just before she whistled one sharp answering chirp. Immediately a sleek spotted cat bounded out of the woods and slapped at Jade's legs.

'Biscuit, what the thundering blazes are you doing here?'

The slender cheetah butted his head against Jade's thigh and chirped again. Avery and Bev lowered their rifles and released audible sighs of relief. 'I might have shot him,' muttered Avery.

Jade stroked the exotic cat's head and back. Biscuit responded by flopping onto the ground and rolling on his back like a giant domestic tabby. Jade chuckled and obliged the cat by rubbing his muscular tummy.

'We weren't in any real danger, Avery, darling,' Beverly said. 'Jade's knee didn't hurt.'

Jade glanced up at her friend. 'My shrapnel wound only hurts when it's going to rain, Bev.'

'*And* when something is trying to kill one of us. At least that's what you told me back in Tsavo.'

'That's impossible, and you know it,' muttered Jade. She stifled her irritation and picked up the broken lead dangling from Biscuit's collar. 'Hmmm. That explains how he got away from Jelani. He snapped his tether.'

'Don't be angry with the lad,' Beverly pleaded. 'He's just a boy.'

'I'm not angry with Jelani, but if I ever see Harry Hascombe again, I'm going to thrash him.' After being shot at and finding both a murdered askari and an elephant left to bleed to death, or die at the hands of scavengers, Jade definitely wanted to hit something, and Harry, her last season's safari leader, seemed as good a target as any. Last June he had connived to trick her into passing on her dead fiancé's legacy to an impostor, Roger Forster. Hascombe claimed he didn't know the man had been a drug smuggler

27

and a murderer, but it didn't lessen his guilt in Jade's eyes. She didn't care to be lied to for any reason. Biscuit had been one of Hascombe's pets.

Avery, who until then had stayed out of the conversation, raised one eyebrow as an inquiry.

'Hascombe could have trained the animal better,' Jade answered, 'and he shouldn't have abandoned the cat.'

'He didn't exactly abandon it, darling,' Beverly said. 'He turned it over to Madeline and Neville to keep for him. After all, with his man Ruta deceased, who would be able to watch him?'

'Quite right,' echoed Avery. 'And after Hascombe decided to give up ranching and turn full-time hunter and safari leader, he couldn't very well drag the poor beast around with him.'

Jade arched her thick black brows and fixed her intense green eyes on Avery. He stammered and shifted his feet before replying, 'Sorry, I didn't quite mean that you are dragging Biscuit around. I meant — oh, bloody hell, I have no idea what I meant. Stop staring at me! You know I hate it when you do that. It gives me goose bumps.'

Jade only smiled a Mona Lisa smirk. 'Harry Hascombe is a lying, thieving, low-down, conniving snake in the grass.' After her dealings with him on her last safari in Tsavo, she couldn't find one iota of respect for the man.

'He's not that bad a sort,' protested Beverly. 'And he tried to do right by Biscuit. He couldn't very well turn him loose. The poor creature would have wandered to some unsuspecting human and then been shot.'

When Jade transferred her hypnotic, predatory stare to Beverly, the pretty blond Englishwoman stuck out her chin in defiance and retorted, 'Anyway, who would have thought that Biscuit would take such a liking to *you*, Jade? He ran away from Neville and Maddy twice before they finally decided you should keep him.'

Jade stroked the big cat and took hold of his broken tether. 'Don't forget Jelani. Biscuit seems to love Jelani.'

As if the Kikuyu boy heard his name, twelve-year-old Jelani came running towards them, breathing heavily. 'Ah, Miss Jade,' he said as he fought to catch his breath. 'He found you. I'm sorry. I — '

Jade raised her hand to cut him off in midapology. 'Jelani, I'm not upset that Biscuit got loose. But I am unhappy that you chose to go trailing after him alone. You could have been hurt. You don't know this forest.' She thought of Captain Smythe's warnings and wondered if she should perhaps heed them for the boy's sake. 'I'm surprised Chiumbo didn't stop you.'

Jelani hung his head, and Jade felt a twinge of guilt for chastising the young Kikuyu. 'I'm sorry, Jelani. I should know that any young warrior who could face down a witch's hyena like you did would not be afraid to follow Biscuit or bother to wait for the headman's permission.'

The lad's black eyes glowed at Jade's reference to his encounter the previous June with a man-eating hyena that had raided his village. Never mind that Jade had already shot the beast before Jelani stuck his knife in it. Jade handed the broken lead to the boy. He took it, squared his narrow shoulders, and scolded the big cat at length in a mixture of Swahili, English, and Kikuyu. Biscuit stood by his side, his tongue lolling. When Jelani finished his diatribe, the cheetah rubbed his head against Jelani's waist and licked his hand as if making a tacit apology for being so much trouble.

'Let's get back,' Jade said. 'It will be dark soon and I don't care to get eaten or shot at — again.'

'And I'm hungry,' Beverly repeated.

★ ★ ★

They dined in midafternoon on roasted bustard that had been smothered in a clay coating and baked under hot coals in a pit. When the fire-hardened clay was cracked aside, the resulting turkey-sized bird nearly fell off the bones, after having spent the day steaming in its own juices. Whole potatoes baked among the coals completed the meal. Jade couldn't remember when she'd enjoyed a bird more. She poured a second cup of her beloved coffee and sipped it. *Pure nectar!* Beverly, she noted, had decided on tea again. Jade grimaced. To her, drinking tea was only a little better than swallowing warm ditch water after the fall leaves had stewed in it for a month.

Jelani ate with Jade and the Dunburys at the trio's insistence. Since the few remaining porters were predominately Wakamba and not interested in conversing with a Kikuyu lad, Jelani didn't mind sacrificing the men's tales for Jade's company. Jade had her own reasons for keeping the boy close. She wanted him to become more than someone's servant or porter, a man forced to eke out a living just to pay the colony's hut tax. Her hope was for him to become a leader of his own people, one who could hold his own against the Protectorate's bureaucracy. Even the tribe's *mundu-mugo*, or spiritual healer, approved her decision. After supper, she motioned for Jelani to move closer to her kerosene lantern and handed him a children's book of Aesop's fables.

'Time for a reading lesson, Jelani. Did you practice today?'

'Yes, Miss Jade, but some of the words are strange to me. I tried to sound them out as you and Miss Beverly taught me, but . . . ' He shrugged to indicate his uncertainty over his success and his general feeling of perturbation over the English language's irregularities.

'Read to us and we shall see.' She smiled her encouragement.

Jelani opened the book to one of the fables and began. ' "The Crow and the Water Pitcher.' There once was a crow who was half-dead from thirst when he saw a pitcher with some water inside. 'Ah,' said the crow, 'now I shall have water and live,' but when the crow tried to put his head into the pitcher, it would not fit, and the water was too far down for him to reach. 'What shall I do?' he said. 'If I do not get a drink, I shall die.' The crow began to . . . ' Jelani paused and pointed to the next word. 'Dee-spair?' he asked.

'That's very close. It is 'despair,'' Jade said.

31

'What does that mean?'

'It means giving up all hope,' answered Lord Dunbury. 'Something you should never do.'

Jelani nodded. 'Now the story makes sense. If the crow gives up, he will die.'

'And did he?' Beverly asked.

Jelani shook his head and turned back to the book. 'Then the crow saw some little rocks. He picked one up and dropped it into the pitcher. He took another and another. He dropped many rocks into the pitcher. The water rose higher and higher till he could reach it with his beak. Then he could take a drink and save his life.'

Jelani looked up and grinned at Jade. 'He was a smart bird.'

'Very,' Jade agreed. 'And what is the moral of this fable?'

Jelani recited the final line of the tale. 'Little by little does the job.'

'A good lesson,' agreed Avery, 'but I should think it could also be 'Never give up' or, perhaps, 'Use your brain when you're in trouble.''

Jelani closed the book carefully and hugged it to his chest. 'I like this book. Some of the animals are very wise and others are funny. I found another story about a wolf that chewed off its own foot to escape from a trap. Do you want to hear that one, too?'

Beverly shook her head rapidly. 'No! It sounds awful.' Then she quickly added, 'But you did very well to read it on your own.'

Jelani shrugged, not understanding her distaste. 'He was a brave animal, but I still like Bwana Avery's books better.'

'You little scamp,' Avery said in mock anger. 'Have you been reading my Tarzan novels?' He jumped up from his seat on a wooden chop box and grabbed the boy.

Jelani laughed as the tall blond man tickled him around the ribs. Biscuit joined in by rearing up and swatting Avery on the backside. Avery lost his balance and collapsed onto the ground as Jelani and the slender cat pounced on top of him.

'All right, all right,' Avery called out between laughs. 'You win. Not fair, two against one.'

The boy and the cheetah desisted, and Avery scrambled to his feet and brushed off his trousers. 'Tarzan wouldn't have stood for that sort of rowdiness.'

'Tarzan spoke a strange language,' Jelani said.

'Ah, you mean Mangani,' Jade replied. 'That's supposed to be the language of the great apes.'

'Do these apes really speak?'

Jade shook her head. 'I'm sure they make some calls to each other, but Mangani is something that the author made up. Much,' she added with a sidewise glance at Beverly, 'like Memsabu Madeline did in her book.'

'She didn't make anything up,' protested Beverly.

'Right. And just when did I ever say to a lion, and I quote, 'You can go back and tell your witch master that I'm not afraid of you or him'?'

'I don't care what you say,' replied Bev with a sniff. '*Stalking Death* is a wonderful book and very true to life. And Madeline is rather like your own personal Dr Watson, dramatizing your adventures. It will be a tremendous smash. She's already sent it off to her London publisher.'

'I say,' said Avery in a gallant attempt to redirect the conversation, 'since we're all reading those Tarzan books, we should learn Mangani and speak it ourselves. Sort of a private code. Won't that be fun?'

'I will make a list of words,' Jelani said. 'I will look through *all* of Bwana Avery's books.' He stopped and glanced up at Avery, a look of hopeful anticipation welling in his large brown eyes.

Avery couldn't resist. 'Yes, you may make a list from my books.' He rubbed the boy's short black hair. 'I'm pleased to see you enjoy reading so much.'

'It is a good idea, Jelani,' added Jade. 'That way you can also practice your writing.' She noticed the sudden frown. 'Yes, I know you don't enjoy that nearly as much as reading, but it's also important.'

Jelani stuck out his lower lip and pouted like any youngster being told what to do. 'I am going to read my story to Chiumbo,' he said, indicating their headman. 'He likes my stories.'

The boy patted his leg as a signal for Biscuit to follow, but the cat opted to stay at Jade's feet.

'That's fine, Jelani,' said Jade, 'but remember your proper bedtime tonight. I'll send Biscuit to guard you later.'

Jelani made a face when Jade mentioned bedtime, but didn't argue the point. Instead, he wandered off, looking for the safari's headman.

'He's a good little chap,' Beverly noted as the

boy left. 'It's very good, what you're doing for him.'

Jade shrugged. 'I'm not doing all that much, but I agree, he is good.' She poked a stick into the fire and stirred up the wood. The fire burned more brightly after she opened up another air passage. A safe distance away, the evening noises started with a tree limb's prolonged groaning, followed by a sharp crack as the branch broke under some elephant's persistent pull. 'He has only an old mother and father, no siblings. It's the least one can do.' She tossed the stick into the fire and added three bigger chunks of wood. 'Besides, Biscuit needed a keeper.'

'Now, don't try to disclaim any interest in the boy, Jade,' scolded Beverly. 'I know you too well for that. You like him and you needed something to give you a purpose in life. There's no shame in caring for someone, you know.' She frowned and shook her head, causing her soft corn silk curls to shimmer in the firelight. 'You've been a lost soul, Jade. I thought you'd snap out of it once you found David's brother, but you haven't.'

At the mention of her deceased fiancé's name, Jade unconsciously reached for his ring, which she wore around her neck as a talisman. British pilot David Worthy had been her sweetheart during the war until his plane crashed in a dogfight in which he had defended her and the evac hospital. He died in her arms, pressing this same ring into her hands with the request that she use it to find his brother. That search had brought her to East Africa and to Jelani.

Beverly watched her friend and scowled.

'Heavens, if anyone needs a keeper, it's not Biscuit — it's you!' She pressed her point despite all of Jade's warning looks. 'Avery and I won't be able to follow after you forever, you know.'

'No one is asking you to,' snapped Jade.

Beverly ignored her and continued. 'It's high time you quit traipsing all over the continent and settled down with some nice man who can watch over you.' She glanced at her husband for support. 'Right, darling?'

Avery decided that discretion was the better part of valor and kept his mouth shut, pretending to be fascinated by his boots.

Jade picked up a stout stick and hurled it into the fire. 'I don't need a blasted keeper!' She rose to her feet and glared at Beverly. 'So if you have any more plans about setting me up, you can just forget it. Both you and Maddy were determined that I should marry that louse Hascombe last year, so I don't put a great deal of stock in your match-making abilities.'

Just then a deep baritone voice sang out from the edge of the forest. 'There's my bright beauty.'

Jade turned and looked straight into the face of Harry Hascombe. 'Spit fire and save the matches! It's you.'

3

Elephants live in a tightly knit society,
dominated by one of the older cows whose
accumulated wisdom allows her to recognize
danger and lead her charges safely to and
from water and food.
— The Traveler

For the third time that day, Jade seriously wrestled with the idea of punching someone in the face. Before, when no actual target stood before her, she'd gained control more quickly, but this time, her target loomed large. Her right hand clenched into a fist, itching to connect with that smug smile. *Just give me one good provocation.*

'What the devil are you doing here, Hascombe?' she demanded. 'I thought I saw the last of your lying, vermin-ridden hide after we hauled you back from Tsavo.'

'Nice to see you, too, Jade.' His gaze ran over her slender figure. 'You're looking particularly fine as always.'

Avery rose and extended a hand towards their visitor, effectively blocking Jade's chances of landing a punch. 'Hascombe,' he said.

'Dunbury,' replied Harry as he shook the young lord's hand. 'Lady Dunbury,' he added as he nodded to Beverly.

She smiled and nodded in return. 'I'm glad to see that your broken leg mended so well, Harry.'

'Thank you,' he replied. 'Kind of *you* to notice.'

Biscuit rose, stretched, and padded softly over to his former master. If Jade hoped the big cat would take a bite out of Harry, he didn't. Instead he sniffed Harry's trousers, then chirped a greeting. Harry put out a rough hand and stroked the cheetah's head. 'And how's my bright beauty?' he asked the cat. 'What are you doing all the way out here?'

Jade decided that hitting the man wouldn't do much good anyway and sat back down on the chop box she'd been using for a seat. She made a point of not offering a chair or a box to Harry. 'He's with me.'

Harry looked around for another of the wooden crates and pulled it up to the fire. 'I can see that.' He sat down and leaned his rifle against his leg. 'What I want to know is why. I distinctly remember leaving him with that coffee farmer, Thompson, and his wife.'

'He kept running after Jade,' Beverly said. 'It was the most amazing sight. Once, he actually followed the scent of her Ford all the way into town to the Norfolk Hotel. When he arrived, he slipped right past the boys out front, went straight through the lobby, and trotted on up to her room just as if he owned the place. And another time he followed her into a party at the Muthaiga Club. That drunken trollop Cissy Estes screamed and stood on a table. That is,

38

before she passed out on it.'

'The devil you say.' Harry shook his head. 'Biscuit was fond of my man Ruta, but I never knew him to act that way even around him.'

'He also likes Jelani, the Kikuyu boy who is traveling with us,' added Avery.

Harry appeared not to hear the last remark. Instead he riveted his gaze on Jade. 'You're a very remarkable woman, Jade, but then I already knew that.'

She returned his stare. Her green eyes, for which her father had named her, bored right into Harry's. Very few people could win a staring contest with her, and Harry didn't bother to try. He glanced back at the Dunburys. 'Well, at least I know Biscuit's in good hands.'

'What are you doing here, Hascombe?' Jade repeated. Her gaze never left his face as she watched for any telltale sign of deception.

Harry stewed a moment under her scrutiny, fidgeting on his box seat. 'I'm leading a bloody damned safari, if you must know,' he finally bellowed.

'You don't need to shout, Hascombe. I can hear you.'

'Sorry,' he muttered. 'It's just that . . . ' He shifted some more. 'You could try the patience of a saint.'

'I think Harry would have appreciated a more cordial greeting, Jade,' said Beverly. 'You've hurt his feelings.'

'Right,' said Harry. He slapped his leg for emphasis. 'Instead I get a bloody interrogation. You used to be friendlier to me, Jade. You even

39

danced with me once, remember?'

For a moment, a memory of that evening jumped, unbidden, to Jade's mind. She saw Harry, looking very handsome in evening kit. More than the image, she remembered his musky male scent and felt his strong arm around her waist, and the smooth grace with which he led her across the floor in a waltz. She shook the thought away. 'I remember. I have an excellent memory. So you're here leading a safari.' As she said it, Jade arched her brows and looked past his shoulder into the woods, as if she expected to see an army of porters and hunters materialize in front of her, a tacit implication that she didn't believe him.

Harry caught the drift of her unspoken query. 'Of course they're not here,' he said. 'I left them at my camp.' He jerked his thumb over his shoulder to the northeast. 'About three miles that way. There's a smaller crater there, a seasonal lake. Unfortunately, it's nearly dry now, so the elephants have abandoned it.'

'I say, I don't mean to criticize. I'm sure you know what you're doing and all, but was that wise to leave them?' asked Avery. 'Your people, I mean.'

'They're perfectly safe. I've got a damn fine headman with them. Name's Nakuru. He's from Tanganyika. Best headmen come from there.'

Lord Dunbury nodded. 'Yes, our man is Chiumbo. He's a Nyamwezi tribesman, I believe.'

Harry's eyes widened in recognition. 'I've heard of him. They say Roosevelt tried to get

40

him, but he was already engaged.'

Avery nodded. 'That's the man.'

'You should feel honored to have him. He's very particular about who he works for, a matter of honor. But I'm surprised to see all of you up here.' Harry nodded in Jade's direction. 'What's Simba Jike got you into this time?'

'Jade's photographing elephants,' Avery said.

'Very exciting!' added Beverly. She looked across to her friend and shuddered when she observed Jade's mouth set in a severe line with obvious loathing radiating from her every pore. 'Um, Jade, darling. Might we show Harry some of your photographs?'

Jade answered in a subdued rumble. 'I'm sure Mr Hascombe is too anxious to return to his people to stay and look at photographs. We don't have a spare tent for him and he won't want to be wandering around the trails once it gets dark.'

Harry retrieved his rifle and stood. 'I believe that is what is now termed a 'bum's rush.''

'If the shoe fits,' Jade muttered.

Harry took a deep breath, touched the brim of his hat, and nodded to the Dunburys. 'Lord Dunbury, Lady Dunbury, always a pleasure. Drop by my camp if you've a mind to. Next crater over. Can't miss us.' He turned to leave when Jade's voice halted him.

'Which one of your people shot at us today?'

Harry turned abruptly, his square jaw clenched in an obvious attempt to control his temper. 'What the devil are you talking about, woman?'

Avery explained. 'This afternoon a bullet

41

passed dangerously close to Jade.'

Harry shook his head. 'I guess that would explain your sour mood, but we're only after elephant, and right now we're just scouting. None of my people fired any shots today.' He turned halfway around to leave, hesitated, and faced Jade once more. 'Perhaps, to be on the safe side, we should each keep track of where the other group is so we don't have any accidents.'

Jade folded her arms over her chest. 'You're telling us you didn't butcher that calf today and leave its mother bleeding to death?' She tilted up her jaw and shook her head. Her short dark hair flashed blue-black in the fire's light. 'I don't believe you, Hascombe. There's nobody else around here.'

Harry jabbed a finger in her direction. 'I have no idea what you're talking about, Jade, but if you think we're all alone up here, you're a damned little fool. Poachers don't tend to introduce themselves.'

'Leave my elephants alone, Hascombe!'

'They're not *your* elephants.' He nodded to each of them and stomped off.

Jade immediately turned on Beverly. 'Did you invite him here?'

Beverly's jaw dropped. She leaned back on her box and put a hand to her chest. 'Me? Why on earth do you think I invited Harry? I was just as surprised to see him as you were.'

'Just before he showed up, you said, and I quote, 'It's high time you quit traipsing all over the continent and settled down with some nice man who can watch over you.'' Jade leaned forward on her own box. 'Let me inform you of something, Beverly. Hascombe is *not* a nice man!'

'I didn't know he was here, Jade. You must believe me.'

Jade heard the hurt in Bev's voice and apologized for offending her. In her own head she couldn't quite figure out why she felt such anger towards Hascombe. Oh, certainly she had cause to resent him. His machinations had clouded everything last June while she'd searched with such desperation for her dead sweetheart's missing brother. And in the end, Harry had been duped by Forster as much as she.

A nagging voice in one corner of her head sneered at her frustration and reminded her that she had once found Harry Hascombe dangerously attractive. The same voice mockingly took note that he still looked in fine figure. Jade scowled. Pure nonsense, she told herself. It didn't help. His mention of their dance together at the Muthaiga Club had already opened the door to her memories and another quickly rushed in. She felt his hot kiss pressing on her willing lips after her bullfighting encounter with the rhino.

Avery's voice broke into her moody reflections. 'Surely you don't think Hascombe's people committed those atrocities? Especially after Captain Smythe informed us that raiders are coming down from the north. Harry's safari might be a fortunate turn of events for us.' Jade frowned at him, and Avery hastened to explain.

'There is safety in numbers. If we banded together, we should be safe.'

'Avery, I can hardly photograph elephants while he runs around and shoots them.'

'But surely we can work out . . . ' He paused midsentence when his wife placed a restraining hand gently on his arm and shook her head.

'Let it go, darling,' she said in a hushed voice. 'We're all tired.'

Avery glanced from his wife to Jade and back again. 'Um, quite right, my love. It has been a long day.' He rose and stretched. 'Are the men keeping watch tonight or is it our turn?'

'You're retiring already? The sun hasn't even set yet.' Immediately Jade regretted her question. After all, they were married and probably dying for some private time, not something easy to achieve on safari. 'Um, go ahead and go to bed if you're tired. Chiumbo has first watch. He'll see to the others.' She didn't move when her friends headed for their tent.

Beverly stopped beside her. 'You should get some sleep, Jade. You're up far too early in the morning, checking your cameras. We'll see that Jelani goes to bed, too,' she added.

Jade kept her gaze down at her boots and sighed. 'You go on. I'm not tired yet. I'll sit up for a while.' When Beverly didn't move from her side, Jade looked up and forced a smile. 'I'm fine. I just want to sit here a spell. Maybe talk to Chiumbo about some of his old safaris. And I need to write up some notes from today for my article for *The Traveler*.'

Beverly nodded and patted her friend's

44

shoulder. 'Don't stay up too late.'

'No, Mother,' replied Jade. She immediately winced as Bev slapped her playfully on the head. After the Dunburys retired, she stirred up the fire with a poker, then tossed another log on top.

Jade didn't really want to talk to anyone this evening. Talking meant thinking and she didn't want to think. She wanted to evaporate, to let all her restlessness rise up as one with the fire's sparks and dissipate into the soft blackness that fell immediately after sunset. In the distance she heard the tubercular-sounding cough of a leopard, followed by the irate screams of some baboons.

She pulled a tattered leather notebook and a pencil from one of her jacket pockets, flipped open the book to a blank page, and paused, pencil in the air. To her left, a rhino snorted from down in the brushy *donga* and from everywhere echoed the explosive snapping of tree limbs. Finally she poured out her impressions of the herds, their tight-knit family units and maternal care. When she reflected on the calf's death and the brave askari's murder, her pencil point snapped under the increased pressure.

Poachers! A spark rose from the fire, and as she watched it drift upward, her mind retreated into a conversation she'd had with her friends after Colridge's party.

They had sat on the Dunburys' terrace, Madeline in her made-over blue dress, Beverly in a moss green silk, the men in evening kit, sipping lemonade as moonlight filtered down through the trelliswork, the air heavy with the perfume of roses.

45

'Mr Percival talked about poachers?' asked Neville Thompson. He uncrossed his legs and leaned forward, his stiff, formal collar undone as he made himself comfortable. 'Jade, this trip could be very dangerous. Surely even you aren't serious about going.'

'I'll be fine. By the way, we got a letter from Pili,' Jade said, trying to change the subject to the young Somali who they had discovered was heir to a small fortune. 'He's doing quite well in school and hoping to start veterinary classes next term.'

'Has there been any more trouble from Mrs Worthy?' asked Madeline. She pulled her shoes off and curled her legs under her to one side after wriggling her toes to ease out the cramps from dancing in tight shoes. 'Is she still contesting her husband's will? From what you told us, she was furious at losing half her estate to her husband's illegitimate son.'

'Mrs Worthy won't bother Pili anymore,' said Avery. Somewhere in the vicinity, a male lion called to his mate in a series of husky roars that ended in a set of short, choppy harrumphs. For the moment, everyone sat very still, drinking glasses in hand, as they listened to the throaty symphony. 'We've seen to that,' Avery continued when the big cat had finished. 'She knows we'll charge her formally the next time she tries anything.'

'So you don't think that runaway carriage was an accident after all,' said Neville. 'I say, is the lad safe?'

Avery nodded. 'Quite safe. We transferred him

46

to a school in Scotland. He may not like the climate, but she doesn't know where he is.'

'And,' added Beverly as she took a cue from Madeline and kicked off her own shoes, 'she can't get her hands on his money, either.' She stretched her long legs in front of her. 'We have it secured in a trust for him. How such a sweet man as David could have had such a horrid woman for a mother is beyond me. To think she actually hired someone to kill her husband.'

'Something we've never been able to prove, either,' added Jade. 'If there was any proof in Roger Forster's papers, they burned with his house.'

There was a brief lull while everyone considered the meaning of that statement. 'I suppose she had Gil Worthy killed so he couldn't bring home another heir to replace her son?' said Neville.

Jade nodded, drained her glass of lemonade, and set it down. 'My only question is, how extensive are her connections in Africa? Olivia Lilith Worthy does not leave many traces behind.'

'Speaking of sweet men, Jade,' said Madeline, as she tried to brighten the mood, 'what did you think of Edmunde, Colridge's son? I believe he took a fancy to you.'

Jade curled her upper lip and imitated a lion's snarl. 'Don't start pushing more men on me, Maddy. First Hascombe, now Edmunde?'

The thought of Harry Hascombe sent a tingle down Jade's spine, which brought her back to the present. She took out her knife and whittled a fresh pencil tip. Soft footfalls approached, and Jade looked up to see their headman regarding her with concern.

'Simba Jike is not tired tonight?' he inquired.

Jade shrugged. 'Actually I am — tired of a lot of stuff, Chiumbo.'

The Tanganyikan sat down next to her. 'It is that elephant cow and her *toto* that upset you. Perhaps you are only tired of death, miss.'

Jade propped her elbows on her legs and rested her chin on her clasped hands. 'I understand hunting, Chiumbo. I've been doing it most of my life. We hunted for food or protection, same as the animals out here. I even partially understand hunting for sport. But I don't understand waste and cruelty. Killing that calf was a waste and letting that cow die slowly and painfully was cruel. I don't understand that. But it isn't the cow and her baby that I was thinking of just now. I keep seeing that poor soldier.' She shuddered. 'Chiumbo, that man was executed. His face was blown away after someone first shot arrows into his gut. That's murder!'

'Cruelty is power, miss. You do not covet power.'

Jade studied the African's face, scarred both by battle and by experience. The firelight highlighted deep wrinkles across his brow and around his mouth and cast a shadow over a badly healed rent that ran from his jaw to his temple, just missing his left eye. She wondered how old he was and decided he must be fifty at least. 'You sound as if you speak from

48

experience, Chiumbo.'

For a few thoughtful moments he watched the fire dance. 'My people are called Nyamwezi, the people who bring the moon. We were traders. We left from Tabora at the new moon and always arrived at Dar es Salaam at the next new moon, so the people there joked that we' — he paused — 'excreted the moon when we came.'

Jade smiled and nodded for the man to continue.

'I made some of those trips with my father. Before we left the village, we would go to the *mahoka* huts, where we prayed to our ancestors and left offerings for them.' His lips tightened, and he scowled, still staring into the fire. 'Then these men you white people call Germans came to our land and destroyed the huts. They mocked our rituals. Chief Isike fought them, and I fought with him as a young warrior. When Isike died, these men took whole villages and forced us to work their cotton farms. Many died. Some of us joined the Hehe tribe to fight these men, who were led by an Englishman named Prince and aided by their missionary people. This man called Prince, he and his lieutenant killed my father. I saw, but I could do nothing. Then our leaders told us to drink and sprinkle ourselves with sacred water from the mountains. They said it would turn the bullets to *maji*, 'water.''

His smile was grim as he shook his head. 'It only turned them to blood, *our* blood. They knew no mercy, Simba Jike. Only cruelty. All these people wanted power.'

'And what do you want, Chiumbo?' she asked.

49

'Do you seek power or revenge?'

He turned to her. 'Men pay me now to lead their safaris. I can say yes or no to their money. That is my power.'

'And why did you say yes to our money?'

'You must sleep now,' he said as he stood. 'I will keep first watch.'

Jade nodded obediently and rose. Biscuit stood with her, and she directed him to Jelani's tent to guard the boy. Suddenly she felt tremendously exhausted. Her head throbbed and her body ached. She rubbed her left knee absentmindedly and stumbled through the tent flaps. Perhaps she should rummage through her kit and find that little bottle of aspirin Beverly insisted she pack. Bev kept telling her that it was a wonder drug and claimed it would help her knee.

She lit the oil lamp and trimmed the wick. The cot looked so enticing, but the assorted aches grew steadily stronger. Jade turned aside, put the lamp in front of her on her camp table, and headed for her pack to find the needed medication, her shadow dancing on the tent's wall.

From behind her came a soft *whoosh* followed by a muffled *thunk*. She whirled and saw an arrow protruding from the center of her cot.

4

It isn't completely clear how elephants speak to each other, perhaps partially with sounds we cannot hear, but anyone who watches a herd for more than an hour knows they do communicate.
— The Traveler

It took a few seconds for Jade to come out of her exhaustion-induced fog and comprehend the wooden shaft sticking out of her thin mattress. For a moment she stared dumbly at it, mouth open, and wondered where it came from. Then it dawned on her that the arrow would have been sticking out of her body if she hadn't opted for pain relief. At that point, the fog lifted in her head, and she raced back outside and peered into the gloom for movement.

Chiumbo read the anger and confusion on Jade's face and ran to her side. 'What is the matter, Simba Jike?'

'Someone shot an arrow into my cot. Did you see or hear anyone?'

Chiumbo shook his head. 'From which way did the arrow come?'

Excellent question, thought Jade. In her haste to find someone, she hadn't paid much attention. A quick inspection of her tent showed the rent where the arrow had entered but little else.

She pulled the arrow out of the cot and showed it to Chiumbo. It looked handmade with a straight wooden shaft that ended in a sharpened bone point. Both the feathers for the fletching and the point were lashed on with thin strips of animal hide. 'Do you know who uses an arrow like this?' She wished she'd paid more attention to the ones in the elephants today.

He shrugged. 'It could be anyone, Simba Jike.' The headman took it from her and carefully directed the point away from both of them. 'You must be careful. Sometimes the tip is poisoned.'

Their movements and conversation soon drew the attention of the Dunburys. They hurried out of their tent as soon as they could slip into their clothes and boots. 'Can't you even go to bed without getting into trouble?' Beverly asked.

Jade scowled. 'I don't suppose you have anything useful to contribute, such as knowing who did this?' She took back the arrow and held it out, tip up, while pointing to the rent in the canvas.

Avery turned to peer into the darkness. 'I say, Jade, have you an enemy we should know about? That makes two times today someone has aimed for you.'

Beverly's jaw dropped in horror. 'Avery!' she scolded. 'I thought we decided that earlier incident was probably a shot gone wild and not someone aiming for Jade. We said as much to Captain Smythe.'

Jade held up her hand to forestall Avery's

rebuttal. 'Once is an accident. Twice is another matter, Bev. I'm inclined to agree with your husband.' She turned the arrow in her hands and studied every aspect. 'Well made. Lightweight but sharp tip. Rather efficient at puncturing skin, I should think.'

'Perhaps one of those Abyssinian raiders?' suggested Avery. 'The back end looks a bit like the ones we saw earlier today.'

'Possibly,' Jade said. 'Whoever it was, I don't think they intended to actually kill me.'

Beverly gasped. 'But it landed in the middle of your cot.'

Jade pointed with the arrow towards her tent, where the soft, flickering glow of her lantern illuminated the interior. 'The lantern was in front of me and they shot from behind me. I think the archer could see my form standing upright. If he'd wanted to shoot me, he could have.'

'But why?' asked Beverly.

'Why shoot at me or why miss?'

Beverly frowned and shrugged. 'Both.'

'Maybe someone wants to scare us away, but if they hit me, they'd run the risk of someone seriously tracking them down.'

Avery nodded vigorously. 'That makes a certain amount of sense and it fits what Captain Smythe told us about the raiders. They probably want us to clear out of the area.'

Jade stuck the arrow, tip first, into the ground near a corner tent peg. Her head pounded, and she rubbed her temples with her fingertips. 'I never took my headache pills,' she said in a soft voice as though thinking aloud.

'Beg your pardon?' Beverly asked.

'Oh, I just remembered that I didn't take my aspirin. That's why I wasn't in my cot. I was trying to find them in my kit.'

Avery let out a soft whistle. 'I say, it's a good job you had that headache, then.'

Jade stifled a yawn. 'Yep. I'd have really needed a painkiller,' she muttered as the situation's irony kicked in. She let the next yawn rip her mouth wide open before she started towards her tent. She hadn't gone more than two steps when a muffled boom erupted from the direction of her tree blind. Everyone immediately ducked, but Jade quickly stood back up again.

'It's all right,' she said. 'That was my flash powder going off.'

'That loud?' exclaimed Beverly. 'The noise at the Muthaiga wasn't half as noisy and we were closer.'

Jade nodded. 'I probably used a bit too much powder this time. That boom is similar to thunder after lightning heats the air. If you were at the blind, you would have seen a very bright white flash first.'

'So something hit the trip wire,' said Avery. 'That's splendid, but I hope you're not planning on checking on it tonight.'

Jade looked longingly into the darkness towards the camera blind and chewed her lower lip. 'No, it can wait until tomorrow, I suppose. Whoever shot my cot might still be out there.'

'Jade,' called Beverly as her friend headed back to her tent, 'what should we do?'

'Double the watch, I guess. I'm going to bed.' Jade yawned again. 'Don't wake me up unless someone actually shoots me.'

Perhaps it was the headache pulsing in her temples in time to her heartbeat. Perhaps it was the memory of the dead askari and the dying elephant's open-eyed terror that she'd witnessed earlier in the day, or the ongoing din of elephants feeding in the distance. Whatever the underlying cause, horrifying sounds and visions wrecked Jade's dreams. All during the night she was beset by elephants trumpeting in rage and panic as they crashed through the underbrush trying to escape an unseen danger. At one point, she saw old Lord Colridge and his cronies talking over a drink at the Muthaiga Club while a herd crashed through the bar behind them. Finally she dreamed the old bull himself stepped out of the morning mists and trumpeted a piercing warning. Curiously, she felt this warning was directed, not to the herd, but to her.

5

The skeptic might counter that elephants could not have anything of importance to communicate, but that certainly has never stopped humans from talking.
— The Traveler

Jade woke at four a.m. and took advantage of the blackness to develop a film roll. Knowing the ill effects of moisture on unexposed film, she continued to use individual film sheets in her trip wire cameras, but she had installed a roll adapter on the Graflex that she carried with her. When she finished, she scanned the developed negative for anything worthwhile and wished once again that she had a complete photo lab instead of a few tins of concentrated chemicals and some developing trays in the spare tent. Red glass covered her lantern and gave her just enough light to see the images. Making prints would have to wait until she returned to Nairobi and Beverly's new house, where the Dunburys had generously added on a full lab just for her use.

'I got you!' she whispered to the big bull elephant in one of the frames. She grabbed a magnifying lens and studied the negative, hoping to find part of the female herd in the

56

background. None of them appeared, but Jade knew that the old boy was on their track. He never ventured farther than a mile from them.

The moment she'd spotted this ancient bull circling the cows, Jade had amended her original intent to photograph only the elephant herds. He traveled alone, as did most mature bulls, his proximity to the cows only tolerated by the herd's aging matriarch. The old dame ruled her herd with an iron trunk, guiding them through the mountain forest in the continuing search for fresh food, and she had little patience for would-be Romeos taking food needed by pregnant cows and growing calves.

Jade looked at the last negative on the short roll and saw the mother cow and her baby as they passed below her tree blind yesterday. The recollection of their subsequent slaughter brought a fresh upwelling of anger to her throat. She wondered if these elephants had been some of the matriarch's own progeny.

Last night's dreams flashed in her mind, and suddenly Jade felt a sense of urgency that made her hands tremble. This outpost was not the sanctuary she'd hoped it would be. She needed to document these giant animals before they and their world evaporated like the morning mists over the crater. Mr Percival, who was forced to spend most of his time closer to Nairobi, must have suspected that as well, which was why he wanted her survey. If the herds were in danger, he could at least limit hunting permits.

'Ja-ade,' sang a clear soprano voice from outside Jade's sleeping tent. 'I say, are you up or are you being a slugabed?'

Jade left the developed negatives hanging from clothespins and tiptoed out of the makeshift darkroom. She slunk around the side of the tent as silently as a real lioness and paused. Then, in a single leap, she pounced behind Beverly and slapped her across the back.

Beverly jumped a foot and shrieked. 'Blast you, Jade,' she said as she collapsed against the tent post, a hand on her chest. 'You scared me! My heart is pounding.'

Jade chuckled, her voice a low contralto. 'I'm sorry, Bev. Truly I am.'

'No, you're not. At least you don't sound very sorry.'

'You're right. I'm not.' She clapped her hands together and laughed. 'I couldn't resist, you know. Don't hurt me.' Her hands rose in front of her face in a mock defensive posture.

Biscuit bounded forward, wanting to join in the romp. He butted his head against Jade, then slapped at Beverly's leg.

'Wonderful. All the cats are attacking this morning,' muttered Beverly. She put her hand to her stomach and grimaced. 'Oof. I feel a trifle green today.'

Jade quieted Biscuit with a gentle but firm touch on the cat's head, then apologized to her friend again. 'Come and see what I've discovered this morning,' she said as she motioned Beverly to the darkroom tent. Beverly waited outside in the misty morning air while Jade slipped in and retrieved the developed negatives.

'Look at this one,' she said.

58

Beverly's soft blue eyes opened wide as she examined the strip. 'He's magnificent! Oh, Jade. I say, well done, old girl.'

'What's Simba Jike done now?'

The deep, purring voice caught Jade completely off guard. She'd been expecting Avery's mellow tenor, not Harry's rumbling baritone. She spun around in an instant, her fists clenched at her sides.

If Harry noticed, he pretended not to. 'Good morning, ladies. I came to invite you to dinner tonight. Lord Dunbury as well, of course.'

'Harry,' Beverly said. 'Good morning. I'm afraid you gave us a bit of a start.'

'My apologies.' He touched his hat brim in an attempt to be polite. 'I wanted to catch you all early before you left camp. Guess I didn't bother to think of the consequences of intruding on you so suddenly.'

Jade let out a muffled snort, which Harry ignored as he did her pugilistic stance.

'So will you join me and my crew for dinner?' He sounded hopeful, almost pleading.

Beverly picked up on it immediately. 'Avery just left to hunt for the pot now, but I can answer for him. We'd be delighted to come.'

Jade snatched the negatives from Beverly's hand. 'I won't be able to join you. I have work to do.' She turned her back on Harry and entered the darkroom tent. The last thing she wanted to do was dine with him. Beverly's lilting voice chattered briefly outside, followed by Harry's muffled response. The tent flap moved aside, and Beverly stepped in.

'Why did you refuse Harry's dinner invitation?'

Jade scowled and nodded to the entrance to indicate she had no wish for Harry to overhear her conversation.

Beverly waved her arm in dismissal. 'Oh, Harry has excused himself to visit with Biscuit.' She took a moment to scrutinize Jade's face. 'You look like hell, Jade. Those dark circles under your eyes are as big as saucers. Didn't you sleep?'

Jade shrugged. 'Yes, but fitfully.'

'Bad dreams again? What was it this time, more plane crashes?'

'No. Stampeding elephants and . . . ' She paused as she recollected parts of her dream. 'Colridge was in it and the commissioner, but I'm stumped if I can figure out why.'

Beverly patted her friend's back. 'Who knows? But you still haven't explained why you don't want to dine with Harry.'

'I don't care to break bread, or antelope, or anything else with that man. I don't much like him and I certainly don't trust him, Bev.'

Beverly shook her head, making her curls jiggle. 'Then wouldn't it be a good idea to see what he's up to?'

Jade's head snapped up. 'Keep your friends close and your enemies closer?'

Beverly shrugged. 'Jade, darling, I do not consider Harry an enemy, but if you do, then by all means keep an eye on him.'

Jade pursed her lips as she considered the situation, then nodded. 'All right, but you tell

60

him. Seeing him again will only ruin my appetite for breakfast.' She picked up some cans of developer and rearranged them in a pretense of being busy.

Beverly laughed at her. 'I already told him you'd come. He'll stop by to get us in midafternoon.' She left before Jade could retaliate.

Jade stuck her head out of the tent and shouted after Beverly, 'He'd better not serve any blasted tea!' She went back into the darkroom tent for a while and considered the advantages of inspecting Harry's camp. She had no idea what sort of people he was leading on his safari or how competent they were at shooting game, but hunters liked to brag. She could find out if they'd killed any of her elephants, especially the calf. Jade frowned at the thought of the calf. Few hunters would brag about shooting a baby. She knew Harry wouldn't.

Harry said they were just scouting right now. Was he lying? How hard would it be to hide the ivory? Large tusks would be obvious, but baby ivory would be easy to stow out of sight. For a moment, she considered the chances of slipping through Harry's camp while Beverly and Avery kept the others occupied. Then she quickly discarded that idea. Hascombe was no fool. He'd know what she was up to. After a little more consideration, Jade decided the best way to find out about the baby ivory was to ask the porters and gun bearers. If she couldn't get to them, perhaps Jelani could.

A smirk stole across her lips. Surely Harry

would like to show off Biscuit to his people, and she couldn't take Biscuit without taking Jelani along. No one would pay any attention to an African boy. To many arrogant whites, the Africans were simply scenery or part of their safari equipment. And even if they did notice him, they wouldn't think twice if Jelani sat to talk with their men.

After a breakfast of leftover bustard on flat bread and a mug of fragrant hot coffee, Jade and Chiumbo, who also acted as Jade's personal gun bearer, left camp to check on her cameras. To her delight, both of the two set for day photographs had been tripped. She hoped the pictures had been taken yesterday afternoon or early this morning and not overnight, but if the flashlight picture showed promise, she'd set them all up for night shots in the future. *That old tusker's dust-bathing grounds ought to do well for a shot.*

Jade checked the cameras for condensation and saw that the lenses were dry. She decided to reset them both in hopes of another day shot and bring them back into camp on her return trip to avoid undue exposure of the lenses to the mountain mists until she saw her results. After making the rounds, she and Chiumbo headed up the mountain with her fourth camera in hand in the hopes of photographing the old bull again.

The problem was finding the bull. Jade knew he sometimes trailed the main herd, but it could be anywhere by now. Based on their last route, the cows might be heading up to the big crater lake at the top of the mountain. If that was the case, he'd be in his favorite bath, water lilies clinging to his back.

Jade scanned the trees for telltale signs of recent elephant passage, looking for broken branches, stripped bark, and polished tree trunks where a large body had rubbed against them. She found some of those indications, but none looked fresh. She pointed up a steep incline and suggested to Chiumbo that they try a shortcut in hopes of catching the herd on the other side of the ridge. He shook his head and led her a few yards to the right into the forest. Then he pointed to a dinner-plate-sized, steaming manure pile.

Fresh droppings!

'Good job, Chiumbo. Someone's been through here recently.'

The trail they found followed the contour of the land around the southern side of the crater, with sharp ravines appearing on their right as the mountain sheered off. More scat littered the ground ahead of them, giving testimony to the number of elephants that had followed this path. Chiumbo took the lead, cautioning Jade to proceed slowly. A trail this fresh meant the elephants could be very close, and the last thing they wanted was to stumble into them. A week ago the idea of running smack into a herd of elephants without knowing they were there would have seemed ludicrous to Jade, but not anymore. She'd witnessed firsthand how silent these massive beasts could be.

That day, she'd been waiting in her first blind, built from brush and set on the ground to the side of a dust-bathing area, when several elephants had emerged like ghosts from the forest right in front of her. The old lead cow had stopped short of her blind and waited, swaying gently from side to side, agitated but not dangerously so. The unexpected blind clearly puzzled her, and as much as she wanted to spray her back with the red earth, she had no intention of leading her troop into danger. Caution eventually won out and the entire herd stepped back into the forest's shadows as silently as they'd appeared.

The saplings along this current trail had been stripped of their branches, and several larger trees bore fresh scars where a thick bough had been pulled down and snapped off to give access to the tender shoots at the tip. This must have been where the herd fed last night, Jade mused.

Chiumbo stopped suddenly and pointed ahead. *Elephants! Dozens of them!* Jade froze. At present there was no breeze, so the herd didn't have their scent, but breezes shifted and twisted in the forest. They'd do better to move off the trail and up into a tree, where they could watch in relative safety.

Jade pointed to a heavily buttressed tree and Chiumbo nodded. The elephants couldn't easily knock it down if they were spotted, and they should be able to see the herd from above. Jade uncoiled a span of rope from her pack and made several loops along its length and another at the end. She next tossed the looped end over a stout branch, slipped the entire coil through it, and pulled. With the rope firmly attached to the branch, they could use the other loops as hand — and footholds to climb.

Chiumbo went first. Jade waited until he was in the branch before she tied her day pack to the rope. After Chiumbo hauled up the pack, he lowered the rope again for Jade to climb. Both of them managed to get into the tree without making undue noise, but Jade wasn't sure the elephants would have paid it any mind anyway. The beasts were clearly absorbed in watching their leader.

From her perch, Jade could barely see the old cow for all the Spanish moss hanging in her way, so she climbed up another tier of branches for a better view. The matriarch kept sweeping her trunk across the trail in front of her, each pass removing a layer of leaf-litter. When the leaves had been cleared away, she started dragging away sticks, first small ones, then larger. Jade watched, fascinated, then signaled to Chiumbo to hand up her camera. This was too good to miss. *What is the old girl digging up? An old blind?*

To her amazement, a gaping hole appeared as the cow hauled away a slender branch. Jade focused and took her photograph. The cow had detected a trap dug in the middle of their trail and deftly uncovered it. From her perch, Jade could see several sharpened stakes in the bottom of the pit, intended to impale the victim, and judging from the size of the hole, elephants were the victim of choice. Once the leader exposed the entire dimensions of the trap, she stepped aside while each of the other cows and the younger bulls took turns inspecting it. Then the entire herd simply walked around the pit and continued on its way.

Good heavens, thought Jade. If the elephants hadn't uncovered the trap, she and Chiumbo might have fallen in and been speared. 'Come on,' she said, 'we need to do something about that pit.'

Jade scrambled back to the bottom branch, and after lowering the pack with the rope, she removed the rope and let it drop to the ground. She couldn't afford to leave the rope behind. They'd need it to get in and out of the pit safely. Chiumbo voiced her thoughts before she could.

'We must pull up the stakes, Simba Jike,' he said. 'The elephants will stay away, but other animals might fall in.'

'I wish we could fill it in,' added Jade, 'but the poachers probably spread the dirt around rather than leaving it in a pile for the animals to see. Blaney Percival told me about these pit traps, but I never expected to see one.'

She tied the rope to a nearby tree, letting the loose end dangle into the pit. Then both she and Chiumbo climbed down it. The trap was only four feet deep, but that was more than enough for an elephant to become impaled. They rocked the stakes back and forth to loosen them in their holes, then yanked them up and tossed them out. 'We need to get rid of these where no one will find them easily. I don't want anyone resetting this trap. We can fill in the hole later.'

'I saw a water hole,' said Chiumbo. 'It is not very full now, but we can toss them into the mud. They will soon be covered.'

'Good idea.' Jade hefted one of the six stakes and followed Chiumbo, who carried two. After two trips, they returned to the pit and threw in the smaller twigs and branches until the hole was only three feet deep.

'A leopard can jump out of that,' said Jade, 'although I doubt a rhino or buffalo could.'

Chiumbo pointed at the lengthening shadows. 'Simba Jike,' he said softly. 'The day now shifts into afternoon. We do not have tents or food. We must go.'

Jade nodded. 'You're right, of course.' She took a swig of water from her canteen and handed it over to Chiumbo to drink. 'The others will get worried if we're late. I'm supposed to dine at Hascombe's camp with them this evening anyway.'

They gathered their supplies and were headed back along the trail when the sound of rapidly approaching footsteps came from a ravine on their left. Instantly Jade flattened herself against the rocky ground and motioned for Chiumbo to do the same. They were just in time. Less than a minute later, eight Abyssinian raiders marched into view beneath them.

Sharp volcanic rocks pressed and bit into Jade's and Chiumbo's stomachs, but they endured the discomfort without a sound. Any movement, any noise, meant discovery from the band of raiders passing below. The first man carried no other burden than his elephant gun, and since it lay cradled across his arms, it appeared that he didn't anticipate any serious confrontation on their route. The next six labored under the weight of two creamy white ivory tusks. One of them had a rifle slung over his shoulder, while the others carried bows. An eighth man trailed with a bow in his hands, an arrow nocked and ready.

Jade waited until the rear guard had just passed below her before she dared to raise her camera. The shutter's click sounded as loud as a gunshot to her ears, and she ducked back down immediately. Luckily the men grunting beneath the weight of ivory made more noise than the camera, so none of them noticed the click.

Once the raiders marched out of sight, Jade and Chiumbo retreated down the elephant trail and hastened back to camp. They stopped only long enough to pick up her other cameras, which had been tripped during the day.

The pair arrived in camp by midafternoon, and Biscuit immediately bounded to Jade and butted his head against her thigh. Beverly looked up from the Tarzan book she was sharing with Jelani, smiled, and started to wave. The wave and her smile immediately vanished when she saw Jade's scowl.

'What happened this time?' asked Beverly. 'Did one of your cameras break down?'

Jade shook her head. 'We ran into raiders.' She watched Beverly's jaw drop in shock. 'Close your mouth, Bev. You look like a codfish.'

Beverly jumped up from her chair and followed Jade to the darkroom tent. 'See here, Jade. You can't just waltz into camp with news like that, then wander off. Come back here this instant.'

Jade emerged from the tent empty-handed. 'I have every intention of telling you all about it. Where's Avery?'

Beverly waved her hand in the general direction of the supply tent. 'He's smoking his pipe and cleaning his rifle.'

'Well, go get him. I'm not telling this twice.'

Beverly returned shortly, dragging her husband by the arm, and Jade launched into her narrative. She kept strictly to the facts as she related direction, number, and weapons. 'That may be all of them,' she said in summary, 'but we can't be certain. No one should take any chances.'

Beverly rolled her eyes. 'By 'no one' I presume you mean everyone except yourself.'

Jade didn't reply, and Beverly let out an exasperated string of mildly vulgar words. Jade arched her brows in surprise. 'There is an impressionable child present in the camp, Beverly, or have you forgotten about Jelani?' She pointed a finger at the boy, who sat on his own, engrossed in the Tarzan book.

'If I may be so bold as to intrude *my* opinion,' Avery began. He held his pipe in one hand and used it like a lecturer might use a pointer. 'I suggest we talk about this with Mr Hascombe's people at dinner this evening. Once we have more information, we can better examine all our options.'

'To hell with Hascombe's opinion,' groused Jade. 'I don't trust him.'

'As we are all only too aware,' added Avery. 'But it doesn't lessen the need for his experience.

He's lived in the Protectorate all his life. We are relative newcomers. And,' he added quickly before Jade could jump in with another rebuttal, 'trust him or not, he deserves to know what's going on.'

Jade conceded his final point with a soft grunt.

'If we knew where Captain Smythe's patrol was, we could alert him,' suggested Beverly.

'Probably gone back to Isiolo to gather up the rest of his men,' said Avery. 'He can't very well arrest a gang of poachers with his one man.'

Jade took a deep preparatory breath. 'Maybe that bloody Hascombe knows where he is. Whether he does or not, we should send a runner with a message to either Marsabit Post or Kampia Tembo to alert whoever is on duty there.'

Beverly grinned. 'That's the spirit, Jade. And I'm sure Harry isn't as bad as all that. You simply — ' She stopped abruptly when she saw the scowl on Jade's face. 'Yes, well. You had better get cleaned up. We'll be leaving shortly, I'm sure.'

Jade passed a hand through her bobbed black hair. 'I have no intention of cleaning up for Hascombe. I'm going to catch a nap while I can, since once we get back tonight I plan on developing my film.'

'Jade!' scolded Beverly.

Jade ignored her friend's tone and slipped into her tent. 'Wake me when that horse's backside gets here.'

The 'horse's backside,' as Jade termed Harry, showed up an hour later and led them to his camp. Jelani walked alongside Jade while Biscuit alternated between tugging at his lead and butting the pair from behind. Avery and Beverly followed Harry, who managed to sidestep every one of their questions about his safari members' identities.

'I would rather wait for formal introductions,' he explained. 'However, I can tell you that they are not professional hunters.' He directed that comment at Jade. 'One man is a banker and another is in manufacturing. Motors, I believe. I'm not sure about the third man. Part of the idle rich, I suppose.'

Beverly expressed her astonishment that he would know so little about the people who'd hired him, but Harry declared that as long as their checks cleared the bank, he was satisfied. Harry's 'three miles' turned out to be as the crow flew. The path itself took a few more tortuous turns before they entered his camp.

Three men and three women lounged in canvas folding chairs set around wooden camp tables, and Jade took them in instantly. Two of the women were Jade's age or younger. One had chin-length, sandy blond hair carefully coiffed in marcelled waves. The other young woman was a peroxide blonde who looked as if she was trying to imitate the more modern screen actresses. Her bobbed hair lay straight except for two tight curls on her forehead, one over each eye. If the effect was intended to be 'vampish,' it looked more ludicrous to Jade. She dismissed both of them as silly.

The third woman appeared to be in her

forties, with a slightly thickened albeit athletic carriage. Her hair, also blonde, was swept back in a less modern but very practical roll from her round face. Jade saw her stare inquisitively at Biscuit, her head tilted as though a new angle would make seeing a sleek African cat on a leash more comprehensible.

Jade had less opportunity to study the men before they acknowledged the newcomers. They all wore khaki-colored bush jackets and heavy trousers tucked into their boots. Two of the three men stood immediately on the guests' entrance and made sharp bows. One of them also clicked his heels together in a military salute.

'Sweet Millard Fillmore on a bicycle,' muttered Jade. 'They're Germans.'

6

Food, danger, maternal love, passion, and security as well as the accumulated wisdom of countless years along ancient trails: these are the topics that make up the elephants' conversations. These subjects are the very essence of life.
— The Traveler

Harry stepped into the center of the group and began the introductions as though the Great War hadn't recently occurred and the English and Americans had never been bitter enemies with the kaiser's empire or felt the brunt of its Big Berthas. Harry first directed his open hand towards a portly, older man with receding brown hair heavily flecked with gray. 'Herr Otto von Gretchmar,' he said. The man inclined his head in a deep bow, exposing a bald spot at the back. 'And this,' said Harry as he indicated the older woman of the set with a polite bow, 'is Frau von Gretchmar.'

The woman smiled. 'Please, you will call me Claudia,' she said in heavily accented English. 'And allow me our daughter, Mercedes, to introduce.' The woman nodded to the girl with the marcel-waved hair, who barely looked up from her immaculately manicured nails. Jade

73

wasn't certain if she was shy, browbeaten, or just incredibly self-centered.

'Pleased to meet you,' said Beverly with a show of impeccable breeding.

The second man jumped into the breach and introduced himself. He looked to be in his midforties with the muscular build of an athlete. He wore his dark brown hair clipped short in what Jade supposed was a military cut, and the traditional saber scar ran across his right cheek. Her suspicions were heightened when he clicked his heels together and bowed. 'I am Herr Eric Vogelsanger from Prussia.'

Since the last two individuals showed no such inclination to introduce themselves, Harry did it for them. 'Herr Heinrich Mueller,' he said as he extended his hand to point out a slender young man still sprawled lazily in his chair. The man peered at them through foppishly long brown hair and smiled. 'And,' finished Harry, 'this is his charming wife, Liesel Mueller.'

Jade noticed that Harry didn't introduce the peroxide blonde as 'Frau' Liesel and wondered just how 'charming' the woman was. She decided she didn't care. Liesel had a petite and well-formed frame but didn't appear any more energetic than her husband until she set her hazel eyes on Avery. She immediately sat up straighter and preened, running a finger through each forehead curl like the proverbial villain curling his mustache.

Jade sidled next to Beverly and whispered, 'Watch out for that one.' She thought she heard Bev snarl in reply. As an afterthought, Jade

74

whispered, 'By the way, I don't speak any German.'

Beverly turned her head and arched her delicate brows at Jade. 'But you studied . . . ' Then her eyes opened wide as she comprehended Jade's plan to eavesdrop. She smiled and whispered back, 'Of course not. None of us do.'

Harry shifted his introductions to Jade's group and identified everyone except Jelani and Biscuit. Jade waited with the instinct of someone well versed in human behavior. Sure enough, one of the women, Liesel, inquired about the cat. Jelani might as well not exist. Yes, Jade thought, her plan to have the boy infiltrate the ranks of gun bearers would work. No one would think anything of it because they didn't even bother to notice him.

'This is Biscuit,' said Jade. She took the lead from Jelani and quietly motioned for him to slip away. The boy grinned at her, enjoying their secret game, and obliged. Jade took a deep breath and resigned herself to enduring dinner.

'Please sit down,' said Harry. He stepped behind a seventh and vacant camp chair and held it. 'Lady Dunbury, won't you have my seat? I'm afraid I didn't think about a shortage of chairs when I invited you. As you can see, I set out three, um, of the best chop boxes for the rest of us.'

Jade maintained her poker face while she watched Harry display his very best company manners. If the act was meant to impress her, at least it succeeded in providing amusement.

'Thank you, Harry,' said Bev as she sat, 'and please just call me Beverly. We've been beyond formality for quite some time.'

Vogelsanger made a sharp bow in Jade's direction and extended a hand towards his seat. 'Fräulein, you will please sit here.' The offer sounded more like a military order than an invitation.

Jade flashed a dazzling smile and shook her head no. 'Thank you, but I would not dream of taking your chair. You looked so comfortable when we arrived.'

Harry still stood beside Beverly, and Jade thought she detected the red flush of momentary embarrassment on his tanned face. She decided to toy with him. 'Why, Harry, aren't you going to hold my chop box for me while I sit down?' Before he could decide what to do, she slid gracefully onto the wooden box. Avery took a spot next to his wife, leaving Harry to sit between Avery and Jade.

Immediately, the camp cook directed two native Africans to serve a savory lentil soup as a first course. Jade noticed that Harry still kept to using practical tin dinnerware rather than the more impressive and fragile china and crystal that other safari companies preferred. She nodded her approval, especially when Liesel Mueller scowled as red wine was poured into her tin mug. Jade turned down the wine and asked for a mug of coffee instead. After that, a palpable silence punctuated only by the occasional slurp from Otto von Gretchmar hung over the group.

Beverly did her best to fill the breach. 'How are you enjoying Africa?' she asked of no one in particular.

76

Claudia von Gretchmar rolled her eyes and placed a hand at her bosom for dramatic emphasis. '*Mein Gott*, but it is horrid this mountain! It is damp and so much noise. I cannot at night sleep.'

'I think it is *wunderbar*,' proclaimed Vogelsanger as the servants replaced the soup with a fragrant stew of game birds and vegetables over a bed of saffron rice, 'but perhaps not so much for the ladies?' He glanced meaningfully at first Claudia, then Mercedes.

'Shooting many animals?' asked Jade with another beaming smile. She thought she heard Mueller whisper, '*Sagen Sie nichts*' (Say nothing) to his companions.

'Herr Hascombe has done the hunting or we would not these fine birds be eating,' said Mueller. 'Do you hunt, Fräulein?'

'Oh yes,' said Jade. 'Generally in self-defense, of course, quite necessary in the Western states, you know. Never know when you need to kill a rattlesnake. But I must admit that I've always enjoyed bringing down the bloviated buffoon. Very dangerous animal, but excellent sport.'

Vogelsanger leaned forward, his interest showing. 'I am not familiar with that animal,' he said. 'Is it a good trophy?'

'Magnificent,' Jade began while Harry squirmed next to her and nudged her right foot with his left.

'Er, I'm sure that Jade is referring to the American *buffalo*,' said Harry. He kicked her foot again.

'I'm sorry you have to rely on Harry in order

77

to eat,' Jade continued. 'I just assumed that you came here to hunt. Perhaps it's all on your game permits. I could read them for you if you're not sure.'

'All this talk of hunting,' exclaimed Liesel Mueller, 'I find it boring.' She leaned across the table towards Avery and batted her eyelashes, heavy with mascara, at him. 'So you are a British lord? You must be very rich. Do you own an automobile?'

'Oh, so you're interested in automobiles?' said Beverly as she edged closer to her husband. 'Jade and I both adore working on them. Tell me, Liesel, what do you find more enjoyable, cleaning a carburetor or the spark plugs?'

Liesel made a face as though she'd eaten a bug. 'I do not know about such things. Automobiles are pretty toys to ride in. I am more interested in *das Kino*.'

'Is that a game or a wine?' asked Beverly.

'I think she means fashions,' suggested Jade.

Liesel let loose an exasperated sigh. 'The moving pictures.'

'Oh!' said Jade. 'You'll have to excuse us. We don't speak German. So you like the cinema?'

'I adore it,' said Liesel. She closed her eyes and crossed both hands over her chest for dramatic emphasis. 'Have you seen Pola Negri in' — she paused to consider the correct translation — '*The Eyes of the Mummy Ma*?'

At the mention of the German actress, Mercedes immediately perked up. 'I would like to be an actress in the movies.'

'Nonsense!' bellowed her father. 'That is not a

proper future for my Mercedes. Your success is with how you marry.'

Jade studied the group's reaction. Mercedes sank into her chair, head bowed. Harry scowled, Liesel Mueller rolled her eyes, and her husband yawned, but Claudia's face remained a complete blank. That is, until Mercedes began to sob. Then Claudia stiffened.

'Mercedes!' she snapped. 'Go to your tent at once.'

Only Vogelsanger looked remotely sympathetic as his gaze followed the girl's retreating figure, but when he turned the conversation away from movies, Jade wasn't certain if he did it to spare Claudia any more distress or for more selfish motives. 'Do you also enjoy motors, Lord Dunbury?' he asked. 'I was telling Herr Hascombe about our newest models.' Liesel immediately groaned aloud as the two men embarked on a discussion of pistons.

'Is this your first trip to Africa?' Jade asked. Vogelsanger, busily lecturing Avery and Harry, did not hear her. Claudia sat quietly, looking at von Gretchmar, waiting for him to speak for her.

'Yes,' he replied.

'I have been to Egypt,' said Mueller. 'It is most interesting if it is sand you like.'

More silence reigned, and Jade contemplated asking one of the other men if she could admire his firearms. If nothing else, the model would give her an idea of what type of game they were after. Before she could voice her question, she heard a sharp whistle. Immediately Biscuit jumped up and ran to the other end of the camp.

79

'What was that?' asked Otto von Gretchmar, his eyes wide in alarm.

'That would be Jelani calling for Biscuit,' said Jade. 'By the way, did I mention that we found someone murdered yesterday?'

★ ★ ★

As soon as Jade had sent him off, Jelani had trotted around to the rear of the tents, back to where the porters, cook, and gun bearers sat around their own fire. The boy heard male laughter and conversation mingled with the assorted sounds that indicated food consumption. His mouth watered as he smelled the aromas of meat and *posho* wafting from the cook pots. Having previously known only other Kikuyu and the few Wakamba men in his own safari, he had never experienced rejection from fellow Africans before and didn't expect any here. It surprised him when it came.

He plopped himself on the ground near a pot of *posho* and started helping himself to the cooked cornmeal when a man sitting opposite scowled at him. The man spoke in a language Jelani did not fully understand but assumed to be Wakamba based on the man's pointed teeth. Whatever his words, Jelani recognized the anger behind them. He clearly wasn't welcome around this fire.

Just when Jelani thought perhaps he should leave, a big man sitting closer to him started arguing with the antagonist. The two traded heated words and angry gestures until the camp's cook came to see what the noise was all about. He listened for a moment to each of the two men.

'*Makelele!*' he shouted. The command that could mean either 'start' or 'stop the ruckus' caused the argument to cease immediately, and the cook turned to Jelani and addressed him in broken English.

'Hey, you, boy. How come you sitting there? You not with Big Bwana,' he said, referring to Harry Hascombe.

'I came with Memsabu Simba Jike and her two English friends to visit.'

'Ayah, they are welcome, but I do not think that Big Bwana invite you.' He jabbed a finger at Jelani.

Jelani stood as tall as his dozen years allowed and folded his arms across his chest. 'I have come with Simba Jike. It is my job to watch her *duma*,' he said, using the Swahili word for cheetah.

The cook translated this for some of the other men and they laughed at his story. 'Then where,' asked the cook, 'is this cheetah and why aren't you with it? Is this a magical animal that disappears?' Again the other men laughed.

Jelani didn't care for this sort of treatment. No one had ever questioned his honor before. After all, hadn't he already proved himself when he helped kill the witch's hyena last year? Wasn't he almost a warrior now?

He put his two middle fingers in his mouth and whistled once, a short, sharp blast. A moment later, Biscuit raced past the other men

81

and butted his head against Jelani's chest. He wrapped his arms around the big cat's neck and hugged him. Several of the men, including the one who had first yelled at Jelani, broke into broad grins and laughed. One of the men scooped a large helping of *posho* and stewed meat onto a slab of flat bread and handed it to him while the cook placed some on a leaf for the cheetah.

Jelani's mouth did double duty as he tried to answer the men's questions and do just service to the food. While he took pride in sharing meals with Simba Jike and her friends, he sometimes thought their food was too spicy and the meals too complicated. He missed the simple taste of *posho*, which reminded him of his mother's hut.

Only the cook and the headman spoke English, and only two others spoke any Swahili. With those men acting as interpreters, the conversation resumed. Jelani explained his job taking care of Biscuit and proudly related his adventure last year with the man-eating hyena that had plagued his village. By the time he got to the part about plunging his knife into the beast's heart, he was on his feet acting out the role, driving an invisible knife into an equally invisible hyena. If he neglected to mention that the animal was already dead when he stabbed it, no one noticed.

Finally, Jelani managed to interject questions of his own. 'Who are these people traveling with your Big Bwana? Are they good hunters?'

The cook, knowing that the reputation and social standing of the entire camp rested on the capabilities of the hunters, puffed out his chest. 'Ayah, they are elephant hunters. Only a brave man would face an angry elephant.'

'I know of Big Bwana,' said Jelani. 'He is a brave man, but I do not know these others. They do not look like hunters.' He shoved more *posho* into his mouth.

The cook stood and motioned for Jelani to come with him. 'I will show you.'

Jelani stood and barked an order to the cat. Biscuit didn't need any order to follow him, but the action impressed the men even more. Jelani followed the cook, and by the time Memsabu Jade called for him, he had discovered the answers to most of her questions. He returned to her with great dignity, head high and back straight, Biscuit's leash firmly in hand.

'Did you have a nice visit with the men, Jelani?' asked Jade when he rejoined her.

'Yes, Simba Jike. *Tarmangani bundolo Tantor.*'

'*Balu Tantor?*' asked Jade. Jelani shook his head no.

★   ★   ★

'I can't recall a more boring evening,' said Beverly once they were settled around the fire back in their own camp. She stretched and grimaced as she worked out a kink in her lower back. 'I suppose I could, but I don't want to.'

'It wasn't *that* bad,' Avery said. He glanced at his wife, who stared back at him and rolled her eyes. 'Well, perhaps it was,' he amended. 'But I'm not sure 'boring' is the right word for his

83

crew. 'Smoldering' is more like it.'

Beverly nodded. 'I know what you mean, my love. One would never suppose from listening to those arrogant, egotistical people that they had just lost the war and, with it, part of the Congo and German East Africa. And then there's Frau Peroxide hoping to make my Avery her next conquest.' She raised her chin and sniffed in disgust.

Avery shifted closer to his wife and put an arm around her in a rare public display of affection. 'Not to fear, my darling. She's as bloody likely to take me from you as they are to regain their territories.'

Jade drained her coffee mug, looked at the empty cup longingly, and rose to refill it. Biscuit lolled at her feet and watched her movements. 'I learned quite a bit.' She finished filling her mug and held out the pot to the others in an unspoken offer. Beverly declined, but her husband extended his half-empty cup. Jade topped it off and replaced the pot.

'Are you going to tell us or leave us in suspense all evening?' Beverly asked. 'And by the way, you still haven't finished your story about that elk and the horse.'

'That can wait,' said Jade. 'I want to tally what we know about Harry's crew. First, tell me what specifics *you* learned about Harry's party, and I'm not talking about their past political history.'

Beverly began ticking off points on her fingers. 'Von Gretchmar is a banker and his wife, Claudia, is a classic wealthy hausfrau who goes to a spa every year in Bad Harzburg to take the

84

cure. Absolutely doting on her *Mann* and terribly short with poor little Mercedes. Not sure she knows one end of a rifle from another.'

'That's a supposition, not a fact,' argued Jade.

Beverly nodded and stuck out a second finger. 'Two, Mercedes does not belong in Africa. And her father has antiquated notions about her proper place. Three, the Prussian, Vogelsanger, loves to talk motors. Whatever business Mueller is in, if any, must not require much supervision from him. He doesn't seem to have a brain in his head, and his wife — ' She raised her hand to arrest Jade's comment on making suppositions. 'I know. Stick to the facts. Just don't get me started on that hussy.'

Jade peered over her mug at Avery. 'And you, Avery?'

He patted his wife's hand in an attempt to calm her. 'Vogelsanger was an officer of some rank. That much seems obvious by his bearing and the crispness of his bush clothes. They also don't seem to be having much luck finding game, especially elephants.' He paused to think as his fingers traced patterns on the back of Beverly's hand. 'They certainly came equipped to hunt big game. Von Gretchmar has a decent enough arsenal with him. He was quite proud of his rifles, some of them of British manufacture but nothing very new.'

'Anything else?' asked Jade.

The Dunburys shook their heads in unison. 'Now, are you going to grace us with your observations?' asked Beverly in mock deference.

Jade bestowed her wry Mona Lisa smile and

85

set down her empty coffee mug. 'That's about it.' She watched and waited until Beverly had just taken a final gulp of coffee before she added, 'And the fact that they're lying about the elephants.'

Beverly sprayed out the mouthful of coffee. 'I'm going to get you for that one, lovey,' she said as she wiped her mouth on her sleeve. 'You did that on purpose.'

Jade chuckled. 'You always were easy to get. Remember that time near Verdun?'

'*Don't* bring that embarrassing incident up ever again, if you please, Jade.'

Jade laughed and clapped her hands together. 'Em-*bare*-assing is right, Bev. Your face wasn't the only thing that turned red.'

Beverly threw her coffee mug at Jade's head. Jade ducked and the mug clattered into the surrounding darkness. A brief rustle followed as some night creature, startled by the missile, ran off deeper into the brush. A leopard coughed its dry, asthmatic chuff from the other side of a nearby *donga*. Jade took comfort in the natural wildness of the sounds, sounds of animals without agendas other than survival.

'I'm sorry, Bev. Really I am.' The barely suppressed grin on Jade's face nearly made a lie of that statement.

'Ahem.' Avery cleared his throat for attention and put his arms around his wife's waist before she could get up and pummel Jade. 'As much as I'm dying to know about my wife's, er, incident, you were about to tell us something about lying. What are they lying about and how do you know?'

'They're lying about the elephants, and I know because Jelani told me just before we left Harry's camp. We used the language of the 'Great Apes' as a code. That was your idea, Bev, remember?'

'What did he say?' asked Avery.

'He said '*Tarmangani bundolo Tantor*,' or 'White man kill elephants.' But when I asked him about *balu Tantor*, or 'baby elephants,' he said no.'

'Jelani?' echoed Bev. 'How does he know? He's just a young boy and he wasn't even around the Germans.'

'Their porters told him. Seems he had a very pleasant chat with the men and boasted about all the wonderful animals we've bagged so far. Of course, they couldn't be outdone.'

'What wonderful animals have we bagged? Outside of some bustards and antelope for food, we haven't attempted to hunt a blooming thing. Did you tell that lad to lie?' asked Avery.

'Of course not. He just included your rhino and our lions and hyena from the last safari. Not his fault they didn't question his time frame.' She poked the fire with a long stick, then tossed the stick atop the flames and watched the fire flare momentarily. In the distance she heard the low trumpeting of an elephant, followed by the explosive crack of snapping tree limbs. *Probably not close*, she thought. Those sounds carried a long distance in the cool night air. For some reason she thought of them as *her* elephants and wondered if she had any business taking that view.

'How many have they killed?' asked Beverly.

'They've taken one of the younger bulls already,' said Jade. 'Jelani saw the ivory.'

'But Harry said — ' began Avery.

'Harry stayed away from the topic of hunting this evening,' interjected Jade. 'And since Mueller muttered to the others in German not to say anything, I suspect Harry told them not to admit to any bagged elephants. He probably knew it would rile me again.'

'So did they kill that cow and her calf?' asked Beverly.

Jade shook her head. 'No, they didn't, which means they probably didn't kill the askari from the King's African Rifles, either. So I guess that means Harry isn't a *complete* scoundrel.'

Beverly stood and stretched. 'I'm relieved to hear it. But I don't understand their reluctance to boast of their trophy. After all,' she reasoned, 'they have a perfect right to hunt elephant. They have licenses.'

Jade arched her black brows. 'Do they?' she asked. 'We're *assuming* that they each have a permit for elephants. Maybe they don't. I wouldn't be surprised if that weasel Hascombe bypassed the game warden. I can't imagine that Blaney Percival issued any permits for elephant hunting up here.'

Avery stood next to his wife. 'I suppose that may be true. Or Mr Percival might have given them permits, but restricted their elephant hunting to the Chobe hills. I *was* rather under the impression that he didn't want the elephants in *this* area hunted. Still, that will be easy enough to check on when we return.'

'I must admit I was taken aback by their attitude when you told them about the dead askari and the poachers,' said Beverly. 'I expected that at least Claudia would appeal to her husband or Harry for protection. She just sat there like a mouse all evening after Mercedes went into her tent.'

'Yes, and Liesel wanted to go out and find them,' added Avery. 'What did she say? Something about wild shifters?'

'*Shiftas*,' corrected Beverly. 'It means raiders.'

'Ack, how romantic,' said Jade, aping Liesel Mueller's voice and accent. 'Imagine to meet a wild *shifta* from Abyssinia.' She rolled her eyes and pretended to gag. 'Tomorrow at first light Chiumbo will send a man off to Marsabit Post to alert the authorities. If no one is there, he's to go to Kampia Tembo.'

Beverly's mouth gaped wide open as she yawned.

'Fair imitation of a hippo, Bev,' joked Jade.

'I've heard all I care to concerning your ill opinion of poor Harry and his boring safari. I'm tired. I'm going to bed.' She turned to her husband and laid a slender hand on his arm. 'Are you coming, darling?' Avery nodded and took his wife's arm. Beverly paused in midstep and looked at Jade. 'What about you, Jade?'

She tried to stifle a smile, but her twitching lips betrayed her. 'I'm not sure Avery's ready for a ménage à trois. I know I'm not.'

Beverly looked in vain for something else to throw at Jade and settled for scowling at her. 'Don't make me slap you, missy,' she said.

Jade hugged herself and rocked with silent laughter. 'Poor Avery,' she said as she pointed to him. 'He's positively beet red with embarrassment.' She wiped a tear from an eye. 'Couldn't resist. But seriously, I want to develop those pictures I gathered up today. I really need to see if this trip wire process is worth the time and film, especially for the night shots. And I want to jot down some thoughts on the night sounds in my notebook. They're almost worth an entire article by themselves, don't you think?'

The Dunburys retired to their tent, and Jade sent Biscuit off to watch over Jelani. Then she began the careful process of developing her negatives. She planned to develop most of the film back in Nairobi. Consequently, she had brought only a small amount of chemicals with her, enough to develop some test pictures and hone her technique.

The nocturnal shot revealed a leopard rather than the hoped-for elephant, but Jade still smiled at the glimpse of hidden life at night in the forest. Leopards were shy animals, and even a profile of one amounted to a good catch. The first day shot showed the rump of an elephant, enough for her to know that the system worked only if the animal would step on the wire with a front foot rather than a hind one. Jade made a mental note to raise the wire height another inch or two.

The last daytime film sheet went into the developer. Jade took it through the series of baths needed to fix the image and held it up to her red-tinted lantern for a better view. At first she couldn't make out what sort of animal had gained immortality in her lens. Then a slow smile spread across her face.

'Well, well. What have we here? Looks like some of our German friends were having their own wilderness experience today. Gracious me.'

Jade clipped the negative to the drying line at eye level. One face, at least, was identifiable amid the tangle of intertwined, half-clothed bodies and disheveled bush gear.

Jade wondered first if Herr von Gretchmar knew that his doting Frau was cheating on him. But who was her lover? The pair stood clenched in a tight embrace, the man's back to the camera. All Jade had in her negative was the back of his head as it nuzzled deep in Claudia's bosom. No discernible bald spot gleamed from this man's thick head of hair, but his one visible ear certainly stuck out far enough. Did Harry's ears protrude like that? *These are big enough to belong to an elephant.* She couldn't recall and wondered if it might have been the younger German of the party, Mueller. She'd have to pay more attention to his and Harry's ears when they next met. Not that it was any of her business. Harry was a grown man; he could do as he pleased.

7

During the day, the forest gives the impression of being entirely devoid of mammalian life. The rhino and buffalo hide in some donga, grazing; the leopard naps unseen in a tree; and the elephants, well, the elephants drift silently like slippered wraiths. Night, on the other hand, introduces a cacophony of coughs, grunts, growls, rumblings, snorts, and screams, all overlain with the reverberating crack of snapping limbs. Sleep is difficult at night.

— The Traveler

Chiumbo pointed to three piles of elephant droppings and held up two fingers, which meant the spoor was two days old. *Blast*, thought Jade. The elephants could be anywhere by now.

'Time for a rest.' She shrugged off her pack and leaned it against a tree. If she'd had her way, they would all have been bivouacking farther into the forest, around the crater lake itself rather than a mile below it. Unfortunately, she hadn't gotten her way. Beverly had felt ill again, and Avery had insisted on staying behind at the base camp with her. Under no circumstances would he let his wife traipse off into the forest with Jade for a few days, and when Jade had suggested that she set up a secondary camp on her own, Beverly grew so distressed and agitated that Jade relented. She had her own theory about Beverly's situation, but decided to keep it to herself until they were ready to talk about it. She wondered if she'd be named a godparent.

Jade ripped off a generous piece of jerked meat, handed it to Chiumbo, and pulled off another chunk for herself. As she chewed, she studied the upper branches of what looked like a mahogany tree for signs of recent feeding. Several other trees bore fresh breaks, some nearly ten feet aboveground. Part of the underlying litter had been crushed deeper into the soil where one of the pachyderms had reared up onto its hind legs for an extended reach.

Jade hadn't believed such behavior possible when Blaney Percival had first described it to her in Nairobi. Then she'd witnessed it for herself from a distance. Better than a circus. Now, *that* would be something to photograph. A shudder of urgency ran through her as though she needed to document everything about these magnificent animals. Suddenly, even tomorrow felt too late. At least all her cameras were set up for night flashes now, one on the way to the old bull's favorite dust-bathing site. She had a good chance of getting another shot of him there.

'Let's head on towards the big lake, shall we, Chiumbo?' Jade suggested. 'Maybe our big gray friends are back from wherever they wandered and stayed put for us.' She pointed to a different trail from the one they'd taken previously. 'We can go that way.'

The two hiked along the wide trail for another hour, following the crater's northern base. Jade assumed it would eventually climb up towards the crater's ridge, perhaps switching back and forth. So far, the slight breeze had stayed in their favor, but as they rounded a bend, the air turned and brought with it a gut-wrenching aroma of rotting flesh. Jade held the back of her hand to her nose and winced.

'Very bad smell, Simba Jike,' Chiumbo said. 'I think maybe we not go on. Not good for a lady to see.'

'We left the 'lady' back at camp with indigestion, Chiumbo. *I* intend to investigate.'

Chiumbo shrugged. 'Lady lions are very bold,' he muttered to himself. 'It is not safe to stand in their way.'

The source of the stench lay another three hundred yards away, hidden under a blanket of scavenging vultures. Jade took her Winchester from Chiumbo and fired one shot in the air. When the birds showed no intention of giving up their meal that easily, she fired another into the thick of them. Most of them half flapped, half ran a short distance away. Jade kicked the rest aside. Five tuskless carcasses lay sprawled before her, all males, a small bachelor herd.

'This is very bad, Simba Jike. It is not safe here.' Chiumbo scanned the forest for signs of movement.

'Whoever did this is long gone. These bodies have been here at least a full day.' She worked her way amid the carnage, looking for clues to the hunters' identity. She found one in the arrows sticking out of legs and guts. She pulled out one and examined the tip. 'What's on the arrows? Does it kill the elephant?'

Chiumbo shook his head. 'Not enough poison to kill an elephant but enough so it is still dangerous. Then men come in close and shoot it with a rifle.'

Jade began yanking arrows out of the elephants. Two broke off near their tips, but a half dozen slid out of the decomposing flesh. She slipped them into her day pack. As an afterthought, she stuck three back in an elephant, pulled out her camera, and took a photograph. Blaney Percival might want a picture as evidence if they ever caught the poachers.

'We might as well go back and leave the scavengers to their dinner. We're not going to find any living elephants walking this trail.'

Chiumbo nodded slowly. 'The elephants will shun this path for a long time.'

A mile and a half from camp, Jade halted abruptly and listened. She placed her hand to her ear and then pointed to the forest. Chiumbo replied to the unspoken question by holding up one hand, fingers spread. Jade nodded. At least five people, maybe more, approached from the south. If the poachers still stalked about in the woods, she and Chiumbo could be in danger. Jade slipped behind a stout tree and waited. Her headman did the same.

The noisy footfalls came closer. Whoever it was needed a lesson in woodcraft, Jade decided. They made entirely too much noise for anyone on the hunt.

'*Verdammt!*'

A stern shush followed this exclamation and exacted some silence, but the spell was broken. Jade had already identified the new arrivals. *Blast! Hascombe's crew.* She waited until they were within twenty yards before she stepped out in front of them.

'Your people must not be very interested in spotting game,' she said. 'You make enough noise to scare everything away.'

Harry Hascombe touched the brim of his hat in a salute. 'Why, Jade. What a pleasant surprise. Nice to see you, too.' He pointed to the rear of the group. 'But we've already been successful. Herr Vogelsanger bagged a nice young bull earlier this afternoon. The boys are bringing up the ivory.'

The Prussian stood at attention, eyes focused above Jade's head, a sneer across his face that the white scar only emphasized. Mueller stood behind him with an annoyed pouting expression, eyes rolling, mouth turned down. Dung coated the sole of his left boot, and he scraped it off on a bunch of nearby greenery. Von Gretchmar merely patted his damp forehead with a pocket kerchief. All the men wore broadbrimmed hats snugly clamped on their heads, hiding their ears from Jade's attempted inspection.

'Indeed,' she replied in as noncommittal a voice as she could muster. She wondered how von Gretchmar had fared. He certainly looked done in by the exercise. Apparently having such wonderful rifles didn't guarantee success. None of the women had come along, but their absence didn't strike Jade as odd.

'*Ja*, but I am surprised in the jungle alone to see you, Fräulein,' said Vogelsanger.

Jade nodded to her headman. 'I'm not alone. Chiumbo is with me, and I'm quite capable of taking care of myself, thank you.' When she saw Chiumbo's face, her eyes opened wider. The tense lines of his mouth, the furrowed brow, the crossed arms: all spoke volumes about his anger and loathing. Well, she thought, he had reason enough to hate Germans, and she decided it would be best if the two of them left now. She turned to go when Harry put out an arm to stop her.

'An askari runner brought a message from Captain Smythe earlier today,' he said. 'Seems there's been trouble in this region.' He searched her face for signs that this was news and found none. 'But then, you already knew that.'

Jade's lips opened a fraction, and her green eyes stared straight at Harry as if to indicate that he was trouble enough. 'We told you we saw Smythe the other day, not to mention the murdered askari and the Abyssinians that Chiumbo and I spotted.' She pointed back down her trail. 'Besides that, there are several carcasses a few miles down there, where someone's been very busy.' She paused and studied Harry's face for an admission of guilt.

He frowned. 'It wasn't us,' he said.

'Didn't say it was. Guilty conscience? What did this runner say, specifically?'

'I got the message secondhand myself,' Harry admitted. 'I was bagging a bird or two for dinner, so von Gretchmar told me about it.'

97

'Oh. Well, thank you for the information.' She smiled at the three men, flashed a bigger smile at their gun bearers, and once again turned to go. Harry stopped her with his next words.

'Just a minute, Jade. I didn't tell you the message yet. This was *fresh* trouble. There was a raid while some Boran women drew water at the singing wells near the mountain base. Several women and children were taken for slaves.'

Jade scowled, and her right hand clenched into a fist. 'One of Smythe's men told you this today?' She paused and thought out the geography. There was a group of wells at the southern end of the volcanic chain, and another to the east. Which was it? Had Smythe sent the runner on to her camp as well, or had he assumed her group had gone, as he'd ordered? She hoped Smythe was hot on the slavers' trail right now, but that also meant the poachers here were not being attended to. 'Do you think it's the same people, Harry? I mean, these slavers and the poachers?'

Harry shrugged. 'Possibly. Possibly not. For years, this entire frontier's been a hotbed for tribal raids by either the Somali or the Abyssinians or some other northern group. Smythe certainly has his hands full — that's for certain. The last man, Captain Ross, was killed in one of those raids.'

'I'll tell Avery and Beverly when I get back to camp, assuming the askari hasn't told them already.' She took one step when she heard the sound of snapping twigs and padding feet. A large quadruped trotted towards her, golden eyes flashing.

The Prussian shouldered his rifle and Mueller slipped behind him, eyes bulging in terror. Jade, hearing the clack of a rifle bolt, spun around, leaped to Vogelsanger's side, and shoved his weapon up just as he fired.

'*Verdammt!* What are you doing?' he demanded. He pulled back the bolt in his Mannlicher to put another round in the chamber. 'It will kill us!' he exclaimed.

Chiumbo stepped forward, hand raised to grab either the weapon or the man; Jade didn't know which.

'Stop!' she commanded, and moved between them. 'It's only Biscuit, my pet cheetah, you idiot. Besides, you could have shot Chiumbo or me.'

The other hunters stared, mouths agape, as the cat loped into view and bounded up onto Jade's chest. She stroked his head and grabbed for his loose lead to hold him. 'Naughty boy,' she scolded. 'You've broken loose again.' Biscuit dropped down and wound around her legs, chirping his greeting. Jade chirped back in reply and scratched the cat's large head just behind the ears while the cheetah purred in pleasure. Jade untangled herself from the lead and glared at Harry.

'Hascombe, you need to teach your crew not to be so hasty. But at least,' she added in a softer tone, 'I didn't see you take aim.' Jade wound the lead twice around her hand to shorten Biscuit's line. 'Now if you, um, *gentlemen* will excuse me, I need to hurry back.' She saw the question form on Hascombe's face and answered first. 'Jelani is probably on his way now to retrieve Biscuit. *He shouldn't be out here alone.*'

'He's not.'

Jade turned suddenly at the sound of an unfamiliar voice. A tall, rangy-looking young man approached them, one arm around Jelani's shoulder, the other gripping a Remington rifle. He had a slightly elongated, narrow face distinguished by a very masculine nose that seemed to emerge directly from the high brow line, and piercing dark brown eyes like doorways into an African night. A thin mustache underlined the distinctive nose, making it look like it was chiseled out of granite.

Jade calculated him to be nearly six feet tall and maybe 160 pounds. He wore the standard multipocketed dun-colored jacket preferred by many people on safari, but there was no mistaking the oil-stained leather boots and the well-worn jodhpurs made of black Leathertex canvas. *Holy socks, a pilot?*

The young man shouldered his rifle, then removed a broad-brimmed campaign-style hat, exposing a thick mop of brown hair cut shorter on the sides but longer on top and parted just off center. One lock flopped down over his forehead.

'And just who in the name of Saint Peter's tailor are you?' Jade asked, careful to keep any trace of hostility or friendliness from her voice.

'Allow me to introduce myself. I'm Sam Featherstone.'

8

Elephants have few natural enemies and so live most of their lives peacefully. However, even in this isolated refuge, they've come to associate the scent of man with death. The elephants have no intention of submitting peacefully, and heaven help the foe that a bull or an angry cow turns against.
— The Traveler

'And *you* must be Miss del Cameron,' continued the young man. When he pronounced 'del,' his bass voice carried just a hint of twang that spoke of the Midwestern United States.

A Yank! Jade immediately regretted her rude question regarding his identity. 'Yes, yes, I am.' She extended her right hand to her fellow American. 'Mr Featherstone, I believe you said?'

The man transferred his hat to his left hand, which still rested on Jelani's shoulder, and shook Jade's hand. 'That's correct. I should apologize for intruding in the middle of nowhere, but I'm a friend of old Dunbury's.' He kept hold of Jade's hand. 'I'd just arrived at your camp and said hello to him and his bride when Biscuit trotted off without so much as a wave bye. When the lad took off after the cat, I offered to go along. Seemed risky for him otherwise, and Avery appeared reluctant to leave his wife.' Featherstone turned his attention to Harry, released Jade's hand, and extended his own to Hascombe. 'Sam Featherstone,' he repeated.

'Harry Hascombe.' They shook briefly, testing each other's dominance in their grip. 'These gentlemen are my guests on safari.'

'Ah, then *you're* the great white hunter.' Featherstone grinned. 'Dunbury told me you were hunting around these parts.' He turned his attention to the three men standing near Hascombe. 'Three Germans, right?' For a moment the smile diminished; then it returned with a mischievous twist on one side. 'Damn fine airplane, that Fokker, although that's not quite how we pronounced it at our airfield. Shot three of them down myself and it wasn't easy. No hard feelings, right? All's fair in love and war, and I confess I *loved* shooting down Fokkers.'

Jade ducked her head and turned her laugh into a cough. Biscuit looked up at her and chirped before padding over to Jelani.

Herr Vogelsanger's brows drew down as he scowled. He pulled himself up in a rigid stance, chin high, nose in the air, and stared at the young American. 'And what,' he demanded, 'means that?' His hands worked in and out of clenched fists.

For a moment Jade worried that the man would haul off his shooting glove and slap it across Featherstone's face in the best European tradition. Judging by his facial scar, dueling was apparently still popular in his culture. She decided intervention was the better part of valor.

'He made a compliment about the plane.' She turned back to the American. 'Thank you for watching over Jelani, Mr Featherstone. I appreciate that.'

'Call me Sam. I was glad to help. He's a brave lad.' Sam patted the boy's shoulder.

Jelani stood beside his protector as though awaiting permission to move. Sam shifted his weight off his left leg and slipped his arm from the boy's shoulder with another affectionate pat on the back and replaced his hat on his head. Jelani took the opportunity to grab Biscuit's lead and scold the cat.

Jade watched the cheetah reply by butting his large head against Jelani. Despite Sam's explanation, she still wondered why Avery and Bev had sent a stranger instead of following the boy themselves.

Almost in answer to her thoughts Sam added, 'Lady Beverly was napping, and as I said, Dunbury didn't want to leave her. Seemed very concerned about her health. It appears she'd done a Daniel Boone on her lunch,' he said, using the American slang that jokingly referred to the fact that the pioneer always 'shot' his supper.

Vogelsanger's tight-lipped grimace still expressed his anger at Featherstone's offhand comments. He opened his mouth to either demand an apology or issue a retort when Harry cut him short.

'We must be getting back to camp.' He looked first at his hunters, then at Jade, and finally at the American pilot. Harry's jaw clenched and he frowned as though he was trying to decide what to do. Sam Featherstone clearly aggravated his clients, but he didn't seem to want to leave Jade behind. 'You should stick with us, Jade,' he said. 'It wasn't a very smart idea coming out here all alone.'

'I told you I wasn't alone.' She nodded once more to Chiumbo, who continued to glare at the Germans, his arms again folded across his chest.

'If it will ease your conscience, Hascombe,' Sam offered, 'I'll be delighted to escort Miss Jade back to her camp.' His dark brown eyes twinkled. 'I'm heading that way anyway. Dunbury has extended an invitation for me to stay.'

Harry's scowl deepened. 'That's entirely up to the lady. We can all walk together.'

Jade looked at the Kikuyu youth, happily engaged in stroking the beautiful cheetah. The last thing she wanted was to put the boy in danger. Since both Harry and Vogelsanger looked as if they wanted to pulverize Mr Featherstone, and Chiumbo appeared willing to take his panga knife to the lot of them, she decided it would be best if they went separate ways.

'I wouldn't want to slow you down, Mr Hascombe, and I'm not sure it's all that safe traveling in your company, especially with that valuable ivory.' She jerked her head towards the newly arrived porters burdened under two large tusks. 'Captain Smythe of the King's African Rifles told us the Abyssinians have come south for ivory raids,' she explained to Sam. 'And Chiumbo and I saw more of their handiwork

104

today. An entire bachelor herd was slaughtered not far from here.'

Out of the corner of her eye she watched the Germans' expressions for any signs of gloating but found none. Mueller maintained his sleepy, calm composure, and von Gretchmar's face still glowed red as though he suffered from the day's exercise. Vogelsanger surprised her the most when he erupted in a volley of mixed German and English.

'*Donnerwetter! Mein* ivory. They must not take it! We must at once leave!'

Jade wasn't sure if he meant leave this spot and hurry back to camp or leave camp entirely. Von Gretchmar seemed to think the latter, judging by his reply. He suddenly came to life and voiced his dissent in breathy puffs.

'So! You decide when we leave? I am not through. I have not got *mein* elephant.'

Sam shook his head and rolled his eyes heavenward. 'Let's get on back, shall we, Miss del Cameron?'

'Call me Jade, and this is Chiumbo, my headman.'

Sam offered his hand, but Chiumbo shifted his feet in apparent confusion and discomfort. Finally he touched Sam's palm lightly with his fingertips and nodded. '*Jambo,*' he said.

'*Jambo,*' replied Sam.

Chiumbo led the group back to camp. Jade went second and motioned for Jelani and Biscuit to follow her. Sam fell in behind them all. Jade turned around momentarily to make sure Biscuit was behaving himself. That was when she noticed Sam's limp. *Another war casualty*. She wondered if the injury had affected his ability to fly, since the rudder was controlled with foot pedals.

'Does it hurt much?' she asked, and nodded to his right leg.

'What? Oh, the leg? No. Got used to it by now. Hardly know it's there. Just lost some flexibility.'

He didn't add anything more, so Jade let the subject drop and turned back around. War wounds were something most veterans didn't care to discuss, which always surprised those who didn't have any. Jade certainly didn't want to talk about her left knee and the fact that it seemed to hurt only when either rain or death was imminent. The latter fact bothered her most. It seemed wrong, contrary to nature and her religious upbringing, as though she were some sort of soothsayer.

'So how is it you just happened to run across Avery all the way up here in the Northern Territory?' she asked over her shoulder. This location was too remote for two men from different continents to just happen to bump into each other.

'It was not an accident or coincidence, as you can well imagine,' he answered from behind her. 'Dunbury and I met in Paris when we were both on leave, and hit it off. We've corresponded since the war. You know, former pilots and allies.'

'Yes, of course,' Jade said, urging him to continue.

'After the war I found myself too restless to simply wander back to Indiana and settle down there. Two of my pals had plans to fly around the country and do air shows. They even offered me a job as a mechanic, since I'm an engineer, but I know they didn't really need me.'

Jade nodded. *Charity*, she thought. That, and the constant reminder that he wasn't the one up in the air, would hurt.

'Have you ever been to New York?' Sam asked.

'Once,' Jade replied, bewildered by the sudden change in topic.

'I went there to see the Museum of Natural History. While I was in New York, I saw an amazing motion picture called *In the Land of the Headhunters*. This man Edward Curtis filmed the Kwakiutl Indians on Vancouver Island.'

'Curtis,' said Jade. 'I heard him talk once in New Mexico. He had a film of the Hopi Snake Dance.'

'That's the very man. Well, to make a long story short, when I got home, I thought I'd like to try my hand at making moving pictures. After all, if he could do it, why not me?' He shook his head and chuckled. 'I bought a secondhand camera and moseyed around out West trying to film buffalo herds. What I discovered was there *aren't* any more buffalo herds, at least not that I could ever find. Then Avery suggested I come to Africa. Said he was now living in Nairobi.'

The trail widened where elephants had pushed a broader swath, so Jade stopped and waited for Sam to join her. Chiumbo insisted on going first to keep an eye out for danger, Jelani and Biscuit in between.

Sam slipped off his hat and ran a hand

107

through his brown hair. 'Of course, Dunbury wasn't actually in Nairobi by the time I arrived. I made a few inquiries, ran into that Blaney Percival fellow, and learned where you'd all gone. Must have missed you by only a few days. Once I convinced Mr Percival that I knew Dunbury, he helped me put together a decent crew, including an old truck.' He flashed a toothy grin at Jade. 'I certainly didn't expect to find a fellow Yank out here.'

'I suppose Avery told you what we're doing here.'

'Yes. Well, briefly. We didn't have much time to catch up before your pet ran off, but he said something about photographing elephants. Rather a coincidence, isn't it? I mean both of us interested in cameras.'

'Do you plan to film animals or — ' Jade clamped her mouth shut, keenly aware of a stabbing pain in her left knee. At that moment Chiumbo stopped abruptly in front of them and stared to their right. Almost immediately came a shrill trumpeting blast and the sound of crashing underbrush.

'That sounds like an — ' began Sam.

'Elephant!' finished Jade. 'Terrified, angry, and headed our way.'

Jade looked around quickly and spied a thick Cape mahogany tree with branches low enough to reach from the ground. 'Climb!' She pushed Jelani towards the tree, clasped her hands into a makeshift step, and gave the boy a boost up. 'Help him, Chiumbo. Then get up there yourself.' The crashing came nearer, and Jade felt the ground tremble beneath her feet.

'Biscuit?' the boy asked as he grabbed a lower limb and hauled himself up into the branches.

Jade shook her head as she removed the lead from the cat's collar and slapped the cheetah hard on the rump. 'Tent!' she ordered, and hoped the cat would head for camp. She needn't have fretted. Biscuit had no intention of staring down a rampaging elephant and tore down the trail as Chiumbo followed Jelani up the tree, pushing him from behind. Another trumpet blast blared from their right, this one ending in a shrill shriek of pain. Jade looked at Sam's injured leg. 'Can you climb?'

'Be right behind you.'

They hauled themselves up to the thunderclap of snapping wood, the elephant's strident peals, and one boom from a heavy-caliber rifle. The earth beneath them shook as nearly six tons of flesh thundered nearer and nearer. Jade swung her leg up over another branch and spied Jelani above her scrunched tightly against the main trunk, Chiumbo's strong arm stabilizing the boy. She tried to smile encouragement when another rifle blast ripped the air. She slid out of the way and reached down to offer a hand to Sam.

'Are you sure we'll be safe up here?' he asked as he swung his bad leg over a limb.

'No, but it's better than being down there in his path,' she whispered. Jade wrapped her long legs around the branch and grabbed hold of an upper branch. She and Sam were ten feet high and somehow that seemed about five feet short of safety.

'I've seen an elephant trample something when it's mad. There's not much left. Right now I'm more worried about the hunters spotting us and shooting us either accidentally or intentionally. Lie low and keep quiet.' She put a finger to her lips and made sure everyone understood. They did. Whizzing arrows and that last rifle shot helped clarify the need for secrecy.

The thundering came near enough that they felt the vibrations in their perch. Several nearby wild coffee saplings snapped and a massive bull crashed into view. A dozen arrows penetrated his thick hide, blood dribbling from each. Jade caught her breath as she recognized the old patriarch that she'd been hunting on film.

He was a magnificent beast with tusks that must have weighed over a hundred pounds each, nearly crossing each other as a testament to his age. One was broken a foot from the tip, the result of an ancient battle for dominance. Both tusks had been polished to a golden amber color like piano keys that had seen innumerable fingers caressing them. Even his wrinkled hide bore dozens of scars like medals of honor. The old bull growled, a low ominous rumble.

The drugged arrows and the frantic race through the forest had taken their toll on the aged giant. The elephant's steps slowed and the great beast staggered once. From behind him came the babble of excited human voices, but none of the people approached close enough for Jade to see or the elephant to reach. An arrow zinged out of the trees and struck the bull in his right hind leg. He screamed another challenge and turned to fight rather than flee.

The bull stood his ground, ears fanned out, trunk raised to catch the scent of his tormentor. From her perch, Jade saw a bloody wound on his side just below the tip of the ear where someone had aimed for a vital spot with an express rifle, but missed. The old elephant made a magnificent image, terrifying in his rage. Jade felt a tear well up in one eye as she witnessed the plight of the forest monarch. Slowly she slithered to the edge of the branch and slipped her Graflex from around her shoulders, determined to pay witness on film to the bull's brave stand.

Two tormentors appeared, and Sam slid his rifle from his shoulder, presumably to pick them off. Jade stopped him with a touch on his arm. 'Too many,' she mouthed as seven more Abyssinians emerged from the shadows. None of them carried any rifles, which meant at least one more remained safely behind cover.

One archer came in too close. A slight breeze brought his scent to the enraged bull and the beast charged. His ears fanned out to the sides and his trunk and tail stuck straight out from either end like a knight's lance as he defended his life and honor. The terrified man launched his arrow in a futile attempt to halt the charge. It stuck in the bull's face, below one eye, but within seconds of being struck, the bull gripped the man in his trunk. The screams of both the hunter and the hunted blended into one, ripping through the forest, as the elephant slammed his attacker to the ground. Trampling feet cut the scream short.

The bull next wrapped his powerful trunk around the end of Jade's branch and tugged. Immediately, she started to scramble backward. A strong arm wrapped around her waist and hauled her back just as the branch snapped like a matchstick less than a foot from where she'd been. Jade acknowledged Sam's timely aid with a nod before she turned her attention back to the battle below her, praying they weren't too exposed now.

With a new weapon in his grasp, the elephant once again charged his attackers, swinging the branch like a club. Jade risked personal exposure and took a picture of the bull. She needn't have worried. Even she couldn't hear the shutter click over the elephant's rampage and no one below her had eyes for anything but the furious animal now on the offensive.

The stout mahogany limb caught one of the poachers on the side of the head and cracked it like a melon. The man's body snapped back from the force, flew into the air, and crashed into a bloody heap five feet from where he'd been standing. In their panic, the remaining men bolted back into the trees behind them, hoping for safety.

For a moment, Jade believed the ancient patriarch would chase the poachers away and win the day. His size and fury more than matched their puny arrows, drugged or not. But the next sound ripped away all hope as it blasted through the forest. The bull met his match with an express bullet to the brain. He toppled to the ground in a thunderous crash. Jade groaned.

Immediately the remaining Abyssinians appeared from their cover and raced to their prize. For the next forty-five minutes the nine men swarmed around the dead bull like ants on a grasshopper, hacking and hewing. The first two pulled machete-like knives from their belts and chopped at the tusks while the others shouted instructions or jumped about in a sort of victory dance. Two of the men carried rifles.

Jade watched to see which of the riflemen would examine the killing shot and publicly acknowledge being the shooter. A lean African dressed in sandals, calf-length drawers, and a long-sleeved tunic glanced at the kill shot, then examined the shoulder wound, which had missed the heart. He pointed to one of his companions, an even thinner man, and laughed. Apparently he considered his companion a poor marksman.

Jade reached for her binoculars and focused on the rifles. One was a double-barreled elephant gun, an English Bland, and one that had seen a lot of hard use, judging by the scratches on it. The other rifle looked newer and definitely too small a caliber to be of any use hunting elephants. She tried to get a better look at it, but the rifle's owner kept dancing around.

One man, the one with the Bland, wanted to take a foot back with him as a trophy, but the others argued against it. By then the tusks fell free and six men hoisted the elephant's two ivory spears onto their shoulders, groaning under the weight. The trophy-hunting poacher decided not to remain alone and fell in behind them. Within

113

minutes, the forest shadows quickly covered any trace of them.

No one in the tree blind moved or spoke for another ten minutes. Jade, for one, needed time to conquer her emotions, and the others took their cue from her. A blend of grief, rage, and despair welled up within her, each vying for dominance. Finally, a lone tear trickled down her cheek. She swiped it away quickly and whispered to the others to climb down.

Jade went first, to make sure no danger lingered. She knew she could climb faster than Mr Featherstone if necessary, but there was no need. All the poachers had gone. Jade called to Jelani to follow with Chiumbo assisting him. Finally she and Chiumbo offered to help Sam. He protested that he didn't need a hand and waited until they moved aside before he continued his descent.

'Psst, Jade.' The whisper came from Jade's left. 'I say, are you all right?'

'Avery!' Jade exclaimed. 'What in thunder are you doing here?'

Avery approached their tree, holding Biscuit by a rope tied to the cat's collar. Sam clambered down, and Avery handed off the cheetah to Jade in order to assist his friend. Biscuit busied himself by first inspecting Jade, then Jelani. Once Sam was back on the ground, the two men shook hands and clapped each other on the shoulder.

'I see you found Jade,' said Avery. 'Thank God you're all right.' He patted Jelani on the head and grinned at Chiumbo.

'We're fine. Better than my old tusker,' said

Jade. The group approached the dead bull with the quiet reverence one expected to see when viewing a fallen head of state.

'The poachers?' asked Avery after a prolonged moment of silence.

Jade pointed to the trampled area nearby. 'That's one of them there.' Only a darkening stain and scraps of cloth remained. Everything else resembled pulp melded into the earth and forest litter. 'And there's another.' She pointed to the man beaten with the tree limb.

'Good for Tusker,' Avery said. 'Wish he'd gotten more of the buggers.'

'Most of them had drugged arrows, but two of them had rifles. At least one was an elephant gun, but I'd swear the other one looked like a German Mauser,' Jade said. Her voice choked as she struggled to maintain a grip on her emotions. *Be darned if I break down in front of Avery, much less a stranger.*

'A Mauser?' asked Avery. 'Are you sure?'

Jade shook her head. 'The man wouldn't stand still long enough for me to get a good look, and it's been a while since I've seen a Mauser anyway,' she admitted. 'Whatever it was, it certainly wasn't an elephant gun. Did you see it, Sam?'

He shook his head. 'Not with any clarity.'

'Chiumbo?'

'I watched the boy.'

Jade walked towards the trees, scanning the ground for a spent cartridge. She found two and picked them up.

She handed the cartridges to Avery while Sam

looked over his shoulder. 'Well, this one looks exactly like one from my English Bland,' he said.

'That's what I thought,' Jade agreed, 'but look at the other one. It's certainly a much smaller caliber.'

Sam took the second cartridge from Avery's hand and inspected it. 'I agree with you, Jade. This could have come from a 98 Mauser rifle.'

'And it looked new,' added Jade.

Avery glanced from Jade to Sam and back again. 'I only caught a glimpse of these men,' he said. 'As motley as that lot looked, I don't see how they could afford either of those weapons. I don't know about the Mauser, but a Bland, at least, is very dear. Any idea how they'd get them?'

Jade shrugged, not ready to voice her thoughts yet, and Sam shook his head. 'Stealing?' he suggested. 'Murder? I suppose there are enough Mausers left over from the war and it's not a stretch to think it could have come from old German East Africa.'

'We need to get back to camp,' said Avery. 'Bev will be hunting us down before long. She went into a complete panic once when Biscuit tore back into camp alone.' He stroked the cheetah's head. 'Thought I'd have to tie *her* down to make her stay behind.'

Jade didn't question Avery's protectiveness. She attributed its recent growth to their increasing desire for an heir. And, if her suspicions were correct, Bev had gotten herself in a family way. Jade made a mental note to quiz her friend in private later.

'How much *did* you see?' Sam asked.

'Very little,' admitted Avery. 'I came back on the double-quick, but they were nearly through hacking off the tusks by the time I arrived. Took a moment to see that you weren't part of the melee. Then I got back under cover.' He looked at them sheepishly. 'Not sure what I'd have been able to do if you had been in danger except try to take down a few of them. Didn't know where you were at first until I got the idea to look up in the trees. I presumed Jade had you all stuck up there.'

'And you were right,' she said. She walked to the dead bull and, with a mumbled apology to the ancient elephant, yanked an arrow from his side. 'It looks like the same type of arrow that . we found with the cow and in my tent.'

'Someone shot an arrow into your tent?' asked Sam. Avery briefly summarized the recent attack.

In the meantime, Jade had pulled another five arrows from the dead bull.

'Are you starting a collection?' asked Avery.

'If I can get ahold of a bow, or make one, I'll have use for these.' She shot a look at the man with the battered head. 'He won't mind if I take his bow.'

'You're going on the hunt?' asked Sam.

'In a manner of speaking,' Jade answered, walking over to the dead man. She pushed the body aside with her boot. 'Blast it! He landed on his bow and snapped it.' She kicked the body back into place.

'Should I ask what she's going to hunt?' Sam whispered to Avery.

117

From the corner of her eye, Jade saw Avery and Chiumbo both vigorously shake their heads no. Jelani stood patiently to the side, waiting for the adults to finish. Jade motioned for him to join her. 'We should leave,' she said. 'Hopefully our runner reached Smythe by now or someone who can get to him.'

'He already knows there are poachers here, Jade,' said Avery.

'Right, but he might not know that they're better armed. Besides,' she added, 'he's got a trail to follow from here.'

'I will follow their track, Simba Jike,' offered Chiumbo. 'Maybe they have a camp.'

Jade mouthed 'later' and jerked a thumb towards Jelani. 'Bwana Dunbury is right, Chiumbo,' she said. 'That is Captain Smythe's job.' She met her headman's eyes and saw that he understood. They'd follow the trail, but not when the boy was around.

'Right,' agreed Avery. 'Glad to see you're finally thinking sensibly, Jade. Now, if you don't mind, we need to get back to camp before my wife starts tracking us.'

★ ★ ★

While the fear and excitement gradually wore down the adults, Jelani showed all the resilience of youth, which intensified as they approached camp. Bwana Avery's friend became a brand-new audience, and the boy, proud of his role in Simba Jike's adventures and of his reading ability, decided to regale the man with some of

118

his expertise. 'Watch,' he announced in the time-honored fashion of children everywhere to indulge adults. 'I will swing from tree to tree like Tarzan in the books.'

He made a leap for one of the lower branches and hauled himself up onto it. From there he took hold of a second, slightly higher branch and swung himself out over the trail. Unfortunately, he ran out of reachable branches and hung as Jade and the others approached.

'Very good, Tarzan,' said Avery as he scooped the boy from the limb and set his feet on the ground.

Jelani frowned and kicked the dirt. 'These trees are no good. The branches are too high to reach.'

'That's because the elephants ate the lower ones,' said Jade.

'*Tantor popo balu-den*,' said Jelani.

'Wait a minute,' said Sam. 'My Swahili may be just shy of terrible, but I didn't understand a word of that.'

Jade laughed. 'Jelani is speaking the language of the great apes from the Tarzan books. Avery brought along several, and Jelani's been reading them. He said the elephants eat branches.'

'Jelani *bundolo dango*,' the boy added as he made a stabbing motion with his right hand. 'I killed a hyena.'

'Good lad,' said Sam. 'I read *Tarzan of the Apes*, but it seems I've got some catching up to do.'

'I will read to you,' said Jelani, and he thumped his chest proudly.

Back at camp, Avery greeted his frantic wife with a gentle hug. Then Sam brought out his motion picture camera and tripod and insisted on capturing what he called a typical safari scene. Jade found his determination amusing, and watched as he directed everyone's activity, from the camp cook's meal preparation to Avery's gun cleaning. Only Biscuit didn't seem interested in following his cues and stalked off to Jelani's empty tent for some quiet. Jelani, a natural ham, managed to be in every scene, and twice Jade watched Sam indulge the boy's vanity at the expense of several feet of film. Finally she came to Sam's rescue by asking Jelani to read and suggested Sam could hear him better if he was sitting next to him rather than standing behind a camera.

Jelani grabbed *Son of Tarzan* from Avery's tent and read until he could barely see the words in the diminishing light. Jade smiled at the boy's fascination with the jungle character and his fictional adventures. Suddenly, an idea popped into her head, and her smile took a menacing twist. If Smythe couldn't take care of the poachers, then she'd draw some inspiration from those tales and handle the poachers herself. They weren't the only ones who could make snares and traps. With just a little luck, she might even acquire a bow without having to make one.

9

Mount Marsabit is covered in forest, not jungle. True, the trees may be evergreen rather than shed their leaves in the winter, but the air is cool, not steaming, and the understory is thin rather than tangled. On some parts of the mountain grow beautiful cedars that make one think of the famed cedars of Lebanon. Walking in these woods, it is easy to forget that you are in Africa unless, of course, you bump into the wildlife.
— The Traveler

The hardest part of Jade's plan had been slipping away from everyone else. Beverly had turned into a regular mother hen recently, but thanks to her increased tendency towards nausea, she opted to stay behind in camp. Jade also had Bev's upset stomach to thank for Avery's decision to remain with his wife. Jelani and Sam were another matter entirely. With that uncanny knack that youngsters have of knowing when something's afoot, the boy wanted to stick to her like a leech, and Sam seemed to think that being a fellow American made them long-lost friends. She didn't want any more friends, especially one that reminded her of the war every time he took a step. In the end, Jade and Chiumbo simply skipped camp three hours before sunrise while the others were asleep. She left a note saying she intended to stay overnight in one of her blinds to get some night shots.

They traveled as lightly as possible. Chiumbo carried a tin filled with dried meat, raisins, and dates on his back in a canvas pack and wielded a foot-long panga knife in his right hand. Jade carried her Graflex with the roll film, and a battery-operated flashlight, in her pack. Two coils of rope hung from her left shoulder, and her Winchester was slung across her right. A bone-handled knife with a five-inch fixed blade hung in a leather case from her belt. Each carried a canteen, and they left the box of food in one of her tree blinds, then cut across country to the old bull elephant's carcass.

Scavengers had already made serious inroads on the elephant's body, but the nausea that welled up inside Jade came more from the feeling of loss than from the sight of ripped flesh and offal. This elephant had lived far too long and sired too many calves to merit this ignominious end. She wasn't sure she could ever look at a billiard ball or a piano again without picturing this magnificent creature.

Chiumbo found the poachers' trail easily, since men heavily burdened with ivory left some impressions, even on the dry ground. They followed the path quickly at first, then moved cautiously as the risk of stumbling on the Abyssinian poachers increased. After several hours, Chiumbo stopped and pointed to the ground in front of them.

'The men have separated here, Simba Jike.' He pointed uphill. 'The ivory went this way.'

Jade stooped beside him and examined the crushed vegetation. 'I agree. The impression is much stronger that way.' She glanced to the left to the other imprint, which led down the mountainside. 'And this track is much fainter, like a man walking lightly. How many men do you think went that way?'

Chiumbo shrugged. 'If they walk one behind another, it is hard to tell.'

'I'm guessing at least one armed man went with the ivory.' She looked up the trail. 'Maybe they're caching it somewhere.' When she looked back down, something about the tracks caught her eye and she leaned over to view them from a different angle. 'This man wore boots. See?' She pointed to a definite heel mark and a partial curve of a right foot. 'The poachers we saw yesterday had flat sandals, didn't they?'

Chiumbo nodded. 'And this man does not walk flat.'

Jade studied the print again. 'I see what you mean, Chiumbo. He walks on the outside of his foot. Interesting.' She straightened. 'I don't recall seeing this print before.'

'Perhaps this man joined the others here,' Chiumbo suggested.

'Yes, that's very likely. So this man in the boots, he might be their leader?'

Chiumbo nodded. 'I think you are correct, Simba Jike. See? There are no marks for a struggle. And,' he added, 'if he leads these men, then he may wear boots and not sandals to show that he is important.'

Jade squatted back down, measured the heel print with her hand, then compared it with her own bootheel. 'About as large as my father's,' she mused. 'Probably not a particularly tall man, then. Dad is only five feet, eight inches, an inch taller than me.' She looked across to Chiumbo, hunkered down on the other side of the track. 'Certainly not as tall as you. By the way, Chiumbo, thank you for stopping Mr Vogelsanger yesterday when he tried to shoot Biscuit.'

Chiumbo merely nodded without looking up.

'Did you recognize any of those men?' she asked, remembering the fierce anger on Chiumbo's face. Perhaps one of them had been involved in the wars with Chiumbo's people. All she had was von Gretchmar's word, which she doubted, that he hadn't been in Africa before, and Vogelsanger hadn't answered at all. 'Did one of them kill your father?'

'No. I only recognized their language.' Chiumbo stood and stalked softly to the outside of the downward trail, then backtracked and did the same for the upward trail. 'I do not see which trail he followed, Simba Jike.'

Jade nodded. Apparently her headman was in no mood to converse about the past. 'Too much leaf litter on the trail to leave a distinct boot mark again.' She nodded up the hill. 'I doubt they carried that heavy ivory too far in one day. We should find where they're hiding it.'

Chiumbo turned to follow the trail uphill. He'd walked several paces before he stopped and

124

waited for Jade. 'Do you not come, Simba Jike?'

Jade shook her head, setting her bobbed black curls in motion. 'I have an idea.' She took out a coil of rope. Her slowly spreading grin spoke volumes on that idea's deviousness, and what her smile didn't say, her flashing green eyes did.

Chiumbo grinned back as he hastened towards her. 'We will set a trap?' He didn't wait for her to answer. 'It would be good to take one prisoner, Simba Jike. I would make him tell us what you want to know.'

'Patience, Chiumbo. I doubt these men ever travel alone, so chances are, even if we catch one, his comrades will cut him down. It's possible all this will do is make them wary enough to go back to Abyssinia.' She sighed. It wasn't exactly justice, but if it prevented more killing and poaching, it would have to serve.

'I understand, Simba Jike. A man should not savor the meat in the cook pot before the game is killed.'

Jade knew this saying was just an African version of not counting chickens, but something about Chiumbo's tone sent shivers down her spine. He was on the hunt. Beyond what he had told her by the campfire, she knew very little about him or his tribe, only that he held the reputation as an excellent headman and as an experienced and brave tracker. Now it seemed he was another war casualty, injured in spirit more than body. Perhaps he led safaris for the same reason she wandered about so much: to escape bitter memories of gore and death. Or perhaps he searched for the men who had killed his father.

'What kind of trap do you want, Simba Jike? Should we spear him?'

'No. It might accidentally kill one of the King's African Rifles. And whatever we set, I don't want to catch a passing animal in the snare,' Jade said. 'This looks like it's also been a game trail.' She looked to Chiumbo for confirmation.

He shrugged. 'I did not see much fresh spoor, Simba Jike, except for one leopard print.'

'Then we don't want to catch a passing leopard. We'll set the real snare off the game trail and put a false one on it.' She pointed to a spot just in front of a large tree braced with thick buttresses that protruded into the trail. 'They will see it and have to step around it, only there's just one way to step around.'

'And that is where we put the real snare,' concluded Chiumbo. 'And the animals?'

'The animals will probably trot right over the false snare, but even if they step directly in it, nothing will happen. It will only look like a real snare to a human.' She looked off to the side. 'Help me find a tree with a branch that will bend.'

Together they found a suitable limb on a tree a few yards down the hill. Jade lassoed the tip, and together they heaved on the rope and hauled it down towards the ground. Chiumbo braced the tip with a log while Jade carved and set up a two-pin toggle trigger that would release the log when someone picked up her bait.

The bait! That took a moment of thought, but only a moment. It had to be something that a

126

human, but not an animal, would pick up. Jade reached deep into a side pocket and pulled out a leather coin purse. Normally she would never have bothered to waste pocket space with money out in the wilderness, but ever since yesterday a plan had been forming in her head. She unraveled a thin strand from part of her rope and tied the purse to the toggle using that strand. To encourage someone's greed, she left the purse partially open and set one coin in the mouth. The illusion was a fallen money bag with coins spilling out. A sprinkling of forest litter over the ropes finished the job.

'That ought to attract one of the greedy bastards,' she announced. 'And that limb is strong enough to fling a smaller man up into the air. With any luck, his bow will go flying off for me to find later.'

Chiumbo grunted his approval. 'And the false snare to drive them here — where they will see this?'

'I'll take care of that, Chiumbo. All I need to do is half conceal a coil of rope and another toggle that won't lead to anything.' She looked back up the trail. 'See if you can find where they took the ivory. Whistle if you do find it.' When she saw Chiumbo hesitate, she faced him. 'What's wrong? Why don't you follow the trail?' She wondered if she'd just asked him to do something menial, a task beneath his dignity.

The tall African took a deep breath before he replied, 'I have never worked for a woman before, Simba Jike. When Bwana Avery hired me, I thought I worked for him.'

127

'And so you do, Chiumbo.'

He shook his head. 'I work for you both by my own choice. You asked me why I said yes to your money. I have heard the stories of you, how you killed a witch, but I did not believe it at first. Women in my tribe would not do such a thing. But I have since learned that white women are sometimes different. When I learned Bwana Avery was your friend, I took his money so I could learn about you. Yesterday, I saw your bravery. And I saw your honor. You would not risk the boy. You waited for him to climb first.'

'He is in my care, Chiumbo,' she said softly.

'And you are in mine, Simba Jike. It is not safe for you alone in the forest. These men are bad. These men who take ivory also take slaves to sell far north.'

Jade nodded. 'Your concern touches me. I'll be careful.'

Chiumbo grunted softly and muttered to himself, 'A lioness is not afraid to be alone.' Then in a louder voice he added, 'I will come back if you do not follow soon, Simba Jike.'

'Thank you, Chiumbo, but you must also be careful, my friend. These same men would kill you.'

He grinned, exposing a row of filed teeth. 'Let them try.' Chiumbo raised a hand in salute and followed the trail uphill, while Jade returned to making her false snare. The trick here was to make it visible without its looking like an obvious deception. The more she thought about it, the more she realized that these men would just step over a simple snare. Then they wouldn't see the

128

bait. No, she needed to drive them off the trail to the right. But how?

She scanned the area for another log and found one about three feet long, and one stout branch three inches in diameter. She whittled the branch to a point and lashed it to the end of the log. Then she threw her second coil of rope over an overhanging branch, tied it around the log, and hoisted it to chest height off the ground. She pushed the log over to the nearby tree trunk and tied it to look as if it could be quickly released. Finally, she set the false snare and trigger. The snare wasn't really attached to the deadfall, but the illusion held that this was a mangle trap that should be avoided at all cost.

Jade stood up and rubbed her left knee, which had started to ache from her squatting so long in one spot. At least, she hoped that was why it ached. Previously, she'd shrugged off Beverly's statement that it hurt just before something attacked her. Now she wasn't so sure. Chiumbo's statement about the slave trading made her nervous. She wondered if he was right. Perhaps this was a dangerous place to be alone. Perhaps she should find him. She turned and nearly collided with a man standing right behind her.

10

Perhaps the most haunting parts of the forest are the brilliant butterflies clustered like gems on the bushes and draped along the thick, silvery Spanish moss.
— The Traveler

Jade stumbled backward onto her own false snare, her right hand grabbing for her knife as she struggled to master her shock and fear. She felt her heart pound in her chest, the pulse drumming through her ears. How had this man crept up on her? Hell's blazes! He hadn't made a sound. As she pulled her knife from its sheath, the man held up his right hand, palm facing her, in a sign of peace. Jade took a wider stance to steady herself and kept her hand on the knife in case it was a ruse.

'Who are you?' she demanded first in English, then in Swahili. As she spoke, she studied the man. He was a native African — that much was clear — but from where? He certainly didn't look like the Abyssinians, nor did he resemble the members of any of the tribes bordering the mountain. Whoever he was, he was ancient, if the parchment-like skin on his face gave any indication. Innumerable wrinkles, resembling the myriad dry ravines running through a barren landscape, showed under the layer of light ash rubbed into his skin, and his sparse hair curled out in white wisps like the mountain's morning vapors, thinning in the sunshine. He wore a frayed gray blanket draped over one shoulder in the manner of many Africans and his feet were bare. The overall effect combined with his silent approach was spectral. Jade suspected it served as camouflage and wondered how long he had stood undetected watching her.

'You are in danger, Simba Jike,' he said. His voice, though cracked with age, held power and strength. 'You must follow me.' He turned and threaded his way past the false snare and down the hill.

'Be careful!' Jade called after him in English. 'I've set a trap there.'

The old man nodded and passed by the coin purse that baited the hidden snare. He didn't turn to see if she followed. Jade gripped her knife more tightly and headed down the hill after him. The thought that he could be leading her into a trap flitted across her mind, but she dismissed it. If he'd meant to harm her, he could have easily struck her down earlier. Besides, something about this man fascinated her. He turned off the visible trail and struck out into the forest, disturbing a cluster of iridescent blue butterflies as they sipped dew off the shrubs.

Her guide maintained a straight track for a few minutes before he paused by a stately tree over one hundred feet tall. Jade recognized it as one that Jelani had called *mukinduri*, claiming it held an excellent remedy for stomach ailments. Since

131

Jade's guts felt as though those butterflies had taken up residence inside her, she thought she could use a cure right about now. The man seemed to recognize the tree, examining its bark, which bore the scars and polish of innumerable elephant rubbings. He turned, put a finger to his thin lips to signal for absolute silence, then proceeded on his way.

While she followed, she scanned the ground for signs. Gradually she began to recognize the marks of an ancient trail, long abandoned. Her main clue was the difference in the age of the trees along their route. These trees were younger ones, which had taken advantage of a bit of open ground to get a roothold. She wanted to ask him where they were going, but the ache in her knee had increased. This time, she paid attention to it because the sound of walking men drifted down the mountainside to her from the upper trail. Jade turned and peered through the timber. She could just barely make out two Abyssinians.

Her pulse quickened as she realized they might also be able to see her, and she followed the old man's example and melted backward into the forest. Her guide beckoned with a hand motion before leading her to a massive fig tree another fifty yards away. Strangler figs were rare on this mountain, but this one dated back centuries, whatever tree the fig initially used for its anchor long choked of life and rotted away. Only a hollow core remained amid a tangled orgy of thickened vines.

The old African nodded towards a gap in the tree's base and then pointed up. Jade ducked inside the dark interior and began climbing, hoping nothing else had sought refuge in the twisted trunk. About ten feet up, the tangle narrowed, making further progress impossible. Something sharp scratched at her cheek and a trickle of blood seeped down to her chin. She felt for a stable perch, and settled herself in. The dead supporting tree's remaining bark sloughed off under pressure, so standing upright was not an option. Jade leaned back against the wall and braced herself with her feet in front of her on nearly opposite sides of the tree. In the dead silence, she detected a muted *whoosh* punctuated by a distant scream. *Success!* Angry voices followed the outcry, and Jade imagined those on the ground worked to release the one whipped up by the bent limb's recoil.

Suddenly the shouts stopped, and the forest again became as still as the grave. Jade tried to imagine the scene outside. The men would have remembered the coin purse and realized the snare was deliberately set, not to catch an animal, but a human. They would be more wary now and a lot angrier. Would they move on and report the incident to their chief? Would he assume the trap was set by rival poachers? Or would these men comb the area for the perpetrator? A sick feeling welled up in her stomach at the thought of Chiumbo. Had they already found him?

At this height, the fig's vines had formed a thin but solid wall, so she couldn't see a blasted thing from inside the tree. *I'll just have to trust the old man to give the all clear.* Then it dawned

133

on her: the old man hadn't joined her inside the tree. Where had he gone? *Sweet Millard Fillmore on a broomstick. How long do I stay in here?*

Her answer came in the sound of snapping twigs followed by the softer brush of carefully placed footfalls that carried down the hill in the cool morning air and echoed lightly in the hollow tree. The men might have thought they were being stealthy, but she'd tuned her senses as sharp as any prey hiding from a predator. To her, the men might have been a charging elephant or a snorting rhino. Besides that, her blasted knee hurt like the blazes. She had received the shrapnel wound in the same bombing raid that had killed her David, and at times she bore it as proudly as her Croix de Guerre medal. At other times, it was just another grim reminder of all she'd lost. Right now it acted as a signal for absolute silence. She didn't want to believe the confounded thing had the ability to alert her to impending danger, but at this point, she was ready to heed its warning.

Jade struggled to control her breathing lest any gasp give away her position. Her thigh muscles cramped as she tensed to brace herself. A chunk of bark pushed against her shirt and gouged her back. She tried to focus on anything else to take her mind off the pain. Unfortunately, what drew her attention from the leg and back pain was some multilegged creature making its way into her open shirt collar and down her chest.

Finally, Jade resorted to her old mantra that she had recited when she'd driven an ambulance along the front lines in France. *I only occupy one tiny space. The shells have all the rest of France to hit.* It didn't help. The vermin in her shirt continued to search out new territory whether she occupied it or not.

The subdued padding of sandaled feet came closer. Had they followed her trail? A twig snapped just outside the hole at the tree's bottom. Jade tipped her head ever so slowly in order to peer down through the gloom. She glimpsed a head poking inside, then pulling back out after a cursory glance. Two voices argued in what sounded like confused conversation. Obviously they had followed her trail, but couldn't figure out where she'd gone after this point. Right now darkness was her ally. *Saints in heaven, don't let them have any kind of light.*

Jade listened carefully, but the men spoke a language she didn't know. Finally she heard one man cut loose in what could only be a vulgar oath, followed by the unmistakable sound of a rifle bolt clacking. She mentally recited a prayer and steeled herself for the bullet.

The rifle blast roared inside the hollow tree, and she instinctively slammed her hands over her ears. Smoke, black powder, and scorched tree bark welled upward. She held her breath, fearing to cough. They didn't know she was in here. Whoever had fired had done so in a fit of anger. She didn't want to be on the receiving end of that anger. This bullet had passed beneath her upraised legs; the next one wouldn't. At least the shock of the rifle blast startled the creature in her shirt to curl up in defense.

She stayed perched in the tree for a quarter of

an hour after the shot, her ears still ringing from the confined blast. That was when the old man poked his head back inside and whispered for her to descend.

'Where were you?' she asked as she landed on the ground, then untucked her shirt and shook out a large millipede.

The old man gave an enigmatic answer. 'I cannot climb.'

'You saved my life, I'm sure,' Jade said. 'Thank you. What is your name, please?'

He pursed his thin, dry lips as though he had to search his memory for a name. 'I am Boguli,' he replied after a time.

Jade looked around and nodded to the hollow fig. 'It is lucky you found this tree. I don't know where else I could have hidden.'

Boguli rocked gently from one foot to the other, a slow metronome-like movement. 'This is an old elephant trail, long unused. I remembered this tree and the trail from my youth.'

'You have tracked elephants?' she asked. She wondered if he had hunted them for their ivory. Probably a family business.

'I have followed the elephants for a long time,' he said. 'I am like a' — he paused and searched for the right word again, as though isolation had made him rusty — 'brother to the elephants.'

Jade didn't quite understand, but then many African tribes held certain animals in high esteem. If his people had revered elephants, even while hunting them, then they might in fact consider them ancestral spirits or other kindred. Suddenly she remembered that Boguli had

136

called her by her Swahili name, Simba Jike, or 'lioness.'

'How did you know I am called Simba Jike?'

Boguli again rocked back and forth from foot to foot. 'You bear the lion's mark on your wrist,' he said, and pointed to her left hand where last year a Kikuyu shaman had stained a permanent trace of a lion's claw.

She glanced at the half-crescent image and touched it. 'Yes, but how did you . . . ' She looked up and the old man had gone, slipping back into the forest as silently as he'd come.

'Memsabu,' Chiumbo called softly from the upper trail. 'Simba Jike, are you here?'

With a parting glance at the rifle hole in the tree, Jade sprinted back up the slope to join her tracker. 'Thank the Lord, you're alive,' she said. 'I was afraid they'd found you. Did they see you?'

Chiumbo shook his head. 'And you are all right, Simba Jike?' He pointed to a scratch on her cheek where the inside of the fig tree had scraped her during the climb. 'You are hurt.' His fists clenched around his own hunting knife's hilt and he ground his teeth. 'I should have killed them.'

'I'm fine, Chiumbo. And no, I don't want you to kill them. That would have brought the rest down on us like angry hornets. I was safe inside a hollow tree.'

'If you had been hurt . . . ' he began.

'But I wasn't.' She stepped forward and gently placed a hand on each of his shoulders, feeling him stiffen at the unfamiliar touch. 'And neither were you.'

'It is good,' he said after a moment's silence.

Jade let her hands drop to her sides. 'Yes, it is good. Now help me reset the snare before we go on, Chiumbo.'

★ ★ ★

After resetting the snare, Chiumbo led the way up the mountain, Jade following closely on his heels. They traveled off the trail as much as the underbrush allowed. Luckily it was thin under the old growth, but that made them more visible, and Jade didn't want to run headlong into any other poachers. She also kept an eye out for Boguli, but the old man had disappeared just as Chiumbo returned. Perhaps Boguli didn't trust anyone other than her right now. They retreated into the shadows and stopped.

'This is as far as I followed, Memsabu,' whispered Chiumbo after they had walked for nearly thirty minutes. 'Then I thought I should go back for you.'

'You did well, Chiumbo.' Jade leaned against a tree to take a drink from her canteen. 'We have no idea how far this trail leads or what's at the other end.'

'It cannot go too far, Simba Jike. I saw those men that you said hunted you by the hollow tree. I hid and watched them go past me. They did not carry packs of food or water with them. Only one had a weapon, a rifle.'

'In other words, they did not look as though they were making a full day's journey,' Jade summarized in a hushed voice. 'That makes sense. Then they must have a cache of supplies just up this trail.' She took another drink and recapped her canteen. 'Either way, this is apparently an oft-traveled route. We need to be even more cautious, Chiumbo.'

Once more she studied the distant forest in hopes of spotting the ancient Boguli, but to no avail. Jade frowned. She should have waited near the hollow tree or at least near the snare. He must have more information about these poachers that she could use or pass on.

Jade slung the canteen around her shoulder and nodded for Chiumbo to proceed. Instead of continuing up towards the volcanic lake at the top of the mountain, the trail narrowed as it wound around to the steeper eastern side. The volcano's cone ascended another five hundred feet on her right, and drifting down from its heights, echoed the staccato bark of baboons fussing from their trees. The forest here seemed drier with more cedars and mahoganies and fewer butterfly bushes. To her left, a squirrel clung topsy-turvy on a tree trunk, as immobile as a picture hanging on a wall.

The amount of volcanic debris increased, and after another ten minutes, Jade spied a rocky outcrop that showed signs of recent human visitation. At least, that was what the nearby stack of firewood indicated.

'Fuel for cooking or keeping animals away,' whispered Chiumbo. 'Someone may be back yet tonight, Simba Jike.'

They waited in the shadows for another fifteen minutes, listening for any sound of life from the recess beneath the outcrop. Finally Jade motioned for Chiumbo to stay put and keep watch while she crept over to the rocks and crouched behind a boulder.

Chiumbo nodded an 'all clear' and Jade slowly eased around her rock. If someone was supposed to be on guard, he was sleeping on the job. More likely, these men didn't plan on anyone's searching for them and hadn't even set a guard. She was right. The place was vacated at least for the moment. Jade motioned for Chiumbo to join her.

Together they inspected the hideout. The rocks blasted away from the top during the last eruption had formed a natural recess nearly ten feet wide and just about as deep. It was almost tall enough for her to stand in upright. All along the right wall lay ivory tusks, stacked like cordwood. Jade counted at least eleven pairs, two large enough to be from bulls. She knew that one of those bulls was the ancient patriarch whose death she'd witnessed. Tucked against the wall lay two tiny tusks, the baby ivory.

Jade's fingernails stabbed her palms as she clenched her fists in anger. Then she again remembered the dead King's African Rifle soldier and her perspective shifted. These elephant deaths were tragic and in some cases cruelly prolonged, but that soldier was murdered plain and simple. He'd died trying to protect these animals. She vowed to make these poachers pay to avenge his death. Driving them from the mountain would not be enough.

'We need to send another runner and report

140

this place to Captain Smythe,' she said.

'What is in those boxes?' asked Chiumbo. He pointed to the back wall.

'I don't know. Maybe food stores.' She took another look around the area for intruders and headed to the back, stooping slightly. 'I'll take a look.'

She left Chiumbo to keep watch again, although, at this point, they were both sitting ducks if the raiders returned to their stash. She counted more on their making some noise as they approached to give her warning. If they were so arrogant to leave this place unguarded, they might feel secure enough to talk loudly as they came near.

The wooden crates were nailed shut, and Jade looked around for something to use as a pry bar. That was when she noticed that one lid had already been removed and simply set back in place. She raised the wooden lid and tried to peer inside, but the back end of the cache was completely in shadow. Jade slipped off her pack and reached inside for her Eveready slide-switch flashlight, a gift from her parents. She prayed the batteries still held power and decided to keep its use to a minimum, but once she beheld the contents, she couldn't stop looking. The box was loaded with Gew 98 Mauser rifles.

'Sweet Millard Fillmore on a tightrope,' she swore.

Suddenly she felt the need to examine the other boxes, too. Scanning the floor with her light, she found the pry bar that had been used to open the first case. She took it up, turned off her light, and set to work raising the lid of another crate. It, too, was filled with the same make of rifle. A third and smaller crate contained ammunition. She left the two crates underneath these unopened, replaced the lids, and put the pry bar back where she had found it before she rejoined Chiumbo. Then she motioned for him to hide with her under cover of the forest while they pondered their next move.

'They will kill many more elephants with all those rifles, Simba Jike,' Chiumbo said.

Jade shook her head. 'No, I don't think so. They weren't elephant guns and the bullets aren't right for elephants. Besides, why would they still be using their drugged arrows when they have all those weapons at their disposal?' She took off her hat and ran a hand through her short black hair. 'It looks more like they're arming for battle. Those rifles might not take down an elephant, but they'd sure kill a lot of humans.' *But what humans?* she wondered.

'What do you wish to do, Memsabu?'

'I wish to send them all to perdition's door,' answered Jade. Then, seeing the confusion on her tracker's face, she added, 'I want to take some of those rifles for evidence, preferably all of them.'

'We cannot carry them all at once, Memsabu. We will have to make several trips. That will be dangerous.'

Jade nodded. 'And if we haul off an entire box, it will also alert them. We need to take the rifles, but leave the boxes behind to look like they are unopened.' She looked back the way they'd

142

come. 'We could do this in stages. First we remove a crateful of rifles here to this spot. Then we start taking as many as we can safely carry somewhere else to hide them.'

'Where?'

She thought for a moment. 'To that hollow tree where I hid earlier today. They should be safe in there. But we need to hurry before we run out of daylight.'

Together Jade and Chiumbo lifted the rifles from the first crate. Jade had nearly left the cache when Chiumbo called to her from behind.

'Simba Jike, there is something else in this box.'

Jade set her rifles down and hurried back to him.

'It is a bag, I think,' he said. 'I felt it when I reached for the last rifle.'

Jade turned on her flashlight. There in the light's soft glow lay a leather drawstring pouch. She picked it up and heard the unmistakable clink of coins inside. She stuck the bag in her side pocket.

'No time to look now. We need to get moving.' She snatched up her armload of rifles and headed out of the cache and into the forest. Since they had emptied the first crate, she set the rifles down on the ground, ran back into the hideout, and carefully replaced the lid while Chiumbo waited for her to return.

'We're already in the shadows here. I wonder how much time we have until we lose the sun,' she said when she rejoined him.

'Not enough time to come back and take the

rifles from the second box, Simba Jike. The night animals will be on the prowl soon.' A leopard screamed in the distance, almost in response to the tracker's statement, and once again, the baboons up at the lake took up their clamor.

'Right, we need to get these away and climb into a tree blind for the night. But I sure would like to set up another snare here before we go.'

'That will take too long, Memsabu. Bwana Avery will cut out my heart if you are hurt.'

Jade heard the urgency in his voice and heeded it. 'I'd be more afraid of Memsabu Beverly, myself, but you're right, Chiumbo. Someone is likely to return before dark as well. But there's something else I want from here before we head back.'

Cautiously, Jade slipped once more into the sheltering rock recess and turned on her flashlight. If these men used this place as a rallying point, they must keep extra supplies here, and Chiumbo had said one of the two men who pursued her to her hiding place had traveled with only a rifle. She shivered as she remembered its blast reverberating in the hollow tree. Perhaps he also owned a bow but had left it behind. If so, she meant to find it.

She started on the wall opposite the ivory and worked her way to the back, shining the beam slowly over each object. Since bows warped easily when wet, she assumed any bow here would be placed farther back to keep it out of the rain and mist. She found it atop a bag of cornmeal.

'Gotcha,' she said as she snatched it up and

144

inspected it. The bow was constructed of several thinner strips of wood tightly lashed together with sinew, making the end result stronger than any one thick limb. The bowstring appeared to be constructed from twisted plant fibers. Handmade and unique, it still bore a close resemblance to the broken bow she'd found next to the dead poacher yesterday.

The urge to search the remainder of this hideout seized her. After all, she rationalized, her knee didn't hurt — well, not too much, surely not any more than one would expect from a wounded knee that had been walked on all day. They couldn't be in any immediate danger, could they? Just how reliable was this ache?

A whistle of ascending notes sounded from the nearby woods, Chiumbo's signal. Someone was coming up the trail. Jade turned off her light and slipped to the opening, keeping as close to the wall of ivory as possible. A quick peek out the opening showed her the way was still clear. She sprinted the short distance to the trees and crouched down, bow in hand.

Chiumbo pointed down the trail, and made walking motions with his fingers. Jade listened. She heard a few voices in the distance, one laughing. She slid the bow around her shoulders and let it rest across her back against her pack. Then she and Chiumbo gathered up the rifles and slipped farther back into the woods, keeping in the shadows.

The need for secrecy overrode Jade's desire to see the poachers. If the raiders caught her and Chiumbo near their cache, they would be killed or sold, neither of which Beverly would approve of. Chiumbo set a silent but steady pace through the forest, and Jade followed. Both of them were in a highly vulnerable position with their arms full of rifles. The irony of being killed with a stack of empty rifles in her arms and a loaded one on her back wouldn't have been wasted on Jade. She nudged Chiumbo from behind and the two hastened their steps.

As they headed around to the more gently sloped northern side, the entire forest became riddled with game trails, some nearly four feet wide. Within a half hour of leaving the cache, they happened upon one that led in the general direction they wanted to go. On the wider trail, the pair could make faster time. Once Jade felt sufficiently far from the raiders, she called a brief halt.

'We need to get back onto their original trail, Chiumbo. The one we followed to the cache. Otherwise, I can't find that hollow tree.'

He nodded just as a groaning creak came from ahead of them, followed by a sharp snap that cracked like a .22 rifle. Jade heard the deep rumbling of gigantic bowels.

'There's an elephant feeding up ahead,' she whispered. 'Another reason to get off this trail.' She wanted to watch the elephant, to pretend nothing else was happening, but the load of rifles bearing down in her arms told her otherwise. *The hell with it.* She set the rifles on the side of the trail, took her camera out of her pack, and crept forward, eager to catch a glimpse of one of the forest giants.

A slight breeze wafted towards her, and Jade caught the strong, acrid scent of elephant. She knew not to trust the breeze, however. In the trees, it took strange eddies and swirls, so it might double back on her and carry her own scent to the beast. She hugged the right side of the trail, ready to duck behind a tree if necessary. A low, hollow rumble, almost soothing in nature, rolled from just ahead, and a higher-pitched whistling squeak answered. *A calf and mother!*

Jade peeked around a tree trunk just as the mother reared up and braced her front feet against the base of a slender olive tree. Her sinuous trunk stretched skyward towards the upper heights and wrapped around one of the fresher, silver-green boughs. Then she pulled the branch towards her until the entire tree groaned and bent downward. At her feet, the calf bounced and extended its own puny trunk up as though it could assist its mother. Jade focused as quickly as possible and took the picture.

The branch snapped with a sharp crack that echoed off the surrounding trees. Mother and branch dropped to the ground, barely making a sound on the soft forest litter. The baby tugged eagerly at the newest and most tender leaves while its mother rubbed her trunk gently across the calf's back. Jade was advancing the roll of film when the breeze shifted.

The female's trunk went up and reached forward, catching Jade's scent. She extended her ears straight out to the sides, a signal that Jade knew meant an imminent charge. Her baby, picking up on its mother's agitation, started to

147

fan its own tinier ears and trumpet, with a high-pitched squeal like a potato whistle. But the cow didn't attack. Whether she lost Jade's scent or became distracted by her baby's antics, the cow pulled her ears back against her head and lowered her trunk to smack her calf to move behind her.

Knowing elephants have poor vision, Jade took advantage of the mother's preoccupation with her young to duck behind the tree again, hoping the mother wouldn't charge what she couldn't see. Step by step, Jade eased back farther from the trail until, once again, the capricious, twisting air currents wafted the elephant's odor to her.

Safe. Something touched her on the left shoulder, and she jumped a foot in the air.

'Chiumbo, it's you. You gave me a fright.'

'This way, Simba Jike,' he whispered, and nodded into the forest. 'I found our trail.'

He had all the rifles cradled in his arms, and Jade relieved him of six as soon as she put her camera back in the pack. Then, as she prepared to follow him into the woods, she looked up the trail to where she'd left the mother elephant and her calf. She could just make out the mother's massive sides and something else. A slender figure stood beside the elephant cow. Jade blinked in disbelief. *Boguli?*

Chiumbo hissed at her to follow quickly. She turned to acknowledge his call, and when she glanced back, the elephant and her calf had moved on. Jade could see no sign of Boguli and wondered if she'd merely imagined him. She took a deep breath, hefted the rifles, and plunged after Chiumbo into the trees.

After another ten minutes of dodging low branches, they emerged beside the poachers' trail close to where they had set the false snare.

'Not much farther now,' Jade said. 'We can stash these and get to the tree blind before it turns dark.'

They skirted the false snare and the real trap, then glimpsed the ancient, regrown path to the hollow fig. Once at the tree, they stacked the rifles inside and covered them with brush. Exhausted, Jade leaned against the fig and inhaled deeply, filling her nostrils with the heady scent of forest litter and humus. She handed a canteen to Chiumbo and took one for herself, drinking deeply. Her stomach rumbled, and she wished they'd brought some of that dried fruit with them.

Jade stretched out her right arm, palm facing her, with the bottom of her pinkie finger resting just on the western horizon. Using her left hand, she positioned two more fingers on top of her right palm until she had filled the gap between the horizon and the sun's bottom. 'Six fingers at about fifteen minutes a finger,' she calculated. 'I estimate we have no more than an hour and a half of daylight left. Probably less once we hit the heavy cover again. We'd better head for the tree blind while we have light.' *And*, she thought as she rubbed her tired calf muscles, *while I still have some energy left in my legs*.

They had started back up to the original trail when they surprised one of the poachers inspecting the snare.

11

There are some dangerous specimens of
wildlife to watch out for and the leopard
ranks as one of them, especially if it feels
cornered. But you should always remember
that the most deadly animals of all are the
ones you didn't see: the ones stalking you.
— The Traveler

'Stop!' She punctuated her order with the
metallic clacking of the Winchester's lever action.
This man might or might not understand
English, but Jade knew that anyone would
recognize the sound of an order being barked
and a weapon to back it up.

The man rose slowly from his stoop, like a
cobra lifting its head in preparation to strike,
and faced them, his rifle hanging loosely in his
right hand, muzzle down. He glanced first at
Chiumbo, who held the panga, then turned his
eyes to Jade. She could read his assessment of
the danger in his slowly spreading grin. Clearly
he didn't think either of them a match for him.

The poacher wore a torn, cast-off military
jacket, unbuttoned over equally worn shorts.
Leather sandals clad his feet. His chest lay bare,
but a nearly full cartridge belt girded his
stomach. She knew that he'd try to distract her

with a gesture, a smile, something to catch her off guard so he could shoot. For that reason, Jade kept her eyes on the hand holding the rifle while she watched the rest of the man with more peripheral vision. He raised his arms slowly, stretching them out as if in greeting, and spoke to her in halting English.

'Greetings, and blessings, lady.' He took two steps towards her. Jade shouldered her rifle and aimed down the barrel. From the side she saw Chiumbo step forward, tensed to spring.

'Stay where you are. Drop your rifle,' she commanded.

The man's grin widened, but he kept his weapon. 'It is no loaded, lady. See? I show you.'

He raised the barrel and pivoted it towards Chiumbo's chest. The action looked almost casual, finger lightly resting beside the trigger, left hand empty. But Jade knew enough men who could shoot from the hip, and at this range, a shot anywhere in the upper body would prove fatal to Chiumbo.

She fired.

In the instant that Jade's shot blasted the rifle from the Abyssinian's hand, Chiumbo leaped forward and grabbed the poacher's left arm. He twisted it behind the man's back as he held his panga to the poacher's throat. The man shrieked in pain, blood dripping from his right hand where Jade had shot him.

'I told you to drop your weapon.' She stooped and picked up the rifle, a Mauser just like the ones they'd seen at the cache, and snapped it open. It was most definitely loaded. 'You lied to me.'

151

'It is not good to lie to Simba Jike,' hissed Chiumbo in the man's ear. The poacher wriggled, but Chiumbo took a tighter grip and held the wickedly sharp knife closer to the man's throat. A tiny thread of blood dribbled down his neck. 'Shall I kill him?'

'No, Chiumbo.' She lowered her rifle. 'I think this man might make a fine hostage.' She picked up the Abyssinian's rifle, set it against a tree, and shouldered her own. Then she retrieved the rope they'd used to make the false snare.

'We'll tie his hands behind him and take him back with us. The command at Isiolo will have questions for him.'

The captured man's black eyes widened at Jade's suggestion as though Chiumbo's threat to execute him was more desirable than to be taken prisoner. The Abyssinian began to protest vehemently as Chiumbo grabbed his bloody right hand and twisted it around to join the left.

'Let me go. Keep the rifle. I can give you gold. White women like gold. Do not take me prisoner. He will kill me like he did the soldier. My death on your hands, lady,' he babbled before adding in a louder voice, 'I will not talk!'

'Oh, be quiet,' snarled Jade. She lashed his wrists together as she would two sticks, then frapped the line to tighten the bindings before knotting the ends.

'Let me go and you will be rich.' The man raised his voice and shouted, 'I will not talk! I will not talk!' He turned back to Jade and hissed, 'Do not look to Isiolo to protect you.'

Jade shoved her handkerchief into the man's

mouth to shut him up. 'I told you to be quiet,' she said. 'Now get moving.' She held the end of the rope in her left hand and gave the prisoner a slight shove to start him walking. He managed one step before a bullet plowed through his skull.

Jade had heard a sharp clap when the rifle bullet struck. Attuned to gunfire during the war, Jade reacted instinctively. Time seemed to slow, and a split second later, she heard the distant crack of a rifle reach her ears. Her mind automatically began to work the math, estimating time lapse between the bullet's sonic clap and the rifle's report, as her body dropped to safety on the ground and rolled off the trail and into the trees.

Three hundred yards.

She saw the captured man halt in midstep, eyes wide in surprise. He stood on one leg for just a moment before he tumbled onto his face, blood pouring from one side of his head.

'Chiumbo!' she heard herself shout, but her headman had paused only long enough to see that Jade was unhurt before ducking into cover himself. In a moment, he was beside her. 'Are you all right?' she asked.

He nodded. 'We cannot stay here, Simba Jike,' he whispered. 'The hunter will kill us next. He will not miss again.'

'I'm not sure he did miss,' Jade whispered back. From her ground-level hiding place she could clearly see the dead poacher's head. The entry wound made a clean, neat hole directly into the brain, a precision shot. The exit wound was small as well, indicating that the bullet used

153

had a full metal jacket, rather than a soft lead nose. *Military issue?* No, this person hadn't missed.

She began to understand why the poacher had shouted his last statement. He wasn't trying to tell her that his capture would be useless; he wanted to convince his executioner. Someone lying in wait who didn't want him to talk to the authorities. But talk about what? Their hideout location? The guns? Maybe what they planned to do with those guns? What was so critical that it merited the man's death? And what was all that blather about white women loving gold?

Jade touched Chiumbo's arm lightly, and they slid backward, deeper into the brush, keeping an ear tuned all the while for the sound of someone stalking them. After another ten minutes of silence, she decided it was safe enough to risk moving again and slowly rose into a crouch. In this position they alternated padding through the forest and pausing to check for pursuit. Neither spoke again until they had covered most of the distance to the tree blind. Only later did she remember the captured Mauser she'd left standing against a tree.

As night fell, the forest around them came alive with the noise of animals feeding, calling, and fleeing. Jade heard something large stumble off to her left, perhaps a buffalo startled from its nap. *As long as it went in the other direction.*

'It's too dark to continue on to camp, Chiumbo, too risky.'

'You stay in the tree house, Simba Jike,' suggested Chiumbo. 'I will go ahead to get help

154

from Bwana Dunbury.'

Jade shook her head. 'No. That's even riskier. We planned to stay in the blind overnight to begin with, so no one is expecting us back at camp. Getting back tonight will only panic everyone, and Lady Dunbury doesn't need to be panicked.'

Chiumbo eyed her thoughtfully, pursing his lips. 'The new bwana, the stone feather man, he will not be happy, I think, when he hears about this.'

Jade sniffed and adjusted both her Winchester and the bow. 'What he thinks is not important. Come on. I'm famished and exhausted.'

Chiumbo smiled, but said nothing in reply. Jade pulled out her flashlight and panned it across the area to get her bearings. A pair of eyes reflected back at her from the brush, but they were too small and low to the ground to belong to a serious predator. A rhino snorted somewhere to the left and the eyes disappeared into the brush, followed by the bristling rattle of quills. *Porcupine*.

'This way,' she said. They found the elephant trail to the blind and hurried the last mile there. Jade felt her legs become gelatinous from stress and overexertion, but her knee didn't ache. As long as it didn't hurt, she felt secure. Danger might lurk all around them, but none was imminent.

They reached the large red stinkwood tree that held the upraised blind, and Jade tugged on a creeper vine. It fell in her hands and brought down a makeshift rope ladder constructed of a series of figure eight knots. Chiumbo insisted on going up first to make certain everything was safe before Jade followed. Once up on the planks, they pulled the rope ladder up after them and collapsed, too exhausted to move.

She might have lain there for good, but a few minutes of the pack, bow, and rifle biting into her back roused her enough to sit up and unburden herself. She also relocated the leather pouch from her trouser pocket to her pack. She drained her canteen as Chiumbo did the same to his; then they attacked their stock of dried fruit and jerky. If the meal didn't excite the palate, it at least quieted their hunger.

'We should take turns on watch,' Jade said. 'I'll go first. I doubt I could sleep right now anyway.'

Chiumbo made himself comfortable against the trunk, gripped his panga, folded his arms across his chest, and closed his eyes. In a matter of moments Jade heard his slow, steady breathing. She cradled her Winchester and took comfort in its presence. It might have been night, but the forest was alive with a cacophony of sounds. She heard either a rhino or a buffalo snort, a leopard cough, and various night birds hoot and scream. Once she even distinguished the deep huffing call of a male lion announcing his presence several miles away.

Over all these noises lay the incessant sounds of elephants feeding through the night. The groans of the trees resembled everything from a wounded animal's cry to the creaking of old floorboards. Sharp, cracking reports snapped from all around and reverberated in the cool night air. Once again Jade reminded herself that it wasn't what she heard that she needed to fear. It was what she didn't hear.

The half-moon rose several hours later above the forest canopy and spilled its iridescent glow over the leaves. Some of it found breaks in the foliage and lit patches of the forest floor below. The dust and litter of the elephant trail glowed in a cool green light as though illuminated from within rather than from above. *Some sort of luminescence*, Jade thought. She vaguely recalled seeing something like that at night on an ocean voyage. A passenger, a scientist by profession, had told her it had something to do with microscopic organisms and chemical reactions. *Most curious.*

Jade studied the cool, patchy glow and, in an attempt to keep herself awake, recollected various lores and myths concerning fairy lights. No wonder people came up with such tales. There was certainly something mesmerizing and hypnotic about the soft greenish white glow to stir the imagination.

Something moved just at the edge of Jade's peripheral vision. A shadow? A shape? She shifted position and tried for a better view. Nothing. Then she saw it again, briefly, a suggestion of a human form standing like a sentinel at the base of the tree, weaving slightly from side to side.

Chiumbo touched her shoulder, and Jade jerked around, startled. The headman smiled and pointed to her, then put his hand aside his cheek, indicating that it was her turn to sleep. Jade nodded, but stole one more look at the tree's base. The vision was gone.

She set her rifle beside her and nestled into the crook of a tree limb. Exhaustion draped over her like a blanket, and she fought one last time for the clarity of mind to think. All reason told her she was wrong, but she could have sworn she'd seen old Boguli standing guard below them.

12

Several African peoples make use of the pre-cious water available from springs at the base of the mountain, including the nomadic Boran and Rendille tribes, who bring their camels and livestock through the deserts. There are even a series of perma-nent wells in the vicinity and the joyfulness with which the people haul up the water has resulted in the name 'singing wells.'
— The Traveler

'Then Chiumbo and I came back to camp at first light,' Jade finished her terse narrative, and studied her companions' reactions. Beverly sat with pursed lips and stared above Jade into the trees. Avery, next to his wife, examined his hands. Jelani lounged against Biscuit and seemed not to have even paid attention. Sam tipped his chair back onto two legs and watched Jade with the same studious expression that she gave to the others. She ignored him. It was Bev's silence that worried her. Beverly was not one to hold her feelings in reserve. Avery spoke first.

'You didn't see who fired that shot?'

Jade shook her head. 'If he had a telescopic sight, he didn't have to be close.'

'But he *might* have been shooting at you,' Avery added.

Again, Jade shook her head. 'The poacher stepped forward and the bullet cut right through his head. Chiumbo was a few yards ahead of him, and I was two steps behind. Hard to imagine someone being that bad of a shot yet managing a clean kill like that.'

Avery looked first at Sam, who shrugged, then at Beverly, who continued to stare above Jade's head. He tried a different line of questioning. 'This old Boguli fellow, might he be one of the local Rendille or Boran natives?'

'He didn't dress like them.'

'He could have been a Merille from Lake Rudolf,' suggested Avery.

Jade rested her forearms on her legs and leaned forward. 'Now, why would a Merille native help me? From what I understand, old Emperor Menelik used to supply them with arms. They ought to be on the side of the Abyssinians, not on mine.'

'Maybe with Menelik dead, they are vying for power amongst themselves,' said Avery. 'This old man, he could be backing someone else. Didn't Smythe tell us that the local warlords change power after an emperor dies?'

Sam dropped the front half of his chair down and spoke up. 'But Menelik's been dead since 1913. Right now his daughter Empress Zawditu rules, with her cousin Ras Tafari Makonnen named as regent. They ran out Emperor Lij Yasu in 1916 for his Muslim tendencies. In other words, the new regime is set in place, at least

160

since 1917. There shouldn't still be all this jockeying for power in the outer regions.'

'Maybe the outer regions don't get news quickly,' Avery said. 'Or maybe they were that last emperor Yasu's main backers. That would explain why they're slow to come around to the new empress and her cousin.'

Sam shrugged. 'What language did this Boguli speak?'

Jade sat up as though suddenly jolted. 'You know, I don't remember.'

'You don't remember?' said Sam and Avery in unison. They looked at each other, eyes wide, mouths agape.

'I think you left quite a bit out of your little story,' snapped Beverly. The sharp edge to her voice startled Jade. Beverly usually reacted with a joke, sarcastic or otherwise.

'I told you everything that happened.'

'Like hell you did!' Beverly stuck out her chin and glared at Jade. 'You don't remember what language this mysterious man spoke?' She scoffed in disbelief. 'And you left out why you set off on such a fool escapade to begin with.' She held up Jade's original note and read it. ' "I am going with Chiumbo to take night shots." ' Beverly wadded up the paper and flung it aside. 'Night shots? You lied to me! This is not some Girl Guides' adventure, Jade.'

For once Jade flinched under Beverly's glaring eyes. 'I'm sorry, Bev. I didn't mean to upset you. I know this isn't a game. Blaney Percival made it quite clear that these poachers mean business.'

'But,' retorted Beverly, 'he didn't ask you to

161

stop them single-handedly. Why,' she continued before Jade could interject, 'do you *always* think that you've been commissioned to go charging off to save the day yourself?'

'I don't always go — ' began Jade. She retreated farther back in her seat.

'Yes, you do!' cut in Beverly. 'At Compiègne, in Tsavo, and now here.' Tears formed in her eyes, turning the normally soft blue orbs into a living replica of the Mediterranean Sea. 'We *do* worry about you, in case you didn't notice.'

Jade put her head down, partly for feelings of guilt and partly out of embarrassment. 'I'm sorry, Bev. I didn't realize you were so worried.'

'Stupid Gypsy,' Bev muttered as she hunkered over and hugged herself. 'You should know we love you and care about you. No wonder your mother sent you away. She probably couldn't stand worrying about you chasing mountain cats and desperadoes anymore.'

Jade saw her chance to stop this interrogation and simultaneously lighten her friend's mood, which, she presumed, was mostly the result of newly blossoming motherhood. 'But that's not why my mother sent me to London, Bev. I started to tell you this before. It was all the fault of that lovesick bull elk. You see, after the elk kicked in the fence and the pony escaped, we sent the dog to herd it back, but Scout — that's the dog — he found the neighbor's Newfoundland instead. She was in heat and — '

'Perhaps this is not the best time, Jade,' advised Avery as he noted his wife's increasingly dark expression.

Jade didn't pay him any heed. 'But we took the puppy, and named it Kaloff — '

'Is that Russian?' asked Sam.

'No, it's a joke. You know, as in Kaloff the dog?'

Sam laughed. 'Oh! Call off the dog. Very good.'

'Right. Well, Kaloff was not very bright, you see, and — ' Beverly jumped up and shouted, 'I don't want to hear about any stupid elk, or pony, or your silly dog!' A tear rolled down her cheek. 'I want you to take this seriously, Jade.'

Jade reared back in her seat, mouth open in shock. She'd never seen Beverly so distraught and she'd certainly never borne the brunt of her wrath.

Avery took his wife by the arms and gently pulled her back into her seat while he murmured soft, placating nonsense. 'There, there, my dear. You mustn't get overwrought. It's not good for you.'

'Or for the baby,' said Jade. Beverly's and Avery's heads both jerked up simultaneously. 'I figured it out myself,' Jade added when the couple began to give accusatory looks at each other. 'No one told me.'

'But how did you guess?' asked Avery. 'Beverly only just told me last evening.'

Jade ticked off the reasons on her fingers. 'Bev's been eating like a starving wolf, she's indisposed each morning, and she's extremely emotional. Bev doesn't generally get emotional,' she explained. 'That's actually the clue that cinched it for me. Heaven knows we've all seen

163

enough gore recently to turn our stomachs, and I've seen Bev bolt down her food *lots* of times.' She held up her hands defensively. 'Don't worry, Bev. Your secret's safe with me. I won't tell anyone.' She turned towards Sam, who still sat quietly, studying the situation. 'You can keep a secret, can't you, Sam?'

He nodded. 'Certainly.' He looked around at the surrounding forest. 'Who would I tell? Of course, in about eight or nine months, the secret will be out anyway, literally.'

Beverly was now sufficiently riled to regain her normal composure. 'Ooooh! Just see if I make either of you two jokers godparents.' She removed her hat and patted her short corn silk curls. 'But I am serious, Jade,' she said as she replaced her hat. 'You go looking for trouble. I swear, you need a keeper.'

Jade ignored the last comment, as it was one that Bev had made before. 'The main point is this: Chiumbo and I found their cache of ivory, weapons, *and* money.' She jumped up from her seat. 'That reminds me, I haven't actually looked at the money yet.'

Avery's eyes widened. 'You didn't hide it with the rifles?'

She didn't bother to reply, since the answer was obvious. Instead, she darted to her tent and retrieved the knapsack by the door. From inside she extracted the leather pouch and carried it back to her companions. 'Let's see what they're using to buy arms with.'

She undid the knot, tugged open the pouch, and spilled the contents into her left hand. She expected to find an assortment of Abyssinian coins, some silver talaris mixed in with a birr, a bessa, or a Mehalek, perhaps even a stray Maria Theresa thaler. She was mistaken. In her hand lay a dozen solid-gold coins bearing a charging elephant on one side and a crowned eagle on the other.

'Tabora pounds,' she whispered. Avery jumped from his chair and snatched a coin from her hand. The others quickly followed suit, eager to see the valued coin of former German East Africa.

'Nineteen sixteen,' said Sam, reading the date. 'Rather a last-ditch effort, don't you think, considering things weren't going all that well for them there? Still, even with the demise of 'Deutsch Ostafrika,'' he said as he turned the coin in his hand and read the flashing inscription, 'these must still be very valuable. If nothing else, for the gold.'

Avery studied the coin's elephant, trunk upraised as it charged forward in front of a mountain scene. 'Rather ironic to think that a coin bearing an elephant is being used to buy weapons to kill the beasts.'

'I doubt that's what these weapons are for,' said Jade. She didn't bother to look up and see everyone's reaction. 'Remember, these aren't express rifles or anything powerful enough to take down an elephant, at least not without heavily sedating it first so the shooter could get right next to it. I think these are being amassed to kill people.'

'Do you mean form an armed raid here in the

northern frontier?' asked Avery.

Jade shook her head. 'I have no idea. They may plan on taking them home and selling them to the highest bidder. Or maybe they plan to wage a war in one of their territories.'

'Could they be selling them down here to someone?' asked Sam. 'I mean, we assume they've purchased them and this gold is all they have left from the bargain. Perhaps they plan to sell them to our friendly neighborhood Germans. Are they from East Africa?'

Jade shrugged. 'Don't know. They say they've never been to Africa before. Chiumbo didn't recognize any of them, but then he wouldn't have seen every German in East Africa.'

'No wonder he had such a venomous look on his face when I walked in on your little party the other day,' said Sam. 'He's from there himself.'

'Right,' agreed Jade. 'From what he told me, he's looking for two men in particular. One, believe it or not, was a Brit named Prince. The other was one of his German lieutenants.'

'Well, he won't find Prince,' said Avery. 'The man got shot in the war. Ironically enough, he was fighting against England and died at the hands of a true British soldier.'

'How do you know that?' asked Beverly.

Avery shrugged. 'I'm not Lord Dunbury for nothing, my dear. I heard many tales after the war before we came out here.'

'I don't know who's buying and who's selling, but these are German-make rifles,' said Jade. 'My bet is that our friends in Harry's camp are selling them to the Abyssinians. For all we know,

Harry may be in on it.'

'And the Abyssinians just happen to be paying with German currency?' asked Sam. He sounded skeptical. 'Maybe you should leave this to the Brits and the local King's African Rifles.'

'Fine,' said Jade. 'I can make a map for you, Bev, and Avery to take back to Isiolo or Archer's Post to get some reinforcements for Smythe. You could go to Kampia Tembo water hole and catch the commissioner there. By the way, has our runner come back yet?'

Avery shook his head no. 'He may have had to travel as far as Isiolo to find an official.'

'I notice,' Beverly said, her tone as close to a growl as her soprano voice could make, 'that you don't seem to plan on going with us.'

'If we all leave, they may get away before anyone can take them into custody. But if I stay here, maybe I can find some evidence identifying the gunrunners. Someone needs to tell the officials what's happening here, and take Jelani to safety. If Smythe comes back without knowing the extent of their armory, many more men may die like the poor askari.'

Jelani, who'd kept silent during the discussion, sat bolt upright on the ground. 'I am not leaving you, Simba Jike, or Biscuit. I can fight these bad men. I'm not afraid.'

Jade smiled at the boy's bravery. 'I know you are not afraid, Jelani. But I am afraid for Biscuit. He keeps getting loose. What if the poachers tried to take him? And if I send him away, I need to send you so that someone can take care of him.'

'But who will keep you safe?' asked the boy.

Sam cleared his throat and shifted in his seat. 'I believe I could guard Miss Simba Jike,' he said. Jade turned and fixed her green eyes on him. Sam ignored her and added, 'Um, along with Chiumbo, of course.'

'I don't need a keeper,' Jade snapped.

'Oh, honestly!' Beverly replied. 'You are the most exasperating person I've ever met, Jade. Avery and I are British citizens in a British colony, so I don't see that any of us is in immediate danger, at least as long as we can keep *you* from antagonizing them. You are the problem, Jade, and I'm not going unless you go, too.' She held up her hand to forestall Jade's forthcoming denial. 'Now, do try and tell us something more about this Boguli person. He's one man who surely has seen something of use to us.'

Jade thought for a moment, searching for any bit of information that she'd overlooked. 'He knew my name. Not my real name, my Swahili name.'

'Most curious,' exclaimed Avery. 'Perhaps he is an old Kikuyu who came up from Nairobi?'

'No,' replied Jade. 'He knows the area too well. He said he remembered that ancient-looking trail and tree from following the elephant herds in his youth.'

'Maybe he's all that's left of some old tribe in the area,' suggested Sam. 'If that's true, he could hold a personal grudge against the Abyssinians. They may have been instrumental in eradicating his people.' He straightened his good leg and

168

leaned forward. 'He could be very useful to us.' He nodded to Jade. 'Do you think you could find him again?'

'Again? I didn't find him the first time. He found me.' She shook her head in amazement. 'The man made less noise than an owl on the hunt.'

'Maybe he will look for you again,' Jelani's young voice piped up from their feet, where he once again rested against Biscuit. 'We could go back to the hollow tree and wait for him.'

The 'we' was not lost on Jade. 'That is a good idea, Jelani. *I* will either return to that part of the mountain tomorrow and look for the old man or find him near the elephant herds. But,' she added with a smile, '*you* will not come with me.'

Jelani thrust out his lower lip in a universally recognized pout. Before he could protest, Beverly came to Jade's rescue. 'Jelani, I need you to stay here with me and help me make a new fishing pole. My other one broke.'

Jade knew there hadn't been any place to fish in since they'd left the Guaso Nyero River, and Jelani surely knew that, too. She doubted that Beverly even owned a fishing pole, but she was fairly certain that at least one of Avery's would show up snapped by tomorrow morning. She appreciated Bev's intervention. Still, Jade did feel a growing anxiety about the others' safety.

'I would still really prefer that the rest of you left,' Jade said. 'If the poachers find out some of their guns were stolen, they might demand them back.'

'As I said before, I'm not leaving without you,

169

Jade.' Beverly's normally melodious voice hissed.

'That's blackmail, Bev,' said Jade. Her friend just smiled.

'Finding this Boguli is a good idea,' interjected Avery. 'He probably won't trust any of us, but he seems to trust you, Jade. Perhaps you can convince him to return to camp with you. Someone should go with you, though.' He looked sideways at Sam.

Jade saw the silent appeal to the American pilot. 'Chiumbo will be with me again,' she said. 'I'm sure Sam has his own business to attend to. Something to film, perhaps? After all, that is why he came here, isn't it?'

'Actually, I spent most of the day filming the Dunburys at home on safari, and I even went back out to run footage of that old dead bull. Thought I could turn this into a picture about the plight of the elephants. So, you see, I'm available at the moment.' He flashed a winsome, boyish grin that showed a lot of white teeth. 'I bet if you got to know me, you might find me an all-round swell fellow. What do you say?'

'I'd say you don't have a leg to stand on. I'm going with Chiumbo to find Boguli.' She stood up and brushed off her trousers.

'Now?' cried Beverly. 'You just got back from one escapade and already you're going headlong into another?'

'The morning is barely begun. I can't waste an entire day, Bev.' Jade took two steps towards her tent before turning back to Sam. 'Actually, you could be very helpful, now that I think about it.'

Sam stood at attention like a soldier awaiting

orders. 'Sam Featherstone at your service, ma'am. When do we start?'

'*We* don't. I have a different mission in mind for you. A reconnaissance run, if you will. I'd really like to gather more information on our German friends. Considering how two of them at least are fanatical about motion pictures, you should be well received. You could offer to film *them* for your safari movie. Perhaps you could take Jelani with you. He's very good at infiltration.'

'I should think most of the camp would be off hunting,' Sam said.

'Exactly,' replied Jade. 'But the ladies might still be in camp, ready to show you around while you film them.' She winked. 'Who knows what interesting things you might capture?'

13

The antiquity of these volcanoes is evidenced by the wealth of life on Marsabit. Over eons, hardened lava gave birth to soil, which nourished grasses, which fed animals. Both plants and animals repaid and replenished the soil by providing it with their wastes and, eventually, themselves. In other words, the soil's current richness owes itself to the three Ds: death, decay, and dung.

— The Traveler

'Whoa! Slow down, partner,' said Sam as Jelani trotted ahead with Biscuit. 'I can walk quickly, but running's not in the cards. Besides,' he added, pointing to the porter walking behind him with the camera and tripod, 'I think Nasero would like it if we slowed down.'

Jelani stopped and waited, frowning in obvious irritation. He held the cheetah's lead, and the big cat paced back and forth as if he, too, was annoyed with their slow pace. 'You talk funny,' Jelani replied. 'I do not understand this running in the cards.'

'Oh, that's a sort of saying from my home. I guess you could say it means I have to work with what I have.'

'Oh,' said Jelani. He fell in step beside Sam

and watched the American walk.

Sam saw the boy's interest and decided he might as well explain. He wanted to win Jelani over for several reasons: one, he genuinely liked the boy, and two, Jade cared for him. 'I hurt my leg in the war,' he explained. 'Someone shot me.'

'Did you kill him?'

'No, I was in an airplane, and it was all I could do to land without crashing.' Sam looked down at the boy to see if he understood. 'Do you know about airplanes, Jelani?'

The boy nodded. 'Memsabu Jade and Memsabu Beverly and Bwana Avery showed me pictures. I think the airplanes are like motorcars that fly.'

'Very good. You understand a lot.'

Jelani shrugged. 'I do not understand why we are going to Bwana Harry's camp. We should be with Memsabu Jade, protecting her.'

Sam took a deep breath. *My sentiments exactly. Blasted fool's errand is what this is.* Well, he thought, maybe he was a fool at that. As a kid, he'd devoured tales of adventure, always wondering if he could have one of his own. It was a dream that hadn't seemed probable while he was working with his brothers on the family farm in Battle Ground, Indiana. Then, while studying engineering at Purdue, he saw his first airplane. He was hooked. What greater adventure could there be than flying? Soon after graduation, he'd heard about an air corps unit forming up in Texas to fight in the war, and Sam was there as fast as the train could take him.

Now, thanks to his injury, he might be

grounded for life. The thought had nearly crushed him until he'd decided on making films as a new means to seek out adventure. And just when he'd wondered about the success of that plan, Avery's package had come: the package containing a smudged carbon copy of a new book, *Stalking Death* by Madeline Thompson.

Sam had read it as he read all adventures, greedily devouring every page. By the middle, he found himself hopelessly in love with what he thought was a fictional character. But Avery and his wife swore the events in it were all true and invited him to come to Africa and meet the heroine. Meeting her, and the thought of all the wonderful wild animals and exotic people to film here, gave him fresh hope. Now here he was, and that seemed to be nowhere. *How the dickens does a pinioned pilot like me, who can't even run, much less soar, stand a chance with a woman like her?* He gritted his teeth together in a vow of determination. She wanted him to spy on the Germans, and by thunder, that's just what he'd do. *And what's more, I'll do a helluva job of it!*

'Our Simba Jike wants to know if these people are working with the poachers,' Sam explained. 'She hopes we can find that out. If they are, then knowing that will help protect her.'

Jelani gave him a sidewise look. 'Do you believe that?'

Sam laughed, shifted his rifle to his other hand, and clapped the boy on the back. 'No, but what Simba Jike wants, Simba Jike gets.'

They arrived at Harry's camp just before

174

eleven, as Otto von Gretchmar and his daughter sat down to a late breakfast. Sam sounded a hearty 'Hello!' at the *boma* gate before entering.

'Good morning,' he said, tipping his hat to the young woman. 'I'm Sam Featherstone.'

Otto von Gretchmar grunted. '*Ja*, I met you the other day. You talked about shooting down the planes.'

'Oh, that,' said Sam with a pshaw and a wave of his hand. 'Just trying to impress the lady, right?' He laughed and watched as the big banker relaxed and grinned. 'But I'm here to make a movie about safaris. I hoped I could film all of you in camp, but I see most everyone is gone.' He turned partway as if to leave.

Von Gretchmar jumped up, tipping his chair. 'But we are here. You will film us dining, *ja?* It will be a present for my little Mercedes. See? You will set up your camera there' — he pointed to a spot where his daughter would be in profile while he took center stage — 'and make the movie. Then I will bring my rifle and act like I go on the hunt.'

What a hypocritical old goat, thought Sam, pretending to do this for his daughter when von Gretchmar obviously wanted the camera on himself. He obliged the man and began cranking out yards of Mercedes sitting demurely eating while Otto ordered the poor cook's assistants around. *This is getting me nowhere.* A glance to the side showed Jelani, equally perturbed, sitting on the ground beside the cheetah.

As soon as von Gretchmar went to retrieve his favorite rifle, Mercedes stepped forward timidly and asked if Sam might film her walking outside the compound. 'I will pretend to hear something, *ja?* And then I will hurry to the gate. Then you will go outside and film me coming out?'

Sam agreed. He was surprised how well the girl understood playing to the camera. She seemed to have a natural intuition about how fast she could move and still have him follow her, and how to play out the drama of soundless acting. Before they relocated outside the gate, Mercedes asked Sam about going to America to become an actress. That was when von Gretchmar returned with his rifle.

'What *ist* this?' he demanded. 'Mercedes, you will sit down.'

'But, Papa,' she pleaded, 'Herr Featherstein is going to tell me how to be an actress. It is what I want above all.'

Her father let loose with a volley of German. Sam did his best to catch anything remotely recognizable, but beyond an oft-repeated '*nein,*' he couldn't glean anything. *Fat lot of good I'm doing here.* Then when Mercedes burst into tears and ran to her tent, Sam debated following her. He didn't need to. Jelani was on his feet in an instant, Biscuit at his heels. *Good lad!*

Sam turned his attention back to von Gretchmar to distract him. 'Young lady not feeling well today?' he asked in as innocent a voice as he could muster.

'Huh?' grunted von Gretchmar in surprise, as if he'd forgotten the American. 'Oh, *ja.* She has the upset stomach, I think.' He frowned and nodded slowly.

176

To Sam, it looked as though the man was only acting the part of a concerned father, and Sam pretended to believe it. 'I should still like to film you showing me your camp. Perhaps we could have you sitting in your tent, flaps back, examining your rifle?' Sam counted on the man's vanity to let him get a look inside at least one tent. He also needed to buy some time for Jelani. He hoped the young woman would welcome Jelani and Biscuit as potential comfort in her hour of distress. Von Gretchmar accepted the offer, and Sam hoisted his equipment and followed the man to his tent.

★ ★ ★

Jelani had spent the better part of the visit sitting on the ground, stroking the cheetah, who lolled next to him. *This is very foolish*, he had thought. *What was Simba Jike thinking, sending us here?* He had looked up and watched the antics in front of him. Did this new American man really think they were helping her by watching a silly man and woman eat? He shook his head and leaned against Biscuit.

Another thought popped into Jelani's head while the cheetah's purr rumbled under him. Bwana Featherstone liked Memsabu Jade. That was very clear. Jelani could see it in the way the man's eyes followed her. A prickling resentment nibbled away at his innards. He knew his jealousy had no basis in infatuation, but he felt bad about losing any of Jade's attention to a newcomer. Hadn't he been the one to welcome

177

her to his country? Hadn't he stood by Memsabu Jade's side when they killed the hyena, and hadn't he been there when the *mundu-mugo* gave her the name Simba Jike? He let loose a small snort of indignation. He should have been by her side now, protecting her.

The bad feeling took another twist. This Featherstone had been a warrior in the white man's big war. He had killed someone. This man had proved himself and had reason to think Memsabu Jade would smile at him. But Jelani knew he himself was not yet a real warrior. He worried about bringing shame to his aging mother and father. They had no other children, no sons except him to give them honor. Was he bringing shame to them? Still, the *mundu-mugo* had told him to go with Simba Jike and her friends and learn to read their words. Well, he had learned one thing. He learned how Tarzan killed when he needed to. Now, there was a warrior! If Jelani got the chance, he wouldn't hesitate to kill anyone who tried to hurt Memsabu Jade.

Just then the silly young woman started crying as if someone had beaten her. Maybe there was something he could do here? He would go to the woman's tent with Biscuit. She would want to pet the friendly animal to feel better. While she did, he would look in her tent. Jelani had no idea what to look for, but he'd seen the inside of enough white people's tents to notice if something seemed strange.

As he had jumped up to follow the woman, he had glanced at Bwana Featherstone's face. The man was smiling. This was a clever idea after all.

* * *

If anyone had asked her later why she decided to follow a newer, fresher elephant trail that morning, Jade couldn't have answered. She had intended only to set up a night-shot camera by a dust-bathing spot, then head straight towards the snare in hopes of finding Boguli again. But once she finished with the camera, she spied this fresher trail heading back south to the crater and had the urge to follow it.

For some inexplicable reason, she knew in her heart that Boguli wouldn't be at the snare. She sensed he hadn't been following the elephants when they'd met; he'd been following her. But if Boguli did still follow the elephants, perhaps he took this trail after them. Or maybe it was the sight of that gorgeous blue butterfly sitting calmly on a moist pile of elephant dung, drinking up the moisture, that she saw as a sign. Whatever her reasoning, she took the trail, pausing only long enough to sketch its location in her battered notebook.

It wound steadily upward, always seeking the easiest climb, but after an hour's trek, Jade reckoned she was reaching forty-five hundred feet at least. The air had cooled noticeably and the trees grew farther apart with less underbrush and more cedars. After a point, it became clear that the elephants didn't feed much on this trail, so she reasoned it must be one linking to the lake and to their favorite bathing grounds. Her pulse quickened, not from exertion, but from excitement. The lake was the one place she'd wanted

179

to be for the past several days, and the thought of so many elephants congregating in one spot tantalized her. After all, she still had a job to do for *The Traveler*.

'Perhaps it is good that we are not seeking the poachers today, Simba Jike,' said Chiumbo as if he read her thoughts. 'If they see we have been in their cave, they will be watching.'

Jade nodded. It seemed as good a rationalization as any. She added her own. 'I thought that old native I met might come up here to be by the elephants. He seems to follow them, and I want to talk with him again.'

By now the trail passed along a strip of trees that ran like a finger, bordering a patch of grassland on the downward side. Looking up, they could glimpse the summit. The line of trees ended at a grass-covered cliff and below them, shining in pristine splendor, lay the lake.

Jade felt her breath catch. 'My stars,' she whispered, 'it's so beautiful.'

Gigantic blue and white water lilies bobbed on the surface until the white lilies moved and exposed themselves for what they were, egrets. Herons, ducks, and coots swam and waded among elephants, dozens of beautiful elephants. A pair of yearling calves splashed at one end, much to the dismay of an elder who turned and swatted at them with her trunk before climbing out of her bath, a water lily stuck on her rump. Close to the shoreline stood a splendid bush, bursting with what appeared to be blue flowers. A duck dived past it, preparing to land, and the 'flowers' fluttered off the bush and landed elsewhere.

Chiumbo broke into Jade's tranquil thoughts. 'It is good there are no poachers up here.'

She sighed. 'Probably because the elephants stay in the water. If they shot them in there, they'd risk losing the ivory.' She looked over to the eastern shore and realized that the cache stood near the base under the protection of the volcano's rocks. No, she thought, she couldn't waste much time up here or there wouldn't be any elephants left to lounge in the protective lake. 'I don't see Boguli. Let's walk around the rim and see if we can spy on the poachers from up above.'

Grasses coated the crater's inner edge, the forest rising up towards the outer rim and falling away down the slopes. Jade and Chiumbo kept just to the tree line, ready to duck behind cover if necessary, as they wended halfway around the crater to the eastern side. Jade had hoped to find an overlook from which to spy down on the poachers' hideout below, but the treetops rising up from the slopes made that impossible.

'Blast!' she whispered. Immediately, the baboons that used these trees for a home started screeching. She remembered hearing them from the hideout and worried that even her whisper could carry down the slope. She motioned for Chiumbo to slip back and waited till they were not directly over the hideout before she spoke again.

'That was a wild-goose chase. We'll head back as soon as we have a bite to eat.'

By three o'clock, they were halfway back to camp when Jade saw Sam standing in the trail waiting for her, rifle in one hand, Biscuit's leash in the other. One of his own Wakamba men, Kalinde, stood near him with his movie camera and tripod.

'Sam! What in blue blazes are you doing here?'

Sam touched his hat brim with the hand holding the leash and grinned. 'Jade, Chiumbo, good afternoon to you, too.' Biscuit tugged at the leash in order to rub his head against Jade's legs. 'Best little tracker in the business,' Sam said, nodding at the cheetah. 'I never would have found you otherwise.'

'I suppose Beverly put you up to this?'

He shrugged noncommittally. 'She may have encouraged me a little, but the idea was my own.' He jerked his head back to the porter and the camera. 'After I got through with my assignment, I dropped off Jelani and Nasero, picked up Kalinde, and went looking for you. I thought you might show me something worth filming out here.'

She pointed back up the mountain. 'There is. A couple miles up that trail sits the most beautiful lake, and it's loaded with elephants.'

'Well, dang,' said Sam. 'I suppose it's too late to head back up there today, isn't it?'

Now it was Jade's turn to shrug. 'Up to you, I suppose.' She resumed walking on, passing the path to camp and heading towards her snare. Sam fell in beside her; his slight limp caused her to slow her pace. She stared at Sam. 'I'm amazed. How did you manage to leave Jelani back at camp?'

Sam pulled off his hat and ran a hand through

his hair. 'Wasn't easy — that's for sure. That boy is determined to go where you go. But Avery stepped in and claimed a need for his help. I think they went hunting.'

'Beverly must have been feeling all right if he was willing to leave her alone. So, did you find out anything of note this morning in Hascombe's camp?'

'Now, the fact that you didn't ask that straightaway tells me you never expected us to.' He watched her face, a big grin on his. When she finally smiled, he clapped his hands together. 'Aha! I knew it. You did send us on a fool's errand. Just for that, I shouldn't tell you.'

'I'm sorry,' said Jade. 'Really I am. I just hate it when Beverly thinks she needs to mother me and sends everyone else after me to play at babysitting. I'm a grown woman. I can take care of myself.'

'Amen to that,' murmured Sam. 'But to give my report, the answer to your question is an unqualified maybe. Hascombe wasn't there. Neither were most of the others. That old fellow, von something or other, was there along with his daughter. That's all.'

'Von Gretchmar,' said Jade. 'He's a banker.'

'He certainly looks and acts like someone who sits behind a desk and pompously orders everyone else around.' Sam puffed out his stomach and his cheeks and strutted along the trail like a bowlegged peacock. Behind them, Chiumbo and Kalinde laughed. 'The man bears a striking resemblance to a bloated walrus.'

Jade chuckled. She couldn't help it. Sam had a

natural gift for mimicry. 'But did you learn anything of use?' she asked again.

'Patience, Simba Jike.' He resumed his regular stride beside her. 'Jelani and I went over with good old Biscuit here in tow.' He nodded to the spotted cat, which walked in front of and a little between them. 'Thought maybe tagging along with the boy *and* the big kitty would make me look more innocent.'

'And you also figured, like I did, that they would pay no attention to an African boy, and someone might say something in front of him that they wouldn't in front of you. I told you, he's good at infiltration.'

Sam grinned, a wide row of teeth shining from under his thin mustache. 'It might have crossed my mind. He's clever. Sharp. Doesn't miss much, and,' he added with a sideways glance at Jade, 'he's absolutely devoted to you. Something I can understand and appreciate.' He grinned again. 'Hard not to be devoted to Miss Simba Jike.'

Jade scowled. 'Get on with your story.' Just then Biscuit grew impatient with their slow pace, slipped behind Jade, and butted her. She handed his leash to Chiumbo.

'I waltzed in there as friendly as a puppy dog. Well, maybe 'waltz' isn't the right word to use,' he added as he looked down at his game leg, 'and I hallooed the camp. Wouldn't want some sleepy Fritz to take a shot at me. The camera's what did the trick. You were right. They seemed fascinated by motion pictures. That little Mercedes certainly wanted to pose. She even asked me about America and becoming an actress, but Herr Papa didn't seem to approve. Scolded her roundly. My German is not very good beyond *Achtung* and *halt*, so I couldn't make out the actual words, but there was no mistaking the tenor of his voice.'

'What did she do?'

'She started crying and ran to her tent. But that Jelani, he went right over there with Biscuit.' Sam shook his head at the memory. 'I'd like to think that he just has a generous heart, but to be honest, I think he saw a chance to take a look around her tent.'

Jade grinned. 'And did he find anything?'

Sam reached into his side pocket and pulled something out. 'I'll let you be the judge of that.' He opened his hand and revealed a gold Tabora pound.

Jade gasped. 'This was in her tent?' In her head she heard the captured Abyssinian say that white women loved gold. Did he mean Mercedes?

Sam nodded. 'On the ground hidden in the shadows of the canvas, to be precise,' he said. 'I think it's too much of a coincidence to find one of those German East African coins lying about their camp, don't you?'

Jade nodded and handed the coin back to him. 'But was it hers, or her father's?'

'I was in Herr Papa's tent filming the old walrus to buy Jelani some time. I didn't see anything out of the ordinary there. Maybe it's from some gentleman who just happened to visit her tent?' suggested Sam. 'Perhaps Vogelsanger?'

'I hadn't thought of that.' She shook her head.

185

'He's a bit old for her, don't you think?'

'She may think so, but I doubt he does. Could be Papa bear is arranging an alliance through marriage. You know, banker and rich industrialist. But there's also that Mueller fellow. He may be dallying with or without his wife's knowledge.'

'Liesel. His wife's name is Liesel, and you may be right, although he doesn't appear to have much interest in anything.'

'And,' added Sam slowly, as if this was an afterthought that had just come to him, 'there's always Hascombe.'

'Harry?' exclaimed Jade. 'It's true he's a scoundrel, but I never figured him for allying himself with poachers.'

'Germans, yes? Poachers, no?' Sam asked in summary.

'The war's over, Sam,' Jade replied.

'Is it?'

Jade ignored this last question. 'Did you show the coin to Avery and Beverly?'

He shook his head. 'Not yet. Didn't want to rile up Beverly, and speaking of riling up Beverly, what was that story you were spinning this morning about that dog?'

'Oh, that. Nothing important. Why do you ask?'

'Avery is my friend, but I don't know his wife well. I thought maybe it would shed a little light on her.'

'Not really. I told Bev earlier that we met all because of a lovesick bull elk. It was after one of our cow ponies.'

'And the pony ran off and the dog went after it,' Sam prompted.

'Right, but the dog made a side trip.'

'I caught that much. That, and you somehow got a pup out of it that you named Kaloff. Very funny. I could use a good laugh about now. What happened after that?'

'I probably shouldn't tell this without Beverly around. She'll get mad if she finds out I explained it to you first,' Jade said.

Sam shrugged. 'Secret's safe with me.' He prompted her a bit more. 'You said the pup was part Newfoundland?'

'Right, but the father was a border collie. Kaloff was cute and big as a yearling black bear but not too bright. He never could quite get the idea of herding. He'd prefer to just pick up something in his mouth and haul it back.'

'And the sheep didn't like that, I suppose?'

'No, but he didn't restrict himself to sheep. I even trained him to fetch my tomcat, Rupert, but Kaloff liked toting carcasses, too. Maybe because they didn't fight back as much as the cat or the sheep. Once he brought back a *big* old dead raccoon. That thing was so bloated you could've played it for bagpipes.'

Sam winced. 'Ick.'

'That's about the size of it. So one day he . . . ' She stopped and listened. 'We've been talking too loudly,' she whispered. 'I hear voices.'

'Sounds like your friend Hascombe and some of his crew.'

'The question is, what else have they been doing besides hunting?'

Just then they heard a *whoosh* followed by a scream.

14

Every gof, or 'crater,' on Marsabit holds some water and consequently is well worth the effort to reach to see wildlife, but one lake in particular surpasses them all. Imagine a bowl of liquid turquoise, a mile across, adorned with blue water lilies and white egrets. Picture a mother elephant stepping into the shallows and coaxing her new baby to join her, spraying him with water, while older calves splash and cavort and still older, more sedate pachyderms lounge. Top this with soaring kites and eagles. This is Sokorte Guda.
— The Traveler

A series of strong invectives followed hot on the heels of the scream. Jade recognized the baritone voice as well as a few of the curses. After all, she'd heard them the previous year in Tsavo. She sprinted the short distance to her snare, then doubled over in laughter.

'Cut me down!' yelled Harry. 'Blast it! It's not funny, Jade!'

Harry hung by his heels two feet off the ground, swaying and spinning like a wobbly pendulum. His gun bearer stood tentatively nearby, studying the ropes for the best way to

188

ease him down without dropping him on his head. Farther back stood Claudia von Gretchmar, Vogelsanger, and the two Muellers, none of whom wanted to get in the way of Harry's fists.

'You're correct, Harry. It's not funny. It's hysterical.' Jade guffawed again and hugged herself as she doubled over in laughter.

'You've really got the hang of this tracking business, don't you, Hascombe?' said Sam.

'What the bloody blazes are you doing, Featherstone?' Harry roared when he spotted Sam placidly cranking his movie camera.

'I'm recording the dangers of safari life for posterity.'

Harry swore again in a rapid stream of curses that conscribed Americans, movie cameras, and Sam in particular to perdition. 'You can't make a film of this!' he bellowed as he spun around to face them again.

'Oh, don't worry yourself, old man. The sound doesn't record at all. No one will know what you're saying. Still suitable for family viewing, unless a few of the brighter kiddies can read lips.'

Jade whooped again. 'Hang on, Harry,' she said as she wiped a tear from her eyes. 'I'll help you down.'

'When you do, Jade, make sure you keep either your profile or face to the camera,' Sam directed. 'A pretty woman always makes the picture.'

'When I get down from here,' roared Harry, 'I'm going to break that bloody camera into bits if you don't stop filming now!

'You'd better stop, Sam,' said Jade. 'As long as Harry keeps swinging his fists around, I'm never going to get close enough to undo the knots.'

'Anything you say, Jade,' answered Sam. 'Watch the camera please, Kalinde,' he said as he limped past Harry. 'Let me help you, old man.' He grabbed a panga from one of Harry's porters and sliced right through the rope.

Harry dropped like a lead weight onto the ground, the impact forcing one last curse from his mouth. Jade hurried over to give him a hand up, and to try to keep him from taking a swing at Sam. She wondered if she'd have an easier time holding back an angry rhino. Sam's brows furrowed as well, as though he disapproved of her hands on Harry's broad shoulders. *Men!*

'Easy, Harry,' she said. 'Temper on safety, like you used to tell me, remember?'

Harry wrenched himself free and dusted off his clothes. 'Was this your doing, Jade?' he demanded, pointing to the snare.

Biscuit, impatient at standing so long, butted Jade again. 'Chiumbo, would you take the cat back to camp?' asked Jade. 'Jelani will end up coming for him otherwise.'

Chiumbo whistled to the cheetah before starting down the trail. Biscuit ran to him, seemingly glad for the chance to leave.

'Now why would I set a snare, Harry?' said Jade. 'I'm photographing wildlife, not hunting.'

'That's not an answer,' Harry growled. Some of his porters, burdened with two tusks, started to set down the ivory and take a break. Harry turned on them. 'Take that on back to camp,' he ordered. 'I'll catch up with you later.'

The men hefted the two four-foot tusks and

resumed their trek. Claudia von Gretchmar patted her forehead and sighed loudly. 'I am tired and hot, and about Mercedes I am worried. I do not want to wait for these' — she hesitated and searched for a word — 'pleasantries to end. I will with the ivory go.'

'What could happen to that child at camp to worry *you*?' asked Liesel, her voice edged with sarcasm. 'You have never worried about her before.' She made a scoffing chuckle. 'And her big, strong papa *ist* there to protect her.'

Claudia glared at Liesel, and Jade worried for a moment that the older woman was going to start ripping the younger one's hair out.

At the mention of Mercedes' name, Vogelsanger's brow furrowed. 'I will accompany you, Frau von Gretchmar,' he said. 'To protect her on the way to the camp,' he added to Harry. He nodded to the others and hastened after the porters.

Jade suddenly remembered the photo negative of a partially clothed Claudia in the arms of another man, an image she'd set aside as meaningless until now. Was Claudia having an affair with Vogelsanger? She'd have to get the negative out and study it again. Perhaps Beverly would recognize the man.

'Well, Jade? I'm waiting,' said Harry after the others had departed.

'Maybe *you* set it and forgot about it, Hascombe,' said Sam. He folded his arms across his chest and leaned against a tree. 'Or maybe *I* set it. Did you ever think of that? Or how about those poachers I've heard about?'

Jade shot a look at Sam that told him to put a sock in his mouth before he started any more trouble. Sam pretended to misunderstand.

'Did you need help there, Jade?' he asked. 'I can coil that rope for you.' He strolled over and took the rope from her hands, making certain that he held them for a moment and that Harry saw it.

He did. He also saw Jade's dark brows shoot up over her emerald green eyes in surprise at Sam's liberty. 'Good idea, Featherstone,' Harry said with a toothy grin at Jade. 'Wouldn't want those pretty hands to get rope burn, would we? I remember how soft they felt when we danced close together at the Muthaiga Club.'

Jade expected the two men to start butting heads together at any moment. *Good heavens! It's rutting season in the forest.* She decided to do her own head butting and attacked another topic. 'Run into any poachers out here yesterday, Harry?'

'Why yesterday?'

'Because someone shot at me again. Thought maybe you saw or heard something. Where were you and your people?' She looked at the Muellers. 'I don't see Otto von Gretchmar and Mercedes. Where's the rest of your group?'

'Is this an inquisition?' Harry snapped. 'Was it your intention to hang me from that blasted tree just so you could interrogate me?' He flexed his hands, clenching and releasing them.

Liesel Mueller patted Harry's tensed muscles and he jerked free. Next she sidled over to Sam and smiled. 'You are an American man, *ja*? I have not seen one before.' She ran her gaze slowly over him, as though she were inspecting a prototype, shifted her rifle to her left hand, and touched his biceps. 'Very nice muscles. Almost as strong as Herr Hascombe.'

Jade watched Liesel's husband to see how he took this display. If anything, he seemed amused by it. Jade wondered if Liesel knew something about yesterday's shooting and was doing her best to distract everyone, so she turned the questions back onto her. 'Frau Mueller, where are your friends? I don't see that pretty Miss Mercedes or her father here. Don't they like to hunt?'

The peroxide blonde slapped her rifle on her left shoulder and posed with her left hip shifted towards Sam and her right hand on her narrow waist. '*Mein Gott*, Mercedes walking? She would out here die.' She sniffed in disgust. 'She is only with us because her papa wishes it.'

'Fräulein Mercedes is not the same kind of woman as you are, Liesel,' said her husband, Heinrich. 'Nor is she brave like Fräulein del Cameron,' he added. 'Mercedes is like a hothouse flower that does not survive well outside of protected walls.'

Liesel's purring smile quickly turned into a scowl as her husband discussed Mercedes so familiarly and raised Jade to the level of a new rival.

Jade recognized the intended compliment towards her abilities. 'Thank you, Herr Mueller. I'm sure a sportsman such as yourself can appreciate the hazards to a delicate young lady.

I'm surprised her parents insisted on bringing her along with them.' She glanced at the trees as though she expected to see the elder von Gretchmar emerge from them. 'But then, he doesn't seem to be cut out for safari life, either. The last time I saw him out of camp, he looked as red as a beet.'

'Von Gretchmar only purchased one elephant license and he bagged his already,' said Harry with a snarl from behind her. 'He only stayed behind with Mercedes so his wife could tag along today.' He stepped in closer till he loomed next to her. 'I'm a patient man, Jade, but my patience is wearing thin.' His voice rose in pitch. 'Now, why all the questions? Especially,' he added, 'since you never answered *mine*.'

'I'm sorry, Harry,' Jade said, her voice dripping sweetness and her eyes wide with innocence. 'Did you ask me something?'

He stared down at her. 'Did you set that trap?' he roared.

'Back off, Hascombe,' said Sam as he hurried to Jade's side.

Harry glared at Sam. The two men were matched in height, but Harry clearly held the advantage on overall size. Jade heard Mueller say something in German about an amusing battle for dominance in the herd and heard Liesel's laugh follow.

Jade shoved Harry out of the way before the situation got out of hand. 'What if I did set the trap, Harry? No one told *you* to step in it.' She heard Sam chuckle beside her and wheeled on him. 'And I don't need anyone else to fight

194

my battles for me.' Sam reeled back a step.

Harry adjusted his hat and retrieved his rifle from the ground, where he'd dropped it when he was snared. 'I'm not sure who or what you were trying to catch, Jade, but if you did set this, then you're playing a dangerous game. One day, you're going to go too far and that pretty little head of yours is going to roll.'

'Is that a threat, Harry?' she called as Harry stomped off down the trail.

He turned, and said over his shoulder, 'Take it for a bit of advice from a friend.'

Mueller tipped his hat to Jade and nodded to Sam as he passed. Liesel ignored Jade entirely, winked at Sam, and sashayed after her husband. Jade watched them till they took the fork towards the north; then she turned back to her ruined snare and sighed.

'Why'd you cut the rope, Sam? I don't think I can reset this one.'

Sam collapsed his camera's tripod and handed the equipment back to his porter. 'Why in tarnation would you want to reset it, Jade? Did you ever stop to think that Beverly and, God forbid, Hascombe are both right?'

Jade turned and studied Sam, her head tipped to one side. 'You don't like Harry, do you?'

Sam blinked. 'Not particularly. But then neither, it seems, do you.'

'But I have reasons. You, on the other hand, just met him.' She continued to maintain eye contact, knowing that the one she scrutinized generally blinked first and looked away from her intense green eyes. 'I find that curious.'

Sam, as if to give lie to her expectations, didn't look away; he just smiled, folded his arms across his chest, and met her gaze. 'Call it first impressions. Now, what are your plans, Simba Jike?'

For the first time, Jade knew she might lose the staring match. She felt like her old tomcat, Rupert, in a back-arching standoff with another equally strong cat. To back down meant to lose face, to take the secondary rank. To continue meant a fight. *What would old Rupert do?* She needed the human equivalent of washing, something to break off the confrontation. 'Pass me the rope. I want to set a deadfall snare over there.' She pointed towards the tree where she'd stashed the rifles. Both she and Sam looked off in the new direction, thereby ending the stalemate equitably.

Sam retrieved the rope from where he'd hung it on a low branch and gave it to Jade. 'I'll help you.' He waved to the porter, still standing aside with his camera. 'Come on, Kalinde. Let's give the lady a hand.'

The three of them headed down the hill and, after a few false turns, located the hollow tree where Jade and Chiumbo had stashed the rifles the day before. To her relief, the rifles hadn't been discovered, and the camouflaging brush showed no signs of disturbance. With Sam's and Kalinde's help, she rigged up a heavy log to a toggle braced in place with several rifles. The end result was that when someone removed enough rifles, the toggle would slip and drop the log onto the victim.

'Not sure it's quite up to Tarzan's standard,' said Jade as she surveyed their work, 'but it will have to serve.' She scanned the surroundings, peering intently past the trees into the shadows.

'Looking for Boguli?' asked Sam.

She nodded. 'He wasn't at the lake where the elephants were, so I hoped he might still be in this area. He's the one who showed me this tree.'

'Old folks have minds of their own, Jade. He's probably moved on. Maybe he went back to his own people.' Sam pulled a watch from a shirt pocket. 'Speaking of going back to your own people, we should be getting back to camp.'

'You're probably right. Beverly will have a search party out for all of us soon.' Disappointed, she turned back up the trail. 'What did you think of Liesel Mueller's comments about Mercedes and her father?'

'Patriarchal German father, a miniature kaiser,' said Sam from behind her. 'He wants to go on safari and never mind what his wife or daughter wants. They must do what Herr Papa says.' He walked in silence for a moment longer, then added, 'Perhaps he is the reason she spends so much time in camp. Maybe she would like to go with the others, but he won't allow it. That could explain why she is so unhappy.'

'Maybe,' answered Jade. She winced as a stab of pain pierced her left knee, and automatically surveyed the trees for danger. She saw none and continued on. 'But Vogelsanger looked to be more concerned about the girl being left with her father than Claudia did. Do you suppose the old man hits Mercedes?'

Sam shook his head. 'I didn't see any sign of bruises on her. I sure wish I could have understood the argument I heard this morning,' he added. 'As I said, my German is very limited. I ignored foreign languages as much as possible at Purdue University.'

'You're a Boilermaker, then,' said Jade as she glanced over her shoulder. 'I never met a — ' Her words choked off as Biscuit charged out of the brush and slammed into her. She saw the streak of blood on the cat's side and touched it. His skin and fur were intact underneath. *Someone else's blood!* 'Chiumbo!'

A rasping growl from an angry leopard nearby answered her.

'Hurry!' she yelled, and took off after Biscuit into the forest, knowing full well that Sam and probably Kalinde could not keep up with her, but unwilling to waste precious time. Just when Jade felt that her lungs were beginning to burst, Biscuit slowed and stopped. The slender cat sniffed the air and hesitated as though uncertain what to do next. That was when she saw Chiumbo lying on the ground, an arrow protruding from his left leg.

Less than twenty feet away stood an angry leopard. Except that the leopard, Jade noted, wasn't snarling at her, Chiumbo, or Biscuit. He faced something out of her vision beyond the trees to her left. From somewhere in those trees, an elephant trumpeted, a shrill rise and fall of notes that reverberated in the forest and seemed to surround them.

The leopard wriggled backward and slapped at

198

the empty air with his paw. His face contorted in a grimace, ears flat against his head as he spit and screamed. The elephant's defiant call blasted the air once more, and the cat turned tail and ran. As soon as the leopard bounded off, Jade raced over to Chiumbo and felt for a pulse. Kalinde ran to her side.

'Bwana Sam told me to drop the camera and run after you.' He looked at Chiumbo. 'Is he dead, Simba Jike?'

Jade shook her head. Before she could answer more fully, she heard the sound of puffing from behind her as Sam approached.

'Is he dead?' he asked, echoing Kalinde's question.

'No,' answered Jade. 'Only drugged from the arrow. But he would have been dead soon if that leopard had gotten to him.'

'I heard an elephant, too,' said Sam as he knelt beside her. 'Must have thought the leopard was after it and scared the cat away. Lucky thing for Chiumbo.'

'Yes, very,' agreed Jade with a sideways glance at Sam. She turned her attention back to Chiumbo. 'I never saw it, but you know, it sounded remarkably like that old tusker that we watched being killed.'

'Another bull,' said Sam as he examined Chiumbo.

The wound had already clotted around the arrow in Chiumbo's leg, testimony to how long he'd lain there. Trying to remove the arrow in the forest would mean reopening the wound and not only risking further blood loss but also attracting still more predators. Jade and Sam decided it was better to leave it in his leg until they could get him to camp.

'Kalinde, run back to camp,' said Sam. 'Bring back enough men to carry Chiumbo and a stout blanket to use for a stretcher. We'll stay here and guard him.'

Twice while they waited, the leopard coughed nearby. The cat hadn't entirely abandoned its potential prey, but it hadn't gathered up enough courage to challenge them, either. Once, they heard the snapping of trees that indicated an elephant herd on the move in their vicinity. Jade and Sam were deciding how to transport Chiumbo out of its path when several low, purring trumpets echoed nearby, and the herd shifted direction and went around them. Finally, after what seemed like forever, they spied Avery trotting at the head of a column of Wakamba men, Kalinde leading them.

'How is he?' Avery asked.

'His breathing is steady,' answered Jade. 'But I've been swatting flies away nonstop. We've got to get this arrow out and his leg cleaned.'

'Beverly's arranging a makeshift hospital in the supply tent,' said Avery. 'It was the only way I could keep her and Jelani back at camp.'

Sam returned for his camera while the others gingerly lifted Chiumbo from the ground and placed him on the blanket. They waited only for Sam to return before they began carrying the wounded headman back to camp. Once they arrived, Jade assisted Beverly in removing the arrow and cleansing the wound. They bandaged his leg and left him resting and semiconscious in Sam's tent while they met for a quick council of war.

'Chiumbo needs proper medical attention, maybe some sulfur if there's any to be had,' said Jade. 'It's essential that you take him to the government station at Kampia Tembo at the foot of the mountain.'

'There's only a hut or two there,' said Beverly. 'The district commissioner must be gone away or our runner would have been back by now.'

'There's good water, and even if the commissioner's not there, he surely has some medical supplies in his hut,' said Jade. 'Get what you can, then head south for Archer's Post. You can make it in a couple of days.'

'He's lucky they didn't shoot him in a vital spot,' commented Avery.

'Maybe they didn't intend to kill him outright,' replied Jade. When the others expressed surprise she explained. 'I think we were supposed to find him near death. Someone wants us to leave in a hurry, which they know we'll do if one of our own is seriously injured. If he were found dead outright, then we might stay and try to take revenge.'

'Their plan worked, then,' said Beverly. 'We're leaving.'

'Yes, you are,' said Jade. 'We cannot risk your baby, or Chiumbo's life, or Jelani's.' She raised a hand to silence Jelani before he could protest. 'You're going, too,' she told him in a tone that brooked no argument. Jelani mumbled something unintelligible and walked away.

201

'I presume you're planning on staying behind, Jade,' said Avery.

'Correct. Somebody needs to keep an eye on these people. Who knows where they'll be by the time you get help sent up from one of the government posts? With any luck, our runner has already reached someone and they're on their way. In that case, I won't be far behind you.'

'But you don't even know who 'these people,' as you call them, are,' argued Beverly.

'I have a pretty good idea. The money I found points to German East Africa. Money also points to a bank and, hence, a banker.'

'You suspect von Gretchmar of running guns?' asked Avery. 'What about Vogelsanger or Mueller? They seem to have money.'

'I'm not sure who's running them, but I suspect someone's at least financing their purchase. Jelani found one of the same coins inside Mercedes' tent this morning when he and Sam paid them a visit.' She looked around for the boy. 'By the way, where did that boy run off to now? I want to thank him for finding the coin.'

'I saw him head towards Chiumbo. One coin is rather thin evidence,' suggested Beverly.

'I agree,' replied Jade. 'But it's certainly more than a coincidence. I need to be free to move around so I can find out if these rifles are coming in or going out, who's delivering them, who's picking them up, that sort of thing. There's more than poaching at work here. There are two men dead already.'

'That's right,' said Avery. 'They killed that

Abyssinian you caught, too. I'd forgotten about him.'

'Well, I haven't, and I can't imagine these poachers would kill one of their own if only ivory were involved. It would be more likely that they'd just lie low until we left.'

'My bet is on Hascombe,' said Sam. 'He's cheated you before.'

Jade arched her brows in surprise. 'I thought you just met Harry. How do you know about what he's done before?'

Beverly jumped into the breach. 'I'm sure Avery or I told Sam something about Harry since he's been here. Anyway, I don't agree that Harry's behind it. He's a British citizen after all. And a good hunter,' she added. 'He wouldn't risk a livelihood leading safaris by killing all the game or doing something illegal. Didn't you tell me his people bought licenses?'

'That's what *he* said,' answered Sam. His tone indicated he didn't believe Harry for one minute. 'He hired himself out to Germans after all. Maybe he made some signal to those porters of his to shoot Chiumbo.'

Jade rolled her eyes in exasperation. *Men!* 'The war's over, Sam. The kaiser lost. The world goes on. Besides, those porters had loads of ivory, not bows and arrows.'

'I think your idea of their financing the operation may be more likely,' said Avery. 'You said you opened at least two crates of rifles and one of ammunition. It's not bloody likely anyone could sneak that past Harry.'

'Which is one of the reasons I'm not entirely

convinced he's innocent,' said Sam.

'Speaking of not innocent, I have something I want you to look at, Bev,' said Jade. She ran to her photo tent and returned with a negative in her hand. 'Take a look at this.'

Beverly held the negative to the light and peered at it as she tried to make sense of the image. Suddenly, her eyes widened. 'Oh, my word. That's Claudia von Gretchmar! But,' she added as she squinted more closely at the negative, 'who is the man she is, um, cavorting with?'

'That's what I hoped you'd be able to tell me,' said Jade.

Avery and Sam both took turns studying the negative until Beverly took it from her husband. 'That's quite enough, don't you think? I have my doubts that you were examining the unknown man in the picture.'

'I can't tell,' said Avery. 'I presume it's her husband.'

'It's not,' said Jade. 'He's balding.'

'Probably Hascombe,' said Sam. 'I don't see that it has much bearing on this, though.'

'I agree,' said Avery. 'So what's your plan, Jade? When do we leave and how do you manage to stay on without being discovered?'

Jade pocketed the negative. 'We need to leave as soon as we can, for Chiumbo's sake, and it has to look like all of us are going. If we start packing now, we should get out of here early tomorrow. I'll make a run over to Harry's camp and inform him of our plans. Then I'll leave with you, in case someone is spying, but I'll double

204

back and hide out in a new location closer to the poachers' cache. We can tuck away some supplies in one of the blinds close by.'

'What about me?' asked Sam. 'Am I supposed to leave as well? Or do I get to have a say in this?'

Jade remembered the recent staring contest and knew that Sam would not back down easily if he didn't like her plan. Beverly was in a family way and Avery was only too glad to be able to move her to safer quarters. Bev, on the other hand, was willing to go because she didn't want to see Jelani hurt or Chiumbo suffer infection. But Sam? Jade had no hold over him.

'You're your own man, Sam. You could set up your own camp and continue to make your movie.'

He looked straight into Jade's eyes with a rakish smile that said, *I have you over a barrel, and both you and I know it*. He glanced quickly over to Beverly and winked before answering. 'I could stay on my own,' he said. 'Or I could pretend to turn tail, too, then sneak off and help you. At this point, I think you're going to need it.'

15

*Elephants are creatures of habit. They
follow the same trails their ancestors took,
feed off the trees that their mothers showed
them as calves, wallow in the same pools.
They also don't like to be disturbed in any
of these activities. If they feel threatened,
they will abandon habit and move on.
More than anything else, they seem to
seek security.*
— The Traveler

Early the next morning before daybreak, while
the others loaded chop boxes and hauled them
down the rocky hill to the two Willys-Knight
Overlanders parked a half mile from camp, Jade
gave the engines a once-over. She'd tightened
and adjusted everything the day they'd set up
camp, but she wanted nothing to go wrong with
their trip to safety. Chiumbo needed as little
stress and strain as possible, and while she
couldn't eliminate tire damage on the lower
mountainside, she could at least reduce problems under the hood.

Sam did the same for his Dodge truck parked
nearby. Then the two of them packed up the
essentials of dried jerky, dates, raisins, gasoline,
water, and ammunition and carried it down the

hill to Sam's truck. At Beverly's insistence, they also accepted a small medical kit complete with iodine and rolled bandages. Over this, they tossed their blankets and a tarp. All the tents went in the Overlanders along with most of Jade's cameras. The fourth one, set for a night flash, was too far away to retrieve in a hurry.

Maybe when this was over, Jade thought, there'd be time to finish her elephant photo study, but she knew the long rains were coming and her chances were fast decreasing. If she returned the next dry season, it would be alone. She wouldn't risk Bev's baby up here.

They decided first to notify Harry's camp. Then Sam would drive off with the rest of them, but only until he and Jade could safely double back and work their way towards the crater. They'd make a base camp there from which they could keep an eye on the poachers.

'How's Chiumbo holding up?' asked Jade when Beverly finished changing his bandages.

She put her hand on her stomach and grimaced while she tried to master her morning nausea. 'Well enough. The wound still looks clean. It smells clean, too, for which we are both grateful.'

Jade put her hand on Bev's shoulder and gave a gentle squeeze. 'You're a good trouper, Bev. Always have been. But you really should take a rest now. Let Avery and our men finish up.'

'Thank you, Jade. I believe I shall sit down for a moment.' She plopped herself under a shade tree after a quick scan for hidden snakes or scorpions. 'Oh, but I could go for a cup of hot tea right about now.'

Jade screwed up her face and stuck out her tongue. 'Tea? Bleah! You keep that up, Bev, and you'll turn your baby into a snooty Brit!'

Beverly laughed. 'I'll brook no comments about Brits from a blasted Gypsy. By the way, you never finished telling me that story.'

'What story? Oh! You mean about the elk? You don't have time for that now. I'll tell you when I rejoin you.'

Bev reached up and took hold of her friend's hand. 'No, I don't want to wait. It may be too . . . ' She stopped, and Jade suspected she was about to say something about it being too late.

Jade sat down next to Bev and patted her leg. 'It's all right, Bev. But if you really want to hear it, I'll tell you. Where did I leave off?' She remembered telling a bit more to Sam but wasn't certain that a discussion of bloated, rotting carcasses was anything Beverly cared to hear in her present condition.

'Something about your neighbor's dog being in heat,' said Bev.

'Ah yes. You can guess the outcome of that meeting,' said Jade with a grin and a nod towards Beverly's mid-section. 'We tried to teach the pup, Kaloff, how to herd, but he preferred to fetch in that big, soft-jawed mouth of his, so we mostly kept him around as a pet. I taught him how to fetch the cat whenever we couldn't locate old Rupert. Well, one day he took it into his huge, silly head that a polecat was just another cat.'

'He didn't herd it, did he?' asked Bev.

Jade nodded. 'Herded it as far as that skunk would go, which wasn't too far. Then after the skunk expressed his, um, displeasure, that idiot dog picked it up and carried it back to us.'

Beverly put her hands up in front of her open mouth with a look of amused horror. 'So what happened?'

'Jade?' a mellow bass voice called from the edge of camp. She turned and saw Sam walking towards her, his limp slight as long as he kept his pace slow. Again she wondered what had happened to him. Had a round of enemy fire penetrated the plane and pierced his leg during a dogfight? Did it hurt his knee, his calf, or his foot? Maybe it was his hip? She never asked because she didn't want to become involved in his life, or have another source of constant reminders of the late war. But it seemed there was no escaping it.

'We need to get to Harry's camp to spread our news,' Sam said. 'We're going to start burning daylight before long.'

Jade looked at Beverly and held out her hands in a gesture of futility. 'Sorry, Bev.'

'Sam is right, Jade. You want to catch them all while they're still in camp. You should take Biscuit and Jelani with you again. The Germans have gotten used to seeing the boy, I think, and might be suspicious if he's not there. Besides, the cheetah will run after you anyway.'

So, once again, Jade found herself standing in Harry's camp, Jelani and Biscuit in tow, with Sam acting ostensibly as their guard. Harry and

Heinrich Mueller sat at the camp table, mugs of coffee in their hands and a platter of biscuits between them. One of the camp servants brought over a second platter of grilled meat, and the fragrant aroma of food and coffee made Jade's mouth water. The two men rose on her entry, but sat down again as she told them to continue their breakfast. She wondered where everyone else was. Possibly sleeping in.

'I see you didn't bring that blasted camera, Featherstone,' Harry groused. 'Afraid I'd smash it?' he asked as he inserted a slab of meat between two halves of a biscuit.

'Back off, Hascombe,' Sam replied. 'We've got more important things to do here.'

'Gentlemen!' scolded Jade to prevent further outbursts. She took a deep breath and tried her best to smile pleasantly. 'Sam's right. We came by to tell you that we're leaving. One of our men is in need of medical attention.' She decided not to be specific in the hopes that any guilty party might inadvertently give himself away.

'Such a bother, these native men,' said Mueller. 'But if you have an elephant license that you have not used, I would buy it from you.' When Jade didn't offer any, the man resumed eating his breakfast as though they'd already left.

Harry scowled at the man's insensitive comment. 'I'm sorry to hear this, Jade,' he said. He set his sandwich back on the table, stood, and walked over to her. 'What happened? Snakebite? Malaria?'

She shook her head. 'Neither. Just a wound but we don't want it to become infected.'

'Well, maybe I have some medicine in our kit you can use,' Harry offered. 'How bad is it?' He took her right hand and held it in his own.

'We don't need your medicines, Hascombe,' Sam said. 'We can treat our own men.'

Harry released Jade's hand and flexed his arms as though he were easing out a cramp. 'Apparently not, Featherstone,' he replied coolly. 'Otherwise you wouldn't be leaving. I thought you came in to make some motion picture. Afraid to stay on your own?'

Sam gritted his teeth and clenched his fists. 'Hascombe, you're going to push too far.'

'We need to make room in one of the Overlanders for our man to be comfortable, so Sam graciously offered to help us haul back some of the gear,' Jade said.

Sam folded his arms across his chest and smirked. 'You should personally know about *that*, Hascombe, right? Didn't they have to do that for you last year when you broke your leg?'

'Stop it!' snapped Jade. 'Both of you, back down.' If she hoped to gain any additional information during this visit, she was mistaken. 'You should take precautions, Harry. The poachers are still out there and it's just possible they don't like our being in their territory.'

'I appreciate your concern, Jade.' He started to clasp her hand again, saw Sam take a deep breath, and thought the better of it. 'Is that what happened? The poachers went after one of your men?'

'Um, he's not talking yet, so we don't know. I'm just passing along some friendly advice. Your

211

people all seem to be intent on bagging their set of tusks, and the poachers might not appreciate any competition. That's the impression I got from Captain Smythe.'

'We'll likely be leaving in a day or two ourselves,' admitted Harry in a lower voice, as if he didn't want Mueller to overhear. 'There are too many people in this group for my taste. They don't stay together, and they don't follow orders. I'm surprised someone hasn't been eaten or gored yet.'

'Anyone in particular?' asked Jade.

'The men are bad enough. Vogelsanger took off before dawn with Liesel Mueller. Blasted Germans act as if they won the bloody war. But the women are worse. That Mercedes is a useless little creature, and her mother is . . . ' He flung out his arms in a gesture of complete bewilderment.

'Maybe you just don't know how to handle women, Hascombe,' said Sam. Jade nearly responded by kicking him in the foot, but stopped herself as soon as the side of her boot contacted his. Somehow it seemed cruel to attack someone's injured leg. She jabbed him in the ribs with her elbow instead.

Harry snorted. 'You're no expert yourself, Featherstone, but,' he added with a flash of teeth, like some predator just before taking a bite, 'I do appreciate your sacrifice. You're giving up completing your picture to protect Jade. I'd hate to see anything happen to my best girl.'

Jade nearly belted Harry herself for that last bit, and it was Sam who tugged on her arm to pull her away. 'We need to get moving,' he said, then looked around. 'Where's Jelani?'

★ ★ ★

Jelani didn't want to leave with Bwana Avery and the others. He wanted to stay with Simba Jike, and he knew that her concern for Biscuit's safety was just a story she made up to get him to go with Bwana and Memsabu Dunbury. It was not that he didn't like them — he did very much — but his place was protecting Simba Jike. And so he hoped to find out something important to tell her, something that would make her realize that she needed him and must keep him nearby. He would remain with her and find the man who shot his friend Chiumbo. Then he would kill the evildoer and be a true warrior.

The last time he came here with the American man, he found a coin in the tent of the young memsabu. Perhaps he would find something else there. He decided to take Biscuit to the lady's tent. If she was inside, he would let her pet the cheetah and maybe she would talk to the cat. White people often talked to animals and told them secrets.

As Jelani approached the tent, he heard a man's voice raised in anger, followed by a woman's tearful sobs and plaintive entreaties. He stopped and listened, but the voices spoke a language he did not know. It was not his native Kikuyu tongue nor the King's English. Neither was it the 'kitchen Swahili' most people used to talk to someone of another tribe or skin color.

He recognized the man's voice as that of the young woman's father. Fathers often scolded daughters. Perhaps she had not cooked his meal correctly. Then he remembered these women did not cook.

Another thought crossed his mind. Memsabu Simba Jike spoke many languages. Maybe she would know what the words meant. He hoped they didn't speak a secret one like he did with Simba Jike the other night. Then Jelani caught a word he recognized: 'nine.' That much he knew at least. It was a number, one less than the fingers on both hands. He crept closer to the tent and listened, softly repeating some of the other words to himself so as to remember them.

'Jelani! It is time to leave.'

He heard Memsabu Simba Jike call his name. Biscuit, too, heard his mistress' voice and chirped in reply. Jelani left the tent, still repeating the last phrase to make it stay in his mind.

★ ★ ★

'Please say that again and slowly,' said Jade once they were out of camp and earshot.

Jelani sighed, expressing his impatience with slow adults. '*Cun — Ig — In — Mack — Un*. I also heard him say 'nine' and 'shmit.' Nine is a number, is it not?'

'In English it is a number, but in German it means no.'

Jade repeated Jelani's phrase several times, putting different breaks between the syllables.

'*König* is 'king,' but *Königin* is 'queen.' That would leave the word *machen*, 'to make.' Perhaps he said *Königin machen?* That would be making her a queen, but that doesn't make much sense.'

'I've heard lots of fathers refer to their daughters as princesses,' suggested Sam. 'Perhaps he was using some term of endearment to calm her down?'

Jelani rolled his eyes and sighed again. 'He was angry.'

'Did you hear anything else? Did the lady say anything?'

'Her voice was very soft and hard to hear,' admitted Jelani. 'Mostly she cried. I think she said 'a rick.''

'A rick?' repeated Sam. 'Eric?'

'Vogelsanger,' added Jade.

'She may have been saying Vogelsanger's first name. Perhaps he is trying to force her into a match with him. He might mean that Eric would treat her like a queen.'

'That's interesting, I suppose, but it hardly helps us,' said Jade. 'Let's go.'

The morning mists had thinned by the time they returned to their own camp, and Sam's porters departed with their loads. The remaining gear was stowed in the cars, and Jade and Sam joined Avery and one remaining man in carrying Chiumbo down to the vehicles. They wedged the wounded headman between canvas tents and bedrolls, where he would be cushioned throughout the bumpy ride. Since Chiumbo was more or less alert, Jade took the opportunity to question

215

him about the attack. He had very little to offer.

'I heard running feet coming from behind, but before I turned to look, I felt a stab in my leg. After that, the earth did not behave right. It tilted and the sun got dark. I could not see, and I fell.' He closed his eyes and gingerly rubbed his temple where a large welt pushed up against a bandage. 'I think I heard a leopard scream and an elephant, but I am not sure.'

Jade placed a hand on his shoulder and smiled. 'You were lucky, Chiumbo. Rest now.'

The big man grabbed her wrist and held it like a vise. 'Simba Jike, I hear you are staying. You must take great care.'

She patted his hand. 'I will, Chiumbo. I promise. And,' she added in order to relieve some of his worry, 'I won't be alone. Mr Featherstone will be with me.'

Chiumbo smiled. 'Ah,' he said. 'Yes, that is good. That is how it should be.'

'Everything is packed, Jade,' said Beverly as Jade finished her good-byes to Chiumbo. 'Avery put all the canned foods in our vehicles and left you with all the jerky and dried fruits.'

'Good. We can't risk drawing attention with a fire to cook.' Jade slapped the front of Sam's Dodge. 'Let's get this wagon train a-moving.'

True to their plan, they drove along as a caravan, Avery in the lead Overlander with Jelani, Beverly driving the second Overlander with Chiumbo, and Sam and Jade following in Sam's Dodge truck. The few remaining Wakamba men walked alongside the slow-moving cars. Since all the extra petrol needed for the return trip had been left in caches along the way, the men had much less to carry, and so were able to help push the cars over the rougher spots. Once when a rock hung up Avery's rear axle, everyone but Beverly and Chiumbo got out and lifted the car's rear end up and over the hurdle.

Sam didn't attempt to drive the Dodge over that rock. Instead, he decided it was a good opportunity for them to go their separate ways. Jelani, who had already made it clear he didn't want to stay with the Dunburys, sat slouched in the front of the Overlander, chin on his fists in a sulk. Biscuit, panting, lay stretched out on top of the chop boxes behind him.

'Jelani,' said Jade, 'you are good and brave and very clever, but I cannot put you in this danger that Bwana Sam and I must face.' She held up her forefinger to his lips. 'No argument. I have a job to do and I cannot do it if I am worried about all of you or,' she added, 'if I have Biscuit underfoot. I'm depending on you to keep him with you.'

Jade reached into her trouser pocket and pulled out a folded sheet of paper. She held it in front of her and waved it to capture everyone's attention. 'I drew a map to the hidden weapons and to the poachers' cache. Give this to the officials at the government station. If you see Captain Smythe before then, give it to him.' She handed the paper to Beverly. 'I also explained how to reach the crater lake. Sam and I will bivouac there.'

Beverly held the folded sheet in her right hand and stared at it silently. Finally, one lone tear dropped on the paper, rolled down a crease, and plopped to the ground, splattering in the dust. Jade turned to Avery, who gave a limp smile as though he didn't know whether to be distressed or apologetic about his wife's emotional state.

'We'll meet you at Archer's Post,' said Jade. 'But leave word at each station along the way just in case there's a change in your plans. You ought to run into someone sooner than later. I hate to think our runner had to go all the way to Isiolo for help.'

'Right,' said Avery, his voice tight when Jade hugged him. He shook hands with Sam, who clapped him on the back. 'Don't stay around here more than a few days. It's too dangerous.'

'Don't you fret at all,' said Sam. 'Just get Chiumbo and the boy squared away and leave the rest to us.'

'You'd better not let Jade get into trouble, Sam,' said Beverly as she choked back a sob. 'She needs a keeper, you know.'

'You can count on me, Beverly,' said Sam. 'I grew up on a farm in Indiana, so I'm an expert at handling varmints.'

'Hey!' exclaimed Jade. Then Beverly chuckled and Jade decided that Sam had called her a varmint only to break the somber mood.

Avery started singing one of the newer songs. 'How you gonna keep 'em down on the farm — '

'After they've seen the Serengeti,' finished Jade. She slapped the door of Beverly's car. 'Off with you, now.'

Jade and Sam watched as the others bounced and jostled their way down the slope, heading

218

towards the desert and grasslands below. She knew they'd stop at the wells near the base to refill all the radiators and water *debes* before continuing south around the mountain to Kampia Tembo, where they'd left their first cache of fuel. If Chiumbo was still without a fever, they would pause for a brief rest, and leave again before dawn rather than risk missing a patrol in the pitch-black of night.

'Let's go before someone sees us,' Jade said. Sam nodded and climbed back into the idling Dodge.

'Are you sure there's a clear path to your lake, Jade?' he asked after he turned the vehicle around. 'Because I don't believe we're going to be able to lift the truck over rocks on our own.'

She shook her head. 'That would be a waste of fuel and water, not to mention time. All we want to do is get the truck hidden away somewhere between here and the lake. We can carry what we need the rest of the way. Besides,' she added, 'I'm not sure how trustworthy your Dodge is.'

'I'll have you know, my dear Miss Jade, that Black Jack Pershing himself used a fleet of Dodge vehicles to chase down Pancho Villa in that border war. I should have thought you'd have known about that since you're from the Southwest. Rumor has it that Villa was so impressed, he ordered one for himself afterward.'

Jade put her hands on her hips and pursed her lips. 'Now that you mention it, I do remember reading about that.'

Sam grinned, tilting the ends of his untrimmed mustache. 'I'd have thought you'd have written one of your famous piss-sonnets about it,' he said, referring to the limericks and humorous poems she had composed during the war.

Jade snapped her head around and scowled at him. 'How do you know about my piss-sonnets? And now that I think about it, what did you mean this morning when you told Harry that he, if anyone, should know about making room for a wounded man in a car? You knew about his broken leg.'

'I've been here a few days, Jade. Avery and Beverly told me a little about their last adventure.'

Jade blew out a short, huffing breath, like a disturbed rhino. 'Sounds to me like they talk too much. Let's get moving. I suddenly feel exposed here.'

Sam inched the car forward. 'Does your knee hurt?'

'What?!' She pivoted a quarter turn and banged her elbow against a canvas day pack balanced behind her. The force knocked loose several papers, which slid partly out. Jade started to push them back into place when several lines of text caught her eye.

'What's this?' She pulled out a sheet and read the first lines of typewritten carbon copy aloud.

Jade put herself in front of the boy like a living shield, bravely faced the slavering jaws of the hideous hyena. With all the cool precision of the gem for which she was named, Jade fired a killing shot directly into the evil heart of the ravening beast. 'Take that, you *toto*-eating monster,' she shouted. 'Eat my bullets instead!'

She snorted in disgust. 'What a lot of driveling, purple prose.' She flipped past several pages and read again.

The rampaging rhinoceros bore down on them with the power of a runaway loco- motive. Blind to pain and bent on destruction, nothing short of a miracle could stop it. Jade snatched a blanket and created her own miracle. '*Toro*,' she cried. The beast spun towards her, giving the men a chance to shoot. Harry watched in admiration, know- ing that he'd never wanted anyone as much as he did that brave, black-haired American beauty.

Jade glared over the top of the paper at Sam, who pretended ignorance to everything but the dried-grass path in front of the car. 'Bev told me that Madeline gave her the carbon copy,' she said. 'Just how did it come to be in your possession, Mr Featherstone?'

Sam took a deep breath, gripped the steering wheel more tightly, and stared straight ahead. 'Do you mind telling me how far I'm supposed to drive?'

Jade ignored his question. 'Did Beverly send this to you? Did she bring you out here to meet me? Because it sounds like just the thing she'd do.' Jade wadded the carbon copy back into the satchel and turned back around, arms folded across her chest. 'No wonder you know so much about Harry and my knee.'

They rode in silence for a few minutes, each staring straight ahead until Sam broke the tension. 'I suppose I'd better tell you everything. I told you I met Avery during the war while we were both on leave in Paris, and that we kept up a sort of correspondence. I wrote to him to toss around the idea of my making a moving picture about buffalo. That's all true.'

Glancing sideways at Jade, he took in the stony set of her jaw and the snap in her eyes. 'The next thing I knew, they told me to get out to Africa as fast as I could. They jumped all over the idea of my filming wild animals and natives. Told me they knew this wonderful American girl I had to meet. Sent me that manuscript and said everything in it was true. I didn't know that they kept it a secret from you till I got out here.' He looked over at her again. 'That's the gosh-honest truth.'

Jade closed her eyes and sighed. Once again she grabbed the ring that she wore hidden under her shirt like a talisman. 'I'm sorry Bev led you astray. I'm sorry you had to leave your camera and equipment back in their car. Maybe in a day or two, when this is over, you can get on with making your motion picture.'

Sam didn't respond at first and the silence built up again, oppressive like the late-morning heat. 'I met David, too, when I was on leave. Seemed like a good man.'

Jade nodded, her hand still clutching the ring. 'I'm sorry, Sam. It's just that — '

'I know, I know,' he said. 'You already told me. I haven't got a leg to stand on.'

The Dodge jerked and bounced along over the hard ground, occasionally dipping down into wallows hidden by patches of grass. The grassland ran in a strip a few hundred yards wide, like a buffer between the desert below and the mountain forests rising to their left. Finally, Jade pointed to a break in the trees on the left.

'Turn in there. We can see how far up it takes us. If my estimate is correct, the crater lake is at the other end of this trail.'

Sam turned into a five-foot gap in the trees where generations of pachyderms had bullied their way through the forest. The trail rose upward in switchbacks forged by lead matriarchs who had found the easiest path to and from the lake. During the wet season, the elephants came down and fed in the lush grasslands. Now in the lull between rains, they had migrated back up into the forest to avoid the sun's heat and to find food in the succulent growing branches and fruits. No elephants had passed this way for nearly ten months and young saplings sprang up in their way, fertilized by giant droppings. Sam drove around them where the trail permitted. Several times Jade got out and walked ahead of the car, hacking at the growth with a panga. Finally, they reached a point where the car couldn't make further progress without considerable assistance.

'We'll leave it here,' Jade said.

'I suggest we make this our home base,' said Sam as he stepped out of the car. He pointed to a large, red-trunked tree beside the trail about twenty feet away. Its thick branches radiated out like wheel spokes with secondary branches creating an interlacing framework.

'We can sleep up there for protection. The lowest branches look to be a good seven feet off the ground. I've got a stout hammock in the back and we can drape a tarp over some upper branches in case it rains.' He saw Jade's frown and added, 'Or we can go on to your tree blind, carry back its wooden planks, and nail them up there.' When she gave the tree another once-over, he pressed his point. 'Anyway, it's convenient. We won't have to haul a lot of gear with us. We've got enough water in the *debes* already, so we don't need to find more at present. It also affords a faster escape if we need it.'

'But I told the Dunburys we'd be at the lake. If they get word to Smythe or someone at the government house . . . '

'Then they'll probably come past here on their way up,' finished Sam. 'At least that's how you drew the map, right?'

Jade nodded. 'All right. You've convinced me. I guess I thought I'd eventually find Boguli up there, but I don't know why.' She studied both her rifle and the captured bow before making a choice and tucked the bow with the arrows under a canvas tarp.

'As I said before, your old native is probably long gone by now,' said Sam as he examined his own rifle.

Jade hung her flashlight from her belt, checked her Winchester for ammunition, added a few rounds, then stuffed more into her pocket. She tucked some jerky into a canvas sack along with a cake of dried dates, and slung the sack and a canteen around her shoulders. Sam picked up his rifle and another canteen and the two of them headed up the trail towards the crest. After an hour's hike, Jade picked up a smaller game trail that meandered east towards the poachers' cache.

Very little stirred along their path, except for the insect life that seemed to thrive in the afternoon humidity. A brief rain shower reminded them that the long rains would start in a month if not sooner. At that point the elephants, annoyed by the constant *plop, plop* of water from the trees, would once again depart from the mountain and feed on the freshened grasslands at the southern base. That was probably when the Abyssinians would also leave. Jade wanted to see the murdering troop all in irons before she vacated the mountain.

She kept their pace easy, so that Sam could keep up. Finally, she recognized the tortuously twisted trunks of a stand of African olive trees and knew that the cache was close by. She held up her hand to call a halt. Both of them listened intently for any sounds of human activity before venturing forward and risking discovery. They heard none. Once again, it seemed the cache had been left unguarded, which meant the Abyssinians had yet to discover the theft of their weapons. It reaffirmed Jade's belief that those rifles had a purpose other than for poaching. Otherwise, someone would have broken open the boxes by now and discovered their loss.

'Wait here,' she mouthed, and pointed to the ground for emphasis.

Sam shouldered his rifle. 'Got your back, Jade,' he whispered. 'Make it fast, though.'

She nodded and, after another quick survey of the area, darted out of cover and into the shelter of the cache. She turned on her light and began a thorough sweep of the ground, one section at a time, looking for anything dropped or set aside that might give her another clue to the poachers' ultimate plans. It was on the fourth pass that she discovered the nest of blankets tucked behind a stack of ivory.

As she panned across the blankets, her light reflected off a small white disk. Jade picked it up. *A button.* A four-holed mother-of-pearl button with delicate filigree edging such as one might see on a woman's blouse. Jade clutched the button in her fist. The hard part was going to be sneaking back into Harry's camp to match it.

16

*Don't imagine for a minute that elephants
are easily chased away by everything new
that appears in their home. Sometimes they
avoid the blinds, bomas, and other man-
made constructions, but it's just as likely
that an elephant will take it into his or her
head to smash the offending object as walk
away from it.*
— The Traveler

Sam stood on the wooden planks that they'd
hauled back from another blind, and inspected
his newly hung hammock. 'That looks mighty
comfortable,' he said. 'It's yours if you want it,
Jade. I can sleep on the planks or . . . ' He let the
rest of his thought dangle. He wanted to say that
they could share it, but didn't dare. One didn't
suggest something like that to a lady. Well, at
least he didn't.

'Sleeping in the truck sounds more uncom-
fortable than on a plank,' said Jade. 'I'll be fine.
Wouldn't think of stealing your hammock, but
thanks for the offer.'

Sam frowned. Had she purposely misunder-
stood him? Probably not. Jade was too
plainspoken to play at deception. He watched
her spread one of the blankets against the trunk

as a nest and felt his breath catch in his throat. *My stars, she's beautiful!* And brave, and intelligent, and everything else he ever thought he'd want in a woman. He'd longed for a life of adventure, and now found that desire all wrapped up in Jade's neat, tidy form. He just had to convince her that he was the man for her, a challenge that seemed more impossible with every passing day. What had he been thinking? That he could saunter into camp and rely on his friendship with Avery to recommend himself to her? *She loves airplanes and respects pilots,* Beverly had said in their letter. *She's an American. You're perfect for each other.* Sam sighed again. Someone forgot to tell Jade — that was all. Well, here they were alone and he'd never get a better opportunity for wooing.

Jade rolled up a second blanket and tossed it over to him. 'You'd better wrap yourself in this, Sam. The nights here get pretty cold, as I'm sure you've noticed.'

'Thanks.' He plopped the blanket on his hammock and took a seat next to her on the plank. Jade opened up her pack and divided out a ration of dried fruits and jerky for an evening supper. He popped a date in his mouth, swallowed, and searched for something to say that didn't sound too corny. 'Beautiful evening,' he said finally. 'The night sky here reminds me of the sky back home, where the stars are so thick you can scoop them up with a spoon.'

Jade nodded. 'Guess that's what the Big Dipper is for, right?' She cleared her throat. 'You know, Sam, I think I owe you an apology, for snapping at you over Madeline's manuscript. I should be mad at Beverly for sending it, but not angry at you.'

Sam wasn't sure that helped his situation much, but he held his tongue and let her finish.

'Anyway, I thought about that Pancho Villa story and I came up with a piss-sonnet, if you'd like to hear it.'

She glanced at him sheepishly under half-lowered eyelids, and Sam felt his innards turn to mush. He nodded.

'Okay,' she said, 'here goes. Old Pancho was running amok, when Pershing came driving his truck. He shot Pancho's hat, and Pancho said that . . . he needed to Dodge more than duck.'

Sam laughed. 'That's wonderful!' *So far, so good*.

Jade drew up her knees, wrapped her arms around her legs, and rested her chin on her knees. Her emerald eyes peered into the forest, but seemed to look beyond it.

'Thinking of home?' he asked, hoping for a tender moment.

She shook her head, her black hair shimmering in the final rays of the evening sun. 'Nope. Thinking about that button we found.' She turned towards him. 'We need to get into Harry's camp and match it to someone's clothes.'

Sam's jaw hung open, flabbergasted. This was hardly the direction he'd planned for the conversation to take and for a moment he was as stupefied as a bullfrog at night that woke to find a bright light in his eyes and a gigging stick in his

229

hide. 'We need to *what?*' he said after an awkward silence. 'Are you crazy?'

Jade refolded her arms in a defensive attitude across her chest. 'You heard me. We need to match that button. My money's on Liesel. She strikes me as the sort who'd do anything for money.'

'May I remind you, Jade, that we're officially gone from the mountain? How are you going to explain our continued presence here when you walk up to the Germans and start examining their clothing?'

She scowled for an instant, then shook her head again. 'But I'm not going to walk up to them. I can slip into their camp when they're gone.'

'They're never all gone,' he said, exasperation in his voice. 'And even if they were, there are always some of their porters around. It's not going to work.'

'Fine,' she snapped. 'And just what do you think we should do, then?'

Sam closed his eyes and took a deep breath before answering. How could anyone so clever be so dang-blasted bullheaded? 'We came back here to spy on the poachers and get more information. Fine. I say we continue to do that. Let's find a place off their trail where we can hide in a tree and watch them. We don't need to do any more than that. If one of Harry's group came there before, chances are, he or she will come back again.'

'Hmmph!' was Jade's only reply. She shoved a handful of dates in her mouth as though saying all conversation was off for the evening. 'I'm going to sleep,' she mumbled between mouthfuls. 'You can take first watch. Wake me halfway through the night.' With that, she stretched out on her board, effectively booting Sam out of the way, and curled up in her blanket.

Sam wrapped his own blanket around his shoulders and sat at the edge of the board, his rifle resting across his lap. It was going to be a long night.

* * *

Jelani woke in the black of night, instantly alert. Something was out there. *No,* he corrected himself, *someone.* He lay still on his blanket between the cars, sorting out the night sounds and listening for the one that had woken him. He heard Bwana Avery's slight snore, and the deep, regular breaths of Memsabu Beverly, Chiumbo, and another man, Abasi, the one who should have been on watch. Closer to him, Biscuit panted rhythmically.

Jelani listened again. Out beyond the scuttling lizards and the shy bark of a bushbuck coming to drink over at the spring drifted the soft sound of a shod foot scratching against rock.

Chirp. The birdlike call came from beyond the spring in the rocks. Jelani recognized it as someone's imitation of a cheetah. So did Biscuit. The big cat raised his head and pivoted his ears forward. *Chirp.* Biscuit started to rise, but Jelani clutched the cheetah's collar and held fast.

So, he thought, *someone is trying to call*

231

Simba Jike's cheetah. Why might that be? Whenever Biscuit went looking for Simba Jike, he went after Biscuit. Someone else, an enemy, knew this. With his free hand he felt for his knife. The bone shaft felt cool and familiar in his grasp as he clenched the hilt.

His passage into manhood lay before him. He would let Biscuit follow this sound and he would tail Biscuit. But he would follow as a hunter, not as the hunted. When dawn broke and Bwana Avery called for them to drive on, Jelani the warrior would climb into the car instead of Jelani the boy.

★   ★   ★

'We already discussed this last evening. You cannot sneak into Harry's camp.' Sam sat perched on the hood of the Dodge, a handful of dates in his right hand, his left hand pointing at Jade as he argued his point. 'The camp is never empty. You'll be spotted.'

'We could create some diversion to frighten everyone out of camp for a moment,' Jade suggested.

'Are you listening to yourself?' he argued. 'A diversion? Do you think you can get a herd of elephants to stampede through there at your command?'

She shook her head. 'That wouldn't be practical anyway. They'd trample any evidence. No, I need something more subtle. If we could snare a leopard, we could turn it loose inside their compound.'

'And they'd all run up and shoot it.' Sam slid

off the hood, landing on his good leg. He took three steps towards Jade and grabbed her shoulders. 'Look at me, Jade. We're supposed to be off the mountain and on our way to Nairobi. If someone in that camp is involved in the poaching, then they cannot know we're on to them. It would be too dangerous.'

She opened her mouth to protest, but Sam simply spoke with more force. 'You *cannot* go into that camp!' He caught the questioning look in her eye, and added, 'And neither can I.'

'You could tell them you decided to stay and finish your motion picture. You've already filmed them once.'

Sam released his hold on her. 'No,' he said softly. 'Somehow I think they might be a little bit suspicious when I waltz in there without my camera. Remember? We sent it back with the Dunburys.' He turned back to the car. 'Now, I suggest we pull out of here and take what evidence you have to the people in charge. Let them deal with this.'

'You never saw that dead soldier, shot in the back of the head like an execution. And they hurt Chiumbo.'

'Which,' he said in a gentle voice as he faced her again, 'is why you need to get out of here. These people are unscrupulous. They are not afraid to kill and they will hurt you, too, if you leave them no other choice.'

'What about you?' she asked. 'Are you perhaps worried about what they might do to you?'

Sam shook his head and grinned. 'I'm more worried about what Avery and Beverly would do

233

to me if I let anything happen to their Jade.' He folded his arms across his chest and leaned back against the Dodge. 'I'm not leaving your side, Jade, and I'm not letting you sneak into Hascombe's camp. So unless you have another idea, we either sit here or we leave.'

Jade studied the set of his jaw and the self-assured way in which he returned her gaze. The resolution on his face said he meant business. This was one man she couldn't seem to buffalo. *Blast!* Her own lips tightened as she mentally ran through her options. 'Fine,' she said after a few moments of deliberation. 'We'll leave tomorrow. But first I'm going to clean out the rest of those rifles in that cache. If these people get away, it's going to be without their weapons.'

Sam rubbed a hand over the stubble on his chin. 'Hmmm. You already took away half a dozen rifles last evening. I'm surprised you didn't tinker with the rest so they'd blow up when they're fired.'

'Interesting idea, but rigging them all would take too long,' she replied. Sam rolled his eyes. 'There's no more room in that hollow tree,' she added. 'We'll have to leave today's take up in this tree instead.'

Sam peered up into the tree. Jade expected he was buying time to think rather than studying the logistics of hoisting rifles. She allowed him his moment, partly because she recognized she was running on emotion and pride rather than common sense, though she'd be danged if she ever admitted as much to him. She'd never backed down from anything in her life, and she surely wasn't about to back down from stopping whoever had hurt Chiumbo and killed that African soldier. But she also couldn't run headlong into trouble, and she found she actually valued Sam's cooler reasoning. She needed a working plan, and if he had one, she'd go along with it.

'Well, are you going to tell me what you're thinking?' she asked.

He tipped his head, his dark brown eyes boring into hers from under his hat brim. 'You do *not* want to know what I'm thinking, missy. But,' he added as he raised his head, 'since you're dead set on doing something, I will give you my advice on this harebrained scheme of yours.' He made a fist with his right hand and raised the index finger. 'One, you've been lucky so far that they haven't set a guard during the day, but they may be wise to you by now and be waiting. It's riskier every time you try to sneak in there.' He raised a second finger. 'Two, I have no intention of carrying any rifles except for my own. Someone's got to act as guard, and since you don't intend to, that leaves me. That means it will take you twice as long to clean them out.' A third finger popped up.

'Three,' said Jade before he could continue, 'you're not up for that many trips with your game leg.' She pointed to her left knee. 'But if I can tough it out today, so can you.'

Sam lowered his hand and folded his arms across his chest. 'Your knee hurts?'

'I spent the night crammed into the crotch of a tree. Yes, my knee hurts.' Jade muttered

235

something under her breath about obstinate Hoosiers and men in general. 'I'll just have to take what I can, then.' She pulled the makeshift rope ladder down from their tree refuge, wound it up, and slung it over her head and one arm. 'I should be able to tie up a bundle and carry it on my back like cordwood,' she announced as she started up the trail. 'Just make sure you have my back.'

'Yes, ma'am.'

They hadn't gone fifty feet from the car when Sam grabbed Jade's arm and pulled her off the trail and into cover. He put a finger to his lips to indicate silence, but she didn't need his warning. She heard the noise, too. A man, heavily winded, by the sound of his labored breathing, was racing towards them from below. As the runner neared, Sam shouldered his rifle and prepared to fire if necessary. Jade grabbed his wrist and shook her head. Then she stepped out of the brush in front of the man.

'Abasi, what are you doing here? Did Bwana Dunbury find Captain Smythe?'

The runner, one of the Wakamba porters, grabbed his knees and leaned over, panting. 'Sam,' said Jade. 'Help me get Abasi to the truck. He needs to sit and drink something.'

They each took hold of an arm and helped him back to the Dodge, where they sat him on the running board and administered water, a few sips at a time. All the while, Jade fought a rising sense of panic as she envisioned first Chiumbo raging in a fever followed by Beverly miscarrying. Just as she began to entertain the horrifying

236

thought of everyone lying in a pool of blood, the exhausted Wakamba found enough breath to speak.

'Simba Jike. You must come. The boy is gone.'

'Jelani is gone?'

Abasi nodded. 'Yes, and Biscuit, also.'

'Was there any sign of a struggle?' asked Sam. 'Did anyone hear anything?'

Abasi shook his head. 'All was quiet. We camped at the foot of the mountain by the desert. The cars were hot. Bwana Dunbury wanted only to stay long enough for the cars to rest, but Memsabu said the headman needed to sleep undisturbed. Still we were breaking camp while the stars still shone. That is when we found the boy missing.'

'Kidnapped,' whispered Jade.

Sam put a comforting hand on her shoulder. 'You don't know that. You know how often Biscuit runs off. He probably found something to chase, and Jelani went after him. I imagine they're both back with the Dunburys by now, safe and sound. But as soon as we can make room for Abasi in the truck, we'll leave.'

Jade shrugged off his hand. 'No. Someone took him. I can feel it.' She knelt beside the winded man. 'Get your breath back, Abasi, and tell us everything.'

Abasi took another sip of water, held it in his mouth to savor the taste, then swallowed. He handed the canteen back to Sam, who put a strip of jerky in the man's hand. Abasi nodded his thanks but did not eat. 'There is not much more to tell, Simba Jike,' he said. 'We heard nothing.

237

We saw nothing. If someone came to our camp and took the cheetah and Jelani, they came as silently as a breath. We called for the boy and for the cheetah with Bwana Dunbury. I looked all over for tracks. We found one footprint. It was the cat's, but the boy's foot lay on top of it.'

'So he followed after Biscuit rather than Biscuit following after him,' Jade said in summary. Abasi nodded.

'Did you see where they went?'

The Wakamba shook his head. 'It is all rocks there,' Abasi explained. 'Tracks do not show.'

'We should go, Jade,' said Sam. 'We have to help them look.' When Jade didn't agree immediately, he twisted his head and stared at her. 'Now!'

She stood and faced him. 'Yes, but if someone from Harry's camp took him, they may have brought him back. They could easily be there by now.'

Sam leaned against the car and nodded. 'Agreed, but if he is with the Germans, it won't be easy to get in and find him without being discovered.'

Jade gripped her Winchester tightly in her fist. 'Then I'll just have to deal with them, won't I?'

Abasi jumped up from his seat. 'Let me come with you, Simba Jike. I will distract them and lead them out of camp.'

'Good. A diversion is just what we need.' Jade glanced at Sam's leg. 'Will you be able to keep up? We're going cross-country. I don't want to risk running into anyone on the trails.'

'Be right behind you.'

They set off at a brisk pace through the forest, grateful for the ancient trees that shaded so much of the ground that there was little understory to hamper their movements or provide a hiding place for a dozing rhino or buffalo. Slight rustles to the side marked the sudden darting movement of smaller animals, rodents and possibly snakes, startled by their approach.

Jade heard Sam's syncopated stride behind her as he kept up with them, and her respect for him went up another notch. It took them a little over an hour to cut straight across and intersect with the original trail that led from their old camp to Harry's, and slightly over another hour to slip under cover of the trees alongside that path. Harry's camp sat in a grassy clearing within the forest. The usual protective wall of brush surrounded it. Jade called a halt to regroup before they ventured into the open. As they settled into position, she thought she heard the low rumble of elephants purring to each other nearby.

Odd. She would have supposed that the herds would stay farther away from the hunters and their guns. But then, low sounds carried far. The elephants might be more distant than she supposed.

Jade pointed to Sam and Abasi, then to her eyes. She made walking motions with her fingers in a wide circle to indicate they should scout the perimeter of the *boma* and get an idea of how many people were inside. They nodded and slipped off to begin their reconnaissance while she watched the gate. The two men had barely left her line of sight when she felt a light touch, like a breath, on her shoulder.

She instantly whirled to face the danger, fell off-balance, and landed on her backside. Her rifle came up, ready. Then she lowered it. Boguli stood before her, still dressed in his worn gray blanket, his skin and sparse hair ashen with dust. He stood with his legs apart, swaying gently from side to side in his own private rhythm.

'I will chase out the men inside so you may go in,' he whispered. 'But the boy is not there. They took him north.'

Jade was too startled to think clearly, still processing the fact that this strange old man, this enigma she'd hoped to reencounter, was standing next to her. 'Where?' she finally whispered, but it was to Boguli's back as he withdrew into the forest's shadows. From her right, she heard Sam and Abasi return. They crouched down next to her, and Sam gave the report.

'We didn't hear any of the Germans or Harry,' he said. 'Of course, some of them could be in their tents asleep. We did hear a few of their porters talking.' He looked at Abasi. 'Could you make out anything they were saying?'

'I put my ear to the *boma* and heard the cook talk about the food — that is all.'

'What do you want to do next, Jade?' asked Sam. 'Shall I walk in there? Maybe Abasi could go in. They probably don't know him.'

She shook her head. 'Jelani's not in there, but I can do a quick search of the tents. Abasi wouldn't know what to look for.'

Sam stared at her, mouth agape. 'How do you suddenly know Jelani's not there?' he asked. 'And just how are you planning on waltzing in unnoticed?'

She put a finger to her lips. 'Shhh. Our diversion is on its way now.' As she spoke, a sound like low thunder rumbled closer, and the ground vibrated under their feet. A sapling snapped in a sharp crack, followed by a symphony of trumpet blasts and low, throaty rumbles.

'Stampede!' breathed Sam. He turned his head towards the sound of the approaching herd. 'We need to get out of here.'

Jade grabbed both his arm and Abasi's. 'No! We're safe here.'

The rumbling grew louder and a dusty fog rolled out of the trees near their side of the compound. The musty, acrid scent of large herbivores wafted over them along with the dust. Jade coughed and fanned away the airborne soil. She saw nine adult females and one young male trot out into the clearing. An aging matriarch whose wrinkled skin bore the scars of innumerable encounters with tree limbs led them.

The herd hesitated for only a moment before they plowed into the *boma*. Under their combined weight the thorn brush snapped like toothpicks in rapid-fire succession, like a chain of firecrackers going off. The lead matriarch raised her trunk and bellowed once before she curled it around a bundle of stout limbs and hurled them into the exposed compound.

The cook and the remaining porters yelled in

241

terror and raced out the *boma* gate and into the forest, thinking only of putting distance between themselves and the rampaging herd. Jade heard a high-pitched, feminine scream and saw Mercedes standing in front of her tent, her open hands in front of her face as though blocking the sight would remove the danger.

Sam started to rise, but Jade held on to his arm. When he looked at her and tried to remove her restraining hand, she shook her head no. So far the elephants had restricted their assault to the *boma* wall itself and hadn't entered the compound. Mercedes was in no immediate danger, but Sam would be if he tried running through the angry herd. Just as he was about to go to the girl's rescue anyway, the young male tossed a branch with a flip of his trunk. It arched up over one of the tents and landed a few feet away from Mercedes, but it gave her the shock necessary to make her bolt after the porters for the gate and the safety of the forest beyond.

'Stay here and cover me,' Jade said as she rose and sprinted behind the elephants and into the compound. She had no idea how Boguli had managed to direct the herd there or even keep their rampage down to an assault on the fence, but she knew the diversion wouldn't buy her much more than a few minutes. Harry and his crew might be near enough to hear the attack and come racing back at any time.

Her first duty was to make sure that Jelani wasn't held captive in the camp. She raced from tent to tent, searching for the boy and calling his name. When she verified Boguli's statement, she

242

darted into Mercedes' tent and quickly searched all the girl's clothing for anything with a missing button. Nothing. Jade stopped and collected her thoughts. If the button didn't belong to Mercedes, then perhaps it was Liesel's. She had no idea which tent belonged to the peroxide blonde, but she'd make a quick search of each one in turn.

Outside, the din from the elephants receded. The herd had completed its destruction of the *boma* fence and was placidly marching off into the forest to resume feeding. Jade had gone through two of the other tents without success when she found a soiled linen blouse wadded up at the foot of a cot. She picked it up and held it by the sleeves. The blouse had identical mother-of-pearl buttons to the one she'd found in the cache, only the top button was missing. Broken threads marked where the button should have been before it was torn away. Had it been ripped off in a fit of passion or in a fight?

Whose tent is this? Liesel's? It wasn't the one that Mercedes ran from. Jade dropped the blouse back onto the ground and headed for the camp table, hoping to find anything to identify the tent's occupant. She discovered nothing on the woman's side that bore any identification, so she headed over to the man's half of the tent. *Somewhere there must be some sort of document. A passport?* She found what she wanted in a small, wooden cigar box: two passports, husband's and wife's. What surprised Jade most was that the blouse belonged not to Liesel, but to the stodgy Claudia von Gretchmar.

17

To the south and west of Marsabit lies the Kaisoot Desert, haven to many animals, especially during the rains. To the north is another matter entirely.
— The Traveler

Heat waves rose up from the black rocks, rippling like the ghostly spirits of long-dead slaves. One of the ghosts must have decided to take his vengeance on Jelani rather than risk the ire of a slaver, for it tripped the boy. Jelani caught himself as he stumbled, and avoided falling on the jagged stones.

The man in front of him stopped, and a second one, traveling behind him, yanked him roughly by the shoulders and half carried, half dragged him to the shade of a large rock pile. Water trickled gently nearby, and Jelani assumed that they had stopped to wait out the day's heat in an oasis.

A few small plants had managed to grab a foothold where the water seeped out of a spring before it all evaporated or fled underground away from the sun. One of the camels, the one with the largest ivory load, plodded over to the greenery and ended the plants' valiant but doomed attempt at survival.

Jelani wanted to be the springwater and join it in its underground flight before he, too, evaporated in the sun's raging heat or worse. He blinked away the dryness in his eyes and studied the men milling around the two camels and the spring. They were northern men, not white but not dark like him. They wore knee-length, loose-fitting robes that might have been white at one time, but had long since taken on the dull color of stale water. Below the robes were ragged trousers and sandals.

He didn't remember meeting up with them until they were already on the march, but then, he didn't remember much at all except following Biscuit, hoping to surprise whoever had lured the cat away. He recalled that the person who called Biscuit kept moving farther away, enticing them both on until Jelani knew he'd gone too far. That, and someone putting a sickly-sweet-smelling rag over his face. When he thought about his capture, another memory hovered on the edge of his mind, like a little kestrel fluttering aloft waiting to capture a lizard. He willed the memory to swoop into his consciousness, but it flitted away instead.

One of the men approached him and thrust a rancid-smelling bag made from a poorly cured goatskin into his shackled hands. Something sloshed inside and suddenly his thirst became a ravenous beast clawing at his innards. The boy fumbled with the leather bung that acted as a stopper. His hands felt numb from the raw leather tightly wrapped around his wrists, but he finally managed to remove the plug with his teeth and spit it into his hand. The water tasted stale and smelled like rotting goat, but he drank anyway. It had been a long march.

What *did* he remember? He struggled to clear his head and think. He remembered waking up when someone hiding in the rocks chirped for Biscuit. He remembered grabbing his knife and letting the cheetah follow the sound in the darkness. But the cat soon outdistanced him. He remembered hearing a shot and finding Biscuit lying in his own blood. Then a gloved hand, the sweet scent like a poisonous flower, and more darkness until he came to, flopped on his stomach across the neck of a camel. His head pounded and he vomited right then and there as the beast lumbered along. One man yelled at him, then grabbed him by the waist and hauled him off the unwashed brute. He remembered his legs buckling under him before he forced them to stay rigid when the same man struck him with a stick and hauled him up on his feet again.

A gloved hand! These men did not wear gloves. The memory came closer but was still out of reach. He choked down another mouthful of the foul water. *What happened to Biscuit?* It was his job to look after Simba Jike's pet cheetah. *Is he hurt?* He wondered what Bwana and Memsabu Dunbury were doing. Did they know he was gone? Were they coming to find him or would they think he had run away? He shook his head to clear out the bad thoughts. *No.* They would not think that. But they would have no idea where to look for him, either, especially if Biscuit could not help them.

Part of him worried that he would be in trouble for letting the slavers capture him. After all, Simba Jike had warned him that there were dangerous men out there, but he never really believed they would hurt him, not while he was with Bwana Dunbury. Underlying all these gloomy thoughts was one mocking, inner voice reminding him that he wasn't a warrior. Not only had he failed to kill Simba Jike's enemy, but her pet cheetah might be dead. She would never welcome him back again. He fought the urge to cry, knowing he could not afford to waste water in tears out here in this rocky desert.

The same man that gave him the waterskin grabbed it away from him and shoved the bung back into the hole. Jelani recognized him as the one who had hit him across the back and shoulders when he could not walk at first. He had a pitted face hidden in part by his short beard. He pointed at Jelani's feet and yelled something to his companion. When the second man shook his head and laughed at him, the first took out his anger on the boy and pushed him down onto the rocks. Jelani felt the rough stones bite into his buttocks and back.

The man continued arguing with his comrade, waving his arms and shouting. Finally, the other pulled his knife from a side slit in his robe and sliced off a length of leather from a camel's worn lead strap. He tossed the leather to the angry man and waved him away. Jelani couldn't understand their language, but he gathered that his antagonist felt he might try to escape while they waited out the scorching heat. It seemed his companion did not think the boy strong enough or foolish enough to risk attempting such a foolhardy trek. To do so without water meant certain death.

The man grabbed Jelani's bare feet and lashed his ankles together. The rough dry leather scraped and sliced into his skin before absorbing some of the blood that trickled out of the fresh wounds. At this point, death in the desert seemed a better option to Jelani than the slavery that surely awaited him. He fought back the rising nausea that came from the rancid water and the pain. He needed to keep his wits about him and think of a way to escape. As the men settled down in the shade of a rocky outcrop to doze, Jelani led his mind back over the lessons he'd learned reading the fables and settled on one in particular.

★　★　★

'Over there. That's one of the cars.' Jade leaned forward and pointed to a block-shaped object in the distance.

After running through Harry's camp, Jade had declined Sam's offer to again search the poachers' cache for the boy. When he pressed her for a reason, all she would say was that Jelani wasn't there, that he'd been taken north. So they hurried back to the Dodge, tossed in their blankets, and drove down the rockiest and most hazardous part of the mountain while it was yet light, continuing after nightfall until a protruding branch smashed a headlamp. At that point, Jade perched on the hood and scouted the ground ahead with her flashlight. Now in midmorning, they contended with rising heat waves that parched their throats and distorted their vision.

'I see it.' Sam hit the accelerator and sped across the rocky ground to the Overlander and the porters left to guard it. Two flat tires explained why the Dunburys hadn't taken both vehicles.

'*Jambo*,' called Jade in greeting. 'Did you find Jelani? Where is Bwana Dunbury?'

The man who also served as cook shook his head and pointed to the northeast. 'Bwana and Memsahib Dunbury found some fresh camel dung over that way. Maybe camel herders, maybe not. Bwana and Memsahib went on, hoping to find them. Maybe they have the boy.'

'Where's Chiumbo? Is he with them?' she asked.

A dark arm rose up from the seat and waved to Jade. 'I am here, Simba Jike. I am fine.' He struggled to rise to a sitting position. 'Memsabu Dunbury said the road north would be hard on me, so she made me stay here. Take me with you. I will make those bad men pay when you find them.' He waved a knife by the hilt.

Jade shook her head. 'No, my friend. Lady Beverly was right. You must stay here and rest.' Seeing the disgruntled frown on his face she added, 'We may need you later. You had best be strong again then.'

'Has Biscuit returned?' asked Sam, If they could find the cat, he could track the boy. The cook shook his head.

'Maybe Avery and Bev found Biscuit already,' suggested Jade as they drove on. She peered out into the rocky ground ahead. 'It's not going to be easy to see their trail, especially once it gets dark.'

'Looks like they thought of that, Jade,' said Sam. 'Look out there.' He pointed at a glittering piece of metal, flashing in the sun. 'If I'm not mistaken, that's a can. They're leaving a bread crumb trail for us to follow.'

Sam, Jade, and Abasi pushed on into the barren territory between Mount Marsabit and Abyssinia. The Dodge jolted and lurched over black volcanic rock, and Sam stopped every half hour so he and Jade could check under the hood and the car for items that had vibrated loose. Part of the exhaust pipe took a direct hit, but they escaped any major damage. Most of the razor-sharp rock was the size of river gravel, and Sam did his best to avoid the larger chunks that could irreparably damage their oil pan.

Nothing relieved the monotony: no wildlife, no vegetation beyond a rare thornbush, and no sign of the Dunburys, Jelani, or Biscuit. Anxiety grew first as a lump in Jade's throat, then swelled into a dull, rhythmic pounding in her temples.

Morning turned to afternoon, and the shadows lengthened as well as the distance between the Dunburys' tossed-out cans. Even their ability to spot these diminished as the shifting shadows from innumerable small rocks played tricks on them. At times their pace slowed to a crawl as all eyes searched for the next marker that let them know they were on the right trail. Jade finally perched on the car's hood for a better vantage point and used her binoculars to enhance her search. By sunset they lost the cans and found the Dunburys instead.

Beverly raced forward and enveloped Jade in a crushing hug. 'Thank the Lord you're here,' she said. 'Abasi, you did very well. Thank you so much.'

Jade gently pushed Beverly away and studied her face. Water marks smeared her grimy face where a few tears had trickled down across the volcanic soot. Those marks spoke volumes to Jade. They hadn't found Jelani, dead or alive. 'Any sign of the boy at all?' she asked.

'None,' said Avery as he put an arm around his wife's shoulders. 'But we found Biscuit. Someone shot at him, and the bullet nicked a lung. They must have left him for dead when they took Jelani.'

'Is it serious? Can he track?' asked Jade. As much as she liked the big cat, her main concern was having him to locate Jelani. Her throat tightened in a knot of panic, and she fought it down. *If anyone has hurt that boy, they'd better pray I don't find them.*

'We patched him up,' continued Avery. 'The wound doesn't appear to be septic. See for yourself.'

He pointed behind her, and Jade turned in time to receive Biscuit's head butt against her thigh. It was as if the cheetah had heard Jade's voice and wanted to reassure her himself. She stroked the cat, knelt down, and inspected the wound under the full bandage wrapped about

251

the cheetah's barrel-shaped chest. The cat strained against his lead, which was tied to the car's rear axle.

'We've had to keep him tied up tightly in the car,' said Avery. 'Even wounded, he wants to find Jelani. Every so often, in between camel droppings, we let him out to sniff a trail for us.'

'Speaking of wounds,' said Beverly, 'did you see Chiumbo? How is he?'

Jade assured her friends that Chiumbo was doing well and anxious to wreak vengeance on the kidnappers. 'Now tell me everything,' she said when she finished her brief report. 'How do you know you're on the right track and why on earth did you stop?'

Avery pointed to the car. 'Had to stop. Everything's come loose under the bonnet, the carburetor is completely fouled, and one of my tires is shredded.' He looked at his watch. 'We've been here for nearly six hours trying to put it all back together.'

'As to being on the trail,' continued Beverly, 'we weren't sure for quite a while. All we could do was look for those blasted camel droppings and assume they were from whoever took Jelani. I hate to think how much time we wasted going back and forth looking for those. But when we found Biscuit, we knew our assumptions were right. Then we found this.'

Avery held up a glove and a rag for them to see. 'These were in the rocks close to where we found Biscuit.'

Jade took the man's leather work glove and the rag and noticed a trace odor, sweet but noxious.

She took a hesitant sniff, then jerked back her head immediately. 'Chloroform!'

'That's what we suspected,' said Beverly. 'Someone held this rag laced with it to Jelani's face. Probably wore the glove to keep the chemicals off his hand. We also found this.'

Beverly reached in her trouser pocket and pulled out a dirty bloodstained handkerchief. 'This was under Biscuit. Jelani must have put it there to try to patch up the cheetah. That's probably when the slavers captured him.' Her voice quavered and a gut-wrenching sob broke from her throat.

Avery pulled his wife to his chest in an enveloping embrace. He caressed her back and kissed the top of her head. 'Hush, darling. They won't kill him or even hurt him. They want him alive and healthy to bring a higher price. And now that Sam and Jade are here, they can continue on and find him. It's going to be all right.'

Jade wanted to add her own reassurances, but the thought of that brave boy being examined like livestock and sold to some northern sheikh filled her with a fresh wave of anger and loathing. She clenched her fists and renewed her silent vow to make them pay. What worried her more than anything was the idea that this was all planned. It seemed too far-fetched to think that Biscuit just happened to wander off and someone shot at him, that Jelani found him, and some slavers who just happened to be in the area captured him using chloroform. No, this had all the earmarks of a staged attack.

Sam saw her tight-lipped mouth and her distant stare. 'Jade, what is it? What are you thinking?'

She continued to gaze out at the featureless landscape. 'That this was not a coincidence. Someone lured Biscuit away, knowing the boy would follow.' She took a deep breath and closed her eyes in a vain attempt to shut out the pain in her temples. 'Think about it. No one shoots at cheetahs. They're harmless. They've never been known to attack humans, and I've never ever heard of them harassing livestock, either. And everyone at Hascombe's camp has seen how Jelani and Biscuit go together, and most of them witnessed the time when Biscuit broke free and the boy came after him.' She looked at Sam. 'You were there, remember?' Sam nodded. 'So if they wanted the boy, they knew to use Biscuit to bring him out, then eliminate the cat so he couldn't follow.'

'But how would they get Biscuit to wander off?' asked Beverly as she pushed away from her husband and dabbed at her eyes. 'The only time the cat goes off, it's to look for you.'

Jade nodded. 'So maybe they have something with my scent on it. Or maybe they lured him with some meat or even called to him.' She didn't add that the cat also knew and liked Harry and might have gone looking for him. 'I'm convinced that at least some of Harry's crew are involved in this gunrunning, poaching operation.'

'So you think this is revenge?' asked Sam.

Jade didn't answer for a while. 'For what? We

were leaving, remember? Or at least that's what they believed. In that case, why not just let us go?' She stroked the cheetah while she organized her thoughts. 'Jelani's been in their camp a lot. I thought they didn't pay any attention to him, but maybe someone did. Maybe this person thinks Jelani heard something that would incriminate him.' She looked up at Sam. 'Or her, if that button is any clue. Remove the boy and remove the evidence.' *And it's my own damn fault for encouraging him to spy on them.*

'What button?' asked Avery.

'We found a woman's button in the poachers' cache. We searched their tents and found it belonged to Claudia von Gretchmar. Jelani's probably been seen snooping in the camp by Otto at least.'

'So they might kill him after all?' moaned Beverly.

'No,' Jade quickly answered. 'No. We'd have found his body with Biscuit's.'

'I'm almost done with the car, I think,' said Avery. 'Another hour should do the trick, and I have a spare tire.'

'We're not waiting for you, old man,' said Sam. 'Sorry, but they've got too much of a head start already.' He looked at Abasi. 'I want you to stay here and help Bwana Dunbury. He'll need another strong arm to take care of that tire. And we want as little weight as possible in the Dodge to get up some speed and keep from digging our own tires into the rocks any more than necessary.'

Jade heard Sam's decisive tone and felt a faint

255

stirring of hope. She had an ally here, a good one. She smiled her gratitude.

Sam caught her smile and stood a little straighter. His eyes sparkled and he returned her look with a nod. 'You ready, Simba Jike?'

'Yes. Let's put whatever we don't need in Avery's car.' They quickly stowed their remaining tarps, bedroll, and packs in the Overlander, eliminating everything but the necessary food, water, medical supplies, and ammunition. Jade slipped the poacher's bow and the arrows into the other car and took only her Winchester. This was not the time for experimenting with another weapon. 'Keep one of the blankets,' she added softly so that Beverly wouldn't hear her. 'We may need it for carrying Jelani.'

Avery came up behind them in time to hear. 'Make certain you have enough medical supplies and water,' he said in a hushed voice. Then in a more conversational tone he added, 'With all this extra weight, I don't think I can tail you without risking the rest of the tires. We'll wait here for one day for your return. If we don't see you by the morning after tomorrow, we'll drop most of this gear by the wayside and follow you.'

'We don't have any cans to leave for markers,' Sam said. 'Hand me that empty chop box back there.'

Avery lifted the box from the Overlander and handed it to Sam. 'Good idea. You can break this up and leave us some wooden markers with compass bearings on it.'

Jade rummaged in the car for Jelani's book of fables as well as the notebook in which he'd been practicing his writing, her hat dropping from her head as she hunkered over the boxes. When she found the books, she felt her throat constrict again as she visualized him proudly reading another story. Then she undid the cheetah's lead from the car and tied it securely to her belt. 'Biscuit,' she called as she squatted down beside the big cat. She held out the two books and watched as Biscuit sniffed them like a hound. Normally sight hunters, cheetahs also relied on scent markers to identify territory. She counted on the cat's sense of smell to help them now. Biscuit flared once, opening his mouth and curling his tongue to catch the taste of the scent as well as its odor.

The slender animal crouched low on his forelegs and sniffed the ground for nearly a quarter of a minute before he lifted his head and stared out at the distant horizon, a high-pitched staccato churring sound, the cat's equivalent of a growl, issuing from his throat. Jade waited, her legs tense, her eyes expectant, as Biscuit stood as immobile as a statue for another half minute. Suddenly the cat chirped a sharp barking sound as though calling to someone. As he bent his forelegs and sniffed the ground again, Jade rose and walked just behind him, letting him take the lead as he picked up Jelani's scent.

Suddenly Biscuit pulled hard at the lead, nearly causing Jade to pitch forward off-balance. She would have fallen but for Sam's strong arm grabbing her waist. Biscuit rebelled against the restraint by turning and first butting Jade in the legs before slapping her ankles with his large

257

paws, his claws scraping her boots.

'He's got the scent,' shouted Jade. 'You *were* on the right track.'

Sam held on to Biscuit's lead to prevent the cat from bolting while Jade untied it from her belt and retied it onto the door handle. She scrambled over the door into the passenger side to be closer to the cat. Sam clambered into the driver's side, and released the hand brake.

'Remember Biscuit's still wounded. He needs to pace himself, Jade,' said Beverly over the noisy sputtering of the car's engine.

'Have you thought about what you're going to do once you catch up to these men?' asked Avery.

Jade's emerald eyes gleamed and she flashed her teeth in a predatory snarl. 'Oh, yes,' she said in a low, breathy tone geared to send shivers down the spine of the listener. She patted the Winchester on her lap. 'I've thought about it a lot.'

Avery's brow furrowed, and he reached across Sam to take hold of Jade's left arm. 'You're not a killer, Jade,' he said. 'Self-defense is one thing, but don't become like these men. Don't kill for pleasure.'

Jade gently pried his hand from her arm. 'Don't worry, Avery. I won't kill them unless I have to. But by the time I'm done, they'll wish I had.'

18

*To the north lies the Dida Galgalla desert, a
wasteland of black lava and vultures, some
of them human.*
— The Traveler

Jelani looked up at the stars and silently thanked
Ngai, the Maker, for creating the night.
Normally it was a time of fear, a time to huddle
in a hut and listen to the roar of the prowling
lion or the cackling laugh of the hyena, but now
it brought relief from the sun's searing heat. It
also brought secrecy.

The small caravan had paused in its
northward trek for a few hours' rest while the
sun sat high overhead and devoured their
shadows. Then, once their shadows dared to
crawl out to the length of a man's pace, they
marched on again. Jelani had made good use of
his time while the slavers slept. As he relieved
himself, he scanned the ground for a sharp rock,
one small enough to fit hidden in his clasped
hands. He found one, about the size of an
arrowhead. While his drowsy guard looked away,
he pretended to stumble, not a hard trick
considering how tired he was. His hands braced
his fall against the barren ground, and he
retrieved his prize.

The men had depended on fear of the blistering desert more than anything to keep him securely in their camp. After all, the waterless wasteland was death to a runaway slave. But the cruelest slaver tied a leather thong around Jelani's neck and attached the other end to the boy's hands. They left him sitting hunched slightly, trusting him to sit or lie still rather than risk the cutting abrasion of the raw leather.

Jelani knew he could not escape them in daylight. Instead, he first worried the leather around his wrist to weaken it. He couldn't break it now, though. They'd see it and only tie him up again, so he slipped the hard black rock into a rip in his waistband to hide it. When night came, he would finish the work.

Then it was night, and the men prepared to sleep by the side of a dried watercourse. Jelani had pretended to faint as soon as they stopped. One man threw the rancid water sack on the ground next to him and tossed something on top of it that was probably supposed to be food, dates by the smell wafting towards his nose. The aroma woke his stomach, which responded by tightening and growling. The hunger pangs nearly drove him into grabbing the scant meal, but he forced himself to lie still and wait.

They left him alone. Soon they would be asleep and he would finish sawing through the thong and slip away. While he lay in his pretend faint, he heard the thumping trot of a camel followed by a new voice. Someone came to the camp, someone the men respected as a leader, if their voices were any indication. The man spoke to Jelani's captors in their own language, but with an accent. He was not one of them. Jelani tried to risk opening one eye to see this man, but he faced the wrong direction, and it was too dark anyway. There was no moon up yet, but something about the accent, about the careful way he spoke, told him the man was white. He understood only two words, spoken with scorn, followed by a sneering laugh. *Simba Jike*. An echo of the man's voice speaking English when Jelani had first been captured rang in his memory.

'*Let Simba Jike find you now. Let her follow you like you did the cat.*'

Determined and hurried strides vibrated the ground as one of the captors stomped towards him. He hoped they wouldn't force him up. It would spoil his entire plan. But the man only grabbed his right leg. He felt something cold slip around it, then felt more than heard the stake being pounded into the ground. They had shackled his foot.

* * *

The black rocks went on forever, while to the rear Mount Marsabit diminished to a hazy blue bump on the horizon. Biscuit followed the scent track easily, impatiently tugging at his leash whenever Sam and Jade stopped to pound a wooden stake into the hard ground and print a compass bearing on it. But Jade saw that the cat was tiring, and judging by the slight limp, his footpads hurt from the sharp, volcanic gravel.

261

Jade rummaged through the vehicle, found another rag, and ripped it into strips, which she wound around the cheetah's feet.

About an hour before the sun set, they found where the slavers had rested during the day. Biscuit hunkered a long time over one spot in particular, and Jade's fist clenched when she saw the rough ground where Jelani must have sat. She took advantage of the last bit of daylight to scan the horizon with her binoculars while Sam poured another can of gasoline in the Dodge and added water to the radiator.

There was no sign of a caravan. Surely they should be getting close, even considering how slowly they'd had to creep along in some spots. Biscuit picked up the exit trail, which appeared to follow a dried waterway. Jade restrained the cat while she took a compass bearing and wrote it on a wooden stake. Then Sam pounded a marker into the ground for Avery and Beverly.

They continued on, Jade sitting on the car's hood with her flashlight in order to spot hazards in the dark. Biscuit needed only a scent and none of them had any intention of stopping for sleep. They hoped the slavers would.

She and Sam hadn't spoken much during their long, slow search beyond an occasional 'Hang on' or 'Watch out for that rock.' Jade had no idea what Sam would do once they located Jelani and his abductors. She just hoped he didn't get in her way.

'Can you see anything at all up there?' he asked from the driver's seat.

'Just Biscuit,' she replied. He still tugged on

the lead, so Jade knew he was on the scent. 'If anything, he seems more insistent,' she added. 'The scent must be stronger. We're gaining on them.'

Sam didn't reply for a few moments. 'I'm not sure how much longer we can go on driving in the dark, Jade. It's getting too dangerous.'

The car slowed as if in punctuation to his statement. She turned on the hood and faced him. 'We can't stop now. I'm not quitting now.'

He brought the Dodge to a halt. 'I didn't say we should quit. But I think we need to proceed on foot. If we are gaining on them, then we need some element of surprise. We're not going to get it with the car. It's sputtering too loudly as it is. We also need to conserve the fuel and water or we won't be able to bring ourselves and Jelani back.'

Jade considered his proposal for a moment as Biscuit tugged at his lead. She wrapped the leash around her wrist once more for a better grip to restrain the anxious cat. Sam was right. As much as she hated to lose time walking, she knew the slavers would hear them coming and be ready for them. They might even try to use Jelani as a shield.

'Shut it off,' she said.

Sam complied, then grabbed one of their medical kits and strapped it to his belt. Both of them took two canteens apiece and their respective rifles. Jade wrote a note to the Dunburys explaining their plan and their last direction, and held the note in place on the driver's seat with a large chunk of basaltic rock.

'Let's go,' she said. Sam replied with a firm nod of his head.

Biscuit, now unencumbered by the car, pulled vigorously at his lead. He chirped once, and Jade shushed him with a gentle voice and a firm hand on his head. The cat led a fast pace despite his injuries, pulling on Jade's left hand until her shoulder ached. She longed to switch hands, but knew she needed to keep the right free to shoot if danger suddenly appeared. After two hours of walking and tripping in the dark, she was ready to hand over the lead to Sam and tugged hard on the leash to halt the cat.

A slight grumbling grunt to her right caught her ear. *A camel?* Perhaps they were closer than they thought. She handed the lead to Sam and held one finger to her lips for silence. They listened again, but the sound didn't repeat itself.

Sam took over as cheetah handler, and Jade massaged her sore shoulder. *Actually, every dag-blasted joint in my body aches.* Even her ankles hurt from twisting her feet over the uneven ground. And so she never noticed the warning ache in her left knee, losing it in the rest of the general pain. Her only clue that there might be any danger was the sudden *thwack* like wood on wood, followed by a dull thud as Sam toppled to the ground. By then it was too late.

'Jade,' he said with a groan, which ended with another *thud*.

'Sam?' Then something struck her from behind and she knew only blackness.

19

Not even the seasonal rains have the ability to bless this desolate and seemingly accursed stretch of land. Despite all the dangers and privations of this barren region, nomadic peoples still guide their caravans and herds across them, bringing trade goods, livestock, ivory, and, sometimes, human cargo to Abyssinia.
— The Traveler

Jelani lay absolutely still and listened for the sound of deep breathing from all the men. Two distinct snores reverberated in the night and told him that no one even bothered to keep watch.

Why should they? They are the predators. They are not afraid of anyone.

He stirred as though turning in his sleep and tested the ankle iron. His heel almost slipped out. Clearly it had been made for a larger captive. He relaxed his leg, lest he clank the rusty chain too much. Then he slipped the rock from its hiding place in his waistband where it had scraped and gouged his side for several hours. Holding the sharp stone by the heel of his hands, he began the slow, deliberate task of sawing away at the weakened leather that bound his wrists to his neck.

Unfortunately, in the dark he couldn't see the thong easily and he inadvertently sliced at his hand and the side of his wrist frequently. That was all right. He remembered that the wolf in the fable had to chew off his own foot to escape his trap. The lesson had been that freedom came at a price, but Jelani knew that a warrior must be inured to pain to conquer. *What was the lesson of the crow's story? 'Little by little does the job'?*

The rock slipped in his hand as his own blood flowed from more and more cuts. Jelani wiped them on his torn shirt and took a better grip. He had to escape tonight and soon. His friends were in danger. They might not want him back after what had happened to Biscuit, but he could not let the same thing happen to them.

The leather strap finally yielded to the rock's sharp edge. His hands were free. Now to release his foot from its prison. Jelani took off his torn and bloody shirt and wrapped it around the chain to silence it. Then he pushed against the iron as he pulled his heel back.

The rusty leg iron might have been made for a larger foot, but it still managed to catch his heel. He took his rock tool and sawed away some of the callus on his heel, taking part of the skin with it. Only by lubricating his foot with his own blood and by scraping off the skin of his heel and part of his ankle bone was he able to finally extricate himself. He gathered up his shirt, wrapping it around his sliced palms as a bandage.

Beside him lay the skin of foul water and the handful of dates. He devoured the dates and

266

forced himself to swallow the horrid-tasting water. There was very little of it, and Jelani's thirst made him wish for more no matter how disgusting it tasted.

He dropped the empty skin on the ground next to the ankle iron and slipped out of the camp and back towards the mountain of the elephants. All the while, two words echoed in his head. *Simba Jike*. He needed to warn her.

* * *

Sensations, more than actual thoughts, worked their way into Jade's slowly awakening consciousness. First came throat-parching thirst, followed by a throbbing pain in her temples. She gradually grew aware of a buzzing sound in her left ear, akin to the ever-present conversational hum at the Muthaiga Club.

I need a lemonade. Where's a waiter when you need one? Maybe I'll just go home. It's too noisy here. Don't these people ever shut up?

'Frightful noise. Someone shooting the lights again. No decency.'

The gramophone wailed out 'The Yellow Dog Blues.' Women in glittering gowns and jeweled necklaces languished in the arms of tuxedoed men whose eyes glowed with a predatory sheen. They danced past the stuffed lion, a Muthaiga Club mascot, its body a patchwork of bullet holes from innumerable target practices.

'Terrible state the colony's gotten in. Blasted train from Mombasa opens the door to too much riffraff.'

'Hear, hear.'

Marion Harris replaced the blues, singing about jazz, trombones, and saxophones, and the dancers erupted into a bedlam of fox-trots and rapid two-steps. The poor lion suffered the indignity of one woman's heels kicking back into its face.

'Commissioner, did you ever uncover what caused that fire at Roger Forster's old place?'

'No. Most suspicious, though. Seemed to have been deliberately set.' This pronouncement was followed by horrified gasps and expressions of shock.

'I thought someone bought the place after the man died on safari last year. I suppose the person who bought it was injured in the fire?'

'No one took possession. Some broker purchased it for a woman in England. A week later it was torched.'

Marion Harris stayed on the gramophone, telling the dancers how men go simply wild over her. One man set his half-empty champagne glass on the stuffed lion's back and scooped up a dance partner. Another half dozen couples left their glasses tipped over on the end tables as they crowded the dance floor, laughing and singing along.

'Met the new chap with the King's Rifles up north? I hear he saw service in Tanganyika during the war. Ought to be able to handle the natives. Tragic how Captain Ross died. Bloody ambush!'

One of the women, tipsy from too much champagne, tripped over her own feet and fell backward until she crashed against the wall and plopped down, straddling the lion. A series of hilarious guffaws erupted. Colridge's son grabbed Jade's arm and pulled her onto the dance floor.

Something tickled Jade's ear. This annoyance was followed by an intense thirst, a gritty cotton-mouthed feeling similar to the only hangover she'd ever experienced, when she and Beverly overdid their Armistice celebration. She tried to sit up, but the dull, throbbing pain pulsed from the back of her head and across her shoulders. *What the hell happened?* The droning hum continued. *Am I still at the Muthaiga Club?*

She shifted again and swatted the annoying fly from her ear. *What is that jangling noise?* The fly resettled around her nostril, searching for moisture. She snorted and shook her head. *Bad idea. Sweet heavens, that hurt.*

Suddenly, her conscious brain sent silent alarms throughout her body. Her pulse quickened, her hearing became more acute, and a faint metallic aroma that she associated with blood assaulted her nostrils. The skin around her wrists sent the message that something hard constricted them. She moved her hand again to swat the pesky fly and again heard the jingling.

Chains!

'Sam,' she whispered. Her throat burned with raw fire as she spoke, and a clot of congealing blood hung from her lower lip. She raised her head, spit onto the ground, and tried again. 'Sam!' This time, a nearby groan answered her.

Jade again attempted to push herself into a sitting position, but discovered that her hands were shackled together with only a foot or so of chain between them. She jammed her right

269

elbow into the ground and used it to gain leverage. When her vision blurred and she nearly swooned, she paused to let her heart keep pace with her head's change in altitude. The spots gradually quit swimming in front of her eyes and she saw that her wrists were tethered, not only to each other, but to Sam's leg as well.

'SAM!'

'What?'

'We have a problem.' She surveyed their situation while he roused himself. As near as she could tell, someone had ambushed them in the dark and left them to die in the desert. Their canteens and rifles had been taken. 'Be careful how you move. I seem to be chained to you.'

Sam raised himself to a sitting position and rubbed his head, wincing from the pain. 'Something hit me in the leg. I remember falling, then . . . ' He paused to recollect the events. 'I think I remember hearing someone behind me and they hit me in the head with a mallet or club or something.' He rubbed his head again. 'Are you all right? Where's Biscuit?'

'Don't know. I think he took off running,' Jade said. 'Probably went on to find Jelani.'

Sam stretched out his free, good leg and tried to reposition himself away from a sharp rock that dug into his thigh. 'I feel like a truck hit me.'

'I heard the blows. I think you're about right. He hit me, too.' She pointed to his leg, the wounded one. 'Did he hit you in your bad leg?'

Sam nodded, then winced from the pain. 'Don't worry — it's not broken. How's your head?'

'I'm all right as long as I don't move too fast. But whoever attacked us only had one decent leg-iron and used it to hold both of us. We're not walking out like this.'

Sam inspected the iron clamped firmly and tightly around his boot. There was no way it would slip off.

'We could cut the boot off, I suppose,' Jade suggested. 'One of these rocks might do it. We just need to be careful not to cut your leg in the process.'

Sam just stared at her, his brown hair flopping over one eye. 'You know, you are not the most fun date I have ever had, lady,' he managed.

Jade produced a rueful smile as she wondered why she brought nothing but disaster to the men in her life. Maybe because she fought entanglements so much. 'Tell you what. We get out of this, and rescue Jelani, I'll make it up to you. Maybe you can give me a tour of Purdue.'

'Mmmm, moonlight on the Wabash River and you. Something to live for.' The smile that spread across Sam's angular face grew so slowly but so inexorably that Jade felt a tingling shiver, not at all unpleasant, race down her spine. He leaned towards her, his face only a few inches from hers. 'Remember when we first met and I wanted to protect you and you told me I didn't have a leg to stand on?'

'Yeah,' she answered warily.

'Well, it seems you were right.'

With that, he grabbed a hole in the knee of his trousers and ripped it open. Then he carefully proceeded to unfasten his right leg.

20

*Anyone who travels north along these cara-
van routes should bring plenty of water with
them. In addition to quantities of water,
remember to take along a goodly number of
blankets. People equate deserts with extreme
heat, not realizing that the nights can
become bitterly cold.*
— The Traveler

Jelani couldn't remember ever feeling so cold.
Even on the mountain of the elephants, the
nights never got this frigid. He shivered. He
couldn't stop shivering. His muscles refused to
obey him, and even his teeth clattered together.
He wished he could put his shirt back on, but
he'd finally ripped it in two and wound a
blood-soaked strip around each foot as some
protection from the sharp rocks. He'd saved one
thin strip to rebind the worst slash on his wrist,
tying it tightly with his teeth. Now his hand felt
numb and tingly.

He had slipped out of the camp unnoticed, as
silent as a snake. At first, he tiptoed, making
certain he made no sound, dislodged no rocks.
Then, when he felt he was far enough away, he
broke into a run and ran until he thought his
lungs would burst. By then his feet were cut and

bloody, so he stopped and used his equally bloody shirt for shoes instead of bandages on his hands.

He had no idea how far he needed to go, only that he must keep moving. He hoped that the slavers wouldn't notice his disappearance until morning and then would decide it was not worth the bother to go back after one boy. He tried to swallow, wished he had some water. Even that stagnant water in that horrid, rotting skin would be better than this thirst.

To his left, the sun rose over the horizon. Soon the cold would stop and the intense heat of the desert day would begin. Should he stop and sleep somewhere? Travel at night? No, the man had said 'Simba Jike' in a terrible, scornful voice, the same tone he had used when he admitted using Jelani as bait to lure away Memsabu Jade. She was in danger. He had to warn her.

Jelani found it harder to put one foot in front of the other. He tended to waver and sway from side to side instead of moving forward. In the morning light, he saw the mountain of the elephants, small, blue, and very far away. Just another step. And another. Simba Jike was there.

He still felt cold, but now his skin also felt clammy. His vision blurred, and he shook his head to clear it. The motion almost made him fall over. He forced his eyes to focus. Something was coming towards him? Was it his friends?

To his utter amazement, a massive bull elephant strode purposefully towards him. His mouth opened in a silent cry, and he collapsed on the ground.

'It's prosthetic!' Jade stared, mouth hanging open in amazement, as Sam held up his boot. A glimpse of artificial leg showed even with the boot top along with attachment points that connected to the stump a few inches below his real knee.

Sam held the bootheel out to Jade. 'Grab hold of the heel and pull,' he commanded. 'I'll try to work the leg out.'

'The blasted thing's prosthetic,' Jade repeated to herself as she took hold of the boot's heel and sole.

'Yes, we've established that. You see,' he added with a grin, 'you were right all along.'

Jade's grimy, olive-toned face flushed a deep rose. 'I'm sorry,' she said. 'I never imagined — I mean, I never meant anything . . . Oh, hell!' When would she learn to keep her mouth shut? And would he expect to hold her to her offer to visit his alma mater? Odd that while sitting in the middle of the Dida Galgalla desert barely cheating death, she would think first about a rash promise of a date made to a man facing death with her. 'I'm sorry, Sam,' she repeated. 'It was an insensitive thing to say. I mean, I knew your leg was wounded.'

He chuckled at her embarrassment as he twisted and tugged on the artificial leg inside the boot. 'You should see the look on your face.'

Jade scowled. 'Can we please keep to the problem at hand?'

'Yes, absolutely,' he said. 'Of course, it's usually easier to get out of the boot when my upper leg is still attached,' he admitted. 'And when there's no blasted leg-iron clamping down on the footgear.'

He leaned backward, gritted his teeth and tugged again. Jade thought she felt something shift inside. 'I think it's coming loose.'

Sam took a deep breath and a firmer grip. 'On three. One . . . two . . . three!'

Jade tipped the bootheel towards her to allow the wooden foot inside to slide back along the heel and lead the way out of the boot. It worked. As the foot came free, she fell backward onto the rocky ground. 'Ouch!'

The ankle iron still surrounded Sam's boot, but without a leg inside, Jade could scrunch up the boot enough to slip the iron off. She tossed the boot back to Sam, who was busily reattaching his leg. Jade nodded at it. 'Shot down?' she asked.

'Not exactly. Machine gun fire penetrated the fuselage and hit my ankle. Shredded it into a bloody pulp. Made for an exciting air battle. Ever try flying without a right foot?'

Jade shook her head. She knew that the rudder controls were operated by the feet and again wondered if Sam was now permanently grounded.

As if he read her mind, he said, 'I've got a friend in Battle Ground, Indiana, who's rigging up a plane for me. One of the Jennies we trained in,' he said, referring to the Curtiss JN-4. 'That is, if I can pay for it. I think I counted too much on making money with these movies. But it's a beautiful plane.' His eyes glowed like that of a lover describing his sweetheart. 'If he can get it fixed up, I can work the foot controls with levers using my hands. Can't wait to get up in the air again. Ever been?'

Jade nodded, remembering the few times David had taken her aloft.

Sam continued his enthusiastic plans. 'Can you imagine making a motion picture of Africa from the air?' He shook his head. 'By thunder, it ought to be incredible.'

As soon as the leg chain had come free of the boot, Jade had felt a moment of hope. She was alive, she was free or nearly so, and she could continue her search for Jelani. Now a new feeling of excitement, of something to hope for besides just surviving, flowed into her lungs and through her veins, sending a tingle to her nerve endings. 'It sounds wonderful,' she answered. 'I can't imagine what that would be like.'

Sam heard the longing in her voice and reached a hand out to take hers, still encased in the wrist irons. 'I can teach you to fly. Since I'll need both my hands to fly, it will be impossible for me to do that and film at the same time. I'll need someone I trust at the controls while I run the camera. Of course, I'd fly first to scout the area.'

For a moment, Jade let herself be swept up in the vision, soaring aloft over herds of antelope and elephants, following the great rivers over uncharted territory. Then the vision faded and was replaced by one of a young boy, chained, helpless, and frightened. She held up her wrists.

'What's wrong with us?' she asked rhetorically. 'Here we are thinking of adventures, and Jelani is still out there in those monsters' grasps.'

Sam never took his soft brown gaze off Jade's face. 'You didn't forget Jelani,' he said. 'And neither did I. You just gave yourself a reason to survive beyond saving him, and that's very important. Otherwise, my dear Miss Simba Jike, I'm afraid you'll go running in there guns blazing — metaphorically speaking, since we don't have any guns — and kill yourself in the process.' He finished reattaching his prosthetic leg and pulled on his boot. 'Now, let's figure out how to break off those chains. They appear to be rather old and rusted.'

Since a hammer and anvil approach seemed to be the only possible option, they searched the area until they found a hefty chunk of basalt to use as a hammer, and another, larger one on the ground that had a chisellike chunk over which they could drape one of the more corroded center links. Jade sat down and braced her feet on one side of the larger boulder and gripped both ends of her chains. Then Sam slammed the makeshift hammer as hard as he could on one side of the link.

Jade felt the shock rip down her arms, and the wrist iron dig against the heel of her left hand. She grimaced, ground her teeth against the pain, and took a firmer grip. Sam waited till she was ready and slammed the rock against the same spot. The link snapped, and Jade fell backward and to her right side. Her hands were separated from each other, but the right one still had a long length of chain that terminated in the ankle iron attached to it.

'Let's try this again and see if we can't break off some of this extra chain,' Sam suggested. He took her hands in his and turned them over, inspecting her wrists for severe cuts. 'You're going to have a bad bruise there,' he said as he gently pushed back the left wrist iron and ran his thumb in a caress over her lion's-tooth tattoo.

Jade felt the sensual touch like an electric shock to her brain. Her pulse jumped. *Gads, why am I reacting like a schoolgirl?* She pulled her hand away. 'I'll get over it. Now break off this long piece.'

Sam untucked his shirt and ripped a strip of fabric from the hem. 'I'm going to wrap this around your right wrist. Maybe we can keep the iron from digging in so hard this time.'

She steeled herself against this newest assault on her senses in the same way she'd readied herself for the first hammer blow. She gritted her teeth. It didn't help. When he touched her right hand, she still felt the fire run from her wrist up her arm and on to her head. Her legs quivered as she sat on the ground, feet braced again, and told herself they were just weak from the walking and lack of water. Her heart didn't believe her, though, and it quickened her pulse again. *Maybe it has something to do with barely managing to stay alive?*

'Ready?' asked Sam as he released her hand and repositioned the chain on the bottom rock.

Jade nodded, not trusting her voice to answer without quavering.

Sam hoisted the hammer rock and struck two blows in quick succession. The chain broke again and left Jade with about ten inches hanging from the right wrist iron.

'Thanks, Sam.'

Sam picked up the remaining chain with the leg-iron and tucked one end in his hip pocket. 'Weapon,' he said in explanation. He wiped the back of his hand over his mouth. 'Now for the boy.'

Jade held out her hand, palm out. 'Sam, I don't quite know how to say this, but I can trot faster than you can limp. You're going to slow me down. I need you to please go back for the Dodge. Go get Avery if you can. He's got some weapons.'

'And send *you* off alone to those bastards?' he exclaimed. '*You* go back for the car. I'll go on ahead.'

She shook her head, and her sweaty black curls slapped her forehead. 'If there's a problem, I might be able to outrun them. You couldn't.' She shot a look at his artificial leg to emphasize her point. 'Look,' she added when she saw the stern set of his jaw, 'we can't risk losing their trail. We have to be close. But the rules have changed now. We don't have any decent weapons. They even took my knife. Maybe I can slip in at night and free Jelani. But I at least have to follow them, and I need you to bring reinforcements.'

Sam nodded. 'I don't like it, but I'll do it.' He started to turn back in the direction of the Dodge, stopped, then spun around and enveloped her in a tight embrace. Catching her off guard, he tipped her back and pressed his dried, cracked lips to her mouth and kissed her. Her lips opened and his kiss enveloped her own wind-whipped mouth.

Jade tasted the salt from his skin and smelled his own musky aroma mingled with the faint remnants of whatever hair tonic he'd last used several days ago. His two-day-old beard scratched her chin, but instead of causing her to pull away, it inspired her to return the kiss with a firm pressure. Her head swam as she slid her left hand up and let her fingers explore his hair.

'Ouch.' Sam released Jade from his kiss but kept a firm grip on her waist. 'The chain is caught in my hair. Ouch!'

'Quit pulling,' she counseled. 'Let me get it.' She freed the errant locks from the chain and brushed his hair back in place. 'This scene isn't playing quite like a Theda Bara movie.'

'Hmmm,' Sam purred.

'What?'

'Oh, nothing. Just imagining you in her role as Cleopatra or Salome. *Very* exciting costumes.' He leaned in to kiss her again.

Jade felt her face flush and turned away. 'Haven't seen those. I was thinking of when she played Cigarette in *Under Two Flags*.'

Sam inhaled deeply, took her by the shoulders, and kissed her on the forehead this time. 'You take care of yourself, Simba Jike. Find Jelani, but watch out for yourself. I'll be right behind you as quickly as I can.'

Jade watched Sam head back at a limping lope towards the abandoned Dodge before she turned towards Biscuit's last heading, suddenly feeling

280

very much alone. She needed water, food, and a decent weapon, but none of that measured up to the need to find Jelani alive.

★ ★ ★

'You must become a *mundu-mugo*.'

Jelani knew then that he was dying, because these words came from the gigantic elephant looming over him. 'I must be a warrior. I must kill . . . '

'No!' The word blared like the trumpeting blast from a bull, issuing a challenge. 'If you kill, then you will also kill your inner spirit. Study from the old *mundu-mugo*. You will lead your people through difficult times.'

'Yes,' whispered Jelani. Then he passed mercifully out of consciousness.

21

*Elephant tusks are more than weapons.
They are tools. With them the beasts dig up
plant roots and peel the bark off trees for
food. Perhaps their most important use is to
gouge out holes in the ground for hidden
pools of water during the dry seasons. Even
other animals depend on the herds to
uncover water.*
— The Traveler

The already intolerable landscape degenerated into a veritable furnace as the rocks soaked up the sunlight. Heat waves shimmered upward, writhing like ghostly dancers and distorting any chance for a clear vision of people on the horizon.

Jade stretched her hand, palm out, her thumb level with the horizon, and measured how many hand widths had passed since she and Sam had separated. She estimated three and perhaps two more fingers. That meant she'd been walking for at least three and a half hours. By now she wasn't even sure she was on the right path beyond the fact that she was heading north towards Abyssinia. Only once had she found any fresh camel dung, and that was two hours ago at least.

Her throat burned; her head ached; her legs moved only out of habit. She closed her eyes against the heat and sent up a silent prayer, gladly offering to endure her sufferings for the sake of the boy's safety. 'Help me find him, Lord,' she whispered. 'Alive.' After all, she thought, it was her own arrogance that had put him in danger. She should have listened to Beverly and left the region. Too late for hindsight. Only one option now — save Jelani — and to do that she had to keep moving.

Vibrating hot air shimmered in front of her, imitating a rippling stream of water. *Don't think about it. Think about something else. Think about music.* She conjured up some little ditty she'd heard playing at the Muthaiga Club and began to hum. Images of gaily dressed women and men outfitted like penguins crowded her mind. Over that, she saw Blaney Percival's face and heard his voice. '*I'll even send word up to Isiolo.*' Oddly enough, in her hallucination Mr Percival wore a loincloth like Tarzan, only he added a starched collar and black bow tie. Jade shook her head. 'Blasted Muthaiga Club. Silly place, full of silly people.'

Then another vision took form out of the wavering air, a person. A hallucination? The apparition strode closer to her with a liquid grace, and Jade blinked. Who else would be walking alone out here in the middle of land that even hell had rejected? *Must be another mirage.* She wished she had her hat for some shade.

Slowly the human shape took on recognizable features. *Boguli!* Jade wanted to laugh out loud

283

and run to him, but her legs didn't want to move, and her throat managed only to eke out a hoarse cackle. The vision beckoned to her.

'Simba Jike. You must go this way. The boy is hurt.'

'Jelani? You found Jelani?' The news that he was still alive lent fresh vigor to her limbs and she broke into a stumbling trot to follow the aging nomad.

They moved about a hundred yards east of Jade's previous course before she spotted the boy. He lay facedown in a crumpled heap among the rocks. Lying next to him, sheltering him from the sun with his shadow, was Biscuit.

Jade choked back a sob. 'Jelani! Jelani!' She knelt beside the youth and carefully ran her hands over his body, checking for serious wounds. The worst were on his feet and hands, but he suffered most severely from lack of water and blood loss. A few flies buzzed around his torn heel, attracted by the dried blood on his makeshift shoes. She started to brush them aside, then saw the chain dangling from her own wrist irons and thought better of it.

'He needs water,' she said. She looked to Boguli and saw he had no water bag himself. *How does that man travel without water?*

Boguli pointed to a winding depression in the dirt beside her. 'It is an old watercourse. All the water is underground. Here it is not too deep. If you dig for it, you will find some.'

Jade looked around for something to use as a digging stick. With no vegetation in sight, she resorted to a chunk of basalt, breaking off a sharp sliver by banging it against another rock. A fragment dug into the heel of her left hand, slicing a shallow slit. Jade flicked out the sliver and ignored the cut.

Then, using her new stone tool, she dug with a vengeance, pouring every ounce of energy into stabbing the hardened earth. As she worked, the hole became a little deeper and wider. Biscuit caught the scent of water, moved beside her, and dug like a dog with his sharp claws.

Within fifteen minutes, a puddle of water seeped into the hole. Jade let Biscuit take a few drinks as a reward for protecting Jelani, while she tore off the bottom half of her shirt. Then she gently nudged the cat aside and dipped the torn shirt into the water to soak it up. She carefully cradled Jelani in her lap and squeezed the wet rag, dribbling water into his mouth. After the third attempt, she saw his throat move as he swallowed. This time, Jade didn't fight back the tears. She let them flow down her cheeks as she continued to squeeze water into the boy's mouth.

'Thank you, Lord,' she whispered. Then she looked up to Boguli. 'Thank you. I might have missed the boy but for you.'

Boguli inclined his head slightly and continued his gentle side-to-side swaying, which Jade had come to know. 'The men who traveled this way have gone on. They will not come back, but the one who took him, he is on my mountain again. I will search for him. When you return to the mountain, I will help you find him.'

Boguli turned and strode away in his slow,

stately manner. Jade watched him go until he once again became a blurry vision in the rippling air.

Her own thirst hollered for attention. Jade gently laid Jelani back on the ground and deepened the shallow hole until the water filled it a few inches. Then she cupped her hands and pulled up handful after handful of water into her parched throat before turning the hole back to Biscuit.

Jelani stirred next to her. She dipped the rag into the pool and squeezed another few tablespoons into his mouth. He opened his eyes. For a moment, he stared at her as if trying to comprehend who she was. Then recognition dawned in his soft brown eyes.

'Simba Jike,' he whispered.

Jade put her finger to his lips and shushed him. Then she scooped him back into her arms and cradled him, rocking back and forth and humming softly to soothe both of them. *He's alive!*

'I'm sorry, Memsabu,' the boy whispered. 'I let myself be captured. I have shamed my mother.'

'Shush. Don't you say that.' Jade had learned that Jelani was the only child of his mother. She knew that his birth had brought dignity to the previously barren woman and that his death before becoming a warrior would be viewed as a terrible tragedy.

'I did like the wolf caught in a trap,' the boy whispered. 'I remembered what the fable taught me.'

For a moment, Jade couldn't comprehend

what he meant. Then a horrifying recognition dawned on her. She immediately inspected his feet, half expecting to see a raw stump on one of his legs. She carefully unbound the bloodier rag on his right foot, mindful not to break open any scabs and restart the bleeding. Instead of a heel on his foot, she saw a sloping gash slicing off the end. The side anklebone also carried a large gash with a flap of dried skin hanging down.

Fully aware of what the boy had endured in order to escape, Jade felt her stomach lurch. She fought back the rising bile, grimaced, and gently rewrapped the wounds. 'I will tell you a story,' she said. 'I will tell you the fable of the lioness.'

Jelani's eyes glowed with expectation as Jade began the tale. 'There was an argument among all the smaller animals as to which one deserved the most praise and honor for producing the most whelps at a birth. Three, said the mother warthog proudly. Five, said the mother hyrax. Four, said the mother mongoose. Finally, they rushed to the lioness and demanded that she settle the dispute, for they knew that she usually had only one child. They asked her, 'How many sons have you at a birth?' The lioness looked at them and laughed. 'Why,' she said, 'I only have one, but that one child is a thoroughbred *lion* and worth more than all your broods.''

Jade stroked Jelani's head and blinked back another tear. 'So you see, Jelani, your mother will always be very proud of you. She had only one son, but she gave birth to a lion!'

22

Motorcars have a difficult time crossing this type of terrain. Camels are definitely a better, albeit less comfortable, choice for transportation.
— The Traveler

The sun had already set and released the night's cool blackness before Jade began the long trek with Jelani in her arms. As much as she wanted to leave immediately, she knew they were all badly dehydrated and wouldn't make it far in the heat. Add to that the fact that they were sitting on probably the only reachable water source for miles around and they had no way of carrying any back except inside of them. So Jade and Biscuit took turns drinking from the seep, and Jade kept squeezing water into Jelani's parched mouth until the boy had enough liquid in him for beads of sweat to form on his skin. Only when she felt able to stand without her head swimming did she risk lifting the boy into her arms.

Biscuit led the way back through the night, at times with his sensitive nose sniffing at Jade's recent trail, but mostly by some unerring sense of direction and excellent vision. Jade followed trustingly, Jelani cradled in her arms. She tried not to think too much, because every time she let her thoughts wander, they flitted right back to her young burden. Then she grew angry and ground her teeth, which didn't help her pounding headache one iota.

She tried thinking about Sam Featherstone instead, but that only confused her. No one had ever been able to best her in a staring match before. Was she losing her touch? Or did she just get weak-kneed over pilots? Her stubborn, independent nature rose to the forefront and taunted her with a terrible play on their recent situation. *Do you really want to be chained to a man?*

That does it! He's not teaching me to fly. I'll get Avery to do it, or better yet, I'll hire a complete stranger. If she ever met Mr Featherstone after this was over, it would be on equal turf. She wouldn't be beholden to him for giving her access to the sky. If she was going to have feelings for someone, she wanted to be certain it was for the man and not for what he stood for.

Jelani moaned softly, and Jade made gentle shushing sounds to quiet him. Once he muttered something about an elephant, but Jade assumed he was speaking in his sleep. Biscuit glanced up at them and made a high, staccato churring sound before he turned back to the trail, invisible to Jade's senses. At this point, she could barely make out the cheetah, his slender shape flitting like a specter in the starlight.

They plodded on, mile after mile, Jade's legs moving again with a will of their own, fueled in large part by the deep welling of dread and anger that pooled in her heart. She turned Jelani's life and health over to God, Biscuit's keen tracking ability, and her legs in that order, but the anger didn't diminish. On the contrary, it grew and festered into something beyond rage, which flashed out as a sudden lashing, then died away, its energy spent. No, this feeling had a life of its own, gestating deep inside her, feeding on her current anguish and on the sight of the limp body in her arms. It fed on every plaintive groan Jelani uttered and each painful step she took as she stumbled over invisible obstacles.

You're not a killer, Jade. That was what Avery had told her. Right now, she wasn't so sure, but she'd certainly welcome the opportunity to find out.

Just before dawn, Biscuit stopped and raised his head, ears flipped forward, eyes scanning the horizon. Then the big cat chirped loudly and loped ahead. After a few yards, he turned and ran back to Jade, butting her from behind.

'Easy, Biscuit. Don't knock me down. Do you see something?'

The cheetah chirped again. This time when Jade searched the horizon, she saw what had agitated him as a vague, blockish shape with two faint glowing eyes took form. *What kind of animal is that?* In her exhausted stupor she mistook the glowing lights for the night shine of a nocturnal beast's eyes. Then she heard the beast's sputtering chug.

A car! 'It's a car, Jelani,' she cried out to the unconscious boy. 'You're going to be all right.'

Jade wanted to run the rest of the way to meet the car, but suddenly she couldn't trust her legs. Instead, she planted her feet farther apart for increased stability and sent Biscuit to greet whoever was behind the wheel. 'Biscuit, fetch,' she said, and the cat took off at a gallop. She could tell the exact moment when the driver spotted Biscuit and hit the gas.

As the vehicle came closer, Jade recognized it as Sam's truck with Sam behind the wheel. Bev and Avery bounced in the seats beside and behind him.

'Jade!' yelled Beverly. 'Jade, darling, we're here.' Her soft blue eyes rested on Jelani, and she sobbed. 'Oh, praise heaven, you found him.'

The car lurched to a stop a few feet from Jade, and Avery leaped over the rear side and relieved her of her delicate burden. 'Is he alive?' he choked out.

Jade nodded. 'Yes, but he needs medical attention and water.'

Beverly clambered out of the front seat and headed straight for the boy. Jade smiled. *Good old Beverly.* She knew exactly what to do and who had first priority.

'Put him in the backseat,' Bev ordered. 'Sam, get the canteens.'

'Already got them,' he replied as he hefted two canteens and handed one to Beverly. He delivered the other personally to Jade. As he approached, her exhausted legs faltered for just a moment and he quickly grabbed hold of her waist and held her up, his right arm clasping her tightly to him. 'Easy, Simba Jike,' he murmured as she unscrewed the lid and drank. 'A little at a time or your stomach will reject it.'

Jade sipped and held the water in her mouth, savoring the taste, before she swallowed. Sam lightly kissed her hair, and she felt another tremor ripple through her. She forced herself to regain her legs, took two good swallows, then handed the canteen back. 'Thank you, Sam. Please give some water to Biscuit. He did guard duty. Used his own body to shade Jelani.' She looked around at the rescue party when Sam released her to tend to the cat. 'Where's Abasi?'

'Abasi and Avery got their Overlander running and didn't wait like we asked,' said Sam. 'Met me just as I made it back to the Dodge. Good thing. They saved me a lot of time going back for them. We gave Abasi a driving lesson. He's taken the Overlander back to Chiumbo.' Sam led Jade to the car and sat her in the driver's seat. Then he found an enamel basin used for sponge bathing and poured water into it for Biscuit. While the cheetah drank, Sam questioned her about the rescue.

'I didn't expect to find you this quickly.' He wiped his sleeve across his forehead and shook his head. 'Frankly I didn't expect to find you at all. I thought I'd lost you.' He reached for her, but Jade forestalled him with a soft touch on his chest.

'Don't think about it. We're here and safe. Thank you.'

'How did you find Jelani? How did you free him?' asked Sam.

Jade briefly related her trek along their last

heading and her encounter with Boguli.

'Boguli again?' said Avery in an incredulous voice. 'Don't you find it just a bit more than a coincidence that this old African happens to be around whenever you have a run-in with these slaving poachers? Are you sure he's not one of them?'

Jade shook her head slowly since anything more vigorous set off explosions of pain between her ears. 'I didn't run into the slavers. Jelani escaped on his own. Hurt himself pretty badly doing it, too.' She looked up at Sam. 'Where's that canteen?'

Sam handed it to her and she took another hit of water. Behind her, Beverly was carefully sponging Jelani's face and hands and applying a tincture of iodine to the cuts on his hands. She heard the boy moan softly through the ministrations and Bev's reassuring voice calming him.

'See if you can find one of those bottles of aspirin, will you please, Sam?' asked Jade. She pivoted as much as possible to see Beverly without hurting her head. 'How is he, Bev?'

'He'll live,' she answered, and started unwrapping the blood-soaked rags on his feet. She glanced up at Jade. 'His temperature seems fine. I expected much worse with heat stress. He said the most curious thing just now.' She shook her head, jiggling the short blond curls, and repeated the words slowly to make sure she remembered them correctly. 'He said the elephant told him to become a *mundu-mugo*.' She looked at Jade. 'Isn't that what his people call their healer? The one who gave you your name and tattoo?'

Jade nodded. 'It is.' She touched the indigo blue lion's tooth drawn on her wrist. 'But I don't understand what he means by the elephant. I suppose he was hallucinating.' Her emerald eyes searched Beverly's watercolor blue ones. 'Are you sure he's all right?'

'Mostly. Thanks to you.' She uncovered his foot and gasped at the bloody, raw heel. 'If we can keep this from going septic, that is. But I can't believe either of you survived this desert.'

Jade saw the pitiful little foot and ground her teeth again. 'We found water,' she explained. 'Boguli told me that we were sitting by an old river channel and the water was only a foot or so underground. I started digging with a sliver of basalt. Then Biscuit got the scent and joined in.'

'Amazing,' said Avery. 'But why didn't this Boguli chap give you any of his water?'

Jade shrugged. 'As near as I could see, the man didn't have any. He was like a camel.' She took the headache pill bottle from Sam, murmured her thanks, poured two pills into her hand, and downed them.

'Then where is he now?' asked Beverly. 'Boguli, I mean.'

Jade took a deep breath before answering. She knew Beverly especially was not going to like this answer and tried to think of an easy way to break it to her. There was none. 'He said the person who kidnapped Jelani returned to the mountain. He said he would track him, then help me find him when I got back.'

The response elicited just the effect Jade had

294

feared. Beverly and Avery rounded on her at once. 'You're going back?' they shouted in unison. Only Sam, Jade noted, said nothing. He stood by the car, arms folded across his chest.

'You're *not* going there,' said Beverly. 'We're taking Jelani to safety. He'll be lucky if he doesn't lose his foot as it is.'

'And there's Chiumbo, too,' added Avery. 'Bev's right. We're through here. It's time to leave this mess to the authorities.' He turned his back as though the argument were finished.

'So far the authorities haven't managed to do anything,' Jade said, 'not even solve the murder of one of their own soldiers. Whoever Smythe left at Isiolo should've sent help when our runner reached them. But you're partly right. *You* are taking Jelani and Chiumbo and yourselves out of here. There's evil behind all this, and *I* am going to find who's responsible, if it's the last thing I do.' She slid over into the passenger seat and motioned for Sam to take the wheel. 'We'll drive you to the Overlanders. Then Sam can drop me off at the mountain before he follows you.'

Sam draped one arm over the steering wheel and gazed at Jade, an amused expression on his face. 'What if I don't want to leave with them?' he asked. 'I don't think you're going to stop me.'

'Hmmm,' she mused. 'Probably not, but don't try and stop *me* or you might just lose your other leg.'

The return trip dragged on. Sam drove, Jade rode shotgun, Beverly cradled Jelani against the worst bumps, and Avery sat behind Sam. If he wanted to attend to his wife and the injured boy, he was prevented by Biscuit, who insisted on staying as close to Jelani as possible to lick his face. Every three hours, they needed to stop and cool the engine. Jelani spoke once, in Kikuyu. Jade thought she heard the phrase *mundu-mugo*. She assumed Jelani was asking for his tribe's version of a doctor.

No one else spoke otherwise, and Jade brooded, her mind turning over every bit of data. Abyssinians were poaching ivory. She'd seen them, seen the stacks of tusks, and when that young askari had found them, he'd paid for his discovery with his life.

But there was more at stake here than ivory. Someone was either purchasing arms from these same raiders or supplying them. Since she couldn't fathom the poachers having such a supply of weapons to sell, she felt certain they were buying them. Why? They weren't the right type of rifle for hunting elephants. Did they plan on selling them to someone else, or were they amassing weapons for some private war in Abyssinia? Or perhaps they planned to carry their slave raids farther south and wanted weapons to fight the British.

Possibly a more important question for her purposes was not *why* but *who*. Who was selling the rifles? And who was financing the purchase? The stash of German East African gold coins and German rifles pointed to Germans' involvement, and there were certainly enough of them running around up there on the mountain. Add to that, Claudia von Gretchmar had been in the cache at least once and lost a button there.

Had she been in a struggle or a romantic tryst?

Jade thought about the photo negative of the woman in the arms of a man other than her husband. She wished she knew who that was. *Harry?* She shook her head. Claudia didn't seem like Harry's type. *And what makes you think you know Harry's type?* Jade asked herself. Just because he had chased after her once didn't mean he always went after young women. Maybe he just liked accessible ones. More than likely, Claudia had been cavorting with the Prussian industrialist Vogelsanger, although he seemed much more interested in young Mercedes or perhaps Liesel. There was just not enough of the man showing in the negative to identify him easily. Even the large ears could be a trick of his head angle.

Wait a minute! Jade remembered the day Chiumbo was hurt. Claudia saw Jade, Sam, and Chiumbo and immediately wanted to go back to camp, ostensibly to keep an eye on her daughter. Did she leave in order to signal to someone to shoot Chiumbo? But it was Vogelsanger who followed after her. *What did he say?* Something about going along to protect Claudia. Maybe they *were* having an involvement. But blast it! His military haircut didn't match the thicker hair in that photograph. That left Mueller and Harry again.

Jade sighed. *Blasted romantic triangles or quadrangles or whatever this one is. Stick to the important facts.* Someone wanted her and her friends off the mountain and had tried to accomplish it using fear before escalating to violence. First someone shot an arrow into her tent; then someone shot Chiumbo without killing him. Only after they left did the criminals actually kidnap Jelani.

Perhaps someone did see his capture and sale as an opportunity for extra profit, but maybe not. More likely Jelani saw or heard something that could identify the mastermind. Jade wished she knew just what German words he'd overheard.

They all knew that she cared for the boy. He was an obvious way to get to her. But why get to her if they thought she'd left? Did they know she'd sneaked back up the mountain? Maybe she and Sam weren't as clever as they thought. Maybe someone knew they'd sneaked back and was determined to get them off the mountain.

Then another thought crept into her brain. Did someone out there hate her so much as to use the boy for revenge? The very idea made Jade fume inside, her anger smoldering, ready to burst into flames as soon as she had a target.

How much does Harry know? She didn't really believe he had orchestrated the incidents, but he might not be above receiving payment for turning a blind eye. After all, how could anyone in his group haul in several boxes of rifles and not have him notice, especially when they'd gone missing? Then she recalled his rather slipshod running of her own safari and thought he might not even notice what personal effects his group carried around, especially not the women.

Jade sat up straighter. That could have been it. Harry wouldn't question what the women brought personally. They could smile and tell him it was private, feminine needs and he'd run off before looking further. It was a near-perfect way to sneak just about anything into an area. Maybe Claudia wasn't such an innocent dupe after all. Well, that was fine with Jade. She had no qualms about shooting a woman. If only she had her Winchester. The beloved rifle had been taken from her along with her knife when she and Sam had been left chained to die in the desert.

By the time they reached Chiumbo, Abasi, and the Dunburys' two Overlanders, Jade's anger had regrown to an all-consuming beast inside her, clawing at her insides to get out. While Avery helped his wife, Jelani, and the ever-attentive Biscuit into the other vehicles, Jade rummaged through the equipment and retrieved the stolen bow and arrows and her hat. Only Sam saw her thin smile and the firm set of her jaw. He put one hand gently on her right hand and met her eyes.

'Remember, Jade, you are not a killer,' he whispered. 'And vengeance is the Lord's.'

She smiled, a seemingly innocent little smile, and nodded once, slowly. 'Yes,' she purred, 'but satisfaction is mine.'

23

There is a duality to many an animal's behavior. A lion will stalk with absolute silence, then roar to create a fatal panic in his prey. Similarly a prey might do its best to stay camouflaged, but once it is discovered, it often advertises its presence with a flashing white rump or bounding leap, as if to say, 'Here I am. I've seen you. You won't catch me.'
— The Traveler

Sam turned off the truck's engine once they were close to the location they'd doubled back to the first time around. 'We can't drive any farther, Jade. It's getting dark, I'm exhausted, and you need some sleep, too.'

She curled up on the seat and leaned her head against the door. 'I'll sleep here.'

Sam climbed out of the truck, went around to the other side, and opened her door, catching her as she spilled out. 'No, you won't. We're not safe down here. I'm going to cover the truck with brush to hide it, and you're going back up that tree.'

Jade shook her head and pinched her arms to rouse herself. 'I'll help you camouflage the truck. Give me the panga. I'll cut, you cover.'

Exhausted, they worked like mindless drones, slashing brush, hauling it to the truck, and stacking the brush in front of the vehicle to prevent detection. It wasn't animals they needed to hide from, but humans. This time, no one must know they'd returned. When they finished, they hauled their meager supplies and themselves up the rope ladder and onto the boards. Jade secured her bow and arrows next to Beverly's rifle, which Sam had borrowed.

'What is there to eat?' asked Sam.

Jade opened the pack that Beverly had replenished, and inspected the contents. 'Dates, figs, a tin of crackers, and some canned meat.'

'No steaks?'

Jade's shoulders twitched as she chuckled silently. 'There is something very ironic about having only dried and salted foods when one has just escaped dying of thirst.' She handed a box of figs and a tin of meat to Sam. 'I don't think I could swallow a cracker if I tried.'

Sam ignored the can of salty meat and popped a fig into his mouth. 'Steak, two inches thick, medium rare.'

'Grilled over an open campfire,' added Jade, playing the game. 'With potatoes baked in the coals.'

'Ears of corn, roasted in their own husks.'

'Do you pull back the husks first and butter the corn, then tie them back over so it's all buttery inside?'

Sam nodded. 'Only way to do it. And coffee. Pots of coffee.'

Jade sighed. 'Nectar of the gods. But I prefer

301

my steak a little less rare. There's nothing like an elk steak, well-done over a mesquite fire.'

'Slathered in ketchup.'

Jade bolted up, eyes wide in horror. 'Ketchup? What are you, a heathen? You don't put ketchup on *any* steak.' She scooted farther away from him. 'I'm not talking to you anymore.' Suddenly her teeth chattered, and she hugged herself. 'Makes me shiver just to think of it.'

'Are you all right?' asked Sam, his face etched with worry lines.

'Cold,' she answered. 'And we left the blankets in the truck.'

He scooted over and put his arms around her, pulling her close. When she stopped shaking, she started to push herself away. 'Thanks. I'm all right now.'

'No, you're not,' he said. 'You've been through hell physically and emotionally. I'm going to make a nest for you in the hammock. All this moss in the trees ought to make decent bedding.' He stood up on the planks and gathered as much of the silvery moss as he could reach and arranged it to cover the hammock. 'Try that out,' he said when he'd finished.

Jade hesitated before crawling into the hammock. 'Where are you going to sleep?'

'Next to you.'

She pulled back, but Sam reached out and took her gently by the shoulders. 'Simple matter of body heat, Jade,' he said as he slid onto the hammock and pulled her in after him.

She plopped onto the moss and nestled up with her back against him, grateful for his warmth.

He wrapped an arm around her and pulled her in closer. 'Do you know what my favorite part of Madeline's book was?' he asked. 'It was when you were changing that tire and met up with the lion. How did she put it?' He started reciting from memory.

Jade faced the immense male lion without a trace of fear, staring into his golden eyes with her own hypnotic green ones. '*Jambo, Bwana Simba*,' she announced in greeting as she raised her rifle. 'You can go back and tell your witch master that I'm not afraid of you or him.'

'What did you do, memorize the book?' She tried to prop herself up on one elbow to see his face, but managed only to get a bunch of dry moss in her mouth.

'Parts of it,' he admitted. 'But that's the point where I knew you were the woman for me.' He toyed with a stray curl on her forehead. 'Jade, you have to know this. I'm in love with you.'

She spat out the moss and twisted around. 'Don't,' she said softly as she put a finger to his lips. 'I'm not ready for someone being in love with me again. I'm not sure I'll ever be ready. It's too hard when you lose them, and I'm too independent anyway, and — '

This time Sam shushed her with a finger to her lips, his dark eyes reflecting the thin sliver of moonlight. 'Well, you know my feeling, so you think about it. And to prove to you how sincere I am, I'll even give up ketchup on my steaks.' He kissed her lightly on the cheek, letting his lips brush against her ear.

Jade laughed. Then exhaustion took over and she drifted into sleep.

★ ★ ★

'Where did your Boguli say to meet him?' whispered Sam the next morning as they peered out from the shelter of trees near Harry Hascombe's camp and up the mountainside.

'He didn't, but I suspect he'll find me. The man is uncanny.' She'd woken alone in the hammock with Sam sitting on the plank nearby, popping dates in his mouth. An impeccable gentleman, he had yet to refer to their night cuddled together against the cold, and Jade felt an upwelling of gratitude. She hadn't felt this emotionally overwrought since David died in a plane crash a few days after he'd proposed.

'From the way you speak of him, he's a rather unusual guardian angel,' Sam said.

'He's no angel,' Jade said, 'but there is something very' — she paused and searched for a way to explain — 'familiar about him.' She scanned the surrounding trees. 'He may be watching us now.' She pulled a piece of paper torn from her field notebook and a pencil stub out of her pocket, placed the sheet on her thigh for a writing desk, and began a brief note. When she finished, she started to rise, and Sam reached forward and tugged on her sleeve as a signal to stop. She glanced at his leg, then at him, as though to ask if it was giving him problems.

He shook his head. 'I'm fine,' he whispered, 'but I'm a little concerned about your plan. You really intend to walk into Harry's camp without consequences?'

'No,' she whispered back. 'But I need to communicate with him. Enlist his help.' She waved the note in front of him. 'If he can get all of them out of camp at once, we could get in there and do a *thorough* search. Somewhere in that camp there must be something tying one of them to the poachers. I'd like to find a stash of those coins in someone's bunk. I just wish we'd find Boguli first, but I can't sit tight and wait for him.'

'You are assuming, of course, that Hascombe isn't part of the plot himself. What makes you think you can trust him?'

He leaned forward to see her face better. 'Are you perhaps harboring any residual feelings for the scoundrel? Don't assume that just because he wanted you once, he won't sell you up the river now.'

Jade sighed and tightened her lips. Once a man started acting even remotely possessive, her independent nature took hold. Now she knew how that cow pony felt when the bull elk kept pursuing it. 'Harry may be a scoundrel, and an opportunistic son of a biscuit who would sell his own mother, but I don't think even he'd ever resort to shooting his own cheetah. He *really* likes that cat.' She turned and met Sam's gaze. '*That* is why I think he's not involved. *Not*,' she added firmly, 'that my feelings about Harry should concern you.' She turned her gaze back

305

to the woods so she didn't have to see any hurt in his face. 'You're a very nice man, Sam, and we've been through a lot together, but . . . '

Sam leaned back against the tree and sighed. 'I take it that means our date to tour old Purdue is off.'

Jade suppressed a chuckle. She couldn't help but admire Sam's indomitable spirit. She turned and faced him. 'You don't really know me, Sam. You love some fiction that Madeline cooked up.' In the back of her mind she wondered if she was making this argument to convince him or herself. *You don't really know him. Maybe you only care about what he represents.* She took a deep breath and continued. 'I'm too — '

'Bullheaded?' he suggested. 'Stubborn, mulish, independent, reckless?'

'Hmmm. Sounds like you know me better than I thought,' she muttered. 'Let's just say I'm not ready for any entanglements right now.' She turned back towards Harry's camp. 'I think the way is clear.' She planned to use one of her arrows and shoot a note into Harry's tent through a gap in the *boma* wall. She knew from the first cursory search in his camp that his tent stood apart from the others, closest to the *boma* gate, putting him in the front line if something came through.

A makeshift quiver manufactured from a square of canvas hung from Jade's belt. She'd ripped the fabric from the Overlander and used Beverly's sewing kit to stitch it into a tube to hold her newest ammunition. Jade extracted an arrow and rolled her note tightly around the shaft. Then, while Sam held the paper in place, she broke off a length of Beverly's sewing thread and tied the note securely to the shaft close to the fletching.

'What does the note say?' whispered Sam.

'It says someone in his camp shot Biscuit and tried to kill us. He should get his group all out of camp immediately and keep them out while I search, or I'll shoot them all in turn, him first.'

'Subtle but effective. What if he's not there now?'

'Then we wait here until he comes back.'

'Let her fly, then,' said Sam as he settled himself to see better. 'Just be sure not to hit Harry with that arrow.' He paused and reflected on that order. 'At least,' he amended, 'not fatally.'

Jade grinned as she slid the poacher's bow from around her back and nocked her arrow.

Harry's crew had already rebuilt the *boma* walls, broken during the elephants' rampage, but either due to carelessness or a lack of available thorn brush, they had left a few gaps. Jade slid her arrow into one closest to Harry's tent and peered through another hole to aim. The camp was actually quiet, but Jade didn't want to risk going in now. Someone might come back soon and catch her before she was finished.

She drew back the bow and aimed for the lower portion of his tent's doorway, then released the string. The arrow pierced the canvas and thudded into the dirt just inside. *Perfect.*

Sam patted her on the shoulder. 'Impressive,' he whispered. 'You're a regular Amazon.' He started to rise, then stopped when he saw Jade stay put, eyes on the camp. 'Let's go,' he whispered. 'We can't wait here.'

Jade never took her eyes off the camp. 'I don't hear anyone.' She looked at Sam. 'I mean *anyone*. Not even the cook. Doesn't that strike you as odd?'

'Do you think something happened to them?' asked Sam.

'Maybe,' agreed Jade. She got up and headed for the *boma* gate. 'I'm going to have a look.'

Sam followed her. 'I'll keep you covered.' He gripped Beverly's Enfield in his hand. They went first into Harry's tent, giving lie to Jade's supposed trust in him. She found blessed little beyond his cot, a shaving kit, a box of rounds for his Mannlicher, a folding chair, and a book. Sam flipped through the book, a novel by Dickens, and paused.

'Find something?' asked Jade, who was busy lifting the cot's mattress to see if anything lay hidden underneath.

Sam held up a photograph. 'Just his bookmark.'

Jade noted the growl when he spoke, dropped the mattress, and went over to look. 'It's me!' she exclaimed. In the photo Jade stood next to her coffee-growing friend and would-be chronicler, Madeline. Both wore formal dresses. 'Must have been taken at the Muthaiga Club,' she said. 'Put it back and let's move on. There's nothing here.'

Under Jade's watchful eye, Sam replaced the picture in the book and slammed the cover shut. 'At least the picture tells me he's not a likely candidate for hurting you. So where to next?' he asked, setting the book back on the table.

'Vogelsanger's.'

They entered each tent in turn. Sam stood at the tent flaps keeping watch while Jade pawed through every item in each tent. By the time they'd searched Vogelsanger's and the Muellers' tents, Jade felt a growing frustration. *Nothing.* Oh, she now knew a lot more about each of them. Vogelsanger read books on machines; the Muellers didn't read at all. Liesel's vanity held no limits, if her cosmetics box was any indication, and she was definitely not a natural blonde.

Jade rubbed her aching back. 'We'll search the von Gretchmars' next, then Mercedes' tent last.'

In the elder von Gretchmars' tent, Jade started with Otto's side. Once again, she lifted camp cot mattresses, flipped through books and magazines, and opened all the boxes. Otto's side of the tent contained nothing out of the ordinary. Claudia's side had already revealed the incriminating blouse with the missing button. She also had a lot more personal items, including a very large and full cosmetics box. Unfortunately, it was evidence of nothing more than a middle-aged woman's desperate grasp on youth and beauty.

Jade shut the lid and started to walk away. She stopped. Something about the box itself caught her attention. It was exactly the same size, shape, and construction as the ones she'd seen in the cache that held the ammunition. *Coincidence?* Maybe she did just happen to pack her beauty kit in an old munitions box, but Jade was more inclined to take it as further evidence that

Claudia, at least, was connected to the boxes now hidden in the cache.

After looking through everything else, Jade started for Mercedes' tent. Jelani had found the gold coin on the floor there. While the girl certainly didn't seem to be capable of this sort of planning, her parents might be using her as a means to smuggle additional materials. Jade noted that she'd never been in Mercedes' tent before.

The interior's simplicity struck Jade most. She'd expected the young woman to have several boxes of clothes, a large cosmetics box, and some sort of camp vanity table. Instead, the tent appeared as spartan as Vogelsanger's. A few books, all in German, lay on a small, collapsible table next to a folding chair. A cracked mirror hung above a washbasin, and a single hairbrush had been placed next to the basin.

'Sam, you're not going to believe this,' she said as she stepped out of the tent.

'Believe what?' snapped an irate female voice.

Jade stared straight into the angry face of Liesel Mueller.

24

This duality applies to elephants as well.
One moment, they are creating enough
noise to wake the dead; the next, they are
silent wraiths. The end result is that you
might bump into one without ever hearing it
sneak up behind you.
— The Traveler

'Frau Mueller,' Jade said as she struggled to explain her presence in their camp, much less in their tents. Mercedes clutched the peroxide blonde's arm, swaying as though she might drop at any moment. Jade decided to take the offensive. She rushed forward and embraced Liesel's hand in hers. 'I'm so glad to see you both alive and safe. I've been terribly worried about you.'

Liesel pulled back and yanked her hand from Jade's. The knee-jerk reaction nearly dropped Mercedes on her backside. 'What means this? What is this worry about us?'

'Here, now,' said Sam. 'You'll make Miss Mercedes fall, Mrs Mueller. Let me help her.' Sam gallantly took the young woman's arm and led her to her tent, leaving Jade to deal with the suspicious Liesel. 'She's all yours,' he whispered out of one side of his mouth.

Jade decided not to try to explain Jelani's abduction, or her and Sam's own trials, as justification for her supposed concern. After all, if Liesel was involved, she already knew about it. Besides, answering Liesel's questions gave the German woman the upper hand, and Jade intended for this to be her own interrogation.

'Has something happened to Mercedes? Is she injured? She looks so pale.' Jade kept a sincere expression plastered on her face, arching her brows, tilting her head, and leaning forward. 'And you, you poor dear,' she added, once again taking Liesel's hand, 'you look exhausted. Shouldn't you sit down and tell me all about it?'

Liesel didn't buy into Jade's routine. 'I do not want to sit down!' she snapped as she again retrieved her hand. This time she wrapped her arms around her chest and tucked her hands underneath, out of Jade's grasp. She stared at Mercedes' tent. 'What is that man doing? He should not be alone *mit* her in her tent.'

Jade realized that she was not making any headway with this tactic. She stood up straight, rested one hand on her bowstring and the other on her hip. 'Mr Featherstone is a gentleman. He is not going to hurt her or take advantage of her, Liesel. Now, what happened? I came here looking for Harry and find the entire camp deserted.' She pointed to the rebuilt *boma* wall. 'An entire side of your barricade has been rebuilt, so something happened, and I'm not leaving until I get an answer.'

Liesel shifted her weight from one foot to the other as though trying to decide what to do. At

312

that time, Sam returned from Mercedes' tent, his body erect, the slight limp lending a bit of dignity to his purposeful stride. Whether it was due to Jade's more direct demand or to Sam's presence, Jade wasn't sure, but Liesel relaxed her grip on herself and answered them.

'We are all of us for von Gretchmar and his wife looking,' said Liesel. 'Eric, he is gone, too.'

'How long have they been missing?' asked Jade.

Liesel hugged herself again and shrugged, her head down. 'Since late yesterday afternoon. Otto, he says, 'Come, Claudia, Mercedes, we take a walk.' He called Mercedes sweet names like a doting papa, but Mercedes did not want to go. Her father, he is not happy at that, but Claudia, she tells him to leave the girl alone.'

Liesel twisted her upper body towards the *boma* entrance and pointed. 'Otto told Claudia the walk would be good for Mercedes, so, *naturlich*, she goes and so does Claudia. When Eric comes back from hunting later and finds they have taken Mercedes out of the camp, he is angry and curses. He does not think she should be here, and he hates Otto because Otto will not let him marry Mercedes. Eric, he storms out of camp alone and does not come back. They were not returned this morning. Harry told *everyone* to look, so we go look.'

'And Mercedes?' asked Sam gently.

'We found Mercedes off the trail collapsed in the bushes. When Harry asked her what had happened, she cried hysterically, so I brought her back.'

Jade and Sam exchanged questioning glances. 'Why didn't Harry go with Vogelsanger when he stormed off yesterday?' asked Jade.

Liesel flapped an arm angrily towards the forest. 'Harry was with *mein* Heinrich hunting. That is all they talk about, the elephant, and the ivory, and the *grosse* trophy.' She sighed and pouted, her lower lip sticking out like a child's. 'That is all those men think of. Eric, he has his ivory, so he leaves them and goes to hunt something else. That is why he comes back sooner than Harry and Heinrich.'

Jade suspected that Liesel resented her personal attractions' taking second place to a pachyderm, and she seemed more distraught over not having some man's attention than the fact that two of her companions were still missing. Jade continued to pry the story from her. 'When Harry and your husband returned, did you tell them what had happened?'

'No!' Liesel tossed her white-yellow hair, the color of sun-bleached straw. 'Harry did not ask me, so I did not say. Maybe I was in my tent.'

Jade felt her impatience rising at this self-centered woman. She tried one last time. 'When *did* you tell him?'

'I heard Harry bellow for Otto and Eric several times after he comes back. I think it was nearly dark, but I pay no attention. I am angry. Then, when I come out for dinner, he asks me if I know where they are. I said I thought they went for a walk.'

'But by then the sun had set and it was too hard to do a proper search, right?' added Sam.

Liesel shrugged again, a noncommittal answer at best. 'Where was Hascombe when you last saw him?'

Liesel looked around as though she expected to see some clues to his location within the compound. 'I think he was just following that big elephant trail, the one where Harry gets caught in the trap.'

'Could you get any sense out of Mercedes?' Jade asked Sam.

He shook his head. 'She wouldn't stop crying, so I poured a glass of water for her from her pitcher. By the time I'd turned around, she'd fallen asleep on her cot. Or maybe she passed out — I don't know.'

Jade nodded towards the tent. 'You had better stay with her, Liesel. We'll try to find Harry and the others.' After Liesel disappeared into Mercedes' tent, Jade turned to Sam. 'Did she say anything?'

'Only some hysterical ravings in German. I tried to memorize what I could. Something that sounded like 'air log' and the other started with 'harem.''

'Harem?' Jade's black brows shot up in surprise. 'Are you sure?'

'Pretty sure. Hard to miss that word. The entire thing sounded like '*Harem skla-vuh.*''

Jade closed her eyes and repeated the phrases to herself several times, trying to put them in context. Whatever had happened, it was something traumatic. But Mercedes hadn't been visibly injured. Had she been deceived? *Deception, lies.* 'Air log, air log. Maybe she was saying

'*Er log*,' which means 'He lied.' I can't think of anything else for 'harem,' but I'm pretty sure '*Sklave*' is 'slave.' If so, then — '

'Then she was saying 'harem slave,'' finished Sam. 'So who lied to her and why would it involve a harem slave?' As he said the last part, his face cleared as though he understood.

'Right,' said Jade. 'Considering Jelani's experience, I think someone was threatening to sell her off north as well. A pretty thing like that would be worth a lot.'

Sam inspected Jade from boot to hat. 'Hmm, makes me wonder why he didn't sell you.'

Jade exhaled a loud *pssh* to indicate her skepticism. 'I'm not exactly the compliant type, which I imagine severely lowers the price. Come on. Let's go find Harry. Liesel said he was following the trail where we snared him. Our secret return is as good as blown wide open anyway.'

'Yes,' agreed Sam as they left the compound, 'but their secret isn't.'

★ ★ ★

By the time they'd reached the eastern base of Sokorte Guda, Jade felt as if she'd done a forced march across most of Africa. She rubbed her injured knee and figured Sam must feel just about as bad as she did.

'Let's stop for a minute,' she said.

Sam plopped down on a fallen cedar tree and rested the Enfield across his lap. 'If you insist.' He reached for his canteen, took a swig, and

316

passed it to Jade. 'I haven't seen anyone yet. Are you sure they came this way?'

Jade wiped her mouth on her sleeve and handed the canteen back to Sam. 'There's been so much traffic on these trails, I'm not sure what I'm tracking anymore. They may have split up at one point. You'd think that if Harry and his crew were anywhere around, we'd at least hear them calling for the von Gretchmars.'

'What do you think about Vogelsanger storming off like that?' Sam asked. 'Did he follow after Otto and kill him and his wife?' When Jade stared at him, he explained, 'Old Prussian sense of honor. He loves Mercedes; he hates Otto; they duel; he kills him.'

Jade shrugged, feeling tired and burdened. It seemed eons ago that she'd walked these same trails looking for the magnificent titans of the forest to capture on film. Her only thoughts then had been of trip wires and flash powder, her only goal to understand the elephant herds. Of course, she'd promised to investigate poaching, but in her wildest dreams she'd never thought she'd see anything. The mountain stood too remotely secluded to be bothered by poachers, who, in her mind, were lazy beings who surely wouldn't want to cross the deserts that surrounded Marsabit, like an island in a dry ocean.

But Jade was a woman of her word, and once she'd seen evidence, she'd intended to follow through with her promise. Now how many had paid a price for her promise: Chiumbo and Jelani close to death, and Beverly's baby at risk? But one death was not on her shoulders: the executed soldier. And even though Blaney Percival had not asked her to find the soldier's killer, she knew the poaching and the execution were linked, two pieces of the same puzzle.

Well, Beverly, Jelani, and the others were out of danger now, safely on the way to Archer's Post. She would not hold herself responsible for Sam. He kept at her heels like some faithful hound at his own insistence, not hers. She frowned. *I'm not being fair. He put his life at risk, too, and not just for me, but for Jelani.*

Blast! If his purpose was to make her more cautious than she'd have been on her own, then it was working. She longed to be free of all tethers, to have no one to account for, to track down every last poacher and shoot him with his own arrow. After this was over, she planned to run off somewhere far away from friends who followed her like the herd followed that matriarch.

The matriarch! Jade suddenly had a mental image of the old cow as she had uncovered the poachers' pit trap on the southern side of this very crater. 'Sam, what if it was Vogelsanger who lied? Think about it. Maybe he never really wanted to marry Mercedes. Maybe he always planned to sell her off.'

'That's a thought. Should we look at the cache for them?'

Jade shook her head. *The pit.* Maybe that was where she'd find the von Gretchmars. If Eric Vogelsanger had killed Otto, he might have tossed his body into the pit, perhaps even tried to stick Mercedes in there before she escaped. She'd have to look. In the meantime, she had Sam to worry about. He'd continue to stick to her if she didn't do something about it, and she really didn't want another person hurt on her account.

'We should split up, Sam. We have a better chance of running into Harry if we do.'

Sam stood his ground. 'Nope. I can just imagine what harebrained scheme you'd hatch up. I'd probably find you riding an elephant or something. I am on you like a tick on a dog.'

Jade sighed. *Just what I need, an overprotective tick. And where in the blazes is Boguli?* She scanned the forest, looking for his gaunt frame among the tree trunks. *Maybe he didn't make it back.* The thought distressed her. She counted on his help, and she respected the aging nomad and hated to think he might have ceased to exist.

At the trail split, Jade gave up on the pit and suggested they proceed towards the poachers' cache. Von Gretchmar and his wife might have gone that way, in which case Harry might also have tracked them that far. They had advanced a quarter of a mile when they heard approaching footsteps.

Sam grabbed Jade's arm and pulled her into the forest's protective shadows. They darted behind the trees and hoped they were hidden from view. While she waited, Jade's mind played over the three possibilities. These could be the poachers walking back to the cache, it could be Harry and his men, or it could be von Gretchmar and Claudia. Each possibility called for its own course of action. The first one required that they stay hidden; the second allowed them to stop Harry and relay what they knew. But if it was Otto and his wife? Jade pulled out an arrow and readied her bow.

Her mind alternated between the persona of a stalker and that of a prey as she waited. She was not prepared for the sight that actually emerged onto the main trail.

25

*Anyone who hunts or photographs wildlife
learns to observe certain behaviors and
interpret them. This gives the individual
some clue as to what his subject is going to
do next. For example, when an elephant
extends his ears and raises his trunk, he is
agitated and might attack.*
— The Traveler

'Captain Smythe!' Jade stood up and stepped out
from behind her hiding spot. Sam emerged from
the other side and stood next to her. 'You are a
sight for sore eyes, sir,' she said.

Smythe stopped abruptly in his tracks. His two
accompanying soldiers stood back a respectful
three paces and held their rifles poised upward
and crossed in front of their left shoulder.
Smythe stared and sputtered once or twice as if
his tongue had quit working properly.

'Miss del Cameron?' he finally said. 'What the
deuces are you still doing here?' He stopped and
studied Sam, pointing a finger at him. 'And who
the thundering blazes is this?'

'Captain Smythe, allow me to introduce Mr
Sam Featherstone. He's an American filmmaker.
Sam, this is Captain Smythe of the King's
African Rifles.'

Sam reached out to shake the officer's hand. 'Glad to know you, sir. We could use your help.'

'Oh? And how is that?'

'There's another hunting party up here run by Harry Hascombe. It seems that three of his people are missing,' replied Sam. 'A German couple, and another man. Hascombe found the couple's daughter on the trail outside of their compound. She's hysterical. We can't make any sense out of her at all.'

Smythe frowned and passed a hand over his cheeks and mouth. 'Indeed. Well, at least she is safe, then,' he said. 'I presume she's under guard at the moment?'

'Not really,' added Jade. 'Everyone else is looking for the von Gretchmars and Eric Vogelsanger. There's just one woman at camp with her.'

The British captain pursed his lips and stroked his mustache while he considered the situation. Then he turned abruptly to one waiting askari, who immediately stood at rigid attention. Smythe spoke briefly in some African tongue to the man, who saluted and trotted off towards the compound. His black skin melted into the forest's gloom until only the red fez atop his head stood out, reminding Jade of the Cheshire cat fading from view with just a smile remaining to mark his spot.

'She'll be under guard soon enough,' said Smythe. 'As for those other three, I'll round up the rest of my men and have a look-see. Wouldn't want some stray leopard to maul them.'

'That's not the entire situation, sir,' said Jade.

'I think they're involved in gunrunning to the Abyssinians. I found some evidence in the poachers' cache which points to it.'

Smythe's toffee brown eyes opened wide, his brown brows tilted upward. 'The devil you say. You found their cache?'

Jade nodded. 'Yes, sir.' She proceeded to outline most of the details of the last few days. 'They have a cache farther up the mountain in a protective overhang. It's full of ivory, but I also found boxes of Mauser rifles as well as a bag of German East African gold Tabora pounds. I also discovered a button from a woman's blouse in the cache. I believe it belongs to Claudia von Gretchmar.'

The captain inhaled deeply and pulled himself up to his full five feet, ten inches so he could peer down his nose at Jade. 'You have been a busy bee, Miss del Cameron.'

'That is not the half of it, Captain,' chimed in Sam. 'One of our men was shot with a drugged arrow and left for dead, an African boy in her care was kidnapped, and we were left chained in the desert to die.'

Smythe snorted. 'And who's to blame? I told Miss del Cameron that these men are dangerous. I ordered her to leave and you have seen, firsthand, the consequences of her blatant disobedience. Now if you will be so good as to take me to this cache, Miss del Cameron, I will do my duty by king and country and take care of this matter once and for all.'

'We can both take you there,' said Sam.

Smythe studied Sam as though he were

inspecting one of his troops. 'You seem a capable chap. I spotted Hascombe and his people on their way up the crater to the lake.' He pointed up the slope. 'Go find him. Tell him to get back to watch the Fräulein so that my man can get back to me and so I don't have more idiots running around to fret about. I'll find his stray people. Tell him to stay put in his camp and wait for me. That goes for you, too. I don't need any more of you people traipsing around here and getting in trouble. I want you all in one spot.'

Sam looked at Jade. 'And what about you?'

'It's all right, Sam,' she said as she placed a hand on his arm. 'I can lead the captain to the caches. At least you know I won't be running around on my own getting into trouble.'

Sam frowned, the ends of his ragged mustache drooping. 'Very well. I'll wait for you at Hascombe's compound.' He glared at Captain Smythe, using his extra two inches of height as a mark of power. 'I'm trusting you to take care of her.'

'I assure you I will.' Smythe moved away for a moment to discuss the new details with his remaining man.

Sam stood next to Jade for a few moments as though trying to decide what to do. His eyes followed every contour of her oval face and olive complexion. They lingered for a moment on her short black curls as they peeped out from under the brim of her old battered felt hat. Finally they rested on her own eyes, the color of spring grass in the dew. He freed one curl from under her hat brim and left it coiled on her forehead.

'You behave yourself,' he said softly. 'Remember, I haven't heard the rest of your lovesick-elk saga.'

Jade nodded and smiled. 'I'll see you later, Sam.' He started to go and she grabbed his arm. 'Wait.' Her voice dropped to a whisper so she wouldn't aggravate Smythe by altering his orders to Sam. 'I think I know where to find either the von Gretchmars or Vogelsanger. Follow the trail south around the crater. There's a pit trap in the trail. Chiumbo and I took out the spikes, but it's still a handy place to toss a body.'

'You think somebody's in there?'

Jade shrugged. 'I don't know, but the poachers made the trap, so either Vogelsanger followed Otto there and killed him and maybe even Claudia or vice versa. Just be careful. Wounded animals are more dangerous, you know.'

Sam nodded to his own leg. 'I know. I'm one of them.'

'Well, get moving there, man,' bellowed Smythe. 'My stars! At this rate the next set of rains will start before you find Hascombe.'

Sam gave one last passing look at Jade as he headed up the narrow trail at a fast, limping walk. Jade, in turn, watched him disappear from view, aware again of a sudden emptiness inside her. *Blast it! This is no time to suddenly go soft.*

'Shall we, Miss del Cameron?'

Jade nodded. 'It's on the east side of the crater. We go this way.' She turned to skirt around the north end towards the cache when her foot slipped and she went down hard on her left knee. 'Ouch! Spit fire and save the matches!'

Smythe gave her a hand up. 'What happened?' he asked.

'I slipped, that's all. Blasted knee gives out easily. Shrapnel wound from the war.'

'Can you make it to the cache?'

Jade marveled at his brusque, businesslike tone of voice. *That's an officer for you. Direct and right to the point. No concern about getting back from the cache, just in getting there.*

She took a few tentative steps and winced. She wondered what it felt like to have an artificial limb like Sam. Did he have ghost pains? Did he have to rely on his knee and thigh telling him when he'd actually planted his boot on hard ground? *Hell's bells. If he can live with that, I can walk with this.* 'Yes, I'll be fine.'

Smythe strode out in front, since he held a rifle and Jade didn't, with Jade leading from behind. Smythe's one remaining soldier brought up and guarded the rear. Once they were under way, the captain called over his shoulder, 'You told that American you would direct me to the caches. That's plural. What did you mean?'

'I held my own raid and took some of the rifles as well as the bag of gold. I hid them elsewhere.'

Smythe stopped so suddenly that Jade nearly bumped into him from behind. He turned slowly, pushed his solar topee back on his forehead, and stared at her with a look of newly found respect in his eyes. 'You stole arms and money from the Abyssinians? Why, my dear Miss del Cameron, it seems I have underestimated both your valor and your foolhardiness.'

Jade frowned, her thick black brows forming a

storm line over her eyes. 'What would you have me do, Captain? Let them go? Let them take their rifles and slaughter some innocent villagers or wipe out more of your soldiers? Aren't you forgetting the one poor soldier I found dead with the elephant? If I could have located you, I would have told you about them sooner. I sent a runner out days ago.'

Smythe's face became stony as his jaw clenched and his lips formed one thin, hard line. 'Miss del Cameron,' he said after a pause during which he seemingly mastered his anger, 'I explained to you before, my men and I have a very large territory to patrol. As it is, we are spread too thin. If you think — '

'If *you* think I have forgotten the sacrifice your soldier made, you are mistaken, sir.' Jade's voice was low, its subdued tone emphasizing her serious intent more than an angry shout could ever do, for it gave proof to her own self-control. 'Nor am I likely to. I have seen too many good men die for someone else's cause.'

Jade held her ground and her gaze until Smythe backed down and looked away. He pressed his hat more firmly on his head. 'Perhaps you should just show me the other cache first.'

'No, sir. It's too far out of the way. The poachers' hideout is closer. Besides, the rifles I've hidden aren't going anywhere and the Abyssinians may be holding some of Hascombe's missing people as hostages.'

Smythe nodded and continued on as she directed. For the rest of the hike, they maintained silence, resorting to hand signals to communicate directions at trail forks. Near the cache, Jade tugged on Smythe's sleeve and put her hand up to signal a stop. Then she held a finger in front of her lips for silence before pointing to the trees. Smythe nodded. They would proceed off the trail.

The captain and his lone soldier took the lead, pushing Jade to the rear as they crept closer to the cache. Jade worried how they would handle this assault with only two armed men and her bow. Surprise could count for something, but if they faced a large number of Abyssinians, they would be slaughtered. Well, as long as she could take some out with her, she'd go down valiantly, and let God defend the right, as the old soldiers used to say.

Smythe held his hand out to the side, palm down, and lowered it, a signal for everyone to drop. Since the cache itself was visible only from the side, they waited silently for a moment, listening for sounds of activity under the overhang. With any luck, Jade thought, it would be empty and they could plan an ambush.

But their luck wasn't that good. From the interior suddenly burst the shouts of an argument. Of the two voices that echoed from the rocky shelter, one dominated and the other pleaded; both shouted in rapid German. Jade recognized them. *Von Gretchmar and his wife, Claudia!* She strained to catch the words, but several conditions hindered her: her position with most of the rock wall between her and the sounds, her lack of practice listening to rapidly spoken German, and the fact that Smythe had pushed her down to presumably get her out of any possible line of fire.

Before he nearly shoved her face in the dirt, she thought she heard Claudia whimpering about a promise that she'd be a queen, followed by something about the gold. So Claudia was involved. And it stood to reason that if Otto von Gretchmar was this angry, then he'd been paid that gold in exchange for the weapons, and his frumpy little Frau had double-crossed him for another man. But who? Vogelsanger? And how did Mercedes fit in?

Jade had no intention of staying flat on her stomach. She rose on her elbows in time to hear von Gretchmar punch his wife. The resounding smack of a hard fist on soft flesh was quickly followed by a surprised cry of pain and the sound of a body falling against wooden crates. Jade was on her feet in an instant, using her nearly squatting position to launch herself just as a sprinter would. She'd taken two strides when a strong arm yanked her back and flung her to the ground. She landed on her backside, just missing her bow.

'Son of a biscuit!' she swore as she struggled to rise. When she did, she faced a solemn African soldier who held his rifle across his chest in front of her and shook his head no.

In the meantime, Captain Smythe had slipped his Webley .455 from its holster and charged the cache. As Jade watched, unable to move past the soldier, she saw Smythe raise his revolver and take aim, his finger on the trigger.

She launched herself at the askari, using

surprise and a few inches of superior height to force him aside. The man stumbled backward as Jade shoved past him. Her efforts to get to Smythe in time were ineffectual. The next sound to reach her ears was the crack of the revolver, followed immediately by a sharp scream of pain.

'No!' she shouted. 'I need him alive!'

Smythe ignored her, and lowered the front of his Webley several inches, evidence that his target had fallen. He fired again.

Jade grabbed for his arm, anger lending strength to her body despite all the abuse it had recently suffered. 'What the hell are you doing?'

Smythe recoiled under the attack of a five-feet, seven-inch, 130-pound human lioness. His hat fell from his head onto the ground as he wrenched his hand back, keeping a grip on his weapon. 'Are you mad, woman?' he demanded.

Jade released her grip and stood back. Her heart pounded, and her fist remained clenched, ready to fight. 'You idiot! *He's* probably not the mastermind here. We needed him for questioning to find out who is running this operation.' She couldn't imagine the portly banker making it off the mountain in time to orchestrate Jelani's kidnapping, or her and Sam's capture, especially not under Harry's nose. More than anything, she wanted the man who had hurt Jelani. Now her rage at having lost a chance to find that out fell on Captain Smythe.

The captain, in turn, turned a sneering smile on Jade. 'Typical female hysteria,' he muttered. 'But you needn't worry. I didn't kill the woman. She'll be useful, I'm sure.'

Jade's head snapped to the side to search the recesses of the cache. She had incorrectly assumed the second shot was for the already fallen Claudia, but the German woman only lay in a sprawl against the boxes, unconscious after her husband's angry blow. No blood marred her clothing beyond the trickle that oozed from her split lower lip.

Smythe pointed to von Gretchmar's body. 'I had to stop him, you know. He would have killed her.'

Jade's eyes followed his outstretched arm to the lifeless body of the banker. Blood stained his shirt in two spots; one bullet had probably penetrated a lung, the other his heart. Then she noticed the revolver lying a few inches from him. 'He had a gun?' Whatever make and model it was, it looked far too small and ineffectual to carry out into the African wilderness, but deadly enough against his wife. Perhaps all was not lost, if Claudia talked.

Smythe holstered his Webley. 'I would appreciate it, Miss del Cameron, if you would refrain from any more such theatrics and leave these matters to me.' He signaled for his one remaining soldier to come forward and issued some orders in an African language Jade didn't recognize. The African immediately trotted into the cache, grabbed hold of von Gretchmar's corpse, and dragged it to the entrance.

Jade wondered why Smythe's men didn't speak English. After all, they were part of the King's African Rifles and might be subject to any number of commanding officers, many of whom might not speak anything other than English and kitchen Swahili. Smythe watched his subordinate prop the body out of sight before returning to stand guard over Frau von Gretchmar.

'That should do for now,' said Smythe. 'And now, Miss del Cameron, if you would be so good as to show me the way to your little hidden cache, I would be very grateful.'

Jade was about to make a comment about von Gretchmar's body becoming an attraction for scavengers when she noticed a gray figure standing like a mist among the shadows. *Boguli!*

26

*But the worst mistake anyone can make is
to assume be knows for a fact what the
animal will do, especially the dangerous one.
Because when you are dead certain about a
behavior, you might certainly be dead.*
— The Traveler

The old man emerged from the dark forest, still
wearing his tattered gray blanket tied over one
shoulder and blending with the shadows as
would an evening fog. And like the fog, he
seemed almost ethereal, his deeply wrinkled face
infinitely serene. As usual, he swayed from side
to side, marking time to some internal rhythm
known only to him. Boguli moved his eyes to
Captain Smythe, then nodded once to Jade.

Smythe had turned to retrieve his fallen
headgear. In the instant Jade gave her attention
to the captain, she noticed the back of Smythe's
head and his oversized ears protruding from his
thick brown hair. Her mind instantly jumped
back to one of the first lengths of film she'd
developed from a trip wire camera, the image of
Claudia von Gretchmar in the arms of another
man.

*Smythe is the leader! Schmit! That's the other
word Jelani heard.* Other memories shouted in

her head. 'Have you had any dealings with the new chap up north? I hear he saw service in Tanganyika during the war.' 'I'll even send word to Isiolo to let the patrol up there know you're coming.' 'Tragic how Captain Ross died.'

No wonder Smythe had killed Otto before he could talk. It was a perfect plan. As a lone officer patrolling this range, he had easy access to the Abyssinian poachers and was able to make a tidy profit for himself. She wondered what his full plan was. Did he buy arms from people like the von Gretchmars to resell to the Abyssinians? Or was he arming them for something else?

Jade remembered both Mercedes' and Claudia's references to becoming a queen and she shuddered as the full scope of Smythe's plan entered her mind, her brain processing this new revelation in the course of a few heartbeats. Then rage and loathing quickly replaced shock and disbelief as she realized that this man stood behind Jelani's torment and pain. Her fist slowly clenched and she tensed her legs to launch herself at her hated enemy.

In that moment, Smythe turned and saw the recognition and fierce determination in Jade's eyes. He rapidly pulled his Webley and leveled it at her chest.

'Well, well, Miss del Cameron, it seems we find ourselves at odds with each other. My employer told me you'd be a formidable opponent and suggested I kill you, but I never really believed it. I thought you'd leave when I told you to.'

'You bastard,' she said, her voice low and

husky. 'I'm going to kill you for what you've done.'

'My dear girl,' he said in a patronizing tone, 'you haven't got it in you.'

Jade sneered, an evil grin playing like a snarl over her beautiful face. 'Oh, just give me a chance, you snake.'

Smythe shrugged lightly and chuckled. 'It's all academic, isn't it? I have a revolver, and you don't. Not even your rifle, although I am curious as to how you got away. I thought I had you and your friend chained very nicely. But no more time for pleasantries. Let's go find that little cache of yours, why don't we? I want my gold back.'

'Find it yourself,' Jade said, and spat at his feet.

'My, my. We are a feisty little creature.' For all the scorn in his words, he kept his revolver trained on her. 'I could shoot you. Perhaps I will.'

Jade hung her head and squeezed her eyes together, forcing a tear to surface. When she raised her head, she kept her now-moistened eyes wide while her lower lip quivered. In short, she looked the very picture of a subdued female. 'Please don't kill me,' she whimpered.

'I knew you weren't so fearless. Of course I won't kill you, but I might hurt you if you don't cooperate,' Smythe cooed. 'I need you to show me where you hid those guns and the money. I can hardly organize my own little revolution without them, can I?' He smirked. 'First, my well-armed private militia will take over one of the richest territories in Abyssinia and become very powerful. But I don't plan to stop there. No, I'm going to be emperor someday. I'll offer my military expertise to the current empress and ultimately gain complete control.'

'So that's why von Gretchmar gave you the money,' said Jade in a breathless tone, as though she were awed by his scheming.

'That fat old fool was merely a delivery boy. He didn't give me the money. I paid it to him for the rifles. Got quite a lot of it when I worked for the Germans in their old territories. Served under another ex-Englishman, Prince. But once it was clear the stupid Germans were losing the war, it occurred to me that I needed a new line of work.'

'So you became Smythe and signed up with the Rifles? Very clever.'

Smythe shrugged. 'Not at first. At first I ran a sort of supply business out of Mombasa. Perhaps you knew one of my contacts? Roger Forster? Then after you fouled that up, we had to disband that operation and sever connections. So I came here. At first I was only ordered to run guns, but then I found an excellent opportunity to advance myself. Put me in a rather neat little position. I'm more of a partner now. But Otto?' He snorted again. 'He only took the risk of supplying me with guns because I promised to make his precious little Mercedes my queen. What he didn't know was that I seduced his Frau and promised her that *she'd* be an empress if she'd only return my gold.'

Smythe spat. 'As if I plan on having either

336

German bitch for a queen. I can make more money selling them, and I will as soon as my sergeant returns with the little Fräulein.' His laugh turned Jade's stomach as he eyed her up and down. 'Maybe if you cooperate, I'll sell you to some nice harem. Otherwise, I'll kill you *after* I shoot off one finger at a time. I know my partner would prefer to see you suffer.'

His partner? She remembered a previous thought. Was there someone out there who actually hated her so much as to use the boy for revenge? Yes, there was, and she suspected she knew who.

Jade hunched her shoulders slightly and drew back in on herself, putting her hands behind her. 'Please,' she whispered again, 'don't hurt me. I'll show you where the money is. And don't let Vogelsanger hurt me, either.'

Smythe kept his Webley in his right hand, the stock held against his side by his right elbow while he gestured magnanimously with his left hand. 'If you think one of those other Germans is my partner, you're mistaken.' He waved his revolver for her to move. 'After you, my dear.'

Jade wasn't certain if her submissive act fooled Smythe or not, but she took the chance that a man as arrogant as he was, especially one holding a gun on her, would hardly believe her capable of treachery. She wanted to end it now, but between his revolver and that soldier who guarded Claudia with a rifle, she knew she didn't stand a chance. No, she'd have to lure Smythe away from his confederates. In the meantime, she slowly collected the dangling chain on her wrist into her closed fists and held them hidden from view.

'No tricks now, missy,' Smythe said. 'Just go on nice and slowly or you'll have a bullet in your shoulder.'

'It's this way,' said Jade as she inched past him towards the trail that would take them not only towards her cache, but also to her original snare. She only hoped it was still in place after all this time. As she headed back into the forest, she looked to the side, trying to catch a glimpse of Boguli, and wondered if the old man could help her. Thoughts of an elephant stampede such as the one that tore down Harry's *boma* flitted across her mind. Boguli, in the meantime, had melted unseen back into the shadows.

Jade led the way to her cache, pausing at every trail juncture to look around, doing her best to appear confused and timid. In actuality, she was looking for Boguli, Sam, Harry, or any other possible reinforcements. She saw none, not even a hidden snake to lead Smythe towards, even though she occasionally forayed onto a narrow meandering path. After all, it wouldn't do to make this too easy for him.

After over an hour of trudging around, Smythe poked Jade in the back with the revolver barrel. 'How much farther?' he snarled. 'You'd better not be leading me on some merry little chase or I'll make good on my promise to deal you serious discomfort. I've heard a great deal about you.'

'No,' Jade wailed. 'You promised not to kill me.'

'And I won't, but I don't think the loss of a few fingers or toes will lower your price too much, and you should fetch a very nice one.' His free hand came up and toyed with her hair.

Jade bit her lip and forced herself not to explode right then and there. He still had his gun trained on her back. She ran through every lesson of patience her father had ever taught her while hunting. Too quick a reaction meant a loss of the prey, and this was one she did not intend to lose. 'It's not far,' she said. 'I'm just trying to make sure I don't miss it. All these trees are starting to look alike to me.'

She knew she was only a few hundred yards away from her snare, but if she led him right into it too quickly, she'd run the risk of tripping it herself. That was when she remembered, it was never reset after she and Sam had cut Harry down. They'd used the rope to make the deadfall by the rifles. She'd have to lead him to the cache and hope he didn't make her retrieve the rifles.

'Well,' snapped Smythe, 'I'm waiting and I'm losing my patience.'

'Down there,' said Jade, nodding down the hill on the ancient elephant trail. 'It's on that old trail.'

Smythe prodded her again from behind. 'You first, lovey.'

Now Jade's every sense was set to high alert. She padded softly but quickly down the antiquated path, her speed giving evidence to her assurance that the rifles and gold lay close at hand. She counted on Smythe's mounting greed to make him careless. She stopped a few yards short of the hollow tree.

'I put it all in there.'

Smythe kept his revolver trained on her as he stepped closer to the shell of a tree and peered inside. His lips spread in a thin, satisfied smile. 'Where's the gold?'

'I put it behind that first tier of rifles,' she lied, knowing Avery had taken the gold with him.

'Show me,' Smythe ordered.

For a split second Jade hesitated. To handle those rifles meant becoming a target for the deadfall, but to say no meant arousing his suspicion. She decided to play on his distrustful nature. Her eyes widened in excitement, and she started to smile and inhale sharply. As soon as she saw he observed her expression, she suddenly cut it off, a perfect imitation of someone who actually wanted to grab a rifle and was suddenly trying not to show it.

Smythe fell for it. 'Stop! You loaded one, didn't you?' He chuckled. 'Clever girl, but not clever enough.' His lip twisted in a snarl. 'Get over there where I can keep an eye on you!' he snapped.

Jade put her hands behind her back and sidled over towards the left side of the tree while Smythe kept his revolver trained on her. Timing and position were critical now. If the deadfall didn't drop, she needed to be just close enough to kick his gun away and slug him hard in the jaw with her fist. If the log did drop, she didn't want to be in its way.

Smythe knelt in front of the tree's opening, his Webley aimed at her midsection. For a moment

340

he studied the stack of rifles, watchful for any trick. Jade and Sam had run the trip line out the other side of the tree so it wasn't readily visible. All she could hope for was that they had done a good job rigging both the toggle and the log that served as the deadfall.

A slight movement in her peripheral vision caught Jade's eye, and she looked over Smythe's back to see Boguli halfway up the trail beckoning to her. She made one slight nod to show she saw him.

'I don't see the pouch,' Smythe growled. He reached into the hollow tree and took hold of the nearest rifle and extracted it. Nothing happened. 'Blasted female,' he muttered.

Time seemed to become suspended for Jade as she waited for him to pull on the right rifle. She became aware of every heartbeat, of the drop of sweat that trickled down her back, of the chain biting into her palms as she tightened her grip. She worried that he would shoot her now that he had found the cache before he ever tripped the deadfall. *Should've left the gold in there and rigged the trigger to it instead.*

'It better be behind this next rifle or I'm going to make you pay for my trouble,' Smythe said, pausing to wink at Jade as though they were sharing a private joke. 'This one seems to be stuck — ' Suddenly his eyes widened as understanding and surprise flashed across his face. He released his grip on the trigger rifle and rolled out of the way. He would have made it if it hadn't been for Jade.

She saw her chance and kicked his gun up into

the air, her leg snapping up with the speed of a rattlesnake. But Smythe was a trained soldier and was on his feet in an instant. He lunged for Jade, who countered by dancing backward and in a circle. The deadfall had gotten hung up, snagged on a limb and ready to drop with just a little more provocation. She needed to keep Smythe in its vicinity while she supplied the force that would drop the log.

She swung her left fist in an uppercut, intentionally missing Smythe by a few inches. He jerked his head back, then, assuming that she fought like a girl, found himself amused by her inept attempt to hit him. Jade counted on his ego, and he didn't disappoint her.

He pointed at his square chin and laughed. 'Come on, darling, not a big enough target for you?'

Jade cut loose with a right hook, only this time she released the chain she'd hidden in her fist. Six inches of hard iron links snapped out and caught Smythe across his left eye before thwacking him on the nose. He roared in pain and grabbed for his face.

'You're going to pay for that, bitch!' he yelled as he grabbed for her.

Again Jade danced out of his reach. This time she feinted with the right hand, then cut loose with another uppercut from her left, followed immediately with a hard right in a one-two punch. Once again she let the chain fly. It slammed into his lower jaw, causing him to bite his own tongue.

This time, not only the chain made contact,

but her fist did as well. The combined force sent the man reeling. Smythe stumbled backward onto the hollow tree. The sudden impact sent just enough of a tremor up the trunk to knock loose the deadfall.

The log dropped, but because Smythe had his upper back against the tree, the log missed his head and only managed to conk him hard in the gut. He fell to the ground, yelling obscenities and swearing a torturous revenge on Jade.

She didn't wait to hear them. By that time she was halfway up the ancient elephant trail following Boguli.

27

The elephant trails on Marsabit are as wide as country roads and about as disorganized, meandering every which way, created as the mood hit someone. Happily, due to the scarcity of large predators, they are generally safe to travel on foot. Even the buffalo on the mountain are shy enough to retreat back into the brush rather than challenge you, unless they are wounded. It is dangerous to try to outrun a wounded bull buffalo. The better part of valor at this point is to stand and fight. That is, assuming you still have your rifle.
— The Traveler

Sam felt as if he'd spent the last several days on the practice field nonstop with the Purdue Boilermakers' football squad, only he was the tackle dummy. Every one of his muscles ached as though they had been repeatedly pummeled, which, when he stopped to think about it, was about right. But what ached more than anything else was his pride. Somehow showing the woman you found most desirable in the world that parts of your body came off didn't seem like the best way to impress her.

That hadn't been his original plan. Ever since

Avery and Beverly had sent him their carbon copy of Madeline Thompson's manuscript detailing their last adventure, he'd been head over heels for Jade. When they told him she had a fascination for airplanes and pilots, he'd decided he would win her. But, hell, if his buddy back home couldn't rig up a plane to operate without foot pedals, he was as good as grounded himself, and now she knew it.

Well, no one could ever say that Sam Featherstone lacked courage and fortitude. He'd stuck by her, pushed his one and a half legs to their limit, and saved both their necks out in the desert. Now that she was safely guarded by Smythe, he'd do as she'd bidden and find that blasted Hascombe and search for that pit trap. After that, he intended to return promptly to Jade's side.

I'll be danged if I'm following Hascombe back to his compound for her to come and compare us side by side. He figured his best chance to win her now was to see her and her friends safely back to Nairobi. If that didn't work, then he'd slip away quietly and not come back until he could fly in.

Where the blazes is Hascombe? Sam picked up a stiff fallen branch and used it to hoist himself up the last of the steep slope, thinking this should be the spot where Captain Smythe said he could find Harry. What he saw first was enough to take away what breath he had left, a stunning view of a bluegreen oval lake replete with water lilies, moss-festooned trees, and flocks of waterfowl. The filmmaker in him wanted to

345

set up a camera on the spot. Even as he watched, he saw gray shapes parading down to the water's edge. *Elephants!*

Then he heard people talking. Someone was coming around the rim trail hidden in the tree line. Sam recognized one of the voices and called out, 'Hascombe!'

Harry stepped around and out into the open. 'Featherstone? What the bloody blazes are you doing here?' Then he stopped and looked behind Sam. 'Where's Jade? Has something happened to her?' He ran the rest of the way to Sam, leaving his small crew behind.

Sam lowered his voice so only Harry could hear him. 'Nothing recently, Hascombe, though we did run into some trouble in the northern desert. We escaped and made it back. Jade's convinced that your German customers are involved with these poachers.'

Harry scowled and rubbed a large hand over his stubbled chin. 'A day ago I would have thought she was imagining things, but the von Gretchmars have disappeared along with Vogelsanger.'

Heinrich Mueller and several Africans joined Harry. 'We saw your wife, Liesel, when she came back to your camp with Mercedes. They're both safe,' Sam said to reassure the man. He counted the number of Africans with them, only six. 'Is this all of you, Hascombe?'

Harry nodded. 'I sent my headman, Nakuru, and the rest of the porters off to the northern craters in case the others went in that direction.' He scowled at Sam from under his hat brim. 'So, what's this all about, Featherstone? What happened to you?'

Sam briefly related Jelani's capture and their own escape, avoiding only the fact that he and Jade had initially doubled back to spy on Harry. *After all* he thought, *Mueller might be a part of this yet.* 'We followed your trail this way. Jade told me there's an old pit trap exposed around the southern side of the crater. She thought it would be a place to look.'

'But you're here alone,' Harry said. 'Just where is our little Simba Jike now?'

'Where she can't get into too much mischief. She's with Captain Smythe. We ran into him over an hour ago. Smythe sent one of his native soldiers to guard the women at your camp, but he told me to find you and send you back to relieve his man so he and the rest would look for Mercedes' parents.'

Harry's eyes widened. 'The hell you say!' he roared. 'I ran into him first thing today. He's the one who told us he'd seen von Gretchmar and his wife up on top here scouting elephants, but we can't find any trace of them, or tracks that they've ever been here.'

'And you've been all over the crater?'

Harry nodded. 'All I can figure is that he saw them head this way, but they changed course before they got there. We'd better get to that pit. They could be in there.'

'The question is,' said Sam, 'did Vogelsanger toss them in alive?'

They hastened towards the place where Jade had said she'd found the pit, and kept a sharp

347

eye out for Vogelsanger or any of the poachers. 'There it is,' said Sam as the edge of the exposed trap first appeared.

Harry ran close and peered in. 'Bloody hell,' he swore. 'It's Vogelsanger.'

Sam joined him. 'He's bound and unconscious, but still alive. Von Gretchmar must have gained the upper hand.'

'Yes,' said Harry, 'but where's von Gretchmar now?'

Two of the porters jumped into the pit and hoisted up the injured Prussian, then clambered out with the aid of their comrades. 'Looks like he's been hit over the head,' said Sam.

Harry untied Vogelsanger's hands while Sam undid the man's shirt and searched for wounds. 'Probably some cracked ribs as well, judging by these bruises.' He splashed water from his canteen on the man's face, then poured a bit into his mouth.

The Prussian sputtered, groaned, and opened his eyes. '*Mein Gott!* Thank heavens you found me,' he said with a moan.

'Where's von Gretchmar and his wife?' said Harry. 'Tell me what you did with them or you're going to find yourself with something worse than a headache.'

Eric struggled to sit up, screamed in pain, groaned, and plopped onto his back again, his hand held at his chest. 'I never found them. Some Englander hit me.'

Sam and Harry stared at each other. 'An Englander?' repeated Harry.

'But the only other Englander left around here

is Smythe,' said Sam. Suddenly his brows contracted in a scowl. 'Then he's . . . ' Sam mumbled as he comprehended the situation.

'That's right,' growled Harry, 'and our Jade is alone with him.'

Harry turned and barked a few orders to his gun bearer and Mueller. 'You take Vogelsanger back to camp. If someone tries to shoot you, shoot 'em first.' He turned back to Sam and nodded at the Enfield in his hand. 'You any good with that?' Sam nodded. Harry pulled his hat down firmly on his brow. 'Then come on, Featherstone. There's no time to waste.'

Sam followed as rapidly as he could, sliding back down the trail more than walking it. In his mind he kept replaying the look of intense hatred and rage in Jade's eyes when she had brought Jelani back to him and her vow to kill whoever'd hurt the boy. As soon as Jade uncovered the truth, she'd stop at nothing to avenge Jelani. Sam only hoped he could reach her in time to stop her from crossing the line from self-defense into murder.

'Don't worry about Jade. She can handle herself,' said Harry as if he read part of Sam's thoughts.

'It's not Jade I'm actually worried about,' said Sam. 'It's what she'll do to Smythe that's got me concerned.'

'What she doesn't do, I intend to finish,' added Harry. 'That man shot my cheetah.'

★ ★ ★

The deadfall had worked but in a limited way. It would be only a matter of seconds before Smythe was on his feet again and in pursuit. Jade regretted that his revolver had landed on the other side of her escape route; she'd have liked to have something more than her confiscated bow for a weapon. Thank the Lord and pompous officers that Smythe hadn't had the foresight to take it away from her. If she could just get somewhere safe enough to lie in wait and get off a good shot. She'd have to rely on Boguli for that.

Would she be able to handle it? She'd pulled this bow only once before and that was to gently fire an arrow into Harry's tent. It had at least a fifty-pound draw weight, and she was running low on energy now. If she tired too much, she'd never get the string back far enough to shoot with any decent force. She'd come close to breaking a cardinal rule of hunters everywhere: never go out with an untried weapon. In addition, her hands stung from the fisticuffs and her knuckles were swelling. She ripped a strip of fabric from her shirt and wrapped it three times around her right hand's knuckles.

Ahead of her, Boguli darted along the ancient trail, his head turning from side to side as though he was searching for something. Behind her, she heard Smythe curse as he scrambled for his revolver. They needed to get out of his line of fire and soon. Almost as if he read her mind, the old man pointed to the right and waved his arm for her to hurry. They slipped into the darkness of the forest just as Jade heard a crack and a high, singing hum as a bullet flew past. It struck a tree with a dull thud.

She grabbed an arrow from her makeshift quiver and held it aloft for Boguli to see. He nodded and began a tortuous route winding back and forth among the trees, keeping the larger ones between them and the enraged captain. Jade, exhausted from her ordeals as well as lack of food and rest, relied on the sheer obedience of her leg muscles to propel her forward. But more than putting distance between her and Smythe, she longed to double back and catch him from behind. She unslung her bow as another bullet whizzed a few feet to her right. At least when she finally got a chance to shoot an arrow, there would be little sound to give her away.

Boguli led her up the hill, all the while avoiding the more well-traveled trails. He seemed to know exactly where the more secretive paths lay and led her into them by obscure routes that were harder for Smythe to spot than an obvious trail juncture. After nearly a quarter of an hour, Boguli suddenly crouched down behind a bush and motioned for Jade to do the same.

Relieved at the chance to catch her breath, Jade took advantage of the respite to nock her arrow. Boguli pointed to her right and slipped into the shadows, walking in a low crouch. Jade followed suit, making certain to keep her body well below the line of bushes. To her left came the sound of heavy footfalls and rapid breathing as Smythe came closer.

The bushes in this spot offered few gaps, and

351

Jade had no intention of stepping in front of Smythe to try for a chest shot. She waited patiently until she heard him pass, counted silently to ten, then slipped out of the brush forty feet behind him. Using every ounce of strength, she drew the bow back to her cheek, sighted, and let fly.

That's for Jelani!

Either the feathers in the fletching were twisted and worn from previous use, or the bowstring was not centered. Instead of flying true, the arrow dipped a bit to the left and struck Smythe in his left buttock rather than in his back as Jade had intended. She heard him scream in pain and rage as he grabbed for the arrow behind him. He turned and fired wildly into the brush, but by that time both Jade and Boguli had disappeared into the forest.

★ ★ ★

'Keep up, man,' Harry hollered over his shoulder to Sam.

The twisting nature of the game trail and the danger of racing headlong into a prowling leopard, a drowsy buffalo, or an ill-tempered cobra kept Hascombe to a brisk walk punctuated by brief jogs along the straighter patches. Sam, unable to run hard for any distance, and hampered by his growing exhaustion, lagged behind, relying more and more on the stout walking stick for support in order to keep up his speed.

'Dammit, Hascombe,' Sam panted, 'you're

making enough noise to alert Smythe and his entire crew. Besides which, you're running off blindly. You have no idea where to look for them now.'

The last part of Sam's statement slowed Harry more than the first. He stopped dead in his tracks and turned to wait for Sam. 'Then tell me, Featherstone, and I'll run ahead and intercept them.'

Sam caught up and took a moment to regain his breath. 'The hell you will. You're not charging in there without me.'

Harry's smile was a devious sneer. 'Afraid I'll save her by myself and win her over, eh, Featherstone?'

Sam scowled. He really wanted to punch this man square in the jaw, but unfortunately, he needed him right now to save Jade. 'No. I just don't want your suicidal charge on my hands.'

Harry snorted. 'To be sure.' He shot a look at Sam's leg. 'Seriously, man, are you going to make it? Did you sprain your ankle?'

Sam massaged his knee and upper thigh, checking that all the buckles and attachments that held his prosthetic limb were still in place. 'Trust me when I say that I feel absolutely no pain in my ankle.'

'Well, I don't intend to carry you,' said Harry as he turned aside and looked down the game trail. 'And we can't dawdle too much, noise or not. So just where are we going?'

Sam took another deep breath, straightened, and briefly studied the terrain. He recognized an offshoot trail as a path that led in one direction to his hidden Dodge, and in the other to the poachers' cache. 'To the villain's lair,' said Sam. 'This time, you follow me.'

★ ★ ★

Jade paused behind a tree and took stock of her remaining ammunition. Six arrows left, hardly enough to launch a fullscale assault if Smythe's men returned. Just how many soldiers did he have in his little army, not counting the Abyssinians themselves? She'd never seen him with more than two or three soldiers. Maybe the real troops were kept at a distance, patrolling other parts of the northern frontier under a junior officer.

For a moment, she remembered the executed man she'd found among the dead elephants. At least one man had remained loyal to king and country. Was he a new recruit sent to join Smythe's ranks? Had he stumbled on only the Abyssinian poachers or had he caught Smythe in the act? Whatever he'd discovered, Jade admired him. There was a man who refused to relinquish his honor even in the face of death. She fingered an arrow before nocking it. *This next one's for you.*

Before she'd sequestered herself behind this tree, Boguli had motioned for her to stay put, pushing his outstretched palm down. The old man himself had wandered off into the forest, presumably to scout. Jade didn't mind. Waiting gave her time to recoup her dwindling strength. It also gave her time to think, and her thoughts kept returning to the dead soldier, hunched on the ground with a gaping hole in place of his face. From there, memories of the slaughtered elephant calf crept in along with the cow that had been left to bleed to death. Finally her thoughts rested on Chiumbo and young Jelani, and once again, Jade lingered there and felt the rage well up within her like a geyser about to blow. She welcomed it. The anger gave her strength and determination. Somewhere in the recesses of her brain she heard Beverly remind her not to get awarded the 'order of the wooden cross,' a term used in the ambulance corps to represent a deceased driver's grave marker. No, getting killed wouldn't bring this man to justice, she decided, and tempered her anger with a dose of caution.

Finally, when her patience had worn itself to nothing, she spied Boguli, a dusty gray shadow thirty feet away. He beckoned for her to follow. With a quick look around for danger, Jade sprinted through the trees towards him. She didn't know where he planned to lead her, but she followed willingly, trusting him.

Boguli took her on a winding path off trail, a route on which she never lacked for a sheltering tree trunk to guard her. It had been over a quarter of an hour since she'd last heard Smythe, and she wondered if he was on her trail or she was on his. The answer came quickly enough when Boguli crouched behind a tree and motioned for Jade to do the same behind a rocky outcrop. Then he pointed to her left. When she peered over the boulder, Jade spotted Smythe standing not fifty feet away, facing down a slight incline.

Jade recognized the spot. It was one they'd passed just before she'd rested awhile. Boguli had once again doubled back. Silently, Jade took her bow, aiming for Smythe's back, but just as she released the string, Smythe squatted to examine a partial boot print. Her arrow flew high this time, and tore under his hat brim and through the cartilage of his right ear.

That's for the soldier you murdered! The next one's for Chiumbo.

Smythe shrieked in pain as the arrow sliced through his right ear's cartilage. Blood splattered his shirt and the surrounding leaves as he spun and fired. The bullet struck the edge of Jade's sheltering boulder and ricocheted off.

She hunkered down into a low crouch and scuttled away crablike as she strove to keep the rocky outcrop between her and the next shot. Smythe fired again, the bullet passing just overhead and into the trees beyond as Jade darted around first one tree, then another. Behind her, the tree bark shattered and pelted her back.

No need for silence now, just speed. With Smythe stuck below the rock outcrop, he had no choice but to backtrack and find a path up to her. Jade planned on being well out of sight by that time, and back in the role of predator instead of prey. Unfortunately, it gave him ample time to reload, and she also lost sight of Boguli as she dodged Smythe's repeated fire. Without him to guide her, she took the only path she recognized, one that, she hoped, led past the only remaining camera blind and a potential hiding place. With any luck, she could use it as a hunter's blind.

Her lungs burned and her leg muscles started to cramp when she finally stopped and collapsed, panting, behind the big mahogany tree where she'd first watched the old bull elephant dust-bathe. Since the day that the bull fell, the herd of cows had left the area, shunning it as though it were haunted. Nothing larger than small animals had prowled the trail. Consequently, her trip wire, upraised a foot so only an elephant or another large mammal could trip it, remained untouched. Jade jumped over it and surveyed the blind up in the trees.

For a moment, she considered hiding up there. If Smythe came by, she could shoot down on him. She changed the 'if' to 'when.' After all, in her mad dash through the forest, she'd surely left a trail that an experienced tracker such as Smythe could follow. Jade pulled another arrow from her quiver and inspected it. Like the others, it had been pulled from the carcass of the dead bull elephant. Consequently, either the shafts or the fletchings bore some damage and might not shoot true to aim. Unless she killed Smythe in one shot, she'd be a sitting duck up in the tree.

Her lips twitched as an idea came to her. She still might be able to make use of the blind as a decoy. Her makeshift rope ladder rested atop a lower branch, its end dangling just within reach where she'd left it. She stretched up, grabbed it, and gave it a tug. The rope with its knotted loops for hand- and footholds fell easily from its perch. She climbed up the first two loops and scuffed the tree trunk with her right bootheel as though she'd hurriedly climbed the ladder, using the trunk for a brace. Then she dropped back to the ground and scuffed the leaf litter before she slipped off to the other side of the trail to wait.

If her plan worked, Smythe would be along shortly, studying the ground for her tracks. He'd see the scuff marks and conclude that she'd only recently climbed up into the blind. While he stood below looking for her and taking his aim, she'd risk another shot at him.

Jade examined her remaining arrows and chose one of the better ones, but when she nocked it, her hands shook as exhaustion caught up with her. Even her thigh muscles trembled. The pain in her left knee made her wince as she attempted to settle into a solid stance, and when she flexed her leg to ease the strain, her calf muscles charley horsed. Jade clenched her teeth as she massaged out the cramp.

A soft crunch arrested her attention, and she froze. *Smythe!* He padded closer with cautious steps, stopping periodically to examine the ground. When he turned his profile to her to inspect the tree, Jade saw he'd tied up his ripped ear with a pocket handkerchief. Blood seeped through it and hung in a congealed stalactite near his lobe. Flies buzzed his head and shirt, drawn by the scent of blood. Other, larger beasts would be attracted by that scent before long. *Let them come!*

Smythe stepped backward into the brush and

squatted down while he considered the tree blind. *Blast!* Jade knew the man had to be clever to keep his superiors in the dark about his operation, but she'd hoped he'd step closer to the tree to at least inspect the scuff marks. Yet when she thought about it, she knew she would have suspected a trap, too. Unfortunately, she couldn't see him well enough to risk releasing the arrow. She'd have to circle around behind him.

Escape routes and risks formed and re-formed in Jade's mind when she spied Boguli slip across the trail several yards past Smythe. Since her ally might have an idea himself, she decided to wait a few more moments in her hiding place before risking a move. She peered past Smythe and into the trees beyond, hoping for a glance of the old African and a clue to his plan, but he certainly knew how to avoid being seen or heard when he wanted.

A trumpeting blast ripped through the dead silence and nearly toppled Jade in surprise. The elephant that announced its anger at the intruders must have been sleeping only a few dozen feet behind Smythe. Jade could only assume Boguli had found the behemoth and startled it.

The plan worked. Smythe burst out of the trees, a look of terror on his face, and wheeled suddenly to spot the beast. He fired twice into the forest in seemingly random shots as though he hoped to startle the unseen animal into running the other way. All this did was arouse the massive elephant into greater anger as another piercingly shrill scream rent the air.

Smythe backed away and tumbled straight onto the calfhigh camera trip wire. He stumbled and fell as the flash powder blazed in a blinding white glare from up in the blind. Jade shut her eyes just in time and, when she opened them, spotted Boguli in the trees just behind Smythe. She took advantage of the latter's exposed position and blinded disorientation, aimed, drew back the powerful bowstring, and fired. This time the arrow flew true and struck Smythe in the back just below the right shoulder blade. His revolver flew from his hands and clattered several feet away.

That's for Chiumbo!

Once again, Jade beat a hasty retreat before Smythe could retrieve his weapon and fire. The man roared in pain, but he managed to find his revolver and shoot twice into the trees where she'd been. By now, his rage dominated all common sense, and Jade knew he'd kill her the first chance he had. After all, there was no more reason to keep her alive and every reason to finish her off before she could reveal his secret.

Her only hope now seemed to lie in beating him to the original cache, where she could hide behind the rocks and take one more shot.

28

Mount Marsabit is home to more than
elephants. A variety of hooved animals
reside there, including the oryx and greater
kudu. Then there is a delightful assortment
of lesser beasts such as the porcupine, the
civet, the honey badger, and that tiny cousin
to the mighty elephant itself, the pudgy rock
hyrax. Most of these smaller animals will
elude even the most watchful eye, but they
can be tricked into taking their own photograph if you set the right trap.
— The Traveler

Her lungs burned as Jade pushed herself to her
maximum and sprinted through the forest towards
the sheltering rocks of the poachers' cache. She
had only four arrows left. If she encountered any
of the poachers on the way, she was doomed.
Consequently she stayed off the trail, keeping
trees between her and any gunfire. Then she
remembered the one soldier left behind to guard
Claudia von Gretchmar. Suddenly the futility of
her plan smacked her full in the face.

*Blast! I'll have to save at least one arrow
for him.* Unless she took down Smythe first and
got his revolver. Then she'd have a fighting
chance. Suddenly, silence and secrecy became as

important as speed, and Jade felt a great longing for her stolen Winchester.

Just when the knot in her right calf nearly became unbearable, she spied the rock outcrop that sheltered the poachers and there, in front of it, stood two guards, the man left at the cache and the one who'd been sent to Harry's camp. For a moment, Jade thought all was lost, but then she noticed that the men in all their arrogant assurance were busy chewing on handfuls of dates. As one calmly spit out a pit and popped another date into his mouth, Jade looked for his rifle and saw it was slung across his back. The other man's rifle lay across one of the crates. Claudia sat huddled in the recesses against the cave wall, casting fearful glances back and forth between her armed guard and her dead husband. Mercedes cowered nearby in Liesel's protective embrace.

Jade kept to the trees as long as she could and waited until one guard stuffed more food in his mouth, and the second sat down as though to nap. Then she erupted from the trees, screaming like a banshee from hell, and raced straight at the startled soldiers.

The standing man spun around and choked on the mouthful of fruit while he struggled to slide his rifle from his back. His hands, still full of sticky dates, couldn't grip the weapon quickly enough to aim and fire, something Jade had counted on when she launched her assault. She kicked up with her right foot. Her boot caught the rifle stock and sent it flying out of his hands. Then she swung a hard right at the man's jaw.

Both whole and broken dates spewed out of his mouth and at least one chunk flew to the back of his throat. He doubled over and coughed, giving Jade the opportunity to send him reeling backward with a left uppercut. He landed with a thud against the second guard, who'd just managed to retrieve his rifle. Both toppled a few inches from Liesel. Jade dived for the first soldier's fallen rifle just as Liesel pushed Mercedes aside and shoved a heavy crate over onto both men.

Two down, one to go! Unfortunately, just as Jade reached the rifle, Smythe staggered into the clearing.

The man's fury and pain were written in blood across his face and shirt and underscored in the deep lines around his eyes and tightly set mouth. In the brief instant that Jade had before he could aim and fire, she read something else in his eyes, a growing stupor from the residual drugs on the arrows, a stupor enhanced by exhaustion. Since she had shot spent arrows pulled from the carcasses of the slain elephants, none of them had enough of the poison to either kill him or render him completely immobile, but their combined effect told on him. It also saved her life.

Smythe raised his revolver in his shaky hands, squinted down the barrel, and fired. What should have taken him a few seconds took him nearly ten, one second more than she needed. Jade snatched up the rifle and rolled just as the bullet zinged past her and struck the rock. Fragments of volcanic stone flew up from the ground and pelted her legs, and her bow's hard wood dug into her back. She settled into a kneeling stance.

As Jade snugged the rifle butt into her shoulder, she prayed the blasted thing was loaded. Without bothering to rise, she worked the bolt action once and fired. The bullet struck Smythe's wrist and blasted the revolver out of it.

He screamed and grabbed his shattered hand. Jade scrambled to her feet, chambered another round, and stepped forward, her rifle aimed squarely at Smythe's chest. In every aspect of his condition, she read the parallel of her innocent friends. She saw Chiumbo's wounds, Jelani's pain and blood, and her and Sam's own brush with death. All that was lacking was the young African soldier's death. Jade intended to complete the parallel. She rested her cheek against the rifle butt and took aim.

Smythe's face paled and he shook his head no, pleading silently for his life. At the same time, he tried to edge away from her, sidling closer to the cache. 'You can't do this,' he croaked. 'I have information you want, about my partner.' Bloody spit drooled from his mouth as he babbled and pleaded. 'You're a woman — you haven't got it in you.'

'How much you wanna bet, Smythe? Willing to bet your life?' She started to smile, but it turned into a snarl. 'Shall I do as Lady Macbeth did? What was it she said? 'Come you spirits that tend on mortal thoughts, unsex me here.' That would solve it, wouldn't it?'

Jade exhaled in preparation for firing. Her finger hesitated for a few seconds on the trigger when two male voices shouted in unison from behind her.

'Stop!'

Jade released the trigger without losing her aim or turning around.

'Nice of you to join us, Sam, Harry. This man is a murderer, a traitor to his country, a smuggler, a poacher, and a slave trader. You're just in time to witness his execution.'

'Don't do it, Jade,' Harry ordered.

'As if you wouldn't?' she asked, her cheek still resting on the rifle butt.

Smythe's eyes jerked back and forth between Jade and the two men, beseeching them to help him. 'She's berserk,' he said, his voice cracking.

'Jade, listen to me,' said Sam. His voice was firm, yet soothing. 'You're not a killer. You drove an ambulance, remember? You *saved* lives. You don't take them.'

'He hurt Jelani!' Her voice broke, and a tear cascaded down her cheek.

'And you saved him,' Sam added, his voice closer as he edged his way to her side. 'If you kill this man, scum though he may be, you'll become like him. Don't do it, Jade. Leave him to the law. I heard him say he has information. We need to get it from him.'

Jade groaned, took a deep breath, and exhaled in a shuddering sigh of resignation as she slowly lowered the rifle. Sam and Harry both rushed to her side, their concern for her overwhelming any thoughts of Smythe. After all, the man was unarmed and clearly in no condition to escape. As if to prove their assumptions correct, Smythe sagged and stumbled to the rocky wall by the cache's entrance.

Harry took the rifle from Jade's hands just as Smythe pulled a knife from his boot.

'Look out!' yelled Sam.

'You can't escape, Smythe,' said Harry. 'Give it up, man.'

'I may not escape, but if I'm going down, I'm taking that bitch with me.'

He raised his hand to hurl the knife as Sam grabbed Jade to pull her behind him, but there was no need to use his own body as a shield. Just as Smythe's hand reached the apex, Claudia von Gretchmar struggled to her feet, a large chunk of volcanic rock in her hand. She brought it down with a hollow thud on Smythe's head and knocked him out cold.

'*Schweinehund!*' she shouted, and spat on his prostrate body. 'That is for betraying *meine* daughter and me.'

29

*The next time you play a game of billiards
or let your fingers run across the piano keys,
think of the life's blood that was spilt to
give you that ivory. It's not just the blood
of the animals; it's the lifeblood of the brave
soldiers and game protectors who guard
the herds.*
— The Traveler

Reinforcements arrived at Harry Hascombe's camp the next day in the form of Lieutenant Fitzpatrick, of the King's African Rifles, and his fifteen askaris.

'Well, this is certainly one for the books,' said Fitzpatrick. 'First your runner staggers into Isiolo with some story about poachers shooting at you and killing one of our men. And just as I get my men together and come out to lend the captain a hand with some reinforcements, I meet up with Lord and Lady Dunbury, who lead me to believe that everything from kidnapping to a potential insurrection is taking place. We come on the double-quick and now you tell me that my own superior officer is a traitor and a murderer.'

'With his own little militia,' added Jade. 'I hope your men manage to round up the rest of these Abyssinian poachers. It seems some of them played the role of his own askaris.'

'Quite so,' agreed Fitzpatrick. 'All but that first poor chap. No wonder Smythe shot him. He couldn't have the man get back to the post and report on his activities. I always wondered why the captain insisted on our patrolling separately. Now I know. But you suspect that he once worked for Germans under Prince in Tanganyika?'

'He admitted as much,' said Jade. 'Let my headman, Chiumbo, take a look at him. I suspect he can identify him as one of the men that killed his family. And take a good look at any of Smythe's personal communications. If my suspicions are correct, someone else was in on this with him. He mentioned as much.' She smiled at the young lieutenant and held out her hand. 'By the way, congratulations.'

He shook her hand, a bewildered expression on his face. 'For what?'

'I suspect you'll be receiving a promotion soon. I don't doubt you'll be the next captain.'

★   ★   ★

'So Smythe planned to eventually become a ruler in Abyssinia,' summarized Avery when everyone but Harry, who had quickly found another client, had returned to the Dunburys' new home ten miles outside of Nairobi. They sat on the veranda of the two-storied stone house, lemonade glasses in hand, and watched the sunset over Beverly's garden. One lone yellow-fronted canary sat on a rosebush and warbled. To their left lay the foundation of a stone stable under construction, where the Dunburys planned to keep horses.

'Yes, a veritable 'man who would be king,' as Kipling put it,' said Jade, Biscuit at her feet. 'He promised von Gretchmar to make Mercedes his queen in return for supplying arms, but he promised the same thing to Claudia behind Otto's back if she returned his gold. In truth, he used both of them and planned to sell them off to someplace like Algeria as soon as he could. The man was totally unscrupulous, doing anything for money.' Jade sighed. 'Ivory poaching, slaving, and gunrunning aren't Smythe's only crimes, intended to fund his dream kingdom. Looks like drug smuggling may have been a side business. He admitted to having worked with Roger Forster before arranging the ambush that killed Captain Ross. Then he headed north into the frontier as the replacement officer.'

'Wasn't Forster the man who smuggled heroin from Mombasa?' asked Sam. 'The man who tried to pass himself off as David Worthy's brother?'

'That's right,' said Jade. 'He also killed David's father, but it was a murder for hire. We always suspected Mrs Worthy paid him to kill her husband before he could produce his illegitimate son.'

'That's a cold woman,' said Sam as he sat back.

'So Smythe stole Jelani as part of his slave

trade?' asked Madeline Thompson, who had joined them along with her husband, Neville.

Jade shook her head. 'Jelani was bait to lure me away. His men shot Chiumbo to get us to leave, but I think he knew we came back. And von Gretchmar surely saw Jelani spy around Mercedes' tent, another reason to take the lad.'

'But how did von Gretchmar manage to get all those rifles in under Harry's nose?' asked Avery.

'They were all in boxes labeled as the women's personal items. As far as Harry knew, they had crates of cosmetics and lingerie and other frippery.' Jade laughed. 'Almost makes me feel sorry for Harry, getting duped again like that. At least we got our rifles back. Smythe had them in his cache.'

Sam's opinion of Harry's predicament came out as a snort. 'I'm glad we found Vogelsanger alive,' he said. 'He's fortunate that Smythe only beat him up and left him bound and gagged in that pit.'

'Why didn't Smythe shoot him?' asked Avery.

'Too many people running around the mountain,' said Jade. 'He probably didn't want to call any more attention to himself with a gunshot.'

'It appears all Vogelsanger was guilty of was trying to protect Mercedes. We know Otto von Gretchmar was up to his neck in this, but whatever happened to Claudia or this other partner Smythe talked about?' asked Avery. 'Didn't he tell you he'd been warned about you?'

Jade leaned back in her chair with her hands behind her head. 'No one could decide how

370

culpable Claudia von Gretchmar was, so the district commissioner settled for chasing her and her companions out of the Protectorate. The last I heard, Smythe refused to speak any more about his so-called distant partner, but they found a letter in his possession written in a woman's hand and signed with an L.'

'An *L*? Then you don't think either Claudia or Otto was this partner he spoke of?' asked Neville.

Jade shook her head. 'I'm guessing the *L* means Lilith, as in Olivia Lilith Worthy. The woman has a double life. To the genteel world, she's Olivia Worthy, grieving widow, but for her illegal activities she uses her middle name. Mr Percival had sent word to Isiolo that I was coming up, so Smythe had time to send a wire and get information about me. Neither of the von Gretchmars had ever heard of me before, but she's one person who had who meets all the qualifications.'

'Lilith Worthy,' repeated Avery in a whisper.

Jade nodded. 'And it appears that she hates me with a passion, presumably because I stopped part of her drugsmuggling ring when I shot Roger Forster, and because she lost half her estate when I produced her husband's other heir.'

Sam leaned forward again. 'Wait a minute! You think this woman, despicable as she may be, is guilty of *more* than hiring her husband's killer?'

Jade nodded. 'Think about it. How would she know who to hire in Africa to begin with unless she already had a connection there? I assumed

371

she'd made contacts from England and built on them, but we've never had direct evidence. Anything in Forster's home that might have incriminated her went up in flames when his house burned down.' She looked over to Madeline in time to see her hastily scribble some notes in a little booklet. 'Wait a minute, Maddy. You're not going to write this up as another novel, are you?'

'And why not?' she said. 'I just received a letter from a publisher in London. They're printing *Stalking Death* and sent a very tidy advance, which will go a long way towards covering the overdraft on our farm. I'm certain they'll buy this one as well. I plan to call it *Ivory Blood*. Doesn't that sound frightfully romantic?'

Jade rolled her eyes and sighed. 'Frightfully.'

Beverly returned from a guest room and sat down on a stuffed chair next to her husband. 'Shhh,' she cautioned. 'Jelani's asleep right now. He's recovering pretty well, but I expect by tomorrow he's going to be demanding to be up.'

'Thank you for keeping him here, Beverly,' said Jade.

'Well, he certainly is better off here than in what passes for a hospital for natives. He's lucky he didn't lose his foot to gangrene. As it is, he's going to be missing a chunk off his heel and it looks like he may lose a few toes. Dr Burkitt hasn't made his final pronouncement yet. I'm just glad that Chiumbo recovered so well. He plans to go home to his people.'

'He left this morning,' said Jade. 'I think he finally feels he can quit searching for his father's murderer.' She closed her eyes and reflected for a moment on her farewell to the man who'd become a true friend.

'You're going home?' she had asked him.

The tall Tanganyikan had nodded. 'My search is over. I no longer need to walk the lands as a guide. I can go back to my people. Perhaps we can begin trading again.'

'And bring the moon to Dar es Salaam,' added Jade with a smile. 'They probably miss it.'

Chiumbo laughed. 'Maybe it found its way to them without us excreting it.'

Jade chuckled. Then her smile took a sad turn. 'I will miss you, Chiumbo. You are a good man and a trusted friend.'

'And you are a good woman, Simba Jike. I am glad to have known you. But a lioness should not live alone. She lives with a lion lord, does she not?' He held up his hand when she began to protest. 'The stone feather man, he is a good man.'

Jade sighed. First Madeline and Beverly — now Chiumbo seemed to think he needed to play matchmaker. 'He is a good man, Chiumbo.'

Chiumbo smiled. 'When I go into the *mahoka* huts to pray to my ancestors, I will pray for you, Simba Jike. May your journeys have happy endings and always lead you home.'

'Where *is* my home, Chiumbo?' asked Jade. 'I can't seem to find it anymore.'

His black eyes peered for a moment into her questioning green ones before he gently laid one finger on her forehead. 'You have been looking for it here,' he said softly, then lightly tapped her chest above her heart. 'But you should look for it here.'

'I only wish Chiumbo was with us that day we first met Smythe,' Beverly now said, her gentle voice breaking into Jade's reverie. 'It would have saved us a lot of trouble.'

'We'd be dead,' said Jade. 'Smythe wouldn't have let anyone escape knowing his past.'

'Is Jelani still insisting on going back to his village?' asked Sam. 'I thought you were all schooling him.'

'We were,' said Jade. 'He's a very bright lad and reads and writes English very well. But he's got this idea that an elephant told him to learn the ways of the *mundu-mugo*. We've actually spoken with the tribe's old healer. He's a greatuncle or something of that nature to Jelani and has been anxious to train him as his replacement. Hopefully, with the education we've given him, he can be a better leader for his people, one that's not so easily taken advantage of by us outsiders.'

Beverly jumped up from her chair. 'Oh, speaking of outsiders, I forgot to give you your mail. Sam, you have a letter from Indiana, and Jade, you have a letter from your mother.' She handed the envelopes around, then waited on the edge of her seat to inquire as to the contents.

Jade studied the rumpled envelope. 'It's been opened already. Bev? Did you open this?'

'Of course not!'

'Well, someone did,' said Jade. 'You can see where the glue tore away part of the paper.' She held out the envelope for them to inspect. Sam took it.

'Jade's right,' he said after a brief study. 'Now,

who would want to read her personal mail?' He handed the envelope back and opened his own letter.

'Maybe Mrs del Cameron opened it herself to add to the letter and didn't reseal it very carefully,' suggested Avery.

Jade didn't bother to reply. She knew her fastidious mother too well to imagine her doing such a thing. Oh, she might decide to add to a letter, but she'd have made out a completely fresh envelope. No, someone was prying into her personal business.

Jade felt a prickling of her neck hairs and wondered if David's mother had hired someone to spy on her. She seemed to have people in her pay all over British East Africa, so it wasn't any stretch of the imagination to think she had an accomplice in Nairobi to keep track of Jade's actions. Maybe she wanted to find out where they'd tucked away the heir to half her husband's fortune, and hoped a letter might reveal it. The prickling increased. She shoved the thought aside and turned to her letter.

'Well,' Beverly said impatiently after a few minutes, 'what does she write?'

Jade folded the letter and smiled at her friend. 'Honestly, Bev, you'd think she was *your* mother. She says she is going to travel to Spain soon to once again try to bring home an Andalusian stud for the ranch. She wants me to join her in Morocco.'

'How nice,' exclaimed Beverly.

'Is your father going, too?' asked Neville.

'No. Dad apparently has his hands full

between lambing season and installing a new irrigation system or something.' She sighed. 'I suppose I should go, although I have no idea what use I'll be. The Spaniards are very possessive of their precious Andalusian horses, and if Mother can't talk someone out of one of those stallions, no one can. Saying no to Doña Inez Maria Isabella de Vincente del Cameron is impossible.'

'By the way,' said Bev, 'speaking of your mother, you never finished your story about that lovesick bull elk.' She settled back into her seat with her arms folded. 'I demand to hear the end of it. You left off when you got some huge mixed-breed dog you named something absurd,' Beverly reminded her.

'Right, Kaloff the dog,' said Jade. 'Not very bright. He preferred picking up sheep to herding them.'

'Yes, yes, you told me he did something to a skunk once,' said Bev.

'And he picked up a dead raccoon carcass,' added Sam. Both Bev and Jade glared at him, Beverly because he knew something she didn't, and Jade because Sam had blabbed.

'Indeed,' said Jade. 'So Kaloff came trotting back with this skunk and I got caught in the middle of it, so we were both forced to spend a better portion of that summer out on the upper pasture with the sheep.'

'No wonder you didn't mind that stinking anti-*laibon* paste you wore last year,' remarked Avery.

'Mother would agree. Anyway, that fall, after

376

the perfume wore off and Kaloff and I were admitted back home, my parents entertained some earl who was pretending to be having an adventure in the Wild West. The man was a bona fide dandy, complete with hair pomade and scented mustache wax.' She paused and pointed down the hallway. 'Beverly, I believe I heard Jelani just now. Perhaps you should check on him.'

Beverly scowled, her blue eyes flashing. 'Oooh. Don't you dare try to interrupt this story again, Jade. You finish it or I'll be forced to take extreme measures.'

Jade flashed a wicked smile. 'Sorry, Bev. I couldn't resist. I'll finish the story. It seems I remarked to our foreman that this duded-up sissy smelled like something the dog toted in. The earl and Mother both overheard me.'

Beverly covered her open mouth with a hand. 'Oh, Jade. How awful!'

'It was,' Jade agreed. 'I don't recall *anything* else ever smelling that bad.' Beverly gasped and Sam yelped in laughter. Jade flashed a toothy grin at them. 'Of course, Mother decided then and there that I had spent far too much time with the ranch hands and needed some refinement. The earl suggested sending me to school in London and recommended Winsor College for Women.' She spread her hands. 'The rest is history.'

Beverly jumped up and hugged Jade. 'And I'm eternally grateful to that elk, the dog, the skunk, the earl, *and* your mother.'

'Hear, hear,' seconded Avery. 'I have a

wonderful idea. I plan on taking the little woman back to London so Beverly can have the best of doctors and so our heir can meet the family. Why don't you both come along?'

Sam, who had remained noticeably silent during the last exclamations, stood. 'I'm going back up to Marsabit in another few days,' he said. 'I want to film the elephants at that big crater lake before the long rains start.'

'Sam, are you sure?' asked Beverly. Her gaze darted back and forth between Sam and Jade.

'Very sure, Beverly,' he said gently. 'I need to salvage my filmmaking career.' He waved his letter in front of him. 'My friend finished fixing that plane for me, but paying for it is another story. I'm going to need the profits from this motion picture to make a down payment. Maybe if I'm lucky, I'll run into that Boguli fellow. Sure wish I'd met him.'

Jade watched Sam with a slight frown as she wrestled with her own reaction to his news. For some reason, she'd taken it for granted that he would be staying in the area for a while, and she didn't know if she was disappointed or relieved that he was leaving. Right now, disappointment was winning out, and she mentally kicked herself for being fool enough to think he still cared about her.

'If you need money, Sam,' offered Avery, but Sam silenced him with a shake of his head.

'I might be able to help you in another way,' Jade said. 'I think I have a picture of Boguli on one of my cameras.'

'You photographed him?' asked Avery.

'Only by accident. He was just behind Smythe when Smythe tripped the camera wire. I forgot about it until now.' She rose from her seat. 'Wait here and I'll develop it.'

Jade hurried out of the Dunburys' house and headed for the outbuilding they'd given over to her for a developing studio. She felt grateful for the excuse to be alone where she could collect her thoughts and bring her conflicting emotions under control. What the blazes was wrong with her? She ought to be grateful that Sam seemed to be letting her off so easily.

She extracted the film from the camera and carefully took it through the various baths to develop the negative. Next she made a positive using the equipment that Avery and Beverly had generously supplied to complete the lab. When the photograph's image emerged from the developing solution, she removed it and clipped it to a line to dry. That was when she first noticed the anomaly in the picture.

'About time,' scolded Beverly when Jade returned. 'I'd begun to think you ran away.'

Jade shook her head, a dazed, faraway look in her eyes.

'What's the matter, Jade?' asked Sam. 'Did the picture blur? That film had been out there in the forest for a while.'

'No. It's remarkably sharp,' she replied.

'Then what's the matter, lovey?' persisted Beverly. 'You look like you've seen a ghost.'

Jade handed the picture to Bev. 'See for yourself.'

Everyone clustered around the picture while

Jade wandered over to the railing and looked out on the well-manicured lawn and typically British rose garden.

'There's Smythe falling down,' said Sam. 'A perfect action shot. But where's Boguli?'

'Look more carefully in the background.' Jade stood with her back to them, listening while they scrutinized the picture. When Beverly and Madeline gasped and the men exclaimed aloud, she knew they'd seen what she'd seen.

'Good heavens!' Sam shouted. 'There's only a shadow behind Smythe, but the shape is as clear as a bell.'

Jade nodded and turned around. 'So you see it, too?'

'Of course we see it, but I don't understand it,' said Sam. 'It's a perfect shadow of a large bull elephant, but you didn't see any elephants around, did you?'

'No, but I heard one, an angry bull. Look more closely. The shadow is all wrong. If there'd been an elephant on the other side of the trail, the shadow would have crossed Smythe. It doesn't. It's directly behind him. Right where Boguli stood. And,' she added, 'look at the tusk. The shadow clearly shows a broken tusk.'

'Bloody hell,' swore Avery. 'That's exactly the same as that old bull that the Abyssinians killed. The one you'd spent so much time tracking. But it can't be.'

Jade shrugged. 'Boguli did say he was like a brother to the elephants.' She turned back to the window. 'I've always wondered if animals had souls. It seems at least this one did.'

AUTHOR'S NOTES

Mount Marsabit was the site of Martin and Osa Johnson's four-year stay, chronicled in Osa's book *Four Years in Paradise*, as well as Martin's book *Camera Trails in Africa*. For more information on the Johnsons and all their African explorations, visit the Martin and Osa Johnson Safari Museum in Chanute, Kansas, either in person or online at www.safarimuseum.com.

Arthur Radclyffe Dugmore also made an early photographic safari on Mount Marsabit. His amazing photographs and descriptions of elephant behavior can be found in the 1925 book *The Wonderland of Big Game: Being an Account of Two Trips Through Tanganyika and Kenya*. Major Dugmore also describes elephant behavior in chapter 10, 'Tembo the Elephant,' in his 1928 book *African Jungle Life*. While his books are out of print, they are well worth locating through book dealers or interlibrary loan.

Some insight into the feudal system of the Abyssinian government of the time can be found in Major Henry Darley's 1935 book *Slaves and Ivory in Abyssinia: A Record of Adventure and Exploration Among the Ethiopian Slave Raiders*. Sir Wilfred Thesiger discusses both his experiences in Abyssinia and trips to Mount Marsabit in *My Kenya Days*.

And finally, if you have never discovered the fun and adventure of the Tarzan series by Edgar Rice Burroughs, you are never too old to start.